P

death's

"Amber Benson does an e........ acters, as well as educating the reader on some great mythology history . . . a fast-paced and very entertaining story."

—*Sacramento Book Review*

"One of the greatest risks but ultimate triumphs of the novel stems from Benson's deft ability to take any myth or belief and make it her own . . . Through the eyes of our story's protagonist, Benson provides a devilish sense of humor and a modern pop-culture sensibility that keep the proceedings light and entertaining . . . Fiercely inventive characterization carries this story throughout.

"In *Death's Daughter*, Benson provides a fun romp that defines the rules of an exciting new universe you'll be chomping at the bit to dive back into time and again. There's action; there's intrigue, redemption, an adorable Hell puppy, and even a hot guy or two. What more could you ask for?" —*Buffyfest*

"An urban fantasy series featuring a heroine whose macabre humor fits perfectly with her circumstances. Sure to appeal to fans of Tanya Huff's Vicki Nelson series and Charles de Lint's urban fantasies." —*Library Journal*

"Amber Benson writes an amusing, action-packed, chick-lit urban fantasy loaded with more twists and curves than a twist-a-whirl . . . Filled with humor and wit, this is a refreshing, original thriller as double, triple, and nth crossings are the norm."

—*Genre Go Round Reviews*

"With a creative story line as proof, Ms. Benson adds writing to her ever-growing list of talents. Set within an intriguing paranormal world, *Death's Daughter* unfolds a seductive tale of power and deception. A great start to a series that will be easy for readers to get hooked on." —*Darque Reviews*

continued . . .

"A clever and well-told story . . . It's also a step outside the current paranormal-fantasy rut but with enough elements in common to please fans of that form as well." —*Critical Mass*

"Amber Benson has created a brash, sassy heroine oozing attitude as she deals with family, business, an angry Goddess, zombie armies, and betrayal in this imaginative blend of assorted mythologies. The snappy dialogue keeps pace with the quick pace while providing a fun touch of self-deprecating humor. It should be interesting to see where Benson takes Callie next." —*Monsters and Critics*

"Multitalented doesn't begin to cover the gifts of former *Buffy* TV-alumna Benson. Her quirky, cranky, and humorous heroine leads readers on a wacky first-person adventure through Hell. Great supporting characters and wild antics keep the pace brisk and the humor flowing." —*Romantic Times*

"Enjoyable . . . One of the novel's best features is the underlying tongue-in-cheek humor that runs throughout the narrative. Readers who enjoy a hefty dose of wit in their paranormal fantasy will embrace this book." —*Bitten by Books*

"*Death's Daughter* is a goofy, funny fantasy that falls into the category of the lightest sort of reading."
—*Patricia's Vampire Notes*

"There's a whole lot of promise here . . . enjoyable." —*SF Site*

"A rich cast of characters and universe." —*Fandomania*

"An enjoyable read, and I will definitely be picking up the next in the series." —*Geek Like Me*

Ace Books by Amber Benson

DEATH'S DAUGHTER
CAT'S CLAW

cat's claw

AMBER BENSON

ACE BOOKS, NEW YORK

THE BERKLEY PUBLISHING GROUP
Published by the Penguin Group
Penguin Group (USA) Inc.
375 Hudson Street, New York, New York 10014, USA
Penguin Group (Canada), 90 Eglinton Avenue East, Suite 700, Toronto, Ontario M4P 2Y3, Canada
(a division of Pearson Penguin Canada Inc.)
Penguin Books Ltd., 80 Strand, London WC2R 0RL, England
Penguin Group Ireland, 25 St. Stephen's Green, Dublin 2, Ireland (a division of Penguin Books Ltd.)
Penguin Group (Australia), 250 Camberwell Road, Camberwell, Victoria 3124, Australia
(a division of Pearson Australia Group Pty. Ltd.)
Penguin Books India Pvt. Ltd., 11 Community Centre, Panchsheel Park, New Delhi—110 017, India
Penguin Group (NZ), 67 Apollo Drive, Rosedale, North Shore 0632, New Zealand
(a division of Pearson New Zealand Ltd.)
Penguin Books (South Africa) (Pty.) Ltd., 24 Sturdee Avenue, Rosebank, Johannesburg 2196,
South Africa

Penguin Books Ltd., Registered Offices: 80 Strand, London WC2R 0RL, England

This is a work of fiction. Names, characters, places, and incidents either are the product of the author's imagination or are used fictitiously, and any resemblance to actual persons, living or dead, business establishments, events, or locales is entirely coincidental. The publisher does not have any control over and does not assume any responsibility for author or third-party websites or their content.

CAT'S CLAW

An Ace Book / published by arrangement with Benson Entertainment, Inc.

PRINTING HISTORY
Ace mass-market edition / March 2010

Copyright © 2010 by Benson Entertainment, Inc.
Cover art by Spiral Studio.
Cover design by Judith Lagerman.

ISBN: 978-0-441-01843-7

ACE
Ace Books are published by The Berkley Publishing Group,
a division of Penguin Group (USA) Inc.,
375 Hudson Street, New York, New York 10014.
ACE and the "A" design are trademarks of Penguin Group (USA) Inc.

PRINTED IN THE UNITED STATES OF AMERICA

10 9 8 7 6 5 4 3 2 1

For my sister

one

Hi, my name is Calliope Reaper-Jones . . . *and my dad is the Grim Reaper.*

There, I've said it—and even though it *did* make me feel like I was taking part in some weird supernatural version of Al-Anon—now that I've gotten it off my chest, I do *sort* of feel better about being a half-human, half-supernatural freakazoid who—you know, let me just interrupt myself for one little minute here because . . . *who the hell am I kidding?*

No matter how many times I say it out loud, I will always be different, always full of self-loathing for the nonhuman part of myself that just doesn't quite fit in with human society even when I'm desperately trying to jam myself into it. I might have *some* Homo sapiens DNA swimming around in my gene pool, but that little bit of human being-ness isn't nearly enough to make me a normal human girl.

No matter how much I want it to.

Okay, I know I sound like a whiner, but all I ever wanted in the whole world was to be *normal*. What's wrong with wanting two *normal* parents, a couple of *normal* siblings, and a *normal* family pet or two? I mean, is all that pretty standard human-family stuff *really* too much to ask for?

Apparently so . . . because there *is* no "being normal" allowed when you're the spawn of the crème de la crème of Supernatural Royalty. Let me just go on the record right here and now and say that being Death's Daughter sucks—and I mean *major, hard-core suckage.*

Of course, as much as I *want* to lay the blame solely at my dad's feet, I have a really hard time being mad at him. Maybe I'm being too lenient here, but at least he was who he was when my mother met him—and there was never any chance of changing that . . . and I mean *ever.* My *mother,* on the other hand, knew *exactly* what she was getting into when she fell in love with the Grim Reaper. She willingly accepted my dad's marriage proposal, willingly took the oath of immortality, and in the process, doomed my sisters and me to an eternity of supernatural abnormalcy!

But try explaining that to *her. She* just gets all weepy-eyed and makes me feel guilty for even daring to mention that she *might* be slightly responsible for my predicament. I mean, there's just no winning with my mother. In fact, to hear *her* tell it, the reason that I was so miserable had nothing at all to do with her *or* my father *or* their unholy union.

As far as she was concerned, I could put the blame right on the doorstep of the Atlanta Humane Society.

It's actually *not* as bizarre as it sounds.

Let me explain:

The story goes that back when she was a normal mortal, and the head buyer for all the Neiman Marcus stores in the Southeast, my mother had been roped into emceeing the annual Atlanta Humane Society Charity Fashion Show by a friend—not knowing that this one charity fashion show was about to change her life, if not for the better, then at least for the *interesting.* She tried every excuse she could think of to get out of it: sick relatives that she had to visit, a sore throat . . . but her friend was immovable and no amount of cajoling or threatening or crying could garner my mother a rain check.

Why the President and CEO of Death, Inc., was at a charity fashion show in Atlanta, Georgia, is another story, but that's where he was and thank God for that. Otherwise, he'd probably have married some dopey Goddess, or other magic-related babe from the supernatural canon, and I would be so full of magical ability that I would be totally unable to hold down a "normal" job. Let alone stay sane at a company like House and Yard, where I am the Executive Assistant to the Vice President of Sales, working to oversee the smooth running of the company that brings you all those "nifty" home and garden gadgets that proliferate the airwaves of the Home Shopping Channel.

Anyway, whatever his reasons for being there, my dad and his Executive Assistant, Jarvis, were seated in the front row, right smack-dab in line with the emcee's podium. Immediately, my dad homed in on the beautiful young woman standing uncomfortably above him, extolling the virtues of a pair of neon pink palazzo pants that some model was wearing as she slunk down the runway.

Enrapturing (his word, not mine), my dad thought to himself, watching the beautiful young woman flip through the index cards she held in her hands as she spoke.

Utterly enchanting.

At that moment, he knew in his heart that he had finally—after many years of searching—made the acquaintance of the love of his life. Before him, high on her podium, stood the future Mrs. Death.

The happy couple quietly eloped six months later.

So, all of the above means that my parents are madly in love with each other, and as long as they continue to enjoy their lives together—and my dad continues to be the President and CEO of Death, Inc.—I and my entire family will continue to be immortal.

I suppose some people would consider this whole "immortality" thing to be, like, the greatest gift a parent could ever give their kid, but I'm here to tell you that it completely, totally, unbelievably . . . *bites*. I mean, imagine losing every person you ever loved to age and decay, while you stayed young and beautiful for eternity—or until you could figure out some way to renounce your immortality without pissing your dad off.

Let me just say that immortality fully screws with your head . . . and I know this from experience.

When I was a teenager, I was in a car crash with two of my best friends, and while I walked away without so much as a scratch, I *did* get the exciting experience of watching my two friends die horrible, agonizing deaths. It was, like, awesome! *Not.*

So, believe me, I *do* know what the hell I'm talking about when I say immortality isn't all it's cracked up to be—even though there are *some* idiots out there that still think being immortal is, like, the cat's meow.

To those people I offer these ten simple words: *Spend a day in my shoes, and then we'll talk.*

In fact, how about you slip into my sexy little size 8 Manolo Blahnik faux zebra pumps that I got on sale at Barneys and try *this* day on for size.

it all started on what I thought was a reasonably normal Thursday evening. I had just shut down my computer, packed up my cute Louis Vuitton knockoff messenger bag—I didn't even know Louis Vuitton *did* a messenger bag until I saw this little number sitting in Times Square—and was getting ready to walk over to the elevator and press the down button, when my cell phone rang.

At least, I thought it was my cell phone.

I dug around in my bag, looking for my stupid BlackBerry wannabe, praying it would continue to ring just long enough for me to follow the sound down to whatever nether region of my purse the dumb thing was seeking asylum in that day. Apparently, my handheld device had something going with my checkbook because I found it wedged—in a strangely *sexual* position—in between the check register and that weird plastic divider thing no checkbook holder ever seems to be without.

Of course, my hand closed on the stupid thing *just* as it stopped ringing, so I immediately pressed the answer key, hoping against hope to catch whoever was on the other end of the line anyway.

Nothing happened.

I put the phone part of the device to my ear, hoping for heavy breathing, and/or other assorted noises, but it was absolutely dead.

"Damn it," I mumbled under my breath, annoyed—and definitely not expecting anyone to say anything in return.

"Hello . . . ?" a voice sang through the receiver.

I almost dropped the phone.

"Helloooo . . . ?" I said in return, my voice completely belying my thoroughly confused state of being. I had definitely heard a serious lack of dial tone only seconds before, so who the hell was poltergeist-ing my PDA?

"Hello . . . ?" the voice on the end of the line said a little more shrilly.

Okay, this is getting just a little bit ridiculous, I thought to myself as I looked down at the phone and saw that the stupid thing wasn't even *on.*

"Okay, listen up. This is Calliope Reaper-Jones. I don't know who you are, or why you've bewitched my handheld device, but this is *so* not funny!"

Without waiting a beat, a low-pitched feminine voice began talking at me like I hadn't spoken at all.

"We will commence tonight with our first session," the voice intoned. "It is imperative that you have a pot of licorice tea and two cupcakes—both in carrot cake—from the Magnolia Bakery waiting upon my arrival—"

"What are you talking about—" I started to say, but was overrun by the voice on the other end of the line.

"Thank you and good day."

"Don't you hang up, or I'll—I'll . . ." I stammered, but it was too late. The voice was gone.

"Crap," I said under my breath as I dropped the phone from my ear and proceeded to stare down at its dead face. I had no idea what the heck had just happened, but it very much sounded

like I was going to have a visitor tonight . . . whether I wanted
one or not.

feeling slightly chagrined about having to go out of
my way for a complete stranger, I hightailed my ass to Bleecker
Street, thanking God that the Magnolia Bakery was open late.
Of course, if I were really smart, I would've totally remembered that they delivered!

After a lengthy wait behind two pierced Goths—the female
one was wearing a leather dog collar and leash attached to
the male one's nose ring—I was able to procure two carrot
cake cupcakes (and a devil's food one for myself). I walked for
a couple of blocks, then, deciding to splurge, hopped into a
taxi, luxuriating in the backseat all the way down to Battery
Park City.

I really do try to walk as much as possible because I *do* live
in the greatest place in the whole world: New York City. I
know I should just get over it already and stop acting like a
tourist, but every time I walk outside my door, I just can't help
being silently thrilled with the beauty of my environs.

Ever since I was a little kid, I had wanted to live in the City
That Never Sleeps. I'd spent my childhood being ferried be-
tween Sea Verge (my family's giant mansion overlooking the
Rhode Island Sound) in Newport, Rhode Island, and a small East
Coast boarding school called the New Newbridge Academy—
but even then my heart belonged to New York.

I don't know what it is about the city that makes it so enticing to me, but seriously, being a denizen of lower Manhattan
is kinda like being high on catnip all the time—not that I was a
cat . . . or had any kind of weird catnip addiction that I was
hiding.

The only thing I did that *might've* bordered on the edge of
addiction was my voracious obsession with acquiring new
clothing, sunglasses, and shoes . . . the trendier the better. Too
bad that all I could afford on the shopping scene these days

was the cute little Al Gore tote bag I'd picked up at the Marc Jacobs store for five bucks the day before.

I had really, really, *really* wanted the amazing blue baby doll dress with tiny pearl buttons going down the front in a neat little row I'd glimpsed in the window, but had had to settle for just the tote when my credit card had been summarily declined at the register. It was just my luck that, although New York boasted some of the best shopping in the world, it also was home to some of the world's highest-priced real estate, meaning that my rent ate up three-fourths of what I took home from House and Yard each week.

Ugh.

Anyway, as the taxi glided to a stop in front of my building, I pulled a wad of one-dollar bills from my bag and shoved it at the driver. He seemed resigned to counting all my sweaty bills, but once he realized I'd given him a three-buck tip, he gave me a wide-lipped smile and tipped his baseball cap to me in the rearview mirror.

I paused, one foot on the pavement, the other still stuck in the cab, and stared, my heart riveted by the pair of ice blue eyes that I saw reflected back at me in the rearview mirror.

I knew those eyes!

I opened my mouth to speak, to say something that would make reality slide back into place, but before I could make a sound, the driver turned his head and gave me a curious look. His dark face was pockmarked and shiny. The two hazel eyes that peered out of his eye sockets bore not even a *passing* resemblance to the eyes I'd just seen.

"You okay, ma'am?" he said, the dulcet tones of his Caribbean accent ripping me out of the surrealness I'd just experienced and plopping me right back into the humid New York City night that surrounded me like a security blanket.

I nodded, realizing that I didn't trust my voice *not* to come out like a squeak if I used it.

All I wanted to do was rewind, to go back a few minutes into the past and see those eyes one more time. There was so much that I wanted to say to the man who possessed them. It just stank that there was no way in Hell—and I meant that literally—that I was ever going to see the guy again, no matter how badly I wanted to.

It was definitely something I'd dreamed about: meeting Daniel somewhere out in the real world, away from all the supernatural weirdness we'd shared together, but unhappily, there was no random run-in on the subway or a surprise bumping into each other at a mutual friend's birthday party in our future. Not because we'd had some crazy falling-out and he'd moved to Timbuktu or Kazakhstan to escape my evil, female clutches. No, the reason I wasn't going to see Daniel hoofing it down Park Avenue anytime in the near future was because . . . Daniel was dead.

He'd sacrificed his own life for my mine during a hard-scrabble battle between the evil demon serpent Vritra and myself almost two months earlier, and no matter how many times I replayed the memory of that horrible night over and over again in my mind, I couldn't shake the guilty feeling that I didn't get to tell him thank you.

Or good-bye.

i took the stairs two at a time, my dark bangs matting to my forehead as sweat poured down my face. There was no air-conditioning in my building, which meant that whenever I opted for the stairs—which was anytime I wanted to leave or return to my apartment since it was a sixth-floor walk-up—I was assured of desperately needing a shower after the fact.

Cradling the box of cupcakes in one hand, I stuck my other hand into the depths of my messenger bag, fumbling for my keys. Like everything that found its way into my bag, my keys were nearly impossible to find. I pulled out my PDA, a toothbrush, and the eponymous tampon from the bag's innards before finally getting a good grip on my keychain and fishing my keys out of the darkness.

I slid the largest key on the chain into the giant, eye-level dead bolt—I always felt like I was in a staring match with the damn thing—and turned the key home. My door swung open and a burst of hot air hit me full in the face, making me wheeze.

"Ugh," I moaned to myself as I flipped the light switch to the "on" position, bathing the apartment in a warm yellow glow. I used my foot to pull the door closed behind me before setting the cupcake box on the arm of my sofa and quickly locking the dead bolt with a heavy, *thunk*like click. I grabbed the cupcake box off the sofa's arm before it could slide off and fall lid first onto the floor, settling it under my arm as I made my way to my tiny eat-in kitchenette. I opened the door to my dorm-sized refrigerator and put the cupcakes (still in their box just to be hygienic) on the bottom shelf, where they would be safe.

When I had first looked at the apartment, I had just been so happy to find something in my price range that I had somehow managed to miss the apartment's big, inherent defect: a kitchen *so* tiny that an adult human couldn't stand up in it without banging against a cabinet or bumping their head on the ceiling. I comforted myself with the fact that I didn't really do all that much cooking so the lack of kitchen wasn't *too* much of a hardship. Although the minifridge *did* tend to fill up once I'd loaded in a six-pack of Fiji water and two bottles of raspberry Kombucha juice—and the bottle of Baileys Irish Cream I'd gotten as a Christmas present the year before didn't really help, either. It desperately needed to be tossed in the garbage if I was ever gonna get anything *edible* inside the Hobbit fridge.

Luckily, I had polished off the last bottle of water the night before, so tonight the cupcakes got the water's old spot.

I closed the refrigerator door and turned around, my feet unconsciously heading for the large, flower-patterned couch that took up half the living room. I was just within couch-flopping distance when I suddenly started sneezing: three vicious sneezes that rattled my brain around inside my head like a Ping-Pong ball and made me see stars.

Feeling the hairs prickle on the back of my neck, I wiped my nose with a tissue I plucked from a box on the coffee table, my eye catching my reflection in the large mirror that hung on the beige wall above the couch.

"What the—" I started to say as I saw a tiny old woman with curly red hair piled high on top of her head reflected back at me in the mirror. She was standing in the middle of my kitchen, filling my ratty old teakettle with water right out of the (germ-laden!) kitchen tap.

"Hey!" I yelped, almost tripping over the edge of the beige and brown area rug that covered most of the living room floor as I scurried across the room. "That's my kettle you're contaminating with tap water!"

My teeth clenched unhappily as I moved to confront the intruder, grabbing a tattered old copy of Kevyn Aucoin's coffee table–sized book *Making Faces* from my bookshelf and wielding it like a baseball bat behind my back. I didn't like anyone invading my territory without my prior approval—no matter how small and old and female she appeared to be. I had learned from experience that even the most benign-looking creatures could prove to be malevolent monsters in disguise.

And I meant that literally.

"Who are you?" I stammered, holding the spine of the book tightly in my sweaty hands.

The old woman didn't bat an eyelash. She just stood there waiting for the kettle to whistle, ignoring me.

"*Who* are you?" I said again, not so nicely this time. Like I said, I didn't like uninvited guests—and I especially didn't like uninvited guests that ignored me to boot! Suddenly, the teakettle began to whistle, and the shrill sound of boiling water screaming through a tiny metal spout was like nails on a chalkboard, making me even more annoyed with the old lady.

"I said, who the hell are—" But the sentence was interrupted by another round of rapid-fire sneezing that made my eyes water and my throat itch.

Raising an eyebrow in my direction, the old woman took the kettle off the eye of the stove, resting it on a lopsided, purple-glazed clay trivet that had my name emblazoned on it in my younger sister's sloping cursive.

Clio had made the trivet for me at one of those "paint your own" pottery stores when she was twelve. It was supercute and it always made me kinda miss my family whenever I looked at it sitting on my kitchen counter—which really wasn't that often, sadly, since I was more of a take-out sandwich gal than a cook.

"You are in need of training much more desperately than your father and mother have led me to believe," the woman said finally, and I instantly recognized her voice as the very same one that had hijacked my cell phone earlier in the evening with a request for carrot cake cupcakes.

"You talked to my parents?" I said, latching onto that snippet of information and allowing a deep feeling of resentment to build inside me.

"They have no right to talk about me behind my back like that! That—that—that . . . *sucks!*"

The older woman snickered at my words, her red curls bouncing like they were in on the joke. I lowered the Kevyn Aucoin book, but didn't return it to its place in the bookshelf. Instead, I kept it at my side just in case.

"They said you were feisty—"

"Yeah?" I stammered, "Well, whatever!"

This only made the old woman laugh mirthfully.

"Don't laugh at me," I howled, starting to feel embarrassed by the situation. This was my apartment, after all, and no strange old woman had any business making me feel like a fool in my own living room/kitchen.

The old woman's laughter died instantly as she began to appraise me.

"So like your mother," the woman said, staring at me like I was a specimen floating around on a slide under an electron microscope. Not a great feeling, especially coming from someone who'd probably been around since the Cretaceous period and had "the art of staring" down pat.

"Whatever," I shot back again, annoyed at being compared

to my mother. My mother and I were *nothing* alike as far as I was concerned . . . at least, God, I *hoped* we were nothing alike.

"Silence," the old woman said, her voice firm yet not un-friendly. She didn't seem to be put off by my *feistiness*, but there was still time. I mean, we had just met, so I was pretty sure I could figure out a way to piss her off before the night was over.

I opened my mouth to say something smart in response (I have a hard time with the whole "think before you speak" thing), but was stopped cold when the curly red hair on top of the old woman's head suddenly came to life, baring two twin eyes that seemed to magically appear at the crown of her head.

Fascinated and repulsed at the same time by the newborn eyes—one was dark brown; the other was such a startling shade of lavender that it looked fake—I almost didn't notice the cherry red mouth resting just above the place where the woman's hairline met the flesh of her forehead. That is, until *said* mouth opened itself right up and began to speak:

"I hope you pay more attention to our words than your mother did," the mouth intoned in a deep, modulated baritone. "Maybe then your obstinacy won't almost cost you your life."

two

There was a loud, apartment-filling *yowl* as the red-haired beast on top of the old woman's head suddenly took flight, crossing the space between us in one giant leap and landing on my shoulder.

I shrieked, fear tearing at my stomach lining, making me want to run *and* pass out at the same time. I tried to shake the giant, unruly hairball off my shoulder, but it was no good. The thing had grown claws, claws that were now sticking into the flesh of my collarbone—probably drawing blood, if I knew *my* luck.

"Get it off me!" I shrieked, taking a step backward and nearly tripping over the coffee table that sat benignly in front of the couch. Righting myself just in the nick of time, I made a face as I felt the creature's warm, yeasty-smelling breath rasping against my cheek.

Ugh!

Just *knowing* the hairball thing's mouth was that close to my face totally freaked me out *even more* than I was already freaking out. What if it decided that I smelled like dinner and decided to take a bite? I was damned if I'd lose an earlobe to the creepy little bugger. I mean, my ears were one of the few things that I actually *dug* about myself. They were small and shaped like tiny, perfect shells. They looked especially exquisite when paired with diamonds and pearls (the fake kind obviously).

"Get off before I throw you off!" I hissed from between clenched teeth, hoping that the hairball creature would take the not-so-subtle hint. The creature must've sensed that it'd only been an idle threat because it continued to sit there, an immobile, orange, talking tumor attached to my shoulder.

I didn't really *want* to touch the thing with my bare hands, but I also didn't want to end up with the hairball as my new favorite permanent accessory—kind of like a miniature Chihuahua, but without the pedigree. Since the hairball was clinging to my skin like a painful tick, I bit the bullet and dealt with the situation, sucking together all my courage and reaching up and grasping the beast around the torso.

"Calmly," the smooth baritone voice whispered into my ear as my hands wrapped around its middle. "Calmly, now."

"Get off of me!" I shrieked again, fear starting to give way to anger as I tried to yank the hairball off me and realized that it wasn't budging.

There was just something about having a hairy, claw-wielding creature of indeterminate species attached to one's shoulder blade that did not make one a happy camper, I decided.

To top the whole thing off, Mr. Badass Hairball Creature weighed a ton, too. It felt like I had a small watermelon perched on my shoulder instead of a fur ball. Besides the extra weight, the creature was *way* warmer than you'd expect—kind of like having an overweight miniheater strapped to your shoulder. I decided that the only way the phenomenon *might've* been relaxing was if you'd encountered it at a spa—but it was definitely *not* pleasant when it was forced on you against your will.

Suddenly, there was a flash of reddish orange in front of my eyes and I felt something soft and fluffy rubbing against my nose. Instantly, I started sneezing again, the quantity and intensity of the sneezes making my head ache.

Damn it, I hadn't sneezed like this since I'd agreed to cat-sit for my neighbor Patience last Christmas and ended up in the emergency room with a respiratory attack—

Wait a minute, I thought, my body racked by another round of staccato sneezes. *The only thing I knew for sure that caused me to have respiratory attacks was . . . well, cat fur. So, it only made sense that I was dealing with my arch-nemesis: the domesticated feline!*

"Get this feline off me!" I said angrily, another sneeze simmering just underneath my words. How much of an idiot *was* I? I should've realized immediately that the hairball monster was nothing but a big, fat, orange and red *kitty cat*!

"Ask Muna nicely, then," the old woman said as she pulled a mug down from one of my cabinets and poured the water from the teakettle into it. "She will only respond when she feels she is being genuinely respected."

I watched the steam pool around the edges of the old woman's mug, willing myself to calm down. *If that voice belonged to a female,* I decided, *then it must be one hell of a butch lady cat.*

"You better get off before I call the Humane Society on your ass," I wheezed, the threat half-swallowed by another sneeze.

I could feel claw digging into bone, which only made me feel crankier. Obviously, I wasn't showing the proper amount of respect toward *her.* My shoulder was probably gonna be scarred for life the rate this whole thing was going. Well, I guessed it was just one more thing I could add to the tally of emotional and physical wounds I'd suffered since I'd allowed myself to become re-embroiled in the family business.

Once upon a time I'd prided myself on being a normal girl with nothing strange lurking in the shadows of my present-tense life—okay, I *did* have a past that I couldn't shake, but it was definitely within my prerogative to ignore it if I wanted to, so there! Now it was all I could do *just* to maintain a quasinormal life *and* clean up the mess that was inevitably left behind when some weird, supernatural entity broke through the "normalcy" barrier I'd carefully constructed around myself. Seriously, I mean, try explaining to your coworkers that the last "vacation" you took was a Devil-guided tour of the bowels of Hell and just see what kind of reaction *that* gets you at the watercooler.

"Would you mind chilling on the couch, or something?" I asked the cat in as polite a tone as I could muster, seeing that there was now a band of cat-induced tightness restricting the flow of breath in and out of my chest.

This was exactly what had happened last Christmas—crazy sneezing fits, followed by wheezing and then the utter obliteration of my ability to breathe like a normal human being. I'd spent Christmas Eve on a gurney in the emergency room, my eyeballs nearly popping out of my head from lack of oxygen. Christmas Day consisted of finding a vet that was open who had the space to board Muffins (my cat-sitting charge) until Patience came back from Tahiti the day after New Year's.

I sneezed again and Muna finally seemed to take pity on me this time. I felt a sharp pinch near my collarbone as the cat used the paper-thin skin like a starting block to propel itself onto the arm of my couch, where it landed with a studied grace before lifting its leg and licking itself in the "you know what" area.

"Ow," I said post–cat leap, hoping for some kind of an apology—I didn't care from whom, the lady or the cat; either one would do—but no apology seemed forthcoming.

"Ow," I said again, a little more loudly this time, rubbing the spot on my shoulder where the cat claws had ripped the skin and hoping that if I called a little attention to the injured area, it would solicit *some* sort of apologetic response. Instead, all the old lady did was pick up her cup of steaming hot tap water—I noticed she'd put some kind of weird greenish black tea bag into the white "I ♥ New York City" mug I'd gotten as a gift from my best friend, Noh, when I first moved to the city—and nonchalantly walked over to where the cat was now

clawing happily at the arm of my Pottery Barn couch. I may've paid only pennies on the dollar for the thing at a floor-model sale—and there may have been a couple of rough spots on the back where the fabric had been torn during its time on the floor—but that didn't mean the dumb cat could use it for a scratching post!

"Stop that, cat," I said, going for strident, but instead settling for a wheeze. I tried to take in a lungful of air, but my lungs didn't seem interested.

Damn it!

The old woman gave the cat a gentle rub under the chin, and said, "That's enough now, Muna. I think we know all that we needed to know. Let's not asphyxiate the poor girl, shall we?"

There was a blinding flash that nearly scorched the tear layer right off my corneas, and instantly I could breathe again, my lungs no longer feeling like they were being compressed inside an iron vise. I wrinkled my nose, testing for any latent sneezes hidden inside my sinus cavity, but thankfully I was sneeze-free.

Satisfied that I wasn't going to suffocate after all, I opened my eyes, prepared for the worst—and boy, was I in for a shocker.

Muna wasn't a cat anymore.

On the arm of my couch—where only seconds before there'd lounged a fat, feline puffball—now crouched a skinny red-haired Minx. The fact that I instantly knew what the creature was called completely amazed me. I had never *heard* the term "Minx" before, let alone known that the species even existed, period. Now here was one of the little creatures sitting on the arm of my couch looking all pert and sassy . . . and very definitely female.

"You're a Minx," I said, like a little kid at the zoo who points at wild animals completely secure in the fact that whatever creature he is pointing at doesn't stand a chance in Hell of getting through the glass barrier to eat him. My index finger still wobbling happily in the air, I could feel the start of a big, dumb smile slowly spreading across my face. Apparently, there was just something about the tiny humanlike Minx that made me feel and act like a ten-year-old.

"Can you get the stupid human to stop gawping, please?" the Minx said, her voice still strangely low and masculine for something so feminine looking.

Well, that yanked the kidlike feeling right out of me.

"Jeez, so sorry for even *existing*," I mumbled as I instantly dropped my hand, glaring at both of them.

"Please, don't take offense, Calliope Reaper-Jones," the older woman said, a slow smile stretching across her face as the skin around her eyes crinkled sweetly. "The Minx can't help being so tart. Imagine what your life would be like if your appearance inspired such childlike wonder wherever you went."

I thought about that for a minute before nodding. I *guess* having the human populace, as a whole, moon over your every move *could* get annoying after a while.

"Sure, I get it. Being cute and adorable and kind of sexy in a little tiny creature/Peter Pan sort of way *could* probably get frustrating for you, I guess . . ." I trailed off as the Minx stared at me.

I wasn't the greatest when it came to deducing someone's height, but if I'd had to guess, I would've said that Muna topped out at about eighteen inches. With her violet, almond-shaped eyes, long, pitch-black hair, and high, cream-colored cheekbones, she was a stunning femme fatale in miniature.

In fact—strange as this may sound—she eerily resembled this Hot Looks doll I'd been madly in love with as a kid. It was actually something I'd inherited from my older sister, Thalia, but I was obsessed with it, dragging it with me everywhere I went like a tiny, human-shaped security blanket. My mother finally threw the doll away when its head fell off. Apparently, it made other people uncomfortable to see a six-year-old kid carrying around a filthy, headless, plush doll the size of a small terrier.

Yes, carting around a headless doll *was* kind of a weird thing to do, but I had my reasons. You see, there was something special about the Hot Looks doll. Something that I'd never told another living soul in the whole world (not even my therapist because I didn't want to give her a heart attack) and that *something* was that *my doll talked to me*.

Yeah, I know, a lot of kids have imaginary friends, but this was completely different. My doll (she said her name was Noodle, which seemed totally appropriate at the time because she was plushy and definitely more flexible than a plate of spaghetti) liked to do *naughty* things.

Now, when I use the word "naughty," you're probably thinking something along the lines of, oh, let's say, eating all the ice cream out of the freezer or not brushing your teeth and not going to bed when your parents tell you to or eating all the Halloween candy out of your sister's jack-o'-lantern bucket . . . but sadly, that kind of stuff didn't even *rate* on Noodle's meter of naughtiness. Let's just say that Noodle's idea of being *naughty* was just a little bit more intense.

Noodle almost made me throw my little sister, Clio, off the side of a cliff once . . . but that's *another* story entirely.

Needless to say, whoever created the Hot Looks dolls must've hailed from the supernatural world because the attitude and the resemblance between my doll, Noodle, and this Minx were pretty freaky.

"Hey, that's not what she meant at all, nitwit," Muna said, interrupting my thoughts as she rolled her eyes heavenward in a move that I recognized right out of my own playbook. "I'm not the frustrating one; it's you imbecilic humans who can't stop staring at me. You're the problem."

Jeez, I only hoped *I* wasn't this petulant and annoying when I was meeting new peeps.

"Muna is just being contrary," the older woman said, the smile still intact on her face. "Of course, one can never ignore the fact that it takes two to tango."

"Look, I appreciate the pearl of wisdom—I really do—but I have one question that needs answering, like, right *now*," I said, sounding louder and angrier than I'd meant to.

"Please, ask your question," the woman said, her voice a study in quiet modulation.

"Okay," I answered, trying to mimic her calmer tone. "Who are you and what do you want—other than to almost asphyxiate me in my own apartment? I mean, you just opened a *wormhole* right into my kitchen and invited yourself in," I babbled, getting myself worked up all over again. "So, like, what the hell?"

Instead of getting all peeved like I'd expected, the little old lady merely laughed, showing straight white teeth that looked shinier and newer than mine—even though she probably had about fifty zillion years on me. I figured it must be magic, because no matter how many Crest Whitestrips I suffered my way through, I would never have teeth as nice as that.

"To begin with, my *name* is Madame Papillon—"

"Wait! I know this one," I said, getting excited because I totally *did* know her name. "You're an aura specialist!"

The older woman slowly inclined her head forward in acquiescence—and for once in my life I actually had an inkling of what it must feel like to know the answer to the final *Jeopardy* question or the correct price of the bedroom suite on *The Price Is Right*.

"You saved my mother's life," I continued, gazing on the older woman with a fresh set of eyes. If she was the one who had saved my mother's life, then she was a formidable woman indeed.

Okay, let's pause for a second because you're probably wondering how someone who's *supposed* to be immortal can die. It's like this: Every immortal has one weakness that can kill them. Some immortals can't touch iron; others die when their heads are cut off . . . The list goes on and on and gets weirder and weirder as it goes. My mother's weakness just happened to be on the more domestic side of things.

My mother's weakness was snoring.

When my parents were first married, my mother wasn't immortal yet, so my dad's snoring hadn't bothered her one bit. But after my older sister, Thalia, was born and my mother was granted her immortality, well, things had taken an abrupt turn for the worse.

My father was beside himself, watching his beautiful young (and newly immortal) wife fading away into nothingness, so he had called in all kinds of experts to help discover the root of the problem. In the end, it had taken a highly gifted aura specialist—Madame Papillon, the little old lady standing in the middle of my living room drinking tea and looking all demure in a cream linen suit—to diagnose the problem and save my mother's life.

Now my parents slept in separate rooms (which had always seemed like a kind of depressing compromise to *me*), but at least they were going to get to spend eternity together. I guess that was *something*.

"And how are you involved in all this? Do you help Madame Papillon with all her important work?" I asked the little Minx.

I didn't mean for it to, but I guess my question came out as kind of condescending, which only seemed to piss the Minx off even more.

"You best mind your tongue," Muna spat at me, her violet eyes narrowed down to two malevolent slits. "I know *your* weakness now and it would only take a few moments to smother you with enough cat hair to—"

"Muna, that's enough," Madame Papillon said sharply, cutting off the Minx before she could finish her sentence. Muna turned bright red with anger, but at least she was silent now.

"I'm sorry about Muna. Like all Minx, she is possessed of a terrible temper," Madame Papillon continued. "Now, as to the reason that I just magically appeared in your kitchen, well, let's just say I was asked—"

There was a loud *ripping* sound and I looked down to see Muna pulling at a loose thread that was hanging from a long tear in the fabric covering the back of the couch. She yanked at the string again, causing the fabric to rip even wider.

"Don't wreck my couch, please," I said, annoyed because it was the only couch I had and I kind of liked it un-ripped-up.

"What? You can always buy a new one, can't you?" Muna replied snidely.

No matter how beautiful on the outside the Minx was, I decided, she was a total megabitch on the inside. Besides which, she didn't have a clue as to what she was talking about. I worked for a slave's wage at House and Yard, so if I wanted to buy a new couch or a new *anything*, for that matter, I really had only one of two options: I could sell an egg (of the human variety) *or* I could sell a kidney—and neither of those options sounded worth putting my body through in order to buy a piece of furniture.

"I want you to understand something, you little snot," I said, glaring at the Minx. "I don't take handouts from my parents. Everything you see in this apartment—including the apartment—was paid for by me, myself, and I, so why don't you just can it."

I had decided a long time ago that if I wanted to live like a real human being, then I was damned if I'd take any money from my father's supernatural endeavors. In fact, up until very recently I'd been living under a forgetting charm so I wouldn't even *remember* that my parents came from supernatural royalty. I was more than happy to believe they were just extremely wealthy jet-setters who hailed from the exclusive enclave of Newport, Rhode Island.

Money I could handle; supernatural stuff . . . not so much.

Muna shrugged. "Well, I guess we better go, then," she said, looking intently at Madame Papillon. "The girl doesn't take handouts."

"Muna." There was a note of warning underneath Madame Papillon's otherwise placid tone.

She turned her attention back to me.

"Whether or not your parents asked me to intercede, the fact of the matter is that you really are in desperate need of my help," Madame Papillon said, her eyes filled with concern.

"Without the proper magical training, I am afraid that you will find yourself continuing to get into situations that you cannot handle."

"I can handle situations," I said defensively. "I can handle lots of different situations. I'm very independent."

Muna snorted.

"Shut up," I said to the Minx.

"The fact remains that you must be educated, whether you like it or not."

I started to roll my eyes, then remembered how obnoxious it was when Muna did it and stopped.

"Look, I appreciate all the worry, but believe me—I have no intention of ever dealing with anything magical or death-related ever again. I am perfectly happy to live my normal life and let well enough alone," I replied.

"It's not really that simple," Madame Papillon said, taking another sip of her tea. "There are creatures who will want to destroy you simply because you are one of the three—two, now that the Devil's protégé has disappeared—in line to take over the Presidency of Death, Inc., when your father abdicates his position."

I sighed.

"I don't want to be Death. Why doesn't anybody get *that*? I have absolutely *zero* interest in all the power and stuff that goes along with the job. I just want to be a boring, run-of-the-mill human being. Is that too much to ask for?"

"Aiming for the stars, huh," Muna drawled sarcastically.

"Didn't you just hear what I said? I don't *want* to aim higher. I like my life exactly as it is."

Well, that wasn't *exactly* the truth, but *they* didn't need to know that. *I* was well aware of how bad my job sucked, that my apartment was too small, that I couldn't afford to buy any clothing unless it lived on the sale rack. I didn't need anyone else to harass me about all of the above. Besides, I really *was* pretty happy with my existence as a whole. I didn't want all the pomp and circumstance that went along with Dad's job. I could live in relative obscurity and be pretty damn happy about it, thank you very much.

"She doesn't want our help," Muna said.

"She just doesn't understand how important this is," Madame Papillon rejoined tersely. They were both talking about me like I wasn't even in the room—something that totally drove me up the wall.

"Look," I said, interrupting their back-and-forth. "I appreciate the concern—I really do—but the Minx is right. I don't want your help."

"That's not the point," Madame Papillon said. "You are in danger, whether you want to admit it or not. Your aura does not lie."

"What do you mean, 'your aura doesn't lie'?" I said, getting a little worried now.

"An aura is an immutable thing, Calliope, but sometimes, in very rare circumstances, it can be changed . . ." Madame Papillon said, then stopped, her mouth set in a firm line.

"Go on," I said, sensing that a really big shoe was about to drop. "Lay it on me."

Madame Papillon looked at Muna, who nodded for her to go on.

"Someone has . . . done something to your aura, Calliope."

"What the hell does that mean?" I asked testily. I absolutely hated it when people dragged out bad news. Better to just get everything out in the open as quickly as possible, as far as I was concerned.

Muna stared at me. Her eyes were full of what I can only term as *pity*—and that scared me more than anything else she could've done.

"Calliope—" Madame Papillon began, but Muna interrupted her.

"My old lady doesn't want to tell you the truth, but I have no problem doing it."

Madame Papillon looked down into her tea mug, verifying the truth of Muna's words. I swallowed hard, my stomach and

GI tract doing flip-flops inside my gut. *This was so not going to be good news,* I decided, feeling sick.

Muna looked deeply into my eyes as if she were trying to plumb my soul, and then, in a very soft whisper, she said:

"*You* don't have an aura at all."

three

"Just kidding," Muna said, obviously relishing the look of horror that she'd just put on my face. "But there *is* something wrong with it."

"There's nothing wrong with my aura," I said tersely. "If there was something wrong with it, I think I would know. I mean, it *is* my aura, for God's sake."

I looked to Madame Papillon for confirmation, only to find her rooting around in my kitchen, her otherwise dignified form buried waist deep in my refrigerator. I'd thought we were in the middle of an important conversation about me and my aura, but obviously Madame Papillon didn't find my problems to be all that pressing.

I watched as she took out the box of cupcakes I'd brought back from the Magnolia Bakery and lifted the lid. Her eyes closed in near ecstasy, she took a deep hit off the cupcakes, the smell seeming to transport her into another dimension.

"Oh my, that's good," Madame Papillon said, her voice thick with passion as she replaced the lid and set the box back in the refrigerator, quickly closing the door behind her like it was full of poisonous insects, not cupcakes. "Carrot cake, is it?"

I nodded. "That *is* what you asked for, isn't it?"

She stared at the door to the fridge, her eyes pinned on the door handle like she was afraid it was going to open of its own volition and once more assail her senses with the aroma of cupcake.

"Yes, that *is* what I asked for," she said, her voice strangely monotone as she spoke, her eyes still riveted on the refrigerator door.

I looked at her quizzically, my aura issues on hold as I tried to figure out what the deal with the cupcakes was. This was total weirdness. The woman had *insisted* on not one, but *two*, carrot cake cupcakes and now she wasn't even going to touch them—just sniff them while they were still in situ? Oh my God, I really hoped she wasn't just gonna leave them in my refrigerator. I could just imagine the magnificent pig-out session I would have if she did—and I didn't even *like* carrot cake. I definitely was *not* gonna let her leave those stupid things in *my* refrigerator for *me* to get fat on.

"You're not gonna eat them?" I asked, fishing around to see what the fate of the cupcakes was going to be.

The aura specialist shook her head.

"I love the smell," Madame Papillon said, finally seeming to snap out of her cupcake trance. "But my immortality would be forfeit if I ever tasted a bite."

It seemed strange to me that this renowned aura specialist was just revealing her killing weakness to me so blithely. I would've kept that secret pretty close to my chest, if it were mine. Of course, she dealt with immortals' weaknesses on a pretty constant basis, so maybe this was just old hat for her.

She looked back at the refrigerator sadly before giving me a wan smile. Then, as if in answer to my unspoken question, she said, "I've shared my weakness with you, Calliope, because I want you to feel that you can trust me with yours."

"Trust you with my weakness?" I stammered, starting to feel woozy with worry. "But I don't know what it is."

Muna rolled her eyes at me again—boy, that number was *really* starting to get old—before leaping off her perch on the couch and landing gracefully on Madame Papillon's shoulder.

"You are an incredibly dense individual," Muna said as she crawled on to the top of her mistress's head and curled up in a ball, her violet eyes closing as she yawned sleepily.

"Why am I dense?" I asked the Minx, but she was asleep before the words were out of my mouth.

Madame Papillon stroked the Minx's arm tenderly and smiled at me.

"Minx exert so much energy while they're awake that they spend more than half of their lives sleeping to make up for it," Madame Papillon said.

She whispered a few words under her breath that I didn't catch, then touched a finger to Muna's near-comatose form and the little Minx instantly turned into a puffy red ball of hair.

"Let's get back to the 'weakness' thing here," I said, not giving a rat's ass about Muna's sleeping habits. This weakness stuff was, like, *way* more important.

Madame Papillon nodded, and I decided that she looked about ten years younger now that she had her Minx pompadour back in place.

"As I'm sure you've guessed, Calliope," the older woman said softly, "felines are your weakness."

Okay, so *that* was why Muna said I was dense. I hadn't cottoned on to the fact that cats were my weakness. I guess it hadn't really registered with me because I had just assumed that if cats *were* truly my weakness, I would've already been dead from my run-in with Patience's cat, Muffins, last Christmas.

Of course, I *was* the supernatural newbie, so how was I supposed to know all the inner workings of immortality?

"But this is something that you must *only* share with the people that you trust the most," Madame Papillon continued, interrupting my thoughts. "Any enemy that discovers your weakness can use it against you . . . with dire consequences."

I swallowed hard. I definitely did *not* like the words "dire" and "consequences" in connection with anything to do with my life. Feeling overwhelmed by all this new information, I decided to file away the "cat weakness" stuff for perusal at a later date . . . when I wasn't feeling like my head was gonna explode.

"Okay, cats are my weakness. Got it," I said, moving on to something Muna had said that I had never gotten a straight answer about. "Now, what was Muna talking about when she said that there was something wrong with my aura?"

Madame Papillon sighed, setting her mug of tea down on my coffee table before settling into the overstuffed softness of the couch her Minx had almost shredded while in cat mode. I noticed that she had used one of the cute little coasters my coworker and friend Geneva had given me on my last birthday, which made me smile giddily.

You see, each coaster was a picture of a different hunk in uniform—one was a policeman; one was a fireman; one was a construction worker—only the kick with *these* coasters was that the material they were made out of was heat sensitive, so that when you put something really hot or really cold down on top of them, they, well . . . *transformed*.

Let's just say that I'd learned a lot about myself since I'd acquired the coasters. I mean, until they'd graced my coffee table, I'd had no way of knowing about my penchant for men in shimmering gold thongs and matching fire-retardant boots!

Forgetting about all the bad news that had just been leveled at me, I waited on tenterhooks for Madame Papillon to pick up her mug of tea and notice her naughty coaster. It only took a minute for my patience to be aptly rewarded. As she lifted her mug, the aura specialist let out a soft hiccup, then started giggling into the palm of her hand like a little schoolgirl.

"I see you got Mr. Fireman," I offered, peering over her to take a quick peek at Mr. Gold Thong—he *was* my favorite, after all.

"These are wonderful," Madame Papillon said, admiring the rest of the "clothed" men in my set—especially Mr. Construction Worker. "Wherever did you find them?"

I shrugged. "I didn't. They were a birthday gift, actually."

"Good gift," Madame Papillon said, smiling, as she poked at the construction worker with her pinky.

I could see the gears starting to shift in the older woman's head—I was pretty sure she was having the exact same thought I myself had had on the (more than) occasional lonely Friday night spent in front of the boob tube—so I wasn't surprised when she set her mug down on the construction worker's able abdomen.

"I had a pretty bad night once, made a huge pot of coffee, then did them all at the same time," I blurted out without thinking, then immediately started to feel embarrassed.

I hadn't *completely* forgotten that my parents had sent this woman and that she might very well be required to go back and give them an in-depth report on the meeting. I could just see my dad's face turn pink when she told him I had quasi-naked construction workers on display on my coffee table.

"We all have nights like that," Madame Papillon said sadly. And I really could believe that she *did* understand the plight of the single, miserable female.

"I had a man once," she continued. "One that I thought was special, but of course, they all make you feel as though you are the only woman in the world when they are using you for your power and success."

Huh? I thought to myself. *What kind of power and success did an aura specialist have that I didn't know about?*

I waited for her to go on, but with only that one piece of information revealed, her lips stayed firmly shut. From the pinched look on her face, I got the distinct impression that no matter how many questions I lobbed in her direction, I was so *not* going to get any more information about her lost bastard-for-a-lover.

I tried another tack.

"So, this whole aura thing? What's the deal? Am I really aura impaired or was Muna just screwing with me?" I asked, taking the other spot on the couch beside the aura specialist.

From this vantage point I could see *just* how grubby my place had gotten in the past few weeks. The kitchen counters were covered in crumbs, the floor needed a good sweep, and there was a layer of dust so thick on the edges of the coffee table that I really thought I might actually be breeding dust mites in it.

I was usually not *that* bad of a housekeeper, but a few months earlier my father had been kidnapped and I'd had to take an unapproved leave of absence from *my* job to go and take over *his* job. All this so that my family wouldn't lose their immortality. Seems like a pretty easy thing just filling in for Pops, right?

Wrong.

There is *nothing* easy about being the President of Death, Inc.

First of all, I had to complete three nearly impossible tasks (*like stealing one of the puppies of Cerberus, the three-headed Guardian of Hell*) just to prove I could handle the job. Next, I had to figure out who had kidnapped my dad and the rest of the executives that oversaw Death, Inc. (*turns out it was my extremely bitter older sister, Thalia, and her demon husband, Vritra—something I so did not see coming*). Finally (*and worst of all*), I had to watch as the only guy who had ever really treated me like I was a beautiful, desirable woman disappeared into the depths of Hell trying to save my existence.

All I have to say is that *I* thought I deserved a little hazard pay for all the shit I'd had to deal with, but of course, no way José was anyone in the *human world* gonna cut me any slack. I mean, they had no idea that the supernatural world even *existed* (*and in tandem with their own world!*), so as far as they were concerned, I had just gone off to Rhode Island to look after my ailing father (*who didn't even have the grace to die and give weight to my excuse*) in our family mansion (*too much info*) in Newport because this was the stellar story (*not!*) my dad's Executive Assistant, Jarvis, had come up with when he'd called the House and Yard office to explain my absence.

Luckily, everyone at work bought his explanation, so when I finally went back, the whole office was sufficiently solicitous about my dad's health . . . everyone, that is, but my überintelligent, überintense boss, Hyacinth Stewart.

And boy, was *she* pissed.

Apparently, the dumb girl that the temp agency had sent over to fill in for me while I was gone had e-mailed one of her friends (*in the middle of a workday*) to bitterly complain about the stupid, fat, ugly, bitchy woman she was working for. The poor girl hadn't learned the most basic lesson that one *must* adhere to when "assisting" for a living in Corporate America: Bosses *love* to read your personal e-mail—seriously, it's like an avocation for some of them—so *don't* write personal e-mails at work. Period.

Needless to say, Hy blamed me entirely for the psychological damage she had had to endure because of my absence. Not *really* my fault as far as I could see, but when you're someone's assistant, you learn very quickly to just grin and bear it. I mean, I really think someone should teach a class in college titled How to Succeed in Business by Nodding and Keeping Your Mouth Shut When Someone (Your Boss) Blames You for Something You Didn't Do.

I think a student's first work experience would be a lot more pleasant after having taken that class.

The ridiculous thing about the whole temp situation was how very *wrong* the substitute had been about my boss. Anyone who worked for her more than two minutes could see that Hyacinth Stewart was a devious and intelligent woman. One who was sharp as a tack and could be more manipulative than Erica Kane on a bender. She was anything but stupid.

Yes, the bitchy part was completely true—I won't fight you on that one—but the fat and ugly stuff? Well, if that was what the girl thought, then she was just a moron. Hy was a beautiful woman, and though she might've been on what one would term the plus-sized side of the scale, I don't think anyone with a brain cell in their head would ever use the word "fat."

Large, maybe, but *never* fat.

I mean, the woman knew exactly how to dress her larger frame so that she was ten times sexier than nine out of ten of the models running up and down Fifth Avenue, portfolios in sweating hand. Seriously, Hy knew exactly how to wrap a man around her finger and make him do whatever she wanted.

Hy knew something was fishy about my absence, but she just couldn't put her finger on what it was. Instead, she'd been Hell on wheels ever since I'd returned, keeping me so busy during the past few months that my life—and my apartment, by extension—was literally falling apart.

Enough said.

When I turned my attention back to Madame Papillon, she was looking at me oddly, almost with pity. I didn't know if it was just because my aura had some serious issues or whether it was only a gut-level response to how completely dirty my apartment was.

"I'm gonna clean it soon," I said, the words just popping out of my mouth.

Madame Papillon looked at me blankly. "Your aura?"

Guess I was just being paranoid about the old apartment, I thought dryly—and happily.

"Can you *get* your aura cleaned?" I asked. Maybe I really didn't have an aura problem if I could get it dry-cleaned or something.

"It can be cleansed," the older woman said, her eyes drawn back to the nearly naked construction worker on the coffee table, "but when someone puts a curse on your aura, you either have to live with it or make the person take the curse off. There's no dry-cleaning service, per se."

I shivered. It was like the woman had read my mind.

"What's *wrong* with my aura?" I asked, swallowing hard. "Is it cursed?"

Curse or no curse, I hadn't really had any problems with my aura recently (or ever) so maybe I could just ignore whatever was going on. The world of "denial" wasn't a terrible place to live in. I mean, lots of other people did it every day from what I could see and they weren't totally Looney Tunes, were they?

"No, your aura isn't cursed," Madame Papillon said, "but there is something *strange* about it. If I didn't know better, I would say that your soul was intertwined with another soul, but that's really only something you ever see in twins. And even that only happens in extremely rare cases."

"A twin?" I exclaimed. I'd always wanted to be a twin! I had spent a lot of my childhood feeling incomplete, like there was something missing, but I just didn't know what it was. Maybe I was a twin! Maybe *that* was what was missing?!

"But you're not a twin," the older woman said, taking a sip of her tea. The pleasant smell of anise wafted in my direction, and I remembered that she had asked for licorice tea with her carrot cake cupcakes when she'd called me earlier. Seemed she'd brought her own tea bag.

Smart lady.

"How do you know? I could be a twin and not even know it!" I stammered. I was *not* going to let the idea of a secret twin be dispelled that easily.

"A true intertwining of souls happens at conception, but your aura . . . has been tampered with recently."

How recently? I wondered. *Like a few months ago recently—because if that was the case, then maybe I wasn't a twin, after all.*

"Do dead people still have auras?" I almost whispered, trying not to let a misplaced sense of hope overwhelm me.

The aura specialist raised an eyebrow, but there was no way she could know what I was thinking. You see, I had *coalesced* (intertwined souls) with someone sort of recently. Not that it had been *my* idea to do the coalescing. Even just the remembrance of the event made me blush.

Let me preface this by saying that I'm not *usually* a lush, but when you're lost in the desert outskirts of Hell with no means of escape, your sense of self-preservation gets all screwy and you'll drink anything.

I was trying to complete one of the stupid tasks that the Board of Death had given me so I could take over my dad's job and save my family's immortality. I was miserable, I was exhausted, I was *lost* . . . and that was when I found myself totally blindsided by a poisoned Midori Sour that magically appeared before me.

Only the quick thinking of Daniel, the Devil's protégé, had

saved me from a fate worse than death: eternal hibernation at the hands of a poisoned girly cocktail.

Ugh!

Daniel had *coalesced* our bodies together—something akin to sex, but even more intimate. I mean, our bodies were *literally* merging together in a way that words do absolutely no justice to, all so that he could absorb half of the poison *for* me. We had both ended up with a couple of hangover headaches from Hell, but I had noticed no other ill effects from the poison . . . *until now*.

Now I find out that there was permanent damage. Our souls were intertwined! I didn't even know if the guy was alive or dead or what—and now we were sharing an aura?

Jeez, Louise.

Madame Papillon shook her head.

"No, your aura—the visible representation of your soul— leaves the body upon death and that is what passes on into the Afterlife for reassignment. So, as long as the body still lives, the aura remains."

"Jesus . . ." I breathed, my heart starting to hammer excitedly in my chest.

"An exception to the rule," Madame Papillon replied in a surprised tone.

"Huh?" I said, my brain only half listening to the woman now.

"Jesus was one of the few exceptions to the rule. He ascended bodily to Heaven, but that was an odd case."

"Excuse me?" I said, my attention slowly returning back to its senses. "Jesus *what . . . ?"*

"There are always exceptions to the rule," Madame Papillon continued, "so, I suppose that my answer to your question *was* incomplete, as you've so succinctly pointed out. A dead person *can* have an aura, as long as *said* dead person is Jesus, or someone of his ilk."

Now I was even *more* confused—and it had nothing to do with Jesus and his corporeal ascension to Heaven. What I wanted to know was if Daniel was still alive somewhere, hiding out where no one could find him. If our auras were still intertwined, then that had to be the case, right?

Or maybe I was just being single-minded and stupidly hopeful. Maybe the coalescing had absolutely *nothing* whatsoever to do with my superweirdo aura issues.

God, the whole thing was totally starting to give me a major-league headache.

Ignoring the throbbing in my head, I asked the one question that I *really* didn't want to ask, but that I really needed an answer to:

"Look, I have to ask you something kind of important, Madame Papillon, but please, please, please, I would be grateful if you would just keep it to yourself—you know, *not* share it with my folks," I finished, grimacing.

She nodded, but I had no way of knowing whether she was really trustworthy or not. She could be a pathological liar and I wouldn't know a thing about it until it was too late.

"Ask your question and I will keep it between us," the older woman said, patting the puff of hair that was Muna. "Even my Minx will not be told tale of this privileged conversation."

Boy, it was starting to feel just like a trip to my therapist's office. Only, *I* wasn't the one paying for the privilege this time.

"I've done some . . . *coalescing*," I whispered, feeling strangely dirty about the whole thing. It's not like Daniel and I had ever had sex or anything, so I don't know why I was feeling like such a prude.

"Oh," the aura specialist said, then cleared her throat. "I see."

"It was done to save my existence, I think, and only the once." I gave her a pitiful smile and she patted my hand in return.

"My poor little one, there's nothing to be ashamed of," chided the aura specialist. "There's nothing wrong with coalescing . . . especially if it was done to help you."

"Could that cause my aura to get all intertwined with the guy's aura?" I asked, feeling like a sixteen-year-old virgin in a sex ed class who hasn't really grasped the concept of how one acquires an STD.

"Yes, I think coalescing could cause something like this to happen," Madame Papillon said sagely. "I've never seen it before, but theoretically it *could* happen."

She set her mug of tea down on top of the construction worker and sighed deeply. She took my hand in her own and squeezed it.

"You asked me if the dead have auras. Was this in reference to the person you coalesced with?" she asked.

I nodded. "I thought he was dead, but now I don't know . . ." I stammered, but she shook her head, silencing me.

"Take this to heart, my dear," Madame Papillon said and I noticed for the first time how beautiful she must've been as a young woman. She had the most exquisite bone structure and truly haunting eyes, eyes that could almost hypnotize you if you weren't careful.

I blinked to dispel the image that I had conjured in my mind of the younger, more beautiful Madame Papillon, and that was when she hit me with it, the one thing that could turn both my heart and brain to mush:

"I have it on good authority that your young man is *anything* but dead."

four

Alone in my messy apartment, I sat on my Pottery Barn sofa and slowly pulled on the piece of thread that Muna had excised from the upholstery, wondering what my next move was going to be.

After the whole emotional blow of finding out that Daniel wasn't dead after all, well, the rest of Madame Papillon's visit had just seemed to fly by. Of course, it wasn't until she and her wily Minx were long gone that I realized exactly how out of it I had been.

I had agreed to let her give me a magic lesson.

And not just any kind of magic lesson, mind you. I wasn't just gonna *spell* something. Nope, I was going to let the aura specialist teach me how to summon and navigate wormholes, something that I had never ever been able to do in my entire life.

All I had to do was summon her and the lesson was mine—free of charge.

My older sister, Thalia—who was now safely ensconced in a tiny cell in the nether regions of Purgatory as she served out the one hundred years of solitude she'd gotten as punishment for her part in my father's kidnapping—had once told me that I was magically inept, that I wasn't even fit to be the *servant* of someone who could wield magic. I was only twelve at the time—and going through a sensitive, pudgy period where nothing about my body and/or mind felt right, so her accusations of magical ineptitude really felt like they were just par for the course. But still, I couldn't *totally* blame Thalia for my feelings of magical inadequacy.

Puberty is when magic really starts asserting itself in young women—must be something to do with all the hormones kicking through their systems—but for me, puberty came and went without magic ever manifesting itself at all. I was horribly embarrassed by my lack of magical talent and even more embarrassed by how ecstatic my father was about my magical duncehood.

While he seemed aware of, but not overly excited about, Thalia's prowess as a magic handler, with me, it was all about discouraging the ability. Something I still didn't 100 percent understand, especially now that he was sending Madame Papillon over to my place for private lessons—and probably paying her more for her time than I made all year.

The one thing that my dad and I did agree on when it came to magic was that it was best to keep the supernatural aspects of one's life under wraps. Especially when it came to letting humanity know anything about you and your abilities. I had taken that idea to heart, trying as best I could to kill all the supernaturalness inside myself. This was part of what had led me to take that forgetting charm, so that no one would *ever* take me for anything other than a human being while I was living out in the human world.

My dad's approach wasn't nearly as extreme; he had just put the kibosh on magic handling in the confines of his house.

Apparently, neither of my sisters had taken that rule very seriously, as both of them were pretty adept when it came to magic. I, on the other hand, couldn't even open a can without a can opener, let alone jump through space and time by summoning a wormhole.

Well, I decided, *I was gonna remedy that one* sooner *rather than later. Then maybe I could figure out how to get my hands on that wannabe corpse, the Devil's protégé.*

I thought back to what Madame Papillon had said about Daniel still being alive and I got both nervous and angry at the same time. How could he just leave me hanging like that, thinking he was dead and off to some other aspect of the Afterlife? I mean, I knew in my heart that I could never do something like that to someone I cared about . . . which then led me to a thought that made me feel even worse than I was already feeling.

Maybe he didn't let me in on this whole still-being-alive thing because he didn't give one rat's ass about my feelings. I was just some girl he had coalesced with once and that was it.

Okay, so I wasn't the queen of self-confidence, but no matter how much my brain kept telling me that I was being a total nut bag and overreacting, the insidious worm of doubt kept creeping closer and closer to my heart.

What if Daniel had faked his own death because he thought I was gonna go all stalker-y on him, or something? I mean, here I was thinking he'd saved my life when he took on the demon Vritra, but maybe that was all just some elaborate ruse to get away from me!

Looking back, I had to admit that I probably hadn't been the nicest person in the world to be around—especially when I thought Daniel and the Devil were in league to steal my dad's job and make my family mortal again—but I didn't think I had done anything weird enough to make Daniel want to stay out of my life forever.

Not that I could remember, at least.

In fact, there had even been a time when I thought that maybe Daniel and I might've been making a sort of love connection, or something. Now, in retrospect, it seemed like the only thing Daniel and I had been making together was bad blood.

Okay, now I wasn't just angry and nervous anymore. Nope,

the two feelings had metamorphosed into something much, *much* worse. A feeling that I had never experienced until right that very moment:

Resentment.

I was a woman scorned and I wasn't going to take it sitting down! I was going to find the jerkoid and make him explain to my face *why* he had pulled the wool over my eyes, no matter how long it took!

This was my new mission in life and I was just going to have to accept the fact that things were *not* gonna be pretty until I got my hands on the man and ripped the truth out of his cowardly little mouth.

Having accepted my new mission, I gave the piece of thread in my hand a good, hard yank, ripping off the entire side panel of the couch's upholstery in the process.

"Shit," I said out loud as I stared at the piece of fabric in my hand, seething.

Daniel, the Devil's protégé, was going to rue the day he ever messed with me, I thought angrily as I looked down at my shredded couch.

Now all I had to do was find the bastard.

And thank God I knew just the person to help me do it.

my younger sister Clio's bedroom looked like one of those retro Japanese sneaker stores you walk by and then have to do a double take because you realize it's a sneaker store only in retrospect.

Of course, her room hadn't *always* looked so sleek and spaceshiplike—it had actually been a much more hospitable environment up until about two weeks before, when Clio had decided to completely remodel her room from floor to ceiling.

For someone like me, who enjoyed sitting in a chair that looked like a chair—and not a wedge of aluminum—the place looked pretty stark.

The floor was silver industrial-grade linoleum stamped

with curlicues that perfectly matched the textured, gray-fabric-covered walls like they had been made to go together. The bed was one of those Tempur-Pedic mattresses set into the floor, so that when its silver, curlicue-covered comforter was all tucked in, it looked exactly like—you guessed it—the floor.

Something I discovered when I stepped on it and, unprepared for the floor to give way underneath my foot, fell on my face.

Not pretty, but not too painful, either.

There was also a large, metal modular workspace in the corner where Clio kept her myriad computer equipment. Beside it was a flat-screen television mounted on the wall, directly in line with the bed. Since I didn't even have a TV in my bedroom, period, the idea of something so big and movie theater–like that you could watch while lying flat on your back and eating Cheetos seemed pretty novel to me.

I wondered how hard it would be to take my own TV—one that was little more than a curio since I didn't have cable—and mount it on the ceiling above my bed, sort of like what they did in motels and hospital rooms. That might be pretty cool, huh?

Then I realized exactly how much I did *not* want my bedroom to in any way, shape, or form resemble a motel or hospital room and decided that it might be best to just leave well enough alone. My little twenty-two-inch TV was doing perfectly fine out in the living room gathering dust.

"I can come back if you're busy," I said as I watched as my little sister sitting in one of those delicious-looking ergonomic chairs in front of her computer, click-clacking away at the keyboard.

I was on the wedge of aluminum that only resembled a chair.

Without missing a beat, she turned her head in my direction and rolled her eyes.

"Whatever, Cal."

"I mean," I said, shifting my weight as I tried to make

myself more comfortable on the aluminum wedge, "if you're busy, I don't want to bother you, or anything."

Her fingers still flying over the keyboard, she shook her head. "Don't be a dweeb, I'm almost done and then I promise to give you my full, undivided attention."

"Oh, goodie," I mumbled sarcastically.

She gave me a sardonic smile, followed by about twenty seconds' worth of fluttering eyelashes, then she went back to her work.

Suddenly, I felt something cool and slobbery licking the top of my right hand. Startled, I yanked my arm away with such force that I nearly fell off the wedge chair and onto the linoleum.

"Goddamn it!" I yelped as I looked down to find our hell-hound puppy, Runt, happily wagging her tail at me. "Don't do that, Runt! You nearly gave me a heart attack . . . Jeez."

The beautiful, black hellhound pup sat back on her haunches and cocked her head at me. I could tell exactly what she was thinking: Calliope Reaper-Jones needs to take a chill pill—and she was so *not* wrong.

"Sorry, Runt. It's been a rough couple of weeks," I said as I reached out to scratch behind her soft, furry ears. She inclined her head forward so that I could get a better purchase on her neck and amp up my scratching. I took that as a sign that she had accepted my apology and didn't hold my being all jerk-y against me.

I looked down into her bright pink eyes and felt an over-whelming sense of love for the beautiful, midnight-colored puppy that had saved my life on more than one occasion. She was an amazing companion and friend, and I really, really, really looked forward to the time when she would develop the ability to talk. Then we could actually have a real conversation, instead of me constantly having to intuit what she was thinking.

I know that normally dogs don't *ever* develop that kind of ability, but since she was the daughter of Cerberus, the Guardian of the North Gate of Hell—and he could talk like no one's business—I got the distinct impression that Runt was gonna have a heck of a lot to say when her vocal cords finally started working properly.

"Uhm, about Runt," Clio said, interrupting my thoughts.

I looked up and saw that she had shut down the computer and was now giving me her "full, undivided attention." I gave my seventeen-year-old baby sister a long, clinical look, noting that she had finally decided to grow out her hair . . . a fact that gave me considerable pause.

Clio had been sporting a shaved head ever since her very cute twentysomething substitute biology teacher had made inappropriate overtures in the dating direction at the beginning of the school year, but now, instead of the baldpate I was used to, about two inches of fluffy black hair stood in its place. I knew that if she was starting to embrace her hotness again, then there had to be a reason for it . . . and that reason could only be of the male persuasion.

Whoever the guy was, I kind of felt sorry for him. If Clio had decided to stop hiding her beauty, then the poor guy was a goner. Seriously, my sister was probably *the* most beautiful person I had ever seen in my entire life—and that included Kate Moss and Christy Turlington—which only gave credence to the rumor that our mother was part Siren.

Only someone with Siren blood could be that amazing looking, as far as I was concerned. My mother was vehement that she was entirely 100 percent human, but I likened that to the old saying: *The lady doth protest too much.* With her pitch-black hair and doe eyes, Clio could send any man to his doom on the rocks of love without even batting an eyelash—just like all good Siren progeny.

I, unlike my two sisters, wasn't born with the gifts of beauty and/or a genius IQ. With my short brown hair and large brown eyes, I was attractive, but not beautiful—and my brain was definitely more attuned to the latest issue of *Elle* than to anything school oriented. Not that I was a terrible student, mind you, but I was definitely *glad* I would never be called on to answer another math problem in my lifetime.

"Earth to Callie," Clio said, bringing me back to reality. I was tempted to blurt out: "So, who's the lucky guy?" but instead, I kept my mouth sensibly shut on the topic, choosing only to reply to Clio's initial statement—as much as I was dying to pry into my sister's love life.

"What *about* Runt?" I asked demurely, tickling the puppy's neck underneath the pink and silver rhinestone halter she was wearing, a place where I knew she particularly loved being scratched.

"Dad didn't tell you?" Clio said, surprised.

"No, Dad didn't tell me anything," I replied, starting to get nervous. What had my dad decided *not* to tell me about now?

"Oh," Clio said, scrunching up her nose, a confused look on her face. "I thought he would've let you know."

"Let me know what?" I said, exasperated by all the pussy-footing around.

"That's why I thought you were in town," Clio continued, ignoring my question. "Because you'd been summoned."

"What?!" I nearly shrieked, feeling like my world was about to tip upside down again. I so could *not* deal with another round of tasks from the Board of Death—no matter whose immortality was at stake.

I guess my sister didn't know me very well if she thought I'd gotten my ass up at the stroke of six on a Saturday morning to take the three-plus-hour train ride from Penn Station to Providence, *then* wait another whole hour for the pleasure of taking the ferry into Newport just so I could deal with a whole bunch of bad-news supernatural business.

Trust me, if I had known I was in the process of being *summoned*, I'd have gotten on the train to Baltimore instead.

"Oh boy," Clio said, looking worried. "You better go see Jarvis. He has all the info."

"Crap," I replied.

As much as I had grown to like my father's Executive Assistant during the time when he had been *my* Executive Assistant—and had helped me fulfill the three tasks the Board of Death had given me in order to take over my dad's job and save my family—I still had absolutely *no* interest in getting a lecture from the faun right then. Literally, there was *nothing* Jarvis loved more than giving me a lecture—and those suckers could go on for *centuries*.

It was sort of sad in a "I have no life of my own" kind of way.

"Do I have to?" I moaned, knowing that if I had been summoned . . . then I had to. "Okay, at least fill me in a little bit, Clio. Who summoned me? Dad?"

Clio shook her head.

"Mother?" I asked, desperately hoping that my mother was *not* the person doing the summoning. The last time she'd asked for a favor, I'd ended up in Hell.

Clio shook her head again as I continued to scratch Runt's neck, her tail thumping contentedly on the floor in a legato rhythm that was very lulling.

"Who?" I moaned, not liking this one bit.

Clio looked down at Runt, then back up at me.

"Runt's dad."

Oh shit, I thought. *Cerberus had summoned me?*

"Did he say why?" I asked, even though I already knew it could only be because of one of two things: He either (1) wanted his daughter back, or (2) was calling in the favor I owed him—and both options seemed incredibly unappealing to me at that moment.

Double shit.

Clio shook her head. "Sorry. That's all I know. Not in the loop." She shrugged.

Great. Clio was as in the dark about this whole thing as I was, which meant I couldn't pick her brain for more succulent little details before having to go and interface with the Jarv-meister.

"Well, you leave me no choice. I guess I'd better go and see Jarvis, then," I mumbled, not *really* wanting to but knowing that I had to.

"Hey, don't tell anyone that I was the one that told you," Clio said suddenly as I stood up, my butt sore from my hard metal perch. "I wasn't supposed to know about it."

"Will do, Captain," I replied, giving Runt a pat on the head before heading for the door. "And thanks for the heads-up."

I was almost out the door before I remembered the real reason I'd come to Newport in the first place.

"Uhm, could you do me a huge favor?" I asked, feeling uncharacteristically annoyed with myself for needing her help. It wasn't like I was a complete mental reject, or anything. I mean, it was totally within the realm of possibility that I could discover Daniel's whereabouts without having to use Clio's phenomenal brain as some kind of human cheat sheet.

Sometimes I wished I were a little less lazy. Maybe life would be more hospitable to me if I actually applied myself to living it properly.

"Callie, your wish is my command." Clio grinned, turning back around from her keyboard and giving me a sisterly wink.

I swallowed hard, not looking forward to the bevy of questions my "favor" was going to invoke.

"Can you tell me how I might get a look at someone's Death Record?" I sort of mumbled, trying to sound as nonchalant as I possibly could.

Clio stared at me, a slow grin spreading across her face.

"And by *someone*, don't you really mean you want to take a peek at your buddy *Daniel's* Death Record?" she shot back at me.

I could see the look of utter curiosity in her eyes and decided that the best defense was a good offense.

"Look, I would love to sit here and chat about boys with you—oh, and by the way, who's the lucky fella?" Clio turned bright red at my words, verifying without any question that she was a smitten lady.

"I don't—" she started to protest, but I raised my hand for silence.

"Like I said . . . I would love to stay and hear all the gory details about your new man," I continued, not letting her get a word in edgewise, "but, you know, I gotta go deal with being summoned and all, so just let me know when you've got that info I needed."

I turned and shut the door behind me as fast as I could, leaving a red-faced Clio unable to say another word. *Yes,* I thought happily, *score one for Calliope Reaper-Jones!*

Little did I know then how *badly* I was gonna get creamed in overtime.

five

The house that I grew up in is huge. Seriously, it's so big that it even has its own name: Sea Verge.

When I was a little kid, I used to worry about losing my friends and never finding them again when we were playing hide-and-seek inside it. The fear was derived strictly from the fact that my house wasn't just a *house* like everyone else's . . . No, my house was basically its own ecosystem. And since seven- and eight-year-olds aren't the most astute creatures in the world, with fourteen bedrooms and nine bathrooms alone in the place, you can well imagine why I would be a little freaked-out.

Just lose one Sally or Mary to the mysterious confines of Sea Verge and no other parent would ever let their kid go and play at *your* house again.

As I got older, I spent more summers than not exploring the inner workings of Sea Verge, so that it ceased to be a place that was alien to me. I think my therapist would say I was just confronting my fears, but I'm pretty sure there was no psychology involved in my efforts. In the end, I was just so damn curious about the place that I wanted to know everything I could about it.

Maybe it did offer some kind of control over my out-of-control life, just knowing the intricacies of the place I grew up in, but after a few summers of intense exploration, I got to the point where I knew every secret doorway, every hidden passage, and every dead end in the place.

My least favorite part of Sea Verge turned out to be the kitchen.

It just wasn't as exciting to me as the rest of the house because it had been completely remodeled when my parents first bought the place. My mother loved to cook, so she'd had the kitchen tricked out with every gizmo and gadget known to modern man, as well as filled the space with so much marble that it reminded me more of a mausoleum than a kitchen—all of which was cool from a culinary perspective, and it did mean that we had the first trash compactor in the neighborhood, but I guess I've just never been all that bowled over by flashy kitchen appliances.

Of course, the kitchen was *exactly* where I found Jarvis. He was making himself a goat cheese (totally ironic, huh?) and sun-dried tomato pesto sandwich on focaccia bread with a side of ginger and jicama salad that my mother's chef, Declan, whipped up when he wasn't feeling particularly moody.

Seriously, you could always tell what emotional state Declan was in by what you found waiting for you in the refrigerator. Fatty, home-style dishes connoted that one of his notorious black moods was on the horizon, while lighter, healthier fare meant he was in a sunnier state of mind.

Go figure.

Anyway, Jarvis seemed so pleased with his artisanal creation that he delicately sliced the sandwich into two equal halves and offered one of them to me. Since I hadn't eaten anything but a gross-out, rubbery breakfast wrap at the train station, I didn't comment on how ironic I found it that a faun was eating goat cheese. Instead, I turned my focus to inhaling my half of the delicious-smelling sandwich as quickly as possible.

"That was scrumptious," I said as Jarvis handed me a paper

napkin and I tidied up the crumbs on my face as best I could. "Anything good to drink in the fridge?"

I walked over to the Sub-Zero refrigerator-freezer combo that my mother had had special ordered in Nantucket white—to match the white, Shaker-style cabinets and the black-and-white veined marble countertops, of course—and opened the refrigerator side. I found a large pitcher of homemade strawberry lemonade waiting for me on one of the shelves and quickly moved it to the kitchen counter. Next, I took out a slim, translucent glass from one of cabinets and poured myself a taste of the good stuff.

"You're like a twelve-year-old boy," Jarvis said as I greedily gulped down my glass of lemonade, burping loudly when I was finished.

"Sorry," I replied, covering my mouth. "God, I was hungry."

Jarvis, who was still eating his own sandwich, raised a delicate eyebrow in my direction.

"You don't look like you're starving, Mistress Calli—" He quickly shut his mouth, pained at not being able to use the word "Mistress" in front of my name.

During his foray as my Executive Assistant, I had forbidden him to call me *Mistress* anything. Jarvis desperately loved standing on ceremony—I think it made him feel like he was in control of whatever situation he happened to be in—but I refused to let him have his way, insisting he call me Callie, or at worst, Miss Calliope—which only made me sound like a second grade teacher or a Jane Austin heroine. Take your pick.

"Miss Calliope, I was just going to say how well fed you're looking these days," Jarvis began again, giving me a smarmy smile. For a guy who rarely wore pants (why wear pants when you've got goat haunches instead of legs!) and was barely four-eleven on a good day, he was a pretty self-assured little devil. Pants or no pants, I guess he knew he could kick my ass any day of the week he wanted.

I gave him a dirty look, not really meaning it—okay, I meant it a little bit, because everyone knows that there's always a grain of truth to any snarky comment someone makes.

And I *had* been indulging more than usual in the office kitchen's assortment of baked goods, so there might well be some merit to what Jarvis was saying . . . but I really, really hoped not. I so could *not* afford to gain any weight, or I'd have to go naked. And I meant that literally—I really didn't have the money to buy anything new if I started splitting the seams on the clothes I already owned.

Fat comments aside, engaging in a little verbal back-and-forth was old hat when it came to my relationship with Jarvis. I knew when he gave me attitude it was only because he liked me. Otherwise, he wouldn't have deigned to talk to me at all, the conceited little bitch.

"The same could be said for you, too, Jarvi," I said, smiling back at him and showing as much teeth as possible. "I'm surprised Declan hasn't mistaken you for a rump roast and put you in the oven."

"Touché," he answered, nodding his approval.

I just have to say now that no matter what I've said in the past about Jarvis, he's a stand-up guy who risked his life to help me. If he hadn't saved me from the clutches of a would-be baddie, God knows where my family or I would be right now—probably trapped in Purgatory with no means of escape, or worse.

Jarvis had always been a loyal and efficient Executive Assistant to my dad, but to me, he wasn't just an employee. To me, he was . . . *my friend*. A friend who *loved* to be annoying and give lectures, but a friend nonetheless.

"So, tell me about this whole summoning thing," I said nonchalantly as I poured myself another glass of strawberry lemonade.

Jarvis sighed, pulled a pair of pince-nez from his immaculately tailored navy suit coat pocket—I was pretty sure it was an Armani number, but since I'm not a real menswear nut, I couldn't be 100 percent certain—and placed them on his hawkish nose. For a faun, Jarvis wasn't half-bad-looking, I decided. Except for the goat flank, shank, and hooves, he kind of reminded me of a less-laid-back Tom Selleck—especially when he was sporting his *Magnum, P.I.* mustache, which was for as long as I'd known him.

"Well, I'm sure you read the notice," Jarvis began, but I stopped him.

"What notice?" I said.

Jarvis sighed again.

"The notice that was left at your apartment by yours truly," he said with exasperation, indicating himself.

"Was it in a red envelope?" I asked, starting to feel a little guilty.

"Yes," Jarvis replied warily. "It was in a *red* envelope. You didn't throw it away, did you? Oh my Lord, you didn't!"

I always hated it when someone had a conversation with you and they didn't let you contribute . . . especially when they passed Go, collected the two hundred measly bucks, and got to the truth of the matter without your help.

I also hated the high-pitched—very British-y—tone Jarvis got when he was extremely upset. Total whine city. Seriously.

"How the hell was I supposed to know it was so important?" I screeched, almost knocking my glass of lemonade over in my agitation. "It was just sitting there for, like, ever."

"Do you *have* no curiosity?!" Jarvis bellowed, the anxious click of his hooves on the wood floor like buckshot. His sharp, intelligent eyes raked mine and I felt so guilty I had to look away. *Damn it, why didn't he just leave me a note or something?* I thought angrily.

"You obviously didn't see the note I left with it, then, did you?" Jarvis hissed.

Oops.

Jarvis stared at me, then shook his head, frustrated.

"I give up," he finished, picking up his plate and putting it in the overlarge side of the kitchen sink that was built for scrubbing pots and pans.

"I repeat," I said finally, "how was I supposed to know?"

Jarvis, his back to me as he washed off his plate, said, "You were just *supposed* to know, or at the very least you were *supposed* to notice my note and read it."

"I'm sorry," I said softly, feeling like a total heel.

I had seen the stupid red envelope sitting on my kitchen counter, and, knowing full well that it contained something I did not want to deal with, I had just casually thrown it away after ignoring it for three days first. The note, too, I guessed, had been chucked in the trash as I remembered paying as little attention as possible to the envelope as I slid it into the garbage.

"Really, I am."

Jarvis turned back around to face me, his mouth set.

"I accept your apology and I know that this was not something you would do on purpose."

Shit! I thought guiltily but nodded my head like the penitent I was supposed to be. A mean thought niggled at the back of my mind, making me wonder if Jarvis knew I'd thrown the envelope out on purpose and was just digging in the knife. I decided not to push my luck—let him think I was too dumb to notice he was trying to manipulate me—and just accept my feelings of total and complete guilt as punishment enough for the day.

"What did the summons say?" I asked tentatively, but Jarvis just shrugged.

"I don't know. I didn't open it."

Damn it! The bastard was enjoying this, I thought angrily, noting the hint of a smile that was slowly transforming his face. He *knew* that I *knew* that he *knew* and he was *enjoying* it!

"You did this on purpose!" I shrieked as I started pacing back and forth next to the polished marble island that dominated the room. "You were just *waiting* for this, *weren't* you?"

Jarvis started to giggle and I swear to God I almost decked him.

"I had a feeling," he moaned between breaths as the giggling became full-fledged laughter.

"Oh, you jerk, you knew I would throw it away and you specifically didn't read it on purpose," I said, my face turning red with anger. "You. *Suck.*"

This only made him laugh harder.

"So, now what do I do?" I moaned, taking an angry sip of lemonade and nearly choking on it.

"I guess," Jarvis said, starting to calm down now, "you go down to Hell and see what the big, three-headed dog wants."

"And what if he wants Runt back?" I said angrily.

This was something that I didn't want to think about. Runt had become like a part of my family and I had no intention of giving her back now. She may have stayed at Sea Verge with Clio, but that was for purely selfless reasons. I mean, what kind of life would a hellhound pup have trapped in a tiny one-bedroom flat in New York City?

A miserable one, that's what.

Jarvis merely nodded at my question. "I assumed that was the reason for your summoning."

Of course, Jarvis had no idea that I owed Cerberus a favor, one that he could collect on at any time, so the thought that I might be summoned for something other than Runt's future wouldn't have occurred to him.

"What do I do?" I asked. "How can I get him to let us keep her?"

Jarvis shrugged.

"That's between you and him . . . and Runt."

I looked up, startled.

"You mean, Runt may actually have a say in this?"

Jarvis shrugged again, then picked up the pitcher of lemonade and put it back in the refrigerator.

"From what I understand about hellhounds, it's the females that you have to worry about," Jarvis said, beginning one of those lectures he so loved to give. "They are the dominant sex of the species—"

"But Cerberus is *huge*. And he has *three heads*," I interrupted.

"Yes, the females may be the smaller of the two due to sexual dimorphism—and they may only have one head—but that doesn't really matter much these days. The females are the ones in control. They choose a life partner to mate with, then after the young are weaned, they go and hunt while the males look after the children."

"Amazing," I said, liking how the hellhounds did business more and more. "So, why is Cerberus the Guardian of the North Gate of Hell and *not* his wife?"

Jarvis shrugged.

"I assume that the females don't want to be tied down, so the job of Guardian would be better suited to a male."

"Interesting," I murmured, wondering how best to put Jarvis's information to use while I was down in Hell.

"How long do I have before I have to go down there?"

Jarvis looked at his watch.

"Forty-seven minutes. The summons expires after that, and you could end up in Purgatory for failure to comply with a direct order from a minion of Hell," Jarvis added quickly.

"Good thing I came to visit when I did," I said, curious at the way fate seemed to work these things out.

"Yes," Jarvis said, eyeing me like I was some alien creature whose actions he could just not comprehend. "*Good thing*, as you say."

I spent the next forty-three minutes sitting in one of my favorite spots in all the grounds at Sea Verge. It wasn't overlooking the water, or ensconced in the English rose garden. No, it was a simple little spot, just a small stone chair really, nestled between a pair of spindly pink tulip trees, but it had always felt special to me. Like it was my place.

Next to the chair was a small stone statue of a little girl kneeling beside a tiny rabbit, her fingers tentatively reaching out to touch the quivering bunny's flank. I had no idea who the girl was, but she always seemed very sad to me. The idea of forever reaching out to touch something that you could never reach . . . Well, it was just really depressing.

I guess that was why I liked the spot so much. It reminded me of me a little bit. *I* was always reaching out to be human but remaining immortal for as long as my dad saw fit to keep me that way.

I looked out past the water, the sound of its foaming bulk gently crashing against the rocks acting like a lullaby to my frayed nerves. Finally, I turned my attention back to Sea Verge itself.

The hands of men may have built our house, but its origins were entirely the brainchild of a woman, the shipping heiress Sophia Miles-Stanton. The legend went that she had drawn up the architectural plans herself in a frenzy of creativity one night and just presented them to her architect the way the Goddess Athena had burst fully grown from her father Zeus's forehead.

The construction of the house took the better part of two years to finish, but while she waited for her dream home to be completed, Sophia was anything but idle. She hired a young man named Edwin Bell, formerly of the landscape design firm Olmstead and Vaux—the very firm that had designed Brooklyn's jewel, Prospect Park—to help her conceive of the gardens that would surround the house.

It was during the course of their collaboration that the upstart young landscape artist fell in love with Sophia, a fact you can see directly in the small tokens of his affection that are interspersed throughout the gardens. Only pink roses—Sophia's favorite—bloom in the delicately sculpted English rose garden; forget-me-nots pop up like clockwork every spring with a pugnacious vitality; summer sweet and wild honeysuckle proliferate along the stone pathways and in the pink tulip tree–shaded overlooks that dot the edge of Sea Verge's grounds.

At the lip of the most northerly cliffs, there are three small stone benches overlooking the water. The benches, all three made from the same polished white marble, are overgrown with a strain of Virginia creeper whose leaves turn a dusty shade of rose at the first sign of autumn, making the benches appear as if they're upholstered in pink fabric. That same vine has become so prolific that it's made its way back up to the main house and has slowly been taking over the entire north side of Sea Verge for as long as I can remember.

One summer my sister Clio and I discovered an inscription hidden underneath the middlemost of the three benches. Time and the salty ocean air had almost destroyed the words, but if you looked closely enough, you could still make them out: "My love lingers here always—EB."

Clio and I thought it was the most romantic thing we'd ever seen . . . until we discovered that Edwin Bell, heartsick over his unrequited love for Sophia Miles-Stanton, had purportedly leapt to his death from that very spot. The official story was that he had accidentally slipped off the edge of the cliff, but still, can you say creepy, anyone?

Needless to say, Clio and I weren't all that supercrazy about hanging out by the benches anymore, so that part of the yard stopped being our favorite place to play in, which I think really pleased my mother. She was always afraid that we were gonna fall off the cliff face or something equally horrible.

This absurd fear of my mother's was something that just didn't compute with me because I'd known my family was immortal from a reasonably early age, and I really didn't understand what difference falling off a cliff made in the grand scheme of things. Maybe it was just a little vestigial *humanness* left inside my mother that hadn't worn off yet, or maybe she was just a nut about people's body parts remaining intact.

Who knows?

Anyway, to this day, whenever I look at the benches sitting out on the headland covered in firm pink leaves, I get the willies.

Barring the "accidental" death of the talented young landscape designer, the day Sea Verge was completed was as glorious a day as there ever was in Newport. People from all over the island trooped up to see the finished project, marveling over the beautiful limestone façade and the overflowing gardens of sweet-smelling flowers and greenery. It was the beginning of an era in Newport. Over the next few decades, the town would see Bellevue Avenue and its surrounding areas become a bastion for the highborn *and* the nouveau riche—a place where money was an anodyne to whatever eccentricity made its home there.

In the end, Sea Verge was *exactly* as Sophia had imagined

it in her mind that feverish night of creation. She felt so much love for the house and its sprawling gardens that she lived there until the very day she died.

I looked at my watch and saw that my time was almost up. I stood up stiffly, my butt sore from the long sit on cold stone, and stretched. As much as I hated going back down to Hell, I knew it was a necessary evil. I would go and see Cerberus, find out what he wanted—if it was the favor, I would do it, and if it concerned Runt, well, I would beg on my hands and knees to keep her if I had to. Having sorted out in my mind how I intended to deal with the Cerberus situation, I began the long march through the gardens and back up to the house.

It was only when I was halfway to the back door that I realized I hadn't thought of Daniel *once* since I'd left Clio's room.

It wasn't a huge victory, I decided, *but it was a start.*

six

I did *not* like Hell.

It was hot and sticky and *extremely* good at ruining whatever outfit you happened to have on. And since I hadn't known a trip to Hell was on the day's agenda when I got dressed that morning, I had *not* known to attire my person accordingly.

In fact, I'd been feeling so good about myself when I'd woken up that morning that I'd forsaken my usual Juicy sweats (my Saturday ritual) for a cute little "impulse buy" Missoni sweater I'd gotten on sale at Loehmann's, pairing it with a pair of black, stretchy stovepipe Seven Jeans that I just adored because they always made my butt look way rounder than it actually was.

The feeling of contentedness continued as I admired my clothing selection in the bathroom mirror. I looked so well dressed and put together that it gave me the confidence to take out the new taupe Steve Madden high-heeled boots I'd just bought (with money squeezed out of my already too tight food budget) *and* had promised myself I would return, unworn, for a complete refund. As I stared at the beauties, I decided that food could be forgone—I didn't really need to eat lunch for the next two weeks, did I?—but a good pair of boots that went perfectly with any choice of ensemble, well, they were worth the forced starvation I was now going to have to endure. Besides, there was always my favorite place at work, the kitchen, to save me from complete anorexia. I knew no one would mind if I filched a few extra blueberry-crumble muffins from the kitchen's stash of work-time goodies, instead of ordering one of those to-go sandwiches (that cost a small fortune anyway) from the downstairs deli.

As I slid the boots onto my feet, they felt so good that I knew, once again, that my decision to keep them had been right. I felt like I was serving destiny . . . and looking fabulous at the same time.

Now, standing in the middle of the kitchen, waiting for Jarvis to open a wormhole in the fabric of time, I realized it must *not* have been destiny's work that morning—or if it had, then destiny was a nasty bitch whom I was prepared to dislike intensely for putting my new boots at risk by sending me to Hell.

"Are you sure you want to go alone?" Clio said as she picked at a piece of cinnamon-raisin toast she'd just pulled from the toaster.

She'd come down a few minutes earlier to let me know that even though all the Death Records were kept in Purgatory, you had to have a writ from the Board of Death in order to get a look at any of them. That was good to know, especially because I was on decently friendly terms with one of the members of the Board of Death, the Goddess Kali. She had been instrumental in helping me rescue my dad a few months earlier and we had sort of become friends during the effort. I knew from my prior dealings with her that she could be moody as an ass and hard to deal with, but ultimately she was pretty fair. Getting her help would be a difficult, yet probably rewarding, proposition, I decided.

"I think that bringing anyone else with me might piss him off," I said, even though I was only half telling the truth. I wanted to deal with Cerberus on my own terms, with no worries about endangering anyone else in the process.

"If you think so," Clio said, crunching into her toast, "but Runt isn't just yours, so, you know, don't let him have her without a fight."

Having heard her name, Runt thumped her tail, and nuzzled my hand.

"I won't make you go back to Hell unless you want to," I said, petting her silken head. Then to Clio, "Just trust me, okay?"

Clio nodded, but I could see that she looked worried. After everything we had been through together, I realized that she still didn't 100 percent trust me. I guess trusting someone to do the right thing and not screw it up was hard . . . and when the whole "not screwing it up" thing dealt directly with the fate of someone (Runt) that you loved, it was even harder.

I took Clio's hand and gave it a firm squeeze.

"I promise I will do everything within my power to make sure that Runt goes where she wants to go and not where her father tells her she has to go," I said, looking right into Clio's eyes. She nodded and I could see that she was trying not to cry.

"I promise, Clio."

I hated to see my little sister cry. She was usually the stalwart one and I was the emotional mess. It was weird to have our roles reversed.

It seemed like the terms "adulthood" and "responsibility" were quickly becoming my new buzz words—even though I had consciously been trying to ignore them. I didn't *want* to be responsible for anyone else—I didn't even want to be responsible for *myself* most of the time—but it seemed like the more I fought it, the more it got foisted onto my plate.

"I trust you, Cal," she said, squeezing my hand back.

Stupid responsibility, I thought to myself wryly. Now I *had* to make sure that Runt stayed at Sea Verge with us, or else Clio was gonna hate my guts for the next century.

"Want some toast?" she said, interrupting my thoughts and offering me a bite of her cinnamon toast. I laughed, shaking my head.

"No, thanks, you know how queasy wormholes make me."

I wasn't very good with the whole "traveling through time and space" thing. I had a very delicate stomach and all the sloshing around your body did inside a wormhole always made me feel like I was gonna throw up my breakfast *along with* my pancreas and maybe my spleen.

Like stuffing something into a blender and hitting pulse, it's a very quick and simple way to travel, but there's always a trade-off for such efficiency . . . *You* get pureed!

"You ready?" Jarvis said, his voice pinched as he prepared himself for the effort of calling up the wormhole. Jarvis was a real pro at it; basically all he had to do was just snap his finger and the ether would instantly start swirling all around him. A minute or two later and there would be a full-fledged wormhole in the middle of the kitchen.

I watched as Jarvis closed his eyes and began to concentrate. The only thought that kept running through my brain as I waited was: How sad and silly was it that I couldn't call up a wormhole for myself? Even Clio could do it and she was only seventeen. Why had I been so averse to learning this little bit of magic that *would* and *could* make my existence a heck of a lot easier? I had no answer for myself. I guess I *did* need Madame Papillon's help way more than I even realized. Which reminded me that I should probably thank my parents for sending her my way in the first place . . . but apparently that was something I'd have to wait to do until they got back from Scotland.

Unbeknownst to me, they had decamped to the Scottish Highlands for some kind of foodie tour/second honeymoon— which no one had bothered to tell me about, of course—and wouldn't be back in the country for two more weeks. Boy, I wish I'd gotten to experience that side of my dad's job . . . I *definitely* could use a serious vacation after all the family and work crap I'd been dealing with recently.

There was a loud *pinging* sound and suddenly the wormhole was there, a black, eddying mass whose sheer power beckoned me toward it. I swallowed hard, my throat tightening and making it hard to breathe. I so did not want to step into that thing even though intellectually I understood *why* I had to. It was funny, but every time I was forced to travel this way, I always found myself wanting to take the stairs instead.

Maybe I could just take the Devil's express elevator down to Hell—I'd done it before—and damn the consequences? I looked around, hoping that some higher power would hear my plea and make my wish a reality, but of course, no express elevator magically appeared in front of me. Cursing my fate under my breath, I did the only thing I *could* do in the situation:

I stepped into the wormhole.

it was just like I remembered it . . . *awful.*

The trip was so bad that once I landed in Hell, I did exactly what my stomach had always threatened to do, but had never done before: I threw up Jarvis's delicious goat cheese and sundried tomato sandwich all over my new boots. Yep, when I stopped retching, I saw that my Steve Madden high-heeled boots had vomit (mostly churned-up tomato) all over them.

"Not the shoes!" I wailed in desperation. I tried to rub them in the sand, but it was a no go. Instead of getting rid of the throw-up like I'd hoped, the sand grains just made translucent scratches in the soft pleather, which the vomit then seeped into.

Crap!

After a few moments of intense grieving for my new shoes, I began to check out my surroundings. Apparently, Jarvis had miscalculated or something, because I wasn't in the right part of Hell. Somehow, I had ended up in the superhot, superyucky desert part of the place instead of in the Marc Ryden–looking foresty part of Hell by the North Gate, where Cerberus lived. I'd spent enough time here in the past to know that I definitely wanted to get out of the desert part as fast as humanly possible, and the only thing I could do to make that happen was to start walking.

It took me three hours and a whole lot of luck, but I made

it. My feet ached from walking in sand, I smelled like vomit and sweat, plus I was way past my forty-five-minute allotted time to meet Cerberus. *Things are not looking good,* I thought as I stepped out of the tree line and onto a grassy verge. Across from the grassed-off section, I saw a long, thin dirt trail that would lead me, hopefully, to the North Gate and to my appointment with Cerberus.

The last time I'd been here was to steal one of Cerberus's puppies, so there'd been a fair amount of sneaking involved. I'd had Jarvis with me at the time, but other than giving me a lecture about the different gates of Hell and what departed souls entered what gate, he hadn't been too much help. Later, he'd been worth his weight in gold, but not in my dealings with Cerberus.

I stepped onto the trail, picking my way across some fallen tree branches, not even *daring* to look down at the mess I had become. Like I said before, when visiting Hell, one does *not* want to wear one's Saturday best . . . and I was living proof of that fact.

"Poor babies," I said out loud, looking down at my shredded boots. "My poor, poor babies."

There was a rustling in the underbrush to my right and I sped up, trying to get away from the sound. I didn't want to get tangled up in any other weird business while I was in Hell. I just wanted to find Cerberus, hear him out, and then get back home, where I belonged—and by "home," I meant my apartment in New York, not Sea Verge.

The rustling in the underbrush got louder, causing me to pick up my pace even more. Whatever was making the noise hadn't gotten close enough to warrant an all-out run yet, but I was totally starting to feel like one of those middle-aged, sweat suit–wearing ladies you saw fast-walking at the mall.

Suddenly, I caught a flash of bright yellow shooting toward me from out of the brush and I took off running. I hadn't really gotten a good look at the thing, but it *seemed* quick and compact and ready to bite my head off without the least provocation.

"Leave me alone!" I screamed, too freaked-out to look back and see if it had gained any ground on me. "I don't taste very good, I swear to God!"

Trying to run in a pair of high-heeled boots is sort of like trying to run barefoot: You step on anything less flat than the road and you end up face-first in the dirt. It didn't take but two seconds for me to step on something hard and round, probably a rock, and go flying. I was moving with so much velocity that I actually think I was airborne for about thirty seconds before I began my descent and landed on the ground, smacking my chin into the hard, compacted dirt. I felt my jaw slam together like a pair of those fake, plastic, windup toy teeth, the taste of blood strong in my mouth. I had impacted the ground so hard that I'd nearly bitten my tongue off.

I ignored the burning pain in my mouth as I crawled to my feet and started running again—"limping" is really the correct term—fear making my heart jump around in my chest in quadruple time. Yep, abject terror is a really great motivator. It kept my feet moving long after the rest of my body had already given up.

After a few minutes of run/limping, I realized that I wasn't being followed anymore, or if I was, whoever was doing the following had no interest in catching me. With my breath tight in my chest and a stitch in my side, I slowed down to a walk and took a tentative look at my supposed pursuer.

Sitting in the middle of the path, about fifty feet behind me, was a tiny yellow dog—not bright neon yellow like I'd thought I'd seen out of the corner of my eye, but a dusty, muted animal yellow.

"Really?" I said under my breath. "Really, *that's* what I was running from?"

I wiped my hands on my jeans, smearing dirt and blood from my abraded palms all over them—hey, they were black, so no one could see—and hobbled back the way I had come. The poor little animal just sat there in the middle of the path, looking cowed. As I got closer, the acrid smell of urine filled my nostrils and I saw that the tiny thing had peed all over itself.

I guess I had scared *it* as much as it had scared me.

"Hey, little guy," I whispered, crouching beside it. "You okay?"

The little animal just shivered as I spoke to it, not responding to my words. I reached out, wanting to comfort it, then immediately thought better of it when I remembered how badly pee stank when it dried . . . *on Missoni.*

"Oh, crap. Whatever," I muttered, picking the little creature up anyway and holding it to me. It looked up at me, still shivering, and licked my face.

"You have foul dog breath and you smell like pee," I said to the little guy as I cuddled him close to me. "I'm gonna smell *just* like you when this all over."

The dog gave a short yip and began struggling to get out of my arms.

"Hey now, boy, calm down," I said, clutching the dog tighter to me. The little animal squirmed even harder and this time toenails were involved.

"Stop that," I began, but stopped when I felt a cold, menacing shadow descend over me. Slowly I looked up, my eyes going wide as I saw exactly *why* the little puppy wanted to get away so badly.

Standing no more than two feet from me was one of the nastiest-looking monsters I'd ever seen. It had four sets of eyes, two of which protruded from the side of its head, and a large, slavering mouth. It had to be double my size, with a prehensile tail that was even longer. As I watched, the creature's tail shot forward, intent on plucking the puppy right out of my hands.

"You can't have him!" I screamed at the nasty beast as I jerked the puppy out of its reach.

The monster squatted down so that it was eyes to eye with me, both of its humanoid-looking legs bending backward instead of the way they were supposed to. It opened its mouth, revealing two rows of squat, square teeth.

"But that's my dog," the creature said in a very normal, if not childlike, voice.

"Excuse me?" I whispered, feeling light-headed. Had the creature just started chatting with me? Was human-monster interaction an everyday occurrence down in Hell?

"This is your dog?" I continued, looking down at the yellow dog squirming in my arms. "Are you sure about that?"

The monster nodded and reached forward with both of its hairy arms.

"C'mere, Bruiser," the monster said and the puppy instantly started wagging its tail and squirming to get out of my arms again.

"You're not gonna eat him, are you?" I asked tentatively, and the monster started laughing, great honking sounds issuing from deep in its sinus cavity. I wanted to ask it what kind of creature it was, but I didn't want it to take offense and eat me, so I stayed mum on the subject.

Instead, I tried to figure out what it was by using deductive reasoning. It appeared to be a hodgepodge of a bunch of different animals all haphazardly thrown together. I noticed that while it seemed menacing, it actually had a velvet-covered black button nose, plush teddy bear ears, and brown marble eyes (all four sets) that were in direct "cuteness" disproportion to the rest of its hulking body.

"Why would I eat my dog?" the monster asked when it had stopped laughing.

"I don't know," I stammered, getting huffy. "Some people eat dogs. They say they taste like chicken."

This only made the creature start laughing again. Feeling stupid, I let Bruiser go and the little dog scampered into its master's waiting arms. The monster's tail shot out and instantly started stroking the dog behind the ears.

"Thanks for helping me find him," the monster said when the dog-master love fest was over.

"No problem," I replied, rising to my aching feet. Whenever I went to Hell, I always left bloodier than I'd come.

"See you around . . . I guess," I called over my shoulder as I started down the path again, cursing my stupidity and the fact that I now smelled like drying dog pee.

"Hey!" the monster called, catching up to me in two seconds flat. "What's your name?"

I sighed. The last thing I wanted was a stalker straight out of Hell. No matter how cute its dog was.

"Callic. Callie Reaper-Jones. What's yours?"

The monster stopped in its tracks and Bruiser gave another short *yip* from his perch in his master's arms.

"You're *her*?" the monster said, gazing at me with unfounded admiration, its four sets of eyes blinking in rapid-fire succession.

"I'm her *who*?" I said, feeling gross and smelly and miserable, and not wanting to continue the conversation with Mr. Monster for any longer than I already had.

Why couldn't Calgon just take me away and never bring me back? Huh?

"You're the girl that bested the Devil and won back Daniel's life."

"Excuse me?" I said, needing the monster to repeat exactly what he'd just said about ten more times so I could take it all in. "Tell me what you just said, but slower and with more information."

The monster nodded.

"I'm Chuck, by the way, and what I said was that you're the lady—"

"I prefer the term 'girl,'" I interrupted, "but go on."

"What? Oh, okay," Chuck continued, a little confused by my sarcasm. "Well, you're the *girl* who beat the Devil—no one does that. You won Daniel's life back so he could leave Hell and ascend to his rightful place—and no one does that, either."

Chuck stopped there, pleased with his knowledge-sharing ability. I gave him an encouraging smile, but inside all I wanted to do was pull my hair out. Apparently, the monster had no experience in elucidating the facts of a situation because I was *exactly* where I'd started with no more information than I'd just had.

Argh!

"When you said that Daniel could ascend to his rightful

place—" I started to say, but was interrupted by a loud *screeching* sound from somewhere deeper in the forest.

Chuck froze, listening. Then, with a hangdog expression on his face, he said: "That's my mom calling. I gotta go."

"Wait," I said. "I just need to ask you a few more questions . . ."

Chuck didn't appear to be listening to me anymore, intent now on getting home before his mother got any angrier, I supposed.

"It was nice meeting you, Callie Reaper-Jones," Chuck said, grinning like the little kid he was. "Just wait 'til I tell my friends I met you!"

And with that, Chuck and Bruiser stepped into the woods and were gone.

"Damn it!" I said, plopping down in the dirt and putting my head in my hands to stop my chin from throbbing. I'd been so intent on pumping Chuck for information that I'd forgotten how much my mouth hurt.

This sucks, I thought to myself as I continued to sit in the middle of the path totally not caring whose way I might be blocking. Luckily, no more unheralded guests appeared and I sat in the silence of the forest for a long, *long* time.

This was turning out to be some day, I thought miserably to myself . . . *and it had only just begun.*

seven

I winded my way through the Valley of Death, traveled past the River Styx, and came to the North Gate without any more runins. While I walked, I *did* keep my eyes peeled for stray dogs and errant monster children roaming the woods. I wouldn't have been at all surprised if Chuck had decided to get together a bunch of his little monster friends and chase me down, so he could show off "the lady who beat the Devil, *etc.*, *etc.*," but I had no intention of being anyone's "show and tell" subject, *thankyouverymuch*.

The North Gate looked very much the same as it did on my last visit to Hell—and this time there was even a delegation of three souls waiting to be let in! I had never seen a soul being admitted into the interior of Hell up close and personal-like before, so instead of just stumbling into the middle of the whole process and causing a scene, I hung back by the trees, watching and waiting for them to make their way through the entrance.

I had *totally* forgotten that the North Gate dealt primarily with pagans, Satanists, and atheists, so it took me a minute to realize that these were three young would-be Satanists I was spying on.

I stepped a little closer and saw that the two males were *twins*, both dressed in matching black T-shirts, black jeans, and black work boots. The female, who upon closer inspection couldn't have been more than twenty, was wearing a black stretchy dress, black leggings, and a bizarrely shiny black plastic cape. All three of them had white pancake makeup slathered over their faces and necks—the girl had added heavy black eyeliner to her eyes, so that she sort of resembled an albino raccoon—and their matching hair color was a shade of Manic Panic called Ebony. Although it had been a very long time since I'd played "Let's shock the parents with a scary new hair color," so Manic Panic might've been calling it something else by now.

As I watched the three little Satanists huff and puff, but not blow anything down, I tried to remember Jarvis's exact words on how the whole Heaven/Hell thing worked.

In my experience, the Afterlife *can* get a tad confusing, so you just have to remember one very important thing: Even when you *think* you have a handle on the way the whole setup runs, it can turn around and surprise the crap out of you anytime it wants.

Okay, let the Jarvis-style lecture begin:

I know everyone thinks Death is just some old, skeletal guy in a robe, skulking around with a scythe in his hand, looking for his next victim, but in actuality, Death is run a lot more like a multinational conglomerate than one might ever imagine. Every person has his or her place in the process—and without their participation, the whole thing would just fall apart into a million pieces.

I mean, even my dad, Mr. High and Mighty President and CEO of Death, Inc., was really just a cog in a much bigger piece of machinery. He has to answer to a higher office, just like everyone else, because, yes, even in Death there are checks and balances to keep one entity or another from trying to stage a coup in the Afterlife.

Far from being a one-man operation, Death was really a bureaucracy, with enough red tape and paperwork to make you ill. In fact, I think my dad spent more time trying to appease his Executives and the Board of Death than he did anything else.

And I knew from experience how hard to please those people could be . . . but I digress. Back to:

"Death 101, or How *Does* That Persnickety Afterlife Work?"

Okay, when a soul dies, it doesn't just magically move on to the next dimension. A soul is actually pretty helpless right after it's passed, so it has to be *collected* by a group of people called *harvesters*. The harvesters usually work in teams of two, using something that I think resembles a butterfly net to scoop up the floundering soul, thus beginning its progression into the Afterlife.

Once a soul has left the earthly plane and moved into the supernatural realm, it becomes solid again. At this point, the harvesters have finished their job. Another person called a *transporter* takes over from there, explaining to the soul the basic principles of the Afterlife and what the process will be like as it transitions from one dimension to the next. The transporter shepherds the soul on its journey to Purgatory, where it is then judged, sentenced, and sent to either Heaven or Hell (based on how naughty or nice it was on Earth).

After the soul has done its allotted time in the Afterlife, it will then be returned to the Soul Pool for recycling—and then the process of Rebirth and Death begins all over again.

When I was a kid, my dad made us watch this documentary on television called *The Power of Myth*. It was really just this mythologist named Joseph Campbell talking to the camera and telling stories.

Basically, he was pitching the idea that all myths are variations on the same themes—if you break them down to their essence—that, whether humanity wanted to believe it or not, different cultures and religions were way more *alike* than they were different.

Afterward, my dad sat down with the three of us, Thalia, Clio, and myself, and explained that Mr. Campbell, who he promised was just a normal human being with no supernatural ties whatsoever, had hit on a very essential truth: that mankind was all the same on the inside, no matter how different they seemed on the outside.

It was only years later, when I was a freshman at Sarah Lawrence, that I found Joseph Campbell's book *The Hero with a Thousand Faces* sitting proudly on a shelf at a used bookstore and remembered so vividly the night that I had first learned that Death was an equal opportunity employer.

Joseph Campbell had the right idea. All you had to do was hang out in the Afterlife for a little while and you'd see that no matter what mask you happened to be wearing, it was always just that . . . a mask. Underneath it, we were all the same.

"I wanna go home!!" the Goth girl shrieked, making my ears ring and reminding me that while we might be the same on the inside, some of us were definitely more annoying on the outside.

"I so did not, like, ask to die," the girl said, her cadence like that of a Valley Girl on speed, "so, like, send me back *right this instant!"*

I realized that the girl was obviously the leader of the group because, along with being the most vocal of the three, she was also the most aggressive. As I watched openmouthed, she marched right up to Cerberus, who was waiting patiently by the towering stone gates, and demanded once again that he send her back to Earth.

While the girl screeched, the two boys she had come with appeared to be about to pee on themselves in terror. I'm sure that during all the Black Magic summoning parties they'd had they'd never really expected to be calling up any beasties from the depths of Hell. Now, faced with something straight out of the *Clash of the Titans* movie, they didn't have a clue what to do with themselves.

I couldn't really blame them for their fear. Cerberus *was* a pretty terrifying fellow. With three monstrous dog heads and a humongous, muscled body, he resembled an overgrown black Lab that was ready to rumble at a moment's notice. Believe me when I say that he was definitely a force to be reckoned with.

I had spent enough time with Cerberus to know that two of the giant dog's heads were dumber than a bag of rocks but relatively normal looking, while the main head, old "Snarly head," as I liked to call him, was supersmart but totally vicious. Its one yellow-colored eye shone like a beacon from the middle of its head, and every time it spoke, it revealed two rows of jagged, limb-biting-off-ly sharp teeth.

As the Goth girl continued with her abrasive invective, I waited for Cerberus to bite her head off or something equally as gory, but instead, he just let the girl go on yammering.

The girl didn't seem at all threatened by the massive three-headed dog—rather the opposite, actually. She just kept running her mouth off while Snarly head stared at her. Of course, I suppose when *two* of the dog's heads were engaged in licking their balls, there was less to be frightened of.

I didn't quite understand why Snarly head was letting the Goth girl drone on until I realized that Snarly head must be impressed by the headstrong girl's lack of fear, not upset by it. Old Snarly was enjoying her diatribe because forthrightness was the one thing he responded to in people—which only made me wish I'd done my research before I used subterfuge to try to steal Runt.

Maybe then I wouldn't owe the guy a favor.

"I have no interest in whether you wanted to die or not. You're dead," Snarly head said sagely.

The girl, shocked, not by Snarly's words but by its eloquent speaking voice, shut her mouth for the first time since I'd gotten there.

One of the boys reached out and pulled on the girl's sleeve.

"Don't make him mad, Chanduthra. He might eat us."

The girl only snorted at her friend's stupidity.

"You heard him, Raphael; we're already dead. So who cares if he eats us? Like, *duh.*"

I had to admit that the girl *did* have a point—even if her acid-laced tongue was extremely annoying.

"But . . ." Raphael babbled.

"Just, like, *shut it*, Ralphy."

The boy glowered at her.

"Hey, don't call me Ralphy. You know I hate that name."

The girl snickered. "But it's your name, *Ralph*."

"ENOUGH!" Snarly head bellowed, its large yellow eye raking over them like a searchlight.

"Sorry, sir," Raphael né Ralph said meekly, his legs quaking underneath him like a little schoolboy's. The girl, Chanduthra, wasn't at all cowed by old Snarly head's outburst.

"Look, mister, it was, like, an accident, you know. No one kicked the candle over on purpose or anything," she said matter-of-factly. Her pale blue eyes looked up imploringly at the three-headed dog.

"If you, like, have to, you can keep Ralph and Richard," she continued. "I won't tell a soul."

I couldn't believe what I was hearing. Was the Goth girl really trying to sell out her friends for her own freedom? What a ballsy chick. I looked over to where Ralph and Richard stood cowering together, shock at Chanduthra's offer clearly apparent on their faces.

"Are you trying to bribe me?" Snarly head said, watching the girl intently. The two dumb heads moved away from their balls, transferring their attention onto Chanduthra. Immediately, they started drooling.

I wondered what *that* meant.

"No," Chanduthra said, "not bribe really, just, you know, like, making an observation."

"And how did you die?" Snarly head asked, moving its great bulk closer to the girl so that the two dumb heads could sniff her better. Chanduthra didn't flinch; just let the dumb heads sniff her up and down without protest.

When they were done with "smell and tell," Chanduthra turned back to glare at the boys, just daring them to contradict whatever came out of her mouth next. She cleared her throat and yanked at the hem of her dress before wiping the sweat off her upper lip with her cape. For a heavy girl, there was very little perspiration going on.

I, on the other hand, was sweating like a stuck pig.

Just another reason why I hated Hell so much . . . *the oppressive heat*.

"Well," Snarly head said, starting to look bored now. "Go on."

I was very interested as to what old Snarly head's next move would be. I had a feeling he didn't get too many souls sassing him right outside the Gate to Hell—*or* maybe I was just naïve and this stuff was business as usual. I had no way of knowing what the protocol was for entering the interior of Hell, so I just stayed put, my curiosity more than piqued as I tried to guess what Snarly head would do with this ragtag bunch of Goth kids.

"We were calling forth the demon Abalam, and Ralphy had a little accident with the candles—"

"I did *not*," Ralph cried out indignantly.

"Shut up, Ralphy," Chanduthra said, licking her lips. "Like I was saying, we had, *like*, just laid the pentagram and were chanting and stuff. Ralph knocked the candle over and, like, everything just started *burning*."

The other twin, Richard, opened his mouth to say something, but another look from Chanduthra silenced him. I couldn't tell which creature the brothers were more scared of: Cerberus, the three-headed Guardian of Hell, or Chanduthra, the Goth Bitch.

"That's not what happened," Richard said, sticking up for his brother finally. "Why are you lying, Sandy? *She* was the one who accidentally kicked—"

Without warning, Chanduthra walked over to Richard and punched him in the gut, hard. The slender young man fell forward, clutching his belly and gagging as he gasped for air. Chanduthra raised her fist high in the air, then pointed it right at Ralph, shaking it in his weasely face as a reminder that she was not above punching him, too, if he crossed her.

"Like, where was I?" the girl said, turning back to face Snarly head, her pale blue eyes glinting bright red in the sunlight.

Wait a minute. Did I just say her blue eyes were glinting red?!

I stared harder at the large, black-clad girl, trying to catch another glimpse of her eyes, but she wasn't facing me anymore. I replayed the last ten seconds in my mind, checking to see if I'd *imagined* the whole thing, if my mind was just addled from the overwhelming heat.

Not getting any help from my compromised memory, I decided I was gonna have to get a closer look at the girl's face in order to discover if there was more to "Chanduthra" than met the eye.

I left my spot in the tree line and moved forward, strategically placing my body between the Goth girl and a small outcropping of rocks about the size and shape of a rollaway hot dog stand. I was well positioned, hidden behind the rocks, so that the girl couldn't see me, but I could get a decent view of her face.

As she continued to talk—explaining in more detail about the candle getting knocked over "by accident" and the lock on the door getting jammed (by accident again, I wondered?)—I watched her eyes for some sign that I wasn't crazy. Ten seconds later I saw it: pale blues eyes, flashing red in the sunlight like an animal's. It only took an instant to realize what kind of game was afoot here.

Our little friend Chanduthra is not alone in that body.

I stood there, unsure of what to do, but then I had the most amazing idea: I would save Cerberus *and* knock my favor out at the same time! It was a perfect plan and I couldn't believe how quickly it had come to me.

I was getting to be a regular genius these days, if I didn't say so myself.

"She's not alone!" I yelled, sprinting forward and throwing

myself full throttle into the Goth girl, surprising myself with
my own strength as I knocked her to the ground.

It didn't take me long to realize that she was a lot bigger
than me—and thus a heck of a lot stronger—but I was able to
hold her off long enough for the twins to join in the fray. They
jumped on their friend, pushing her into the dirt and pummel-
ing her back so that I could make my escape.

"The demon they called. It's inside her!" I yelled at Snarly
head as I stood up and dusted myself off—but instead of the
enthusiastic thank-you I was expecting, the big yellow eye just
stared at me, indifferent.

"Aren't you gonna help them?" I said, watching the twins
work frantically to keep the angry Chanduthra subdued, but
old Snarly head did nothing

"Did you even hear what I said?" I asked again, starting to
feel peeved at the three-headed dog's lack of interest in the
quickly escalating situation.

Finally, Snarly head blinked its giant, yellow eye and
sighed.

"Yes, Miss Reaper-Jones, I am apprised of the situation.
Now, if you'll excuse me . . ."

The ugly, one-eyed head closed its eye and instantly the
two normal dog heads started barking like crazy, sounding off
some kind of hellhound alarm. I watched, dumbfounded, as the
giant stone doors flew open, expelling a small army of creatures that looked *exactly* like my little buddy Chuck, only bigger and with longer tails, but with the same teddy bear ears and
button eyes.

The creatures instantly circled the scuffling would-be Satanists, pulling the two boys out by their collars, so that they
could focus all their attention on Chanduthra. I heard a low
hissing sound and one of the creatures stepped forward, its
four pairs of eyes like laser beams, pinning themselves to the
girl's thrashing body. The creature lifted its right hand just as
the girl opened her mouth to scream, but strangely, nothing
happened. Instead, I watched as her whole body was engulfed
in a pale violet light, making her skin seem translucent, almost

like she had become an X-ray of herself. I could clearly see the writhing shape of another creature trapped inside her, hiding within the girl's corpulent frame.

At this point, I didn't know if this was, like, the coolest thing I'd ever seen or the grossest, but it was definitely the most transfixing. I couldn't stop staring at the Goth girl and the otherworldly violet light that encircled her.

There was a loud *ripping* sound that filled the air, and then the creature started to separate itself from its host. It was as if the thing inside her were her child, but she was birthing it through her skin rather than her womb. I continued to watch, horrified, as her skin began to stretch and buckle, then slowly split apart so that the thing inside could finally emerge.

Like a snake shedding its scales, the creature shed the girl's skin, letting it pool to the ground around him like a human-skin coat. As it stepped into the light, covered in the mucus-y afterbirth of Chanduthra's sinew and guts—and nothing else—it gave me a wide smile.

It was pretty apparent the thing was male—although I have to say that I've seen much bigger penises in my day—and he was much taller than the Goth girl had been. He had a mop of wet brown hair tied in a knot at the very top of his pointed head, adding even more height. He possessed long, almost skeletal arms and legs, and a barrel chest and porcine neck, which sat oddly on such sticklike appendages. The most interesting aspect of the man's countenance was his bright red skin. He resembled a lobster after it had been in the pot too long—only without the claws and stalked eyeballs.

"Hello, everyone," he said, his tandoori red skin glistening in the heat of the day. He turned to me and bowed. "I guess you caught me."

Snarly head opened its massive yellow eye and shook its head, sending a string of drool shooting from its mouth and right onto my Missoni-covered shoulder.

What did I say about wearing nice clothes in Hell?

"Don't encourage the girl, Abalam," Snarly head said, a

long sigh escaping from its massive jaws. Then: "Are you ready for your return to the excrement pile?"

"Please, I beg of you," the demon implored, dropping to his knees, hands clasped together in supplication. "You may send me to any place of your choosing, but please, please, *please* do not send me back to the excrement pile! I cannot bear the place anymore . . ."

"You know that is not my choice to make," Snarly head said, looking none too pleased with the errant demon. "I cannot choose what place in Hell you must work in. You can take any changes to your position up with the Devil himself."

The excrement pile, I wondered to myself. What kind of terrible thing did a demon have to do to get itself a commission working *there*? And even more worrying than that, what sin did a person have to commit to get judged worthy of being sent to the excrement pile in the first place?

I was dying for more details, but before I could ask any questions, Snarly head shot me a nasty look as if to say, "I know exactly what you're thinking and you had better keep your mouth shut if you know what's good for you." Taking its nonverbal advice, I decided that I didn't *really* need to know anything about the excrement pile after all. Unlike a few other folks I could name, *I* had zero interest whatsoever in getting on the bad side of the Guardian of the North Gate of Hell.

"Thanks for the fun, kid," the demon said, turning back to me and flashing a toothy grin. "I ain't been that near a smokin' female body in about a thousand years."

"I don't know what you're talking about—" I started to protest, but he gave me a wink.

"See you on the other side, sweetheart."

Cerberus's two dumb heads bayed again, and there was another flash of violet light from the older Chuck-like creature that had done the X-ray thing with its eyes a few moments earlier. It shot out a paler violet light this time, engulfing the demon and making its eyes roll up into its head. As the light intensified, the demon's hair started to smoke and then *poof* . . . The demon was gone.

Once Abalam was no more, the Chuck-like creatures circled the trembling twins—one of which (they were identical, so how was I supposed to know which was which?) was crying— and gently herded the boys toward the stone gates. I tried to sneak a peek inside the interior of Hell as the long-tailed Chuck-like creatures made their exit, but all I could see was a great mass of swirling black nothingness pulsing just inside the gates.

Whatever it was, just a few seconds of staring into its depths made me clench my teeth so hard that my mouth started aching again and a trickle of blood pooled at the side of my lip.

As I closed my eyes and willed away the pain, I heard the stone gates close with a loud *crunch*. When I opened my eyes again, the twins and their guards had disappeared, leaving me outside with Cerberus—and the oozing afterbirth that was once a Goth girl named Chanduthra.

I felt slightly dirty after my run-in with the demon (something to do with his job at the excrement pile, maybe?), but it wasn't even like we'd touched for more than three seconds, so I didn't know why I felt like I needed to take a shower so badly—maybe it was just the combined smell of dog drool and dog pee, mixed in with all the sweating I'd been doing since I'd gotten to Hell, that was making me feel so foul.

Before I could ask Cerberus what exactly was going to happen to the demon now that he'd pulled a no-no and tried to escape, one of the dumb dog heads licked the side of my face, adding to my dog drool collection.

Maybe I could start a line of cologne called Eau de Dog Drool, I mused. *You only wore it when you* didn't *want to attract a man.*

I sighed, knowing that I was just gonna have to go with the flow and accept the fact that I was nothing more than a large, soft-bodied chew toy for one of the three-headed hounds of Hell to play with.

God, I just hoped my dry cleaner could get the drool stains

out of my sweater—I couldn't bear to throw a Missoni in the garbage, no matter how bad it stank.

"Calliope Reaper-Jones," Snarly head said, spraying a little more drool in my direction as it spoke, its voice low and full of menace.

I tensed, expecting the worst.

"You're late."

eight

"I *may* be late, Mr. Cerberus, sir," I said, trying not to sound defensive, "but it's not my fault."

I knew it sounded lame. *Everyone* says that it's not their fault when they show up at the Gates of Hell, but seriously, this time it really wasn't my fault—I just didn't know how best to explain this to Cerberus without sounding like a liar.

"I was in Hell *exactly* when I was supposed to be," I continued, deciding that the best thing I could do was to be absolutely honest about my whereabouts up until that very moment, "but Jarvis must've screwed up the wormhole or something because I ended up right where I always end up when I go to Hell . . . *the desert*."

Snarly head didn't say anything, so I took that as my cue to go on.

"I really, *really* hate that part of Hell, but I've been there more times than anywhere else in this *sweatbox*—"

Snarly head snickered, seemingly amused by my choice of words, but still it did not speak.

"Anyway, I had to *walk* all the way here, which it turns out is a really long way, but then I found this dog and then this monster kid—kind of like the ones that shoot violet-colored light out of their eyes, only smaller—"

"They're called Bugbears," Snarly head said, interrupting me, "and they work for the Devil and live in the woods surrounding the Northern and Western Gates."

"Okay, *interesting*," I offered, glad to know at least what to call the creatures from now on. "So, then I saw that you were dealing with those Goth kids and since I'd never seen anyone enter the interior part of Hell before, I decided to just hang out and watch—that was okay, wasn't?" I queried.

Snarly head blinked twice and the other two heads just panted. I didn't know what that meant, but I decided to take it as a passive—very passive—yes.

"And then I saw the girl wasn't really a girl, but something else—"

"How astute of you," Snarly head said dryly. Apparently, Snarly head wasn't in the mood to answer direct questions, yet sarcastic asides seemed well within its capacity, which makes for great conversation . . . *not*.

"By the way, how did the demon get inside the girl in the first place?" I asked.

"When you call a demon, you not only allow him into your dimension, but you also offer him succor at your own breast."

"Excuse me?" I said.

Snarly head sighed.

"Abalam was allowed to possess the girl's body because she called him. He then sacrificed the two brothers so that he could stay on that plane. He had no idea that her body had been so ill-used that it would have a heart attack from all the stress and die. And thusly, he would be returned to the Afterlife."

"Yeah, for sure he never planned on *that* happening," I said. "What a prick."

Snarly head only nodded.

"A prick? I don't know about that. But stupid? Yes."

I was starting to feel a little camaraderie with Mr. Snarly

head, so I decided to just take a stab at getting him to let me out of my favor.

"Hey, since I helped you out with the whole Abalam thing and all, could we just call it even-steven and discharge my favor—"

Snarly head snorted, the other two heads joining in gleefully. Instinctively, I knew they were snorts of derision at *my* expense, but I decided to soldier on, ignoring the attitude Cerberus was throwing around. If I started back-talking, he might call for a Bugbear escort and then I'd end up stuck in Hell with the two Goth twins. Anyway, I wanted something from him (to keep Runt at Sea Verge) so it was best to appease the beast, not piss him off.

"The harvesting team realized that a possession had occurred, so I was forewarned. You were of no help to me . . . only a hindrance," Snarly head said, enjoying my discomfort immensely.

I sighed and rethought my approach. I decided that if I could make him forget that I was late, then I'd at least done something.

"*But* if you already knew that there was a demon inside of that girl," I added obsequiously, "then I guess that's not really worth a favor, is it . . . ?"

I trailed off, biding my time.

"No," Snarly head said, considering.

"So, what favor may I do for you, then, O great Guardian of the North Gate of Hell?" I said, bowing my head in supplication. Maybe I was overdoing it, but there *was* a lot on the line here.

I looked up and saw Snarly head mulling over what I'd just said.

"I'll make a deal with you, Calliope Reaper-Jones. One that will be mutually beneficial to both of us," Snarly head proposed, taking a step closer to me so that its words would not be overheard by anyone or anything but the other two heads.

"Anything you wish," I murmured, but in the back of my mind a little voice instantly started fretting over what *exactly* I might just have agreed to.

"There is a man named Senenmut, a talented architect that worked on some of the great Egyptian monuments. For reasons unknown, he has been *removed* from the system—even though his soul was due here at my gate centuries ago," Snarly head said, giant yellow eye unblinking.

So far, so good, I thought. I could get the supernatural yellow pages out and dig up this guy easy enough.

Not.

"Of course, I have no way of knowing where Senenmut is, or even if he still exists. As far as I have been able to ascertain, he has never stepped inside any of the other Gates of Hell, but I cannot say if he was ever smuggled across Heaven's shores. His soul might very well have been returned for renewal upon his death and no one thought to erase him from my book."

"You mean, he might be someone else now?" I asked curiously.

I was always acquiring new pieces of information about how Death worked. I had no plans for needing the information in a work-related way, but I didn't want to look like a total loser when Jarvis got going on one of his lectures about the Afterlife.

All three heads nodded in unison at my question.

"But wouldn't he still retain some memory of his old self?"

Snarly head thought about this for a moment, then nodded.

"Yes, it's rare, but in some cases, a soul can retain a vestige of its former memory," Snarly head conceded.

"Uhm," I said, "I don't mean to be a pain in the ass, but do you have any ideas, or leads, or whatever, on how I might discover this guy's whereabouts? I'm not really much of a PI, but I'm pretty sure you already knew that."

"I can only assume that if you find his Death Record, then you will find the man, in whatever form he now resides in," Snarly head said, offering the only help I was gonna get out of him.

"You said earlier that this would be a mutually beneficial undertaking?" I inquired. I wasn't gonna just do *something* for *nothing*, favor or not. I wanted Runt and this was my ticket to getting her.

"Yes, I did say that, didn't I," Snarly head mused. "You are still in possession of my daughter, Giselda. I would be willing to broker her freedom from Hell if you were to do this small favor for me—"

"And the favor I owe you for trying to steal Runt—I mean, Giselda—in the first place? That would be discharged, too?"

Snarly head nodded in consent.

"We don't need to sign anything or something, do we?" I asked. "Your word is good enough—"

"MY WORD IS LAW!" Snarly head bellowed.

Crap, I hadn't even *meant* to offend the three-headed beast, but that was exactly what I had done. I was a terrible negotiator.

"Of course it is," I murmured. "Just double-checking."

Snarly head glared at me, just a crack of yellow revealing itself between the massive eyelids. The other two heads continued to pant. Apparently, the heat in Hell got to the folks who lived here, too. I wondered why the Devil didn't try putting on a little air-conditioning every once in a while. Might be pretty good for morale.

Of course, it would render the adage "Not a snowball's chance in Hell" kind of obsolete.

As I stood there, weighing my options, I could feel a bead of sweat snaking its way down from my hairline and insinuating itself into the folds of my sweater. I really *was* gonna have to wrap things up if I was gonna have any chance at all of getting the Missoni dry-cleaned before every stain I'd gotten on it set.

"Okay, done. I agree to the deal," I said, since all other options seemed moot.

Snarly head smiled, the first smile I'd ever seen cracking its ugly beast of a countenance. It kind of gave me the chills. The little voice inside my head was still babbling about what I'd gotten myself into, but I ignored it, making myself think of Runt's cute little mug instead. If this is what I had to do to secure her freedom, well, consider it done.

Both of the dumb heads came forward and licked each of my hands in turn. It was the weirdest way I'd ever sealed a deal—and minorly unpleasant to boot.

"If you fail in your mission, Calliope Reaper-Jones," Snarly head said after I had been double licked by its brethren, "you will forfeit all rights to Giselda and she must be returned to me, no questions asked, your favor will not be discharged, and you will remain beholden to me until I see fit to release you from your debt."

"What do you mean when you say the word 'beholden'?" I asked quietly.

Snarly head smiled again and this time I felt a definite creepiness set in.

"You will become the Guardian of the North Gate in my stead."

I swallowed hard, the heat and the magnitude of my situation making me feel faint.

"I had a feeling you were going to say something like that."

"Do you accept?" Snarly head asked, long, sharp teeth revealing themselves beneath the now-waning smile.

There really wasn't a choice. I was between a rock and a really, really, *really* hard place. I shifted my weight from one foot to the other, my jeans sticking to the salty wetness of my body like a second skin.

"I'll do it."

Snarly head lowered its face so that it was mere inches from mine. I could smell the stench of rotting meat on its breath and I almost gagged. Its face was so close to mine that the great unblinking yellow eye looked like a giant fried egg plastered to its face.

"Calliope Reaper-Jones, you have twenty-four hours to complete your task . . . *or else you are mine!*"

I know I should've just turned around then and there and let Cerberus have his big dramatic moment, but I couldn't do it. Not because I didn't want to, but because I needed his help getting back to Sea Verge.

"*Uhm*, sorry to spoil the climax and all, but could you, uh, call up a wormhole so I could get back to Earth?" I asked tentatively.

Snarly head blinked and I was gifted with another blast of rotten-meat breath right in my face.

Yummy!

"I suppose I could," Snarly head said, raising itself back to its normal height.

"Thanks," I replied, once again feeling like a dimwit for not being able to call up my own wormhole and disappear.

I really needed to remedy the situation—and fast—so that I didn't have to rely on the kindness of strangers to get me where I needed to go. It was annoying *and* totally embarrassing at the same time.

"By the way," Snarly head said, "this is for you to take with you."

Something cold, solid, and about the size and shape of a gold Amex card magically appeared in my right hand. Little digital numbers flashed across its face faster than I could read them.

"What *is* this?" I asked curiously, feeling its weight in my hand.

"It's a rubidium clock," Snarly head replied. "It will let you know how much time you have left, down to the exact Planck unit."

As I stared at the rubidium clock, I suddenly felt a gentle breeze playing with the hair on the back of my neck. I turned around to find the wormhole Cerberus had opened for me right in the ether of Hell. I slid the rubidium clock into my pocket and stepped inside.

i found clio and Runt waiting for me in the kitchen when I returned. They both looked perturbed but hopeful as I landed on my ass in the middle of the spotless whitewashed oak floor and promptly collapsed into a nauseous heap.

"You okay down there?" Clio said, munching on something creamy and beige that looked surprisingly like a Nutter Butter square.

I nodded, but just the *thought* of food being consumed nearby made me want to hurl whatever stomach juices were left in my stomach after the last time I'd thrown up.

Apparently while I was gone, Clio had eaten two pieces of toast, an orange (whose peel now sat in a Jenga-like clump on the counter), and a container of yogurt, and was now working her way through a shiny red package of Nutter Butters. This was tantamount to a binge for my usually calorie-conscious kid sister, so I could only surmise that she had been worried about me while I was gone.

This thought made me feel all warm and loved . . . until she started yelling at me when I tried to explain why Cerberus had summoned me down to Hell.

"You *what?*" Clio shouted, bits of uneaten Nutter Butter spraying in my direction in response to what I'd just told her.

"There was nothing I could do," I moaned. "My hands were tied."

"And if you don't find this guy in twenty-four hours— what then? We lose Runt?" Clio said, her eyes wide with dismay.

I nodded, not liking it any more than Clio did—but she hadn't been there! She didn't know how *little* wiggle room Cerberus had given me . . . or how intimidating it was to deal with a three-headed hellhound who could rip you in half with just one bite.

"Look, how hard can it be?" I surmised, my stomach feeling less heave-worthy now that I was back on my feet and functioning. I could even watch Clio munching on the Nutter Butters without too much distress.

"Have you ever *been* to Purgatory and seen the Hall of Death, where they keep the Death Records?" Clio asked. "It's a huge place, and if you even got that far, you'd need a letter of release from Dad or someone on the Board of Death to look at the stupid files anyway."

I shrugged.

"I don't think *that* will be a problem."

I figured it wouldn't be a huge deal to talk my friend the Goddess Kali into giving me the release form I needed—and if she balked at my request, well, I could just do what I usually do and wing it.

"You can't just wing it, Callie," Clio said as if she were reading my mind. "Yeah, I know how you operate, and don't even think about it. There's so much security in the Hall of Death that it's ridiculous. They'd sniff you out in two seconds flat."

I scowled at my younger sister as she leaned against the marble slab–covered kitchen island, not at all appreciating her negative attitude.

"And how do you know all of this?" I asked, trying to keep the snippiness out of my tone.

Clio sighed, then stuffed another cookie into her mouth. As she chewed, I could see her struggling with how much information she wanted to divulge to me. Which only made me wonder *what* exactly my little sister got up to when I wasn't around—and once again I found myself curious about the mystery man my sister had to be seeing. Now wasn't an appropriate time to give her the third degree, but I definitely intended to get the information out of her at a later date . . . whether she liked it or not

"It's not what you're thinking, Cal," Clio said finally. "It's just . . . I sort of promised Dad that I wouldn't tell anyone about it. And I don't want to piss him off or anything—"

"Tell anyone about *what*?" I blurted, exasperated by my sister's hedging.

"About the internship he got me in the Hall of Death last summer—"

"He got you *what*?" I stammered, not entirely believing I'd heard her correctly.

"I wanted to know more about what Dad did for a living, so I asked for an internship at Death, Inc."

"Oh, okay," I said, confused.

"Are you mad at me?" Clio asked, looking at me nervously, her hand distractedly petting the top of Runt's head like it was Buddha's belly, ready to grant her an extra helping of Luck.

"Why would I be mad?" I said, squirming inside for some reason.

"I don't know . . ." Clio offered, her words trailing off into the unsaid.

I shrugged.

"Look, there's nothing to be mad about, Clio. Why would I care?"

Clio exhaled, releasing the tension in her jaw and shoulders I hadn't even noticed was there until now.

"Thanks, Cal," Clio said, smiling. "But please don't tell Dad I told you, okay?"

I nodded, *my* jaw and shoulders now acquiring the tension Clio's had just lost. I didn't really know why I felt so unbearably weird inside about the whole thing. I mean, it wasn't like *I* wanted to work for Dad or anything. Still, the fact that he'd just let Clio chill in Purgatory without any supervision all summer made me feel kind of, well . . . I guess the correct word would be "jealous."

"It's not really a big deal, Cal, but you have to believe me when I tell you that security was, like, *extremely* tight."

"Okay, security's tight. I get it, Clio," I said, gathering more confidence as a plan began to form in my mind. "I'm not just gonna go in there and improvise. I've got a plan and it's great. So, everything's gonna be just fine and dandy."

Clio didn't look at all reassured by my little speech.

"You promise," she said after a moment's hesitation.

"I've got the whole thing figured out," I said, the words just flowing out of my mouth without my brain paying the least little bit of attention to them.

"*Trust* me."

nine

"Hey, Jarvis," I said, the smile fixed so securely on my face that I just *knew* he was going to suspect something. "I have a *huuuuuge* favor to ask you."

Clio, Runt, and I had scoured the house for an hour looking for the faun, only to find him sorting manuscripts in Dad's library. He looked up briefly from his work when we first entered the room, but didn't for one minute stop what he was doing. Usually I'd have been annoyed by his lack of attention, but since a "distracted" Jarvis meant a less "suspicious" Jarvis, it made my job of pulling the wool over his eyes that much easier.

"Yes?" Jarvis said as his eyes flicked in my direction, then quickly returned to the ancient, calfskin-bound manuscript he was holding in his manicured hands.

Realizing it was now-or-never time, I moved farther into the large, well-appointed room and sat down in one of the stately brown leather wingback chairs that were flanking the matching brown leather couch that was the centerpiece of the room. Clio and Runt stayed firmly in the doorway (for moral support), but I was essentially on my own for this one.

I guess it serves me right, I thought to myself. *Any girl who*

*makes a dumb deal with a full-grown hellhound deserves all
the trouble she gets.*

"Well . . ." I began, then instantly started worrying about
getting dog saliva all over the buttery leather upholstery. With
the time crunch, I hadn't had two seconds to change my
clothes, so I hopped back up onto my feet again and moseyed
over to the other side of the room, taking up residence beside
the huge, inlaid mahogany fireplace.

I could just see the look on my dad's face if he came home
and found dog drool on one of his prized wingback chairs. It
would *not* be a pretty sight. Already there'd been Hell to pay
when I'd sort of trashed his study a few months ago.

In *that* room, I'd unconsciously doodled all over his desk
set, turning the brown leather binding into a wannabe Ror-
schach test. Granted, it was a dumb thing to do, but I *had* been
under a lot of stress at the time. Stickler for accepting personal
responsibility that he is, my dad totally made me replace it—
and no matter what anyone tells you, leather-embossed desk
sets are not cheap!

"Yes . . . ?" Jarvis intoned again, looking up at me over the
lenses of his pince-nez like he was channeling some kind of
uptight schoolmarm.

The more time I spent in Jarvis's company, the more feminine I judged his behavior to be. I didn't know if this was because of the clipped British accent and European sensibility, or
if it just meant that Death's Executive Assistant, Jarvis De
Poupsy, was batting for the "other team."

I was about as unhomophobic as they came, so it didn't really matter either way to me, but I was *definitely* curious about
Jarvis's sexual orientation. Leaving thoughts of Jarvis and his
choice of "bat" for another time, I cleared my throat.

"Well, like I said before, I need a huge a favor."

Jarvis gave me a piercing stare that was not at all deadened
by the half inch of pince-nez glass that it was filtered through.
I swallowed hard, my mouth so dry and prickly I might as well
have been back in Hell.

"Go on," Jarvis said as his fingers slid through the pages of the manuscript he was holding.

"Well, my boss at work—"

"The zaftig woman with the incredible sense of style?" Jarvis said, interrupting me.

"Yes, the zaft-whatever woman with the incredible style," I answered, nodding.

"She's quite attractive."

Boy, after Jarvis said that, you could've heard a pin drop. I looked over at Clio, who raised an eyebrow. Only Runt seemed unfazed by Jarvis's statement.

"You think so?" I asked curiously, and immediately a deep scarlet blush began to creep up the back of Jarvis's neck, across his cheeks, and into the roots of his meticulously maintained sideburns. His face was so flushed that I was surprised the pomade in his hair didn't start melting down his neck.

"Do you have a crush on Callie's boss?" Clio said from her spot by the doorway. She had a devilish smile on her face, making her look even more adorable than she already was. I had a feeling she was never gonna let Jarvis live this one down.

"I will not even honor that absurd question with a response," Jarvis said hotly as the manuscript he had been holding slipped through his fingers and landed with a soft *thud* on the dark parquet floor.

Clio snorted, which only made Jarvis turn redder. Trying to escape our scrutiny, he knelt down and picked up the book, taking longer than he should have so he could collect himself. When he stood back up, the blush was fading, but I could still see annoyance festering in his eyes.

"She makes your palms sweat, huh?" Clio said, sidestepping the pince-nez that Jarvis immediately threw in her direction.

This kind of adolescent display from my dad's Executive Assistant was highly amusing, but definitely not something I wanted to extend if I was going to get Jarvis's help. I needed him happy, not ready to throw something at Clio's head.

"Sorry, Jarvis," I said, retracing my steps back to a more normal state of play. "We shouldn't tease you like that. My bad."

Jarvis scowled at me.

"Clio, apologize to Jarvis."

Clio opened her mouth to protest, but I gave her a warning glance. If she didn't apologize, I was never gonna get Jarvis to do what I needed him to do. He'd say no just to spite us.

Runt seemed to know exactly what was at stake here—her future, of course—because she stuck her muzzle into Clio's backside, pushing her forward as if to say, "Apologize." Surprised by the friendly shove, Clio shut her mouth and looked down at Runt. Our adorable hellhound puppy looked back up at her with large, pleading pink eyes, and Clio sighed.

"All right," she said under her breath and then to Jarvis, "I'm sorry I made fun of you."

Jarvis gave her a smug look.

"You made me lose my place in the manuscript," he said.

Clio looked at me and I nodded.

"I'm *sorry* I made you lose your place in your manuscript."

Jarvis smiled at Clio's discomfort, but still looked moderately peeved; definitely not a good time to try anything underhanded on him. I ran my finger across my throat, indicating that I was going to abort the mission, but Clio shook her head forcefully, indicating that I should continue.

Jarvis's eyelids lowered to slits as his stare slid from my face to Clio's. Obviously he had sensed that there was something untoward brewing between us, but before he could ask either of us what was going on, Runt—of her own initiative—padded over to Jarvis and gently placed the pince-nez she'd retrieved from the floor into his hand. He wiped the dog saliva off the tiny glasses with a handkerchief he retrieved from his coat pocket, then gave Runt a gentle rub behind the ears. She closed her eyes, enjoying the attention.

Situation diffused by a hyperintelligent hellhound, I mused happily. *Score two for the Calliope Reaper-Jones team!*

"Attention hog," Clio muttered under her breath. As grateful as I was to Runt, my sister *did* have a point; our pup was shameless when it came to getting her ears scratched.

"So, as you were saying?" Jarvis murmured, dropping his

sharpened gaze from my face and returning his attention back
to his manuscript.

If he was willing to forgive and forget so easily, I decided,
who was I to argue with him? This thought gave me the wherewithal to muddle forward with my half-baked plan.

"Uhm, yes, you see, my boss—the well-dressed one—wants
me to do some research on a new product line we're develop-
ing . . ." I began, the words I'd initially planned to say slipping
right out of my mind as my mouth continued to move of its own
volition. It was becoming blatantly obvious that Clio was right.
I relied *way* too much on my improv skills to get by in this life.
Sometimes I could talk out of my ass and everything would just
make sense, you know? But other times . . . well, my "seat of
the pants" attitude didn't exactly fly.

This was one of those times.

"Uh-huh?" Jarvis said, setting the manuscript down on an
Empire-style wooden side table and returning his scowl to my
face. "And what kind of line might that be?"

I didn't know what to say. My brain literally froze inside
my skull so that I couldn't think, I couldn't talk . . . I could
hardly breathe.

"Uhm, yes, what kind of line is it?" I said loud enough for
everyone else to hear even though it had been said primarily to
get my brain out of "blank" mode. "It's a new series of filing
accessories!"

Jarvis stared at me blankly, then a sly smile stretched across
his lips.

"Liar."

I opened my mouth, shocked.

"I am not," I replied defensively.

Jarvis looked heavenward, the sly smile still turning up the
corners of his mouth. "You are lying, Mistress Calliope. Through
your teeth."

I started to protest, but Jarvis held out his hand Fran
Drescher–style.

"Talk to the hand."

"Jarvis," I began, "we've already spoken about the Fran Drescher hand so I'm very surprised you'd still want to use it anymore."

I turned to Clio so that I could better explain.

"Jarvis used 'the hand' on me when he told me Dad had been kidnapped. I explained to him that the gesture was very dated and should be listed as a 'do not use,' right along with the catchphrases 'snap' and 'all that and a bag of chips.'"

Clio looked befuddled.

"Who's Fran Drescher?"

I sighed and returned my attention back to Jarvis, whose face was the color of a clown's nose.

"And there you have it. Out of the mouths of babes."

Jarvis glared at me.

"Point taken, but that still does not mean that I accept your story."

"Okay, fine," I said, throwing up my hands in frustration. "*Don't* believe me."

"I think you are lying and I will not be a party to whatever crazy scheme the two of you have dreamed up," Jarvis countered with a sniff.

Clio raised her hand.

"I'm just here for moral support."

"Both of you suck," I said, plopping down into one of the wingback chairs, this time not caring one whit whether I got dog saliva on it or not.

Clio came into the room and perched on the arm of my chair.

"Jarvis," Clio began, "Callie really needs your help."

Jarvis studied the glass in his pince-nez, looking for streaks and finding none.

"Continue," he said, sliding the handkerchief into his pocket and setting the pince-nez back on the bridge of his hawkish nose.

"My dumb-butt sister made a deal with Cerberus. If she can get her hands on the Death Record of one of his errant souls, we can keep Runt out of Hell and up here with us," Clio said, reaching out her hand. Runt was immediately on the alert, padding back to Clio for more patting.

Jarvis took a deep breath, then slowly let it out through pursed lips.

"That is a tall order, indeed."

Clio nodded.

"So, now you see why we need your help?"

Jarvis nodded, looking over at me with concern. I knew I was being a baby, sitting in the wingback chair and sulking, but I just didn't have the energy to do anything more constructive.

"Why didn't you just ask me for my help, Mistress Calliope?" Jarvis said, the tone of his voice not hostile like I'd expected, but soft and probing as it effortlessly pulled me out of my black mood.

"I, uh, just thought you'd say no," I offered meekly.

If I'd really taken the time to think about it, I would've realized that I always expected to have to manipulate a situation to get people to do what I wanted them to do. I didn't know why my brain was wired that way, but it was. The truth was when it came to just being honest and asking someone for help when I needed it, I was a complete and utter coward about the whole thing.

"Mistress Calliope, I am your friend. All you have to do is ask for my help and it is yours," Jarvis said as he sat down in the other wingback chair and reached out, patting my shoulder.

I couldn't believe how great Jarvis was being about the whole thing. Instead of taking the opportunity to ridicule me, he'd been kinder to me than I had any right to. A big, wet tear slid down my face and I was so surprised that I didn't even make a move to wipe it away.

"Really?" I asked, another tear plopping onto my cheek.

Jarvis nodded.

"If you want me to take you to Purgatory, I will. But . . ."

Of course, there was always a "but," I thought to myself wryly.

"Go on. Hit me," I said, gritting my teeth.

Jarvis looked taken aback.

"I couldn't! Really. No matter *how* impossibly you've behaved—" he gasped, his face blanching the color of a skinned potato.

"No, I mean, hit me with whatever the 'but' is." I snorted, stealing a peek over at Clio, who was trying hard not to laugh, her hand looped into the back of Runt's pink rhinestone halter.

"Oh my," Jarvis murmured, covering his mouth with his hand, shocked as he realized what he'd just implied.

"Nice one, Jarvi," I said, giving him the biggest, toothiest grin I could manage. He just shook his head, chagrined. After a moment, he looked up, his face composed.

"I suppose it's a simple request, really," he began hesitantly, "but one that would mean the world to me."

I waited, wondering exactly what kind favor would *seem* simple to Jarvis, but would be like pulling teeth for me.

"I would like an introduction."

Well, that one caught me completely off guard.

"An introduction?" Clio asked, apparently just as surprised by Jarvis's request as I was.

Jarvis nodded, looking nervously between us.

"I want to meet the zaftig one."

I almost choked on my own saliva.

"You wanna *what*?" I said, my voice coming out three octaves higher than normal.

"I would like to meet your boss."

I shook my head.

"No, I heard you the first time."

Clio tried to catch my gaze, eyes wide with shock. She had never met my boss, Hyacinth Stewart, but she had heard tale of the woman—and how badly she overworked me.

Of course, Jarvis wouldn't find this request petrifying, I thought miserably. *He obviously had a crush on the woman, which meant that no matter how overbearing and frightening she really was, she could do no wrong as far as he was concerned.*

"I can't believe you thought *this* was a small favor, Jarvis," I said out loud, but the little faun must've thought I was joking because he didn't seem the least bit bothered by my words— either that, or he just didn't care *what* I thought.

"So, you'll do it, then?" he said, his dark eyes shining with eagerness. He was even more excited than when I'd let him explain the inner workings of Death, Inc., to me down in Hell—and I thought he'd been animated back *then*.

"I don't know what she'd say about meeting *you*." I sighed. "I don't think she has any idea that fauns even exist."

Jarvis nodded as if what I was saying required some serious thought.

"Well, I could always use a spell," he said, looking nervously between Clio and me. I think he was waiting for our approval and I didn't have the heart not to give it to him.

"I think we should just wait before we start messing with any magic," I offered, resting my chin on my hand.

"Yes, yes . . . of course, you're completely correct," Jarvis said, nodding his head. "We should just wait and see what the situation calls for."

"But there is one other thing that I think you should know before I say yes to this insanity," I added, not liking any of this one little bit. I had a very good idea that the only thing Jarvis was heading for when it came to dealing with Hyacinth Smith was heartbreak.

Well, on the lighter side, at least now I didn't have to do any more guesstimating as far as Jarvis's sexual proclivities were concerned; now I knew *exactly* what team my dad's Executive Assistant played for. Jarvis was a BBW lover (for the acronym-impaired, that's: Big Beautiful Women), and more power to him for his discerning taste. Actually, to tell you the truth, it made me like the little faun even more than I already did.

Too bad the BBW *he* was obsessed with would chew him up and spit him out before he'd even realized what'd happened to him.

"She's married . . ."

"But recently separated!" Jarvis chimed in.

He's been doing his homework, I mused.

"Then you know she has a kid."

Jarvis broke into a sly grin.

"Oh, is *this* all you were worried about?" he said, his fingers caressing the well-oiled ends of his mustache like the villain of an old-time movie serial.

"Yep, that's all," I replied.

Isn't that enough? I thought to myself.

"I really don't foresee any of that being a problem, Mistress Calliope," Jarvis said, sitting farther back in his chair. "No, I do not foresee that being a problem *at all.*"

As I watched a devious little smile overtake Jarvis's handsome face, I actually started to rethink my whole position on the subject. Maybe it was Hy that was in for a little heartbreak.

"Okay, then. We have a deal," I said, resigned to the idea that something about this trade-off was bound to backfire in my face.

I stuck out my hand to shake on it, sealing the deal, but Jarvis wouldn't reciprocate. Instead, he held up his finger to stop me, then reached into his jacket pocket and pulled out his monogrammed handkerchief, draping it over my hand like some kind of antidirt sheath. Only *then* would he shake my hand.

"Yes, we have a deal," the faun said, grinning like a schoolboy at me. "Besides, the sooner we get our hands on that Death Record, the sooner I can get my hands on those *lovely lady lumps.*"

As soon as those very out-of-character (or maybe they were more in character than I realized) words were out of Jarvis's mouth, Clio and I exchanged horrified glances. I could see that she was thinking the exact same thing I was: In just *one* sentence, Jarvis had done the impossible. He'd embarrassed *both* of us more than we had ever been embarrassed in our entire lives . . . *and* he'd taken all the fun out of a particularly awesome Black Eyed Peas song.

"Okay, horn dog," I said, rolling my eyes in Jarvis's direction. "Let's go to Purgatory."

ten

In the beginning, God looked at the universe that he/she created and saw that it was good.

The Angels would oversee Heaven, while the Devil took care of Hell. Both sides seemed happy with this arrangement and it all looked like it was going to start off swimmingly . . . until God got to Purgatory.

It seemed that the balance between Good and Evil that God had created by divvying out Heaven and Hell so fairly had left the stewardship of Purgatory—the way station by which the two planes were connected—open to subversion by any Tom, Dick, or Harry from both sides. If either Heaven or Hell were to overrun Purgatory and claim it as its own, the precarious balance between the two planes would shift and life as we know it would cease to exist.

Forever.

God, being the superintelligent creative force that he/she was, caught this flaw in his/her otherwise pretty awesomely crafted creation and decided that whatever being he/she picked to run Purgatory would have to be the *ultimate* in impartiality. This entity would need to possess both Good and Evil inside themselves, so that they would not judge one side with more ill will than the other. They would need to be extraordinarily fair, but also completely willing to make the hard, gut-churning decisions that any good boss has to make sometimes.

After much trial and tribulation, God had an epiphany. He/she couldn't believe that the solution had been staring him/her right in the face from the very beginning. The creature most suited to run Purgatory *and* oversee Death was none other than the simplest of God's creations.

The answer to God's problem was: *humanity*.

my father was only thirty when he was tapped for the job of Death.

Up until then he'd been an idealistic young man, born into poverty, who had managed to pull himself so far out of the muck that he'd become one of the wealthiest land developers in all of North America. The most supernatural thing anyone could've said about him at the time was that he had an almost magical way of creating money out of nothing. Other than that, he was completely, utterly, totally normal—or at least that was what he thought.

There was no way for him to know that he'd *never* been normal, not even when he was an embryo swimming in his mother's belly.

You see, in every generation three individuals are born who have the propensity to become Death. This person can live an entire human existence totally oblivious to the fact that they carry this "specialness" inside them, written into their very DNA. Nevertheless, it's there, dogging them their whole lives, waiting for the one shining moment when they might be called upon to fulfill their supernatural destiny.

When you become Death, one of the perks of the job is that you and your family are granted immortality. So, as you can imagine, job longevity is pretty high, which means that only a few people ever get called up to vie for the job, period. Because the "old" Death has to abdicate his/her position of his/her own free will before any of these "special" individuals get called in for a job interview, the chances of learning the truth about oneself get even slimmer. In fact, the majority of them *never* learn how "special" they truly are—but for those individuals who *are* shown the truth, it's a pretty life-changing experience.

Most humans aren't even aware that the Afterlife exists at all, let alone able to grasp its inner workings in one sitting, so you can imagine how unsettling the whole situation can become.

After they've terrified the crap out of the poor interviewees, the Board of Death gives the possible "new" Deaths three tasks to fulfill—there used to be thirteen, but there was so much bitching about the time it took to complete them (we're talking *years* here) that the Board of Death finally eased up on the requirement. The tasks differ for each individual so that no one can cheat off anyone else—apparently, human beings can't be trusted as far as you can throw them—and in the end, the person who completes his/her set of tasks first becomes the new head honcho in charge of Death.

I myself (with the help of Jarvis, Runt, and my sister Clio) had experienced the tasks firsthand—and completed them— but that still didn't mean I thought the Board of Death had the right idea about the whole thing. Of course, my dad had gone through this rigorous trial to secure his position as the head of Death, and he had ruled Purgatory for the past century or so with a mixture of fairness and firmness that garnered him the respect of all the denizens of the Afterlife, so there must've been some merit to the endeavor.

Speaking of my dad, it had actually been his idea to treat Death like a corporate entity. He'd spent his human life dealing in trade and commerce and figured that the same principles could be applied to the running of Purgatory and the collecting of souls. He had instigated the creation of Death, Inc., instilling his new charges with a sense of responsibility and a healthy respect for a job well-done. He had restructured the antiquated system so that instead of a hodge-podge of different groups grudgingly working together to secure souls after Death and guide them through the Afterlife, now everyone was part of one company, one community if you like, that worked together in harmony.

He had also completely renovated Purgatory itself. When he had inherited the place, it was nothing more than a giant fortress made of brimstone (because it's indestructible) and held together by sheer will. There were no offices, no executive structure to the business—the sole governing body within Death was the Board of Death, but it was rarely called into session *except* to supervise the succession of the "old" Death to the "new" Death—and there was so much infighting that sometimes souls got lost in the shuffle.

My dad saw all this and decided that the time was ripe for a change. He created a new hierarchy within Purgatory, establishing a single Executive Board—with himself as President and CEO—that oversaw a much larger delegation of Vice Presidents and Managerial Executives. Each continent had its own Vice President, and below them, running each individual country, were the Managerial Executives. The Managerial Executives looked after the local Managers, who in turn liaised with the harvesters and transporters and basically made sure that the business of Death ran as smoothly as possible.

My older sister, Thalia, had been a member of my dad's Executive Board (she had held the title Vice President of Passage for a while), but when she realized that no matter how well she did by the company, she would never attain the highest position (President and CEO), she went kind of mental and tried to force my dad out of his job with the help of the vicious demon Vritra, whom she had married in secret when she was sent to take over the Asian offices of Death, Inc. Her plan had been foiled, but—even though it was an isolated incident—it did make me seriously wonder if my dad's system of corporate leadership wasn't going to open him up to more of these kinds of attacks in the future.

As far as I could see, a democratic approach to Death was a neat idea in theory, but when those below you craved power, there was no way to stop them from just reaching out and trying to take it—regardless of how egalitarian you think you've made your system.

Anyway, my dad didn't just restrict his renovation to the inner workings of Purgatory; he also upgraded the building itself. He had the Hall of Death completely redone, added a whole wing of Executive Offices, even built a cafeteria that was so huge it could seat every employee of Death, Inc., in it at the same time. He had also restricted the use of Purgatory to corporate work only.

Before his installation as the new Death, Purgatory had been used as a sort of prison, where souls could be held without judgment for as long as Death saw fit. There was no such thing as habeas corpus then and my dad, who had lived his human existence in America, thought this was bullshit. He knew what could happen when a soul's rights were violated (slavery anyone?), and he refused to allow this practice to continue in Purgatory. Upon taking charge of Death, he immediately liberated all the prisoners that were being held in Purgatory unjustly, sending them out for judgment and release to Heaven or Hell. Now only very high-level political prisoners were held there—but only after they had been judged and sentenced by an outside court made up of jurors unaffiliated with Purgatory.

Looking at all the things he'd done since he'd taken office, it was pretty apparent that my dad was kind of an amazing guy. I wish I could say that I'd always known about *all of the above*, but the truth was that the first I'd heard about it any of it was from Jarvis, sitting in my dad's library while we hashed out a plan to break into the Hall of Death and steal one very important Death Record (and get a peek at anther one!). Clio, it seemed, was well aware of my dad's triumphs because she spent the whole time nodding her head in agreement as Jarvis explained them all to me.

I guess you could say I'd been out of the loop for a long time—and I had—but the real reason I was so in the dark about my dad's life was because I hadn't *wanted* to know anything about it. I'd spent my childhood aware of, but relatively incurious about, my heritage, and then as a teenager I'd made a concerted effort to bury that aspect of myself so far down into my subconscious that it was like it didn't even exist at all.

Had anyone asked me why I'd chosen to disinherit myself from my family, my stock answer would've been that I'd seen my two best friends killed in a car accident and after that I hadn't *wanted* to be immortal anymore—living forever while everyone and everything you love dies? I don't think so—but if I really wanted to be honest with myself, I supposed the real answer lay buried deep in my psyche. The truth was that I'd been living in denial for a very long time . . . and the saddest part about the whole thing was that I had personally chosen this half existence for myself.

I'd even taken that stupid forgetting charm to help me compartmentalize the "supernatural" part of myself away from my "normal" consciousness; that was how badly I did *not* want to get involved with the "family" business. Of course, back then I'd had no idea that my future self would be called into service to help save my dad and that there would be absolutely nothing I could do about it. That the forgetting charm would be so easily reversed and I'd be forced to deal with reality once more.

If I'm really being honest with myself, then I should just be *completely* honest, right?

Well, you see, when I was nineteen years old, I did something stupid, something that scared me and made me feel totally out of control, and because of this *one* stupid thing, I had barred myself from the supernatural world forever.

At least at the time that was what I had hoped.

it was the Christmas break of my junior year at Sarah Lawrence. I'd had a crappy semester; a really hard-core professor in my creative writing class had hated me on sight and had made my life a living Hell. It was the first time I'd ever wanted to quit, leave school, and run away to Siberia.

The rub was I knew if I left school, my dad would use it as the open window with which to drag me kicking and scream-

ing into the family biz. He had been determined from each of
our births that my sisters and I would come and work for him.
My older sister, Thalia, had acquiesced immediately. She loved
the fact that our dad was Death, that the family was immortal,
and that if she played her cards right, she could end up with
more power than she knew what to do with. I, on the other
hand, had always been certain that my destiny did *not* lie in the
supernatural world; I was pretty sure I would end up writing
for my favorite fashion magazine, *Vogue*.

I'd gone to school itching to get away from the future I
knew was waiting in the wings for me. I knew if I didn't get
my butt in gear and change a few minds, I was gonna get rail-
roaded into a career that I did *not* want. It had taken me almost
three years, but I had finally gotten up enough nerve to tell my
dad exactly what I had planned for myself—and if he didn't
like it, well, screw him.

In some ways, I liked to think my disinterest in what he did
came directly from him. He had been very strict about my
sisters and me never using magic in his house. He said that he
had his reasons, but he never justified them to us. Thalia had
gone underground, breaking Dad's rules, but not flaunting it in
his face. When she finally went away to school and was no
longer under his thumb, she had very openly let the family see
how adept she had become at magic. The interesting thing was
how proud my dad seemed of her magical prowess.

Still, he made sure that Clio and I knew that the magic
Thalia could do was no better than a parlor trick. He drummed
it into our heads that magic was *not* necessary in his trade.
That magic only caused more problems than it solved. I guess
I believed him because I stayed away from the stuff like it was
anathema.

Anyway, that Christmas break I had made the decision to
confront my dad. I would tell him that he was out of luck, that
I was gonna go to New York City the *minute* I graduated and
there was absolutely *nothing* he could do to stop me. I had
planned out the whole thing to a tee. I knew how I would get
him alone, the exact words I would use . . . I had even imagined

the five hundred different reactions he was going to have to my speech.

The only thing I couldn't have planned was that Thalia would come in and steal my thunder before I'd even had a chance to get my storm going.

I'd taken the train to Sea Verge the day before Christmas Eve, sporting a miserable cold I'd gotten from one of my roommates, so I wasn't in the best of shape when I arrived at its front door. In fact, I'd blown my nose so much on the trip that I looked like an alcoholic, all broken capillaries and red, chapped skin. I had brought only a small valise with me because I didn't plan on staying too much past Christmas dinner. I had a New Year's date with a couple of friends, and I wanted to get back to school as soon as possible.

Besides, I'd only promised my mother that I'd come for Christmas—nothing more, nothing less.

The woman had called me at least five times since Thanksgiving, pleading with me to spend the Christmas holidays with my family that year. I hadn't wanted to go, but since I needed to talk to my dad anyway, I decided that the least I could do was spend some "quality" time with the family and make my mother happy at the same time—at least for a couple of days. I was pretty sure that once I told my dad the news, the crap was really gonna hit the fan.

I'd let myself in when I got there and had gone straight to my room. All I wanted to do was to lie down on my bed and sleep, undisturbed, for the next twenty-four hours. Of course, once Clio realized I was home, she was in my room almost jumping up and down on my bed with excitement. Apparently, Thalia had arrived right after me and she was about to drop a bombshell on the family . . . the *entire* family, which included me, apparently.

I didn't have the heart to be a bitch and tell Clio to get out, that I didn't give a damn *what* Thalia was gonna do, that she could turn herself into a toad and I could care less. So, instead of getting the sleep I desperately needed, I followed Clio right into the eye of the storm.

The Christmas tree looked incredible.

A huge blue spruce, it stood twenty feet high, shimmering like a snowflake before me as I followed Clio down the stairs and into the large, heavily decorated winter wonderland that was our living room. My mother was an amazing interior designer, and every year she would outdo herself when it came to the Christmas decorations.

She always went all out on holidays, but Christmas was different because it was her favorite. She would spend months preparing everything down to the last detail, her good taste conjuring up the most amazing holiday spectacles imaginable.

When I was little, she and I would consult about the decorations for the year, sketching out our plans on heavy cream drawing paper, giggling as we sipped hot chocolate or spiced cider from thick Christmas mugs. I had loved this time with my mother so much that I had actually begged God to never let me grow up. I knew down deep in my soul that once I got older, the magic would disappear and our decorating parties would cease to be . . . and sadly, I hadn't been wrong. The minute I'd hit puberty, my mother and I had started arguing and we really hadn't stopped since.

As Clio and I made our way through the huge, crepe paper snowflakes that were exquisitely wrapped around the base of the tree, I caught sight of my parents sitting on one of the black and cream toile couches beside the fireplace. Thalia was standing in front of them, dressed in a black Armani suit, her Jimmy Choo heels clicking in a staccato beat as she paced across the black-and-white marble tiled floor. Her long dark hair was pulled back at the nape of her neck in a tight chignon.

She looked up when she heard Clio and me come in, and the smile on her face was full of self-satisfaction.

I had never been very close to Thalia, even when we were kids. There was something cold about her that I found difficult to deal with. Clio and I had never talked about it directly, but I knew my younger sister felt exactly the same way about Thalia that I did.

"Oh good, the prodigal daughter has returned." Her voice

was like cracked ice. "Nice of you to join us, Calliope. I was just going to tell Father all about your little secret."

"Excuse me?" I said, pulling a tissue from my pocket and sneezing into it.

I felt like crap; I looked like crap . . . I mean, I hadn't had a shower in two days and the comfortable sweats that had become my sickbed uniform stuck to me like mummy wrappings. I really didn't have the mental wherewithal to deal with my sister's screwed-up psychobabble bullshit. I wished with all my heart that I'd just crawled into my old bed and never gotten up again, I felt that cruddy.

Thalia glared at me, her eyes locked on the tissue I held like a crumpled dove in my hand. I raised an eyebrow in her direction and she took a step back like she was scared I was gonna get germs on her or something.

"What secret?" Clio asked, looking up at me, then over at Thalia, a worried frown pinching her pixie face. Neither of my parents moved a muscle. My dad just stared at me, his face drawn and pale. Even his lion's mane of unruly hair seemed more subdued than usual.

Thalia laughed and it was *not* a pretty sound. For the first time in my life, I realized that I'd never heard my sister laugh unless it was at the expense of someone else. It seemed like the only thing that ever drew any mirth from her revolved around meanness and self-aggrandizement. She looked at me, her head inclined curiously. She was waiting for me to respond to her charge, but there was no way José I was gonna take the bait. I just stood there, waiting for her to play whatever trump card she had up her Armani-clad sleeve.

It was a Mexican standoff with neither one of us willing to give an inch. Finally, Thalia shook her head, losing patience with my unwillingness to sink to her level. She had always taken the lead when we were children, and I was forcing her to do it again.

"Well, if Calliope won't tell you, then I will," she said, her excitement barely contained beneath a veneer of frost.

I gritted my teeth, bracing myself for what I knew was coming. Somehow Thalia had found out that I wasn't joining the family business, that I planned to go to New York City and seek my fortune there instead.

At least, that was what I thought she was going to say.

"Calliope Reaper-Jones is a liar and a cheat. She plans on selling out the family the minute she graduates from school."

I stared at her. I had absolutely *zero* idea what she was talking about. *Sell out my family? To whom? And why?*

Thalia didn't stop there. No, she continued on, enjoying the confusion and fear she was creating.

"I've been secretly working with the rest of the Executive Board to discover who's been leaking insider information about Death, Inc., to the Devil. And we think we've found our source," Thalia said, her eyes glittering as they raked across me.

"That's bullshit," I railed, knowing exactly where this was going. "I don't even know anything about Dad's job!"

Thalia shook her head, laying on the fake pity with a trowel as she went on.

"Everyone knows that you don't want to be immortal, Calliope. It's common knowledge. You can't deny it."

"So I won't," I shot back, sneezing again three times in quick succession. "But I don't sell people out, Thalia. *Ever.*"

"I have evidence to the contrary," Thalia said tartly, her eyes never leaving mine.

"I don't care *what* you have," I nearly screamed, anger flaming inside me.

Thalia took a step toward me, a Joker-like grin spreading across her fine-boned face.

"You are a traitor, Calliope Reaper-Jones," she spat at me.

That was it. That was the straw that broke the camel's back. I had had enough . . . even if I didn't consciously know it. The anger that had been building inside me came to a head and I could feel its power ripping through every cell in my body as it clawed its way out. My mouth froze into an elongated frown, a weird, growling noise escaping through my compressed lips.

Before I understood the extent of what was happening to me, I had a total *Carrie* moment and the human part of myself slipped away into unconsciousness.

When it was all over, my sister Thalia was a big, fat toad sitting underneath the Christmas tree.

I've only ever heard Clio's side of how the thing went down, but I'm pretty sure it was a real doozy, because after that my dad readily accepted the idea that I would *not* be joining Death, Inc. Of course, Thalia really was full of crap about me being some kind of familial traitor, because when my dad returned her to her normal form, she totally admitted that she was on a fishing expedition, just trying to scare any pertinent information out of me. How could she know I would go all ballistic on her?

It was only years later, after she had engineered my dad's kidnapping and tried to take over Death, that I realized what the whole Christmas extravaganza had been about. Thalia was looking to discover two things: what my power level was and whether I could be bullied out of her way.

She was also planting a seed of distrust deep inside the hearts of the rest of our family. One that she hoped would grow and flower, so that someday she could pick it and use it to destroy us all forever.

And sadly she almost accomplished exactly that.

eleven

As I stared up through the pea soup–like morass that seemed to envelop the Purgatorial skyline, I decided that the huge brimstone, steel, and glass skyscraper that housed Death, Inc., was kind of reminiscent of the building from the opening sequence of the film *The Hudsucker Proxy*.

I wasn't 100 percent sure why that particular thought had come into my mind, but I suspected it had something to do with the feeling of "corporate desolation" that the film inspired, an ambience that Purgatory was especially notable for. After all the weird intermingling I'd seen between the mortal world and the Afterlife, I wouldn't have been at all surprised to find out that the film's production designer had actually stumbled his/her way into Purgatory and been unduly influenced by the place.

This "corporate desolation" ambience not only pertained to the one inhabited part of Purgatory—the gigantic brimstone keep that my dad had renovated into a retro, Americana-style skyscraper only a decade or so after he'd ascended to the Head Honcho-ship of Death—but also to the empty wastelands that made up the rest of the place. Well, I say empty wastelands—I'd always heard that the place was completely unpopulated—

but Jarvis had informed me that recently there'd been rumors of creatures escaping out of Hell and disappearing into the emptiness in search of a better life for themselves and their families. Of course, there was no proof of this, other than a few rumors, but still, the wasteland was so dark and barren that I couldn't imagine wanting to escape into it, no matter how bad my lot in Hell might've been.

Excrement pile, anyone?

In fact, I had spent most of my life trying to stay as far away as possible from the place as I could. As a kid, I had just never really been all that interested in what my dad did for a living. I had never asked for a tour of the Death, Inc., offices, or—like Clio—asked for an internship in any of its departments. I'd kept myself so busy in the human world that I'd had no need to explore the supernatural side of my life.

Now when I looked back at my childhood, I wondered how it was possible *not* to be impressed by my dad. I mean, just the building alone he'd designed was such an amazing piece of architecture that it should've attracted my artistic sensibility. Still, I had always been much more excited about spending time with my mother, finding her interests to be more in line with my own: fashion, interior design, and food.

Yes, my dad may have run a multinational corporation almost single-handedly, but my mother was a genius of *design*. When she biannually redecorated Sea Verge, I was there at her side, watching her work. When she went on one of her massive shopping trips to New York City—where she bought only the most fashionable of designers—I begged for her to let me tag along and watch the whole endeavor, wide-eyed.

As far as I was concerned, *those* were the glory days of my childhood, creating lasting memories in my young, supple mind. I had fought as hard as I could to stop the strange, fantastical world that my dad inhabited from getting *any* purchase inside my brain.

Thinking back, I suppose those early memories were what had initially drawn me to New York City. My mother had treated the place like it was the fashion and cultural Mecca of the world, and since fashion was the one thing that really floated my boat, it just seemed like the perfect place to live as an adult. Of course, those memories were created when I was a kid (and living off my parents' dime), so what appeared to me then as a magical place where clothes grew on trees and luncheons at the Russian Tea Room came standard with every visit wasn't exactly the world I encountered when I officially moved there.

Even though New York City wasn't *exactly* as I remembered, I didn't regret my choice for a minute. I loved the City and I enjoyed struggling in it. I also knew that no matter what bad stuff someone found to say about my character, they could never accuse me of not working my butt off. The City demanded that of you and I willingly gave up my pound of flesh in order to stay there.

"Come on, now," Jarvis said, whispering in my ear as he stood, watching me marvel at the looming building that housed Death, Inc. "Shake a leg."

"I'm coming," I said, pulling my eyes away from the gargantuan brimstone skyscraper and following Jarvis through the revolving glass front door.

Jarvis made it into the lobby without any problem, but somehow I got caught in the revolving door just as a tall cadaverous man in a too-short suit stepped in from the other side. He didn't seem to notice that I was inside the revolving door with him because he gave his side such a hard push that he was immediately ejected out the other side, but I was caught spiraling around the circumference of the door twice. When I was finally able to escape the door's vortex, I found that I was right back where I had started.

Outside.

I hate this door, I thought to myself as I let out a frustrated sigh and thrust myself back into the spinning glass for another round. This time no one was trying to exit from the other side, so I was able to navigate the door without another roundabout fiasco, but as I stepped into the well-air-conditioned lobby, I was suddenly filled with a sense of déjà vu so strong that it couldn't have been déjà vu at all.

I had been here before. I just didn't know it was part of Purgatory at the time.

The memory snuck into my brain unbidden.

I was waiting here in this very lobby with Jarvis right before I'd gone upstairs to meet with the Board of Death and receive the three tasks I had to complete in order to save my family, my dad, and his job. In my mind's eye, I saw Jarvis and myself sitting over in the small vestibule; me browsing through a magazine—was it *Elle*? I couldn't remember—while Jarvis tried to explain how the Office of Death had come into being.

I vaguely remembered him explaining The Fall and the creation of Heaven and Hell and me, like a numbskull, muttering something about Adam and Eve. Thinking back, I must've looked like a real idiot to Jarvis. No wonder he treated me with such disdain. I hadn't known *anything* about my family or the Afterlife, and I had *flaunted* my lack of knowledge in his face like a badge of honor.

At that moment, I was overwhelmed by the need to open my mouth right then and explain to Jarvis that I finally understood why all this stuff was so important to him. That I really needed him to forgive my ambivalence, because it just came from insecurity and fear, not a true dislike of my dad and the business he gave his life to.

"Jarvis," I began, looking down at the little faun who had stood beside me even when he hadn't known if I was fit to take over my dad's job or not. "I'm—"

Before I could continue that thought, a thin woman in a fifties-style golden mohair skirt suit walked over to us and wrapped her arms around Jarvis, nearly choking him.

"Jarvis, darling," she purred as she reluctantly released him. "It's been forever. Still living the good life on Earth?"

Jarvis looked over at me, embarrassed for some reason.

"I suppose so, Evangeline," he murmured before turning

and beckoning me over. "By the way, this is Calliope Reaper-Jones."

Evangeline's mouth dropped and the cat-eyed plastic frames she was wearing slid down her nose as she stared at me.

"Jarvis, you're kidding?" she exclaimed. "*This* is the daughter? The one that . . . you know."

Jarvis nodded as the woman reached out to shake my hand like I was Ed McMahon offering her a million dollars. It didn't take a mirror to know my face was turning beet red. Now *I* was the embarrassed party. I ran a hand through my disheveled hair, hoping I didn't look as bad as I thought I did. I hadn't had time to change out of my dog drool ensemble before we'd left, so I was feeling particularly uncomfortable in what I was wearing.

I knew I should've borrowed something from Clio, I thought miserably as the nice woman continued to yank my arm up and down vigorously.

"Nice to meet you," I said through gritted teeth.

All I wanted was to fade into the wallpaper (or in this case, steel, since the whole space was fashioned out of the stuff) and disappear. I hated being the center of attention. It just made me feel all weird and discombobulated, like I was a balloon some little kid had let go of at the fair that was sailing so high it was about to enter the stratosphere.

"You as well, darling. You as well."

She gave me a quick once-over as she dropped my hand, appraising me with a sharp eye, but seeming to like what she saw. Even though there was no judgment behind her eyes, once again I wished I'd taken the time to change my clothes. At least I'd done a cursory wash of my face and hands in the foyer bathroom, spritzing myself with the Esteban jasmine-scented room spray my mother kept in all the bathrooms in the house. I had no idea whether it was safe to spray that kind of stuff on your bare skin, but I was willing to take the risk if it meant I wasn't going to stink anymore.

Clio had wrinkled her nose in disgust when I'd come out of the bathroom, but hadn't said a word. I guess she decided that me stinking of jasmine was better than me stinking of dog drool.

"Are you going upstairs?" Evangeline asked Jarvis, but I could tell that she was more curious if *I* was going upstairs.

"We're just going to the Hall of—" I started to say before Jarvis stamped his hoof hard on my toes, instantly shutting me up.

"I'm giving Miss Calliope a little tour of the building. She's only seen the lobby and the Board of Death's domain," Jarvis said, his voice smooth as butter. "Her father thought it best she acquaint herself with the rest of the building."

"Of course," Evangeline said as she licked her lips.

"So we must be going. We are already late for one of our meetings," Jarvis continued, grabbing my arm and leading me toward the bank of elevators that presided over the back of the lobby.

Evangeline gave me a curious little wave as I followed Jarvis's lead, then before I realized what was happening, I was being bodily forced into an open elevator by my faun escort. As soon as the doors shut, Jarvis let out a long sigh and slumped against the side of the elevator.

"What floor?" I asked, looking at the panel of buttons that seemed to stretch almost to the elevator's ceiling. I didn't take an official tally, but there had to have been at least one hundred buttons on the steel-plated sucker.

Jarvis looked up and shook his head.

"Please press button seventy-three," Jarvis said, starting to relax a little.

"Okay," I said, counting two at a time until I hit seventy-three and pushed the button.

"Now press twenty-one."

I counted again, pushed the correct button, and suddenly the elevator shot upward so quickly that I fell forward, catching myself against the smooth steel of the elevator wall.

"That's better," Jarvis said, not at all fazed by the rapid ascent the elevator was making.

"Who was that woman?" I asked as I held on to the elevator wall for dear life.

"She's the Secretary of Passage. She used to work with your sister Thalia."

"No way," I said, feeling woozy, more from having touched an enemy than from the elevator's speed. "And she had the gall to shake my hand?"

Jarvis shook his head.

"She had nothing to do with your sister's kidnapping plot," Jarvis replied. "At least, the Board of Death cleared her of any complicity. But still, it's always best to keep people like her at arm's length. She's very ambitious and *extremely* calculating."

I nodded.

"*And* it was very strange, indeed, to see her in the lobby. She has no need to use the lobby entrance. She has access to her office via wormhole. I suppose the only thing that makes any sense is that someone clued her in to our arrival and she scurried down to make sure she accidentally 'bumped' into us," Jarvis finished unhappily.

"How would someone know that we're even here?" I asked curiously. "You didn't tell anyone we were coming and neither did I."

Jarvis sighed.

"They keep a log of all wormhole transport in and out of Purgatory. No one is supposed to have access to it, but that means nothing. Information can always be had here for a price," Jarvis said uneasily.

"Crap."

Jarvis nodded in agreement.

"Crap is definitely apropos, Miss Calliope."

At those words, the elevator came to a smooth stop and the doors slid open, revealing a small, cramped antechamber. It was probably no less than fifteen by twenty-five feet, but it felt smaller. The walls were done in a shade of pale green that I could only call "sickly mint" and the floors were made of neatly fitted white linoleum squares. There was a tiny brown reception desk in the back flanked by four metal folding chairs. As I followed Jarvis out of the elevator, I realized that there was no one in the room, not even behind the reception desk.

The elevator doors shut with a loud *screech* that nearly made me jump out of my skin. Jarvis seemed oblivious to the sound as he beckoned me to follow him over to the reception desk. As we passed the first metal folding chair, I realized that I had been wrong. We were not alone in the room, after all. An almost-transparent figure sat hunched in one of the chairs, its hands clasped together expectantly, watching us.

I paused midstep as I realized I was seeing my first ghost. Part of me wanted to stop and get a better look, but I could feel a steady hum of weird energy emanating from the thing, making the hairs on the back of my neck stand on end.

I felt Jarvis's warm hand on my arm and let him lead me away.

"Stay far away from that Shade," Jarvis hissed under his breath. "Only the Devil makes creatures such as those."

I nodded, not needing to be told twice.

Before I could ask Jarvis any more about the creature, I heard a loud *buzzing* sound—which made me jump—immediately followed by another, longer *buzz*. I looked over and saw Jarvis pushing a little button on the desktop. Beside it sat a tiny golden plaque that read: PRESS FOR SERVICE.

I expected someone to appear instantly, but apparently things ran at their own speed in Purgatory. Jarvis knew the drill because he shrugged and walked over to one of the folding chairs facing the Shade and sat down. I didn't want to stand at the reception desk by myself, so I hightailed it over to the chair beside Jarvis and plopped my butt into it.

We sat there for what could have been an hour—but was probably more like three—waiting for God knew what to happen. I tried to put things in perspective; the Shade had been sitting there longer than we had, so he had it worse than us, but that didn't really make me feel any better.

I pulled the little rubidium clock out of my pocket and looked down at it, watching the numbers whiz by.

"How much time do I have left?" I asked, not really expecting it to respond, but suddenly the numbers on the face stopped whizzing, and in their place I saw: twenty hours, seven minutes, thirty-six seconds, 5.4×10^{-44} s.

Now, what the hell does that last equation mean? I wondered to myself. *Maybe it is that weird Planck-unit thing Cerberus was talking about.*

But before I could give it any more thought, a door behind the reception desk—one that I hadn't noticed being there at all—opened and a small, slim, dark-haired girl in a yellow shirtwaist dress came out, her porcelain features set in a bland mask. She looked over at the ghost and nodded, then turned to Jarvis, a smile lighting up her face.

"You'll be next, Mr. De Poupsy."

Jarvis inclined his head in response. "Thank you, Suri."

She gave Jarvis a wink before turning back to the Shade. I watched her, surprised to witness her face instantly resetting to its previous state of detachment as she moved to address it; she obviously didn't care for the creature any more than we did.

"This way, sir," Suri said, her voice neutral.

The Shade didn't seem to notice the girl's coolness toward it as it stood up and followed her out of the antechamber.

"Weird," I whispered as the door closed on the Shade's back and I slipped my rubidium clock back into my pocket.

Jarvis nodded.

"You called it a Shade?" I asked, curiosity always a bad habit of mine.

"Well, I don't have much experience with creatures like that," Jarvis began, "but yes, it's called a Shade. It's a soul that has chosen to be released from the Wheel of Samsara—that's basically the cycle of reincarnation—so that it could remain in Hell and offer its services to the Devil."

"Creepy," I said, shivering. "Why doesn't it have a body?"

"It does, but the Devil is a wily fellow, as you know, so when he sends his minions to do his bidding outside of Hell, he keeps their bodies with him, forcing them to return to

Hell once they have completed their task or forever remain disembodied."

I had never heard anything so awful in my life—someone keeping your body hostage so you can't run away? That was just plain mean.

"He's a real jerkoid, isn't he?" I said, my mind instantly returning with gut-churning fear to the memory of the one face-to-face I'd had with the Devil.

The jerk had pitched me headfirst into a bottomless pit at the edge of Hell, so that his protégé, Daniel, could take over my dad's job instead of me. Luckily, God had intervened and I hadn't been forced to spend my life in free fall like the Devil had intended.

Wasn't I just a lucky little ducky?

"He's the worst of the worst, but necessary," Jarvis replied. "Very necessary."

I nodded. I completely understood what he was driving at. Without the Devil, Evil wouldn't flourish, and then Good would overwhelm the world, creating an imbalance in the universe. You had to have both of them—Good and Evil—or else things just didn't work properly. Weird, but true.

Before we could continue our conversation, the invisible door behind the reception desk opened again and the cute girl in the shirtwaist dress stepped out into the antechamber, dark pigtails bouncing at the sides of her head. She motioned to us and we stood up.

"This way, please, Mr. De Poupsy," she said cheerfully, no sign of the insipidness she'd shown the ghostly Shade. "It's always such a pleasure to see you."

And with that, we followed our guide through the doorway and into the Hall of Death.

twelve

The Hall of Death was like nothing I'd ever seen before.

If the antechamber was a model in Spartan chic, then the actual Hall itself was the antechamber's antithesis. Part medieval monastery, part steel, skeletal behemoth, the Hall was nothing if not an architectural masterpiece. A hulking monster of a place, it had been created with such an intermingling of old-world munificence and cold modernity that standing before it made me feel as if I were in some kind of hallowed temple.

Sturdy, interlocking limestone blocks that appeared as if they'd been cut by hand stretched so far beyond my field of vision that I couldn't see where the hallway ended. Each block fitted so elegantly with the next that even when I looked, I couldn't find a mortar seam. The floor was hewn out of larger blocks of the same limestone, but its length was covered in long Oriental carpets fashioned in repeating patterns of black, crimson, and russet. Upon closer inspection, I saw that each carpet contained such a wealth of intricate detail that no two had been woven alike.

Each one contained a plethora of animals, heavenly bodies, and other strange symbols—some of which I had never seen before, making me wonder if they might be the letters of some archaic dead language that had ceased to be spoken by human tongues anymore. However you cut it, the carpets were beautiful and so fragile looking that it almost seemed sacrilegious to be treading upon them.

On each side of the passage were arched, open doorways that led into smaller rooms containing long, thin wooden tables and matching benches, neither of which looked very comfortable. Every table had three green glass reading lamps set on top of it, giving off a warm, scholarly glow. Here and there I spied people reading from huge, ancient tomes—some of them taking notes, others just casually flipping through pages. In the far corners of each room we passed, I saw hulking suits of medieval armor standing at attention, arms ramrod at their sides, helmets obscuring the faces of anything or anyone that might be hiding inside.

At the side of each archway, a tall, flickering torch stood sentry, filling the Hall with the scent of burning cedar, a smell that was somehow comforting and invigorating at the same time. On some of the walls we passed hung rich tapestries from the medieval period, representing two-dimensional interpretations of crusading knights and their infidel victims.

Some of the tapestries were superviolent—one even showed a guy getting his guts pulled out—while others offered more sedate imagery. I wanted to stop and look at a couple of the ones that had animals on them—animals I had never seen before, like this one crazy creature that had a lion's body, an eagle's head, and a set of rainbow-colored wings—but Jarvis grabbed my sleeve and wouldn't let go.

"Follow me, please," Suri said, her voice pleasantly chirpy. "And please don't touch anything, thank you."

"Sorry," I said, embarrassed that she had caught me edging toward one of the bloodier tapestries.

She had a slight accent that made me think Arabic might've been her native language once upon a time, but it was so obscured by a Mid-Atlantic twang that it was hard to tell.

As we followed our guide down the hallway, I looked up,

dazzled by the more modern part of the structure: especially the intricately woven steel frame that made up the foundation of the glass-enclosed ceiling. It was like staring up through the hulking skeleton of a transparent beast. I had no idea how the thing was even possible because, from what I remembered, we were somewhere in the middle of the giant brimstone and steel skyscraper, not at its apex.

There should've been a whole other floor of offices directly above us, not empty sky. This meant that the clear blue sky we were looking at through the glass was either some kind of high-tech 3-D hologram, or it was just a really quality piece of magic.

My vote was for magic.

Either way, it was a marvel to behold, the transparent glass allowing a curtain of soft, pale light to trickle down into the hall, melding with the smoky incense from the torches to create a hazy atmosphere that made the Hall feel like a veritable bastion of mystery.

As the hallway stretched beyond us with no apparent end in sight, I had the impression that our movements were being watched. I wasn't sure who the culprit was, but I got a funny feeling every time we passed an empty room—like there might *really* be knights in that armor, ready to slit your throat if you even thought about thinking about touching something.

I caught Jarvis's eye, shifted my gaze to one of the suits of armor we passed, and opened my eyes wide, in query. Jarvis instantly caught my meaning and nodded. Okay, so I wasn't crazy. There *was* something creepy-crawly about the dormant knights we kept seeing. Suddenly, something clicked inside of my brain and I remembered what Clio had said about how tight the security was in the Hall of Death.

Those suits of armor weren't just ornamental decorations like the carpets or tapestries. No, *they* were the security she had been referring to.

Big, scary creatures in medieval, hammered metal zoot suits were totally gulp-worthy!

As I stared at a heavy steel broadsword resting against one

of the knights' hips, I decided that I was definitely going to
keep my hands and feet to myself. I so did *not* want to go head-
to-head with something that could cut me up into tiny, little
slivers of human flesh with only a couple of chop-chops. Even
immortality was a tough sell when your body was in a million
pieces that just wouldn't stick back together, no matter how
much superglue you used.

"Almost there," Suri promised with a big smile that revealed
two rows of tiny corn kernel–like teeth.

She had turned around to make sure Jarvis and I were right
behind her, but something unexpected must've caught her eye,
because suddenly Jarvis and I were barreling into the back of
her stationary form.

"What the—" I started to say, but before I could get the
words out of my mouth, Suri was pushing past me, her eyes
blazing. I moved to follow her, but Jarvis grabbed my hand.

"Stay right there, Mistress Calliope," he murmured, his
voice barely a whisper. I looked over at my friend, but he
merely shook his head and indicated for me to watch Suri.

Together, we stood in the middle of the hall, staring as our
guide picked up speed, her body moving with a kind of grace-
ful power I had only seen in animals—specifically giant cats.
And I had definitely seen enough National Geographic shows
to know what damage lions and tigers could do when they
were pissed off.

We watched as Suri barreled down the long hallway, her
legs seeming to grow longer as she ran. Without warning, she
veered off course, her body like a missile bound for one of the
numerous small reading rooms I'd glimpsed through the curved
archways. As she disappeared inside, I yanked Jarvis back to
me by the arm, dragging him closer so that I could get a better
look at what was going on. He dug in his heels, but I was
bigger—I had a good few inches (and not so good pounds) on
the little faun—so he had to follow me.

"I wanna see," I said, moving us *even* closer.

"This is most irresponsible—" Jarvis began, but was cut off

abruptly when we were shoved out of the way by two armored knights, broadswords drawn.

I slammed into one of the walls, but I kept my grip on Jarvis, so he didn't fall and get trampled by the marauders.

From my new vantage point by the wall, I was still close enough that I could *just* peer inside the little reading room. At first, all I saw were the knights' receding backs, but once they'd joined the fray, I had a pretty good view of what was going down.

Suri, like some fantabulous Jet Li character come to life, was trying unsuccessfully to subdue the Shade we had seen back in the antechamber. I immediately saw why she was having such a hard time battling the evil thing. It was noncorporeal, so no matter how many times she attacked it, she just slid right through it to the other side.

One of the armored knights tried to approach the Shade, but Suri held up her hand to stop him. She pointed to the now-defunct knights that had originally been in the room. Both of them were on the ground beside the reading table, their bodies nothing but twisted hunks of scrap metal now. I couldn't figure out how the Shade could have completed that kind of handiwork without a body, but I didn't doubt for a second that it had had some hand in the deed.

Out of the corner of my eye, I caught sight of something long and furry—a tail, I decided—shooting out of the room and down the hall. I tried to follow its progress, but my eyes were quickly drawn back to the reading room by the sound of a loud crash.

Two more knights had bitten the dust, and now Suri didn't just look frustrated—she looked *pissed*. The Shade, on the other hand, didn't seem at all perturbed by the situation. Instead, it kind of gave off the vibe that this was exactly how it had intended things to go down.

Suddenly, the Shade turned its head, its attention now on me. I took an involuntary step back, my brain reeling as something cold and probing slid inside it. I gasped, reaching out for

Jarvis's shoulder to steady myself. The world around me disappeared, my vision clouded by flashes of gold and ebony and scarlet. I shut my eyes, but this had no impact on the strange flashes. In fact, it only seemed to make them worse.

Panicking, I opened my eyes again, hoping that reality had decided to return, but now Jarvis and the Hall of Death were completely gone, replaced by the blurry image of a red folder. And the harder I looked at the folder, the less cohesive it became, more like an afterimage, actually, or the phantom picture you see behind your eyelids when you've closed your eyes after a long bout of staring.

It's not what you see, but what you don't.

The words entered my brain, unbidden.

I blinked, and without any further adieu, the red folder was gone and I was back in the Hall of Death, furiously clutching Jarvis's shoulder, my fingers like talons.

"Hey, Jarvi?" I whispered in the faun's ear. "Why does this feel like a setup?"

Jarvis looked at me, askance.

"What do you mean?"

I shook my head. "I just have a feeling that *this* isn't the main attraction."

Jarvis narrowed his eyes.

"You had a vision."

It wasn't a question.

I shrugged my shoulders uncertainly.

"Maybe. I don't know," I said as the sound of metal crashing into limestone pervaded the air around us.

"All right, where shall we find this 'main attraction,' as you so succinctly put it?" Jarvis said abruptly.

I shrugged again. "I don't know. It was just a feeling I had. How am I supposed to know what the hell it means?"

Jarvis pursed his lips, not liking it at *all* when I got whiny on him.

"What does your gut say?" he said slowly, letting the words hang in the air.

I shrugged.

"I don't know."

Jarvis let out a long breath, trying not to lose his patience. "Think, Miss Calliope."

"Okay, okay. I'm thinking," I murmured, hoping to get him off my case by at least *trying* to do what he wanted of me.

Okay, I thought to myself, *what does my gut say?*

I'd never really paid all that much attention to my gut before—unless you counted feeding it when it was hungry, but I was pretty sure that that wasn't what Jarvis had meant. I inhaled deeply, focusing on the feeling I'd had about the Shade, but after a few moments of careful contemplation, nothing was forthcoming.

"It's not working!" I hissed sharply, annoyed by the situation and wishing fervently that I'd just kept my mouth shut about the whole "feeling" thing in the first place.

Jarvis sighed and took my hands. At his touch, I was flooded by a sense of calm so intense that I nearly started snoring—I was that relaxed.

"What are you doing?" I asked drowsily, barely able to keep my eyes open.

"Close your eyes, Mistress Calliope."

He didn't have to ask me twice. I closed my drooping eyelids, the world going black around me.

"Now," Jarvis continued. "What do you *see*?"

Free from the onslaught of thoughts that usually assailed my brain when I tried to go to sleep, I let my mind wander in the darkness behind my eyelids. Without any heavy lifting on my part, I found myself descending through the darkness until it suddenly gave way to a torrent of pure light so bright and inviting that I let it engulf me.

When consciousness returned again, I discovered that I wasn't in my head anymore—and that was when I realized I wasn't in my body, either!

I'd left my body only, like, twice before, and I'd ended up right back inside someone else's body two seconds later, so neither experience had been totally terrifying—especially the first time, when I discovered that the fellow I was inhabiting was a total hottie with a physique so tight it'd made my head spin.

But this time was different; this time I hadn't been immediately stuffed back into another person's body like the meat inside a soul tamale. Instead, I was a floater, completely unfettered from my (or any other) physical form, free to go wherever the heck I wanted without anything or anyone to stop me.

Enjoying my newfound freedom, I looked around and saw that I was back in the Hall of Death. Part of me wanted to go into the room where Suri and the armored knights were still battling the Shade, but something, some kind of inner voice, drew me away.

Not here, the voice whispered to me.

I let it guide me across the Hall to where my body stood immobile; its hands clasped with Jarvis's, its eyes shut in utter concentration.

It was weird to see myself from an "outside my body" perspective. I had always thought that my slim frame was too boyish—part of the reason I tried to dress it in as much feminine-looking stuff as possible—but from this side of the looking glass, I realized that maybe I was being too critical of myself. I'd put on a few pounds recently and my butt and boobs were looking markedly rounder than they'd been before. Also, my face was a little fuller, giving my features a less angular look. All in all, I thought I was looking pretty saucy, if I *did* say so myself.

Maybe, I decided, *I wasn't such a bad catch, after all. Lose the dog drool ensemble and I was heading into pretty damn near presentable territory.*

Before I could linger too long gawping at myself, the inner voice that had led me away from Suri and the Shade began urging me to continue on.

This way, the voice said. *Hurry.*

Leaving my body and Jarvis behind me, I floated down the main hallway, my eyes scanning each archway and adjoining room as I passed it, waiting for the little voice to tell me what to do next. For a long time there was only radio silence, then as I neared the end of the hallway, the little voice kicked into high gear.

Turn here. Now, it nearly shrieked.

I did what it said, even though as far as I could tell, there was no doorway to turn into, only a large tapestry hanging on the wall, portraying a unicorn with a small golden cat sitting serenely at its feet, and to their right was a gallant knight, his head inclined forward in an elegant bow.

This way!

The voice goaded me forward and I dubiously complied, but instead of hitting solid limestone like I'd expected, I was surprised to find myself inside a small alcove hidden behind the tapestry.

Up there, the voice said.

I looked up and saw metal rungs embedded into the limestone wall, leading upward into darkness. I headed in the voice's direction, not even pausing to think about what might lie in wait above me.

Hurry! the voice intoned. *Hurry!*

I floated up, past the metal rung ladder, noticing that each separate rung was engraved with a different symbol. I was able to decipher only a couple of them, but those were the easy ones: a unicorn and a serpent. The others were more intricate and abstract, similar to some of the patterns I'd seen in the carpets on the floor of the main hall. I wondered again if the symbols were actually words and decided I would have to ask Jarvis about it the next time we weren't in the middle of a crisis situation.

As I reached the top of the ladder, the voice heralded my arrival.

You're here! Hurry!

I had no idea where "here" was, but it definitely wasn't anyplace I'd ever been before. First of all, it was very dark, with only one tiny overhead light that shone faintly down from right above, barely illuminating the two-foot area where I was hovering. The murky lighting made it hard to see what was around me, but I could sense I was in some kind of corridor. One that was so narrow it could hold only one human-sized body at a time. I couldn't see how long the corridor stretched in either direction because of the lack of light, but directly in front of me I found row upon of row of neatly filed peach folders.

Just as I started to peer down at one of the folders to read its label, the row began to shift and I realized that the files were mechanized so that you could call up exactly what folder you needed without having to sort through the whole row by hand.

The system kind of reminded me of a horizontal version of the setup they had down at my local dry cleaners: totally efficient, but kind of annoying if you went past the item that you wanted. I had seen Mrs. Wu, the owner, flipping back and forth in frustration through the hanging rows of freshly plastic-ed clothing on more than one occasion.

The row in front of me kept moving, so I floated to my right, hoping that if I changed my proximity to the stack of folders, it would stop flipping. Instantly, the light that had been above me extinguished—and another light directly above my new position flipped on. I looked down to find that I was standing in front of a whole new set of file folders, only these guys were blue, not peach. I wanted to look down and read the label on one of these blue folders since it was still stationary, but I was afraid that if I floated any closer, it would start shifting like the other row had.

Suddenly, I heard a low *pop*. I followed the sound with my nonexistent eyes, expecting to see only darkness, but instead one of the weird overhead lights flipped on about fifty feet down the corridor. As I realized what had made the light turn on, my breath caught in my nonexistent throat and I, without meaning to, found myself racing at hyperspeed down the corridor. I wanted to call out, but since I had no mouth, I could do nothing but hover and watch as the handsome, dark-haired man with the ice blue eyes pulled a red file out of the stack in front of him and extracted a thin brown piece of paper from inside it.

Daniel, my mind screamed, but it was no use. All I could

do was watch as he replaced the empty file, looked around to make sure no one had spotted his larceny—*Me! I saw it!* I wanted to yell out—and then folded the piece of paper, slipping it inside his coat pocket.

The whole thing took less than a minute, and then the light flipped off again and he was gone. I could only imagine he knew some other secret access point and that was how he'd made his daring entrance and escape, but I was too upset by the encounter to follow him or ask him what exactly he thought he was doing gallivanting around Purgatory when he was *supposed* to be dead!

The only thing I could bring myself to do was look down at the file folder he'd replaced. I knew it was the right one because he'd replaced it too quickly and hadn't gotten it back into its spot properly, causing a corner to stick out where it should have lain flush with the other folders.

The row of red folders remained silent as I looked down at the label, my heart lurching as I read what it said:

DANIEL SMITH, THE FORMER DEVIL'S PROTÉGÉ

I barely had two seconds to digest what the label said before I felt a sharp tug on my soul and I found myself being dragged, unwillingly, back into my body.

thirteen

I gasped for air; my lungs felt like two deflated balloons flopping around painfully inside my chest. It didn't seem like I'd been gone for very long, but by the frightened look on Jarvis's face—and the lack of oxygen I'd experienced upon my return—I wasn't so sure. Either way, I didn't think there'd be any permanent brain damage, but it definitely made me not want to have a repeat performance anytime soon.

"Are you all right?" Jarvis said, worry tightening his face, making him look drawn and tired. Even his mustache seemed the worse for wear.

I nodded, still trying to catch my breath and readjust to having a corporeal form again. We were interrupted by the crash of metal striking solid wall, the sound splitting the air around us. We turned in unison, observing the pained throes of an armored guard as it slid down the limestone wall behind Jarvis and crumpled into a heap at his feet. Two seconds later Suri's airborne body followed suit, landing with such force that it caromed down the middle of the Oriental-carpeted hall like a skipping stone. The young woman didn't stay down for long, though. Like a supple marionette, she was instantly back on her feet again, her whole body snapping itself into place as if her limbs were being mysteriously maneuvered by a series of invisible, but interconnected, strings.

Eyes wild, Suri let out a piercing war cry that made the hairs on the backs of my arms rise, then she leapt back into the fray. I followed her progress, noting that there were now *eight* armored knights involved in the battle, each of them wielding some kind of massive sword or battle-ax. They handled their weapons with such ease that they might well have been made out of Styrofoam instead of steel.

The Shade now stood on top of a long table, surrounded by the hulking knights, but being outnumbered nine to one didn't faze it. I heard another war whoop and watched as Suri did a front handspring, landing only a few feet away from the edge of the tabletop, balled fists straining at her waist the only indication of her extreme agitation.

Suddenly, I felt the heat of the Shade's stare on me again and I looked up, my belly churning as its eyes locked onto mine. I felt a tug at my brain and then I was fighting against my own soul as it tried to disconnect from my body and go floating away again.

Help me, a voice said urgently inside my head. It was the same voice I'd heard when I was bodiless. I hadn't paid much attention to whom the voice might belong to before, but now I listened, waiting for the tell that would confirm my suspicions.

Please, help me, Callie.

I knew that voice.

"*Daniel,*" I breathed, the word barely a whisper as it slipped from my mouth, but it was enough to snap the connection. Almost instantaneously I found myself back in possession of my body again. I let out a relieved breath, my body shaking as I realized how close I had come to losing control of my soul.

It didn't take a brain surgeon to figure out was going on. Somehow, Daniel had separated his soul from his body, leaving the corporeal side of him free to slip into the Hall of Death and steal his own Death Record. I could only assume that the weird soul blending we had engaged in months earlier was the reason why our souls were able to call each other out and communicate so intimately.

It was hard to reconcile this Shade with the Daniel I knew. Still, something within my heart recognized this *thing* as Daniel, so I was just going to have to listen to what the little voice inside my brain told me to do and trust that everything would work out all right.

Jarvis heard my exhalation and looked up quizzically. I shook my head, hoping that he would understand my wordless plea for silence. He started to open his mouth, then quickly shut it again, nodding. Without another word, he reached out and took my hand, giving it a firm squeeze.

I turned my attention back to the fight already in progress, an idea forming in my head as I watched the knights inch closer to their prey. I didn't know why Daniel was trying to steal his own file, but he had asked for my help—

Suddenly, all the collected feelings of anger and hurt bubbled to the surface of my heart, and I was so full of rage that I wanted to tell Suri *exactly* who the Shade was and what he'd been doing upstairs with the Death Records. I could feel the nasty words just itching to leave my mouth, but I swallowed them back as I realized something important: No matter how angry I was with the stupid former Devil's protégé, no matter how much I detested him right at that moment for making me think he was dead . . . in the end, all I really wanted to do was run over and kiss the crap out of him.

The realization that I was in love with Daniel hit me like a ton of bricks. I was so *not* prepared to find my heart beating in double time at the mere thought of putting my lips on his. It was ridiculous, a totally crazy proposition—and it didn't matter one whit that my heart felt one way while my brain was holding down the opposite opinion. I was just giddy to be within a hundred feet of him—soul or body, either one was fine by me!—saccharine as that was.

I took a deep breath, strangely relaxed now that I had finally stopped denying the obvious, and began to assess the situation. Daniel's soul still stood on the table, his way blocked by the armored knights. Suri, her body a tightly coiled mass of muscle and sinew, crouched by the table's edge like a snake readying itself to pounce. As I watched her, she shoved a hank of thick black hair behind her ear, her face a mask. I had no idea what she planned on doing to subdue Daniel's soul, but since I now had a vested interest in the outcome, I needed to intervene before she made mincemeat out of him.

"Stop!" I yelled, my voice firm and controlled. Under normal circumstances, I was a bit of a coward, but knowing that Daniel's safety was at stake filled me with a sense of purpose, making me feel like one of those preternaturally strong mothers who can lift a full-sized car off her kid when normally it's all she can do just to carry her shopping bags out of the grocery store by herself. Whether I wanted to or not, I was gonna keep this new persona going long enough to make sure no one I cared about got hurt.

"Hey, stop it!" I yelled, striding forward so that I was standing just underneath the archway that led into the room. Suri looked up, startled by my presence.

"I can stop him," I said confidently.

Suri just stared at me, eyes narrowed in suspicion. I gave her my most winning smile, but she just continued to stare at me as if I were speaking in another language.

We stood there, staring at each other like we were in some kind of Mafia standoff, until I heard a clipped voice behind me say:

"Do you not realize who she *is*?"

I felt Jarvis step up beside me, flanking my right side as if he were my bodyguard. I flashed him a quick smile, which he returned before giving Suri such a look of intense concentration that I thought she might melt into a puddle right then and there. He may have been almost a head shorter than me—*not* that I was a behemoth at five-six—but there was just something about Jarvis that inspired respect, no matter how high you towered over him.

Suri looked from Jarvis to me, then back again, before shaking her head. She seemed a lot less sure of herself now that I had the faun in my corner. I was digging the odds more and more now that the two-person standoff had magically become a three-person hustle.

"*This*," Jarvis continued, his tone dripping with disdain directed right at Suri, "is *Calliope Reaper-Jones*."

It took a moment for Jarvis's words to click, but when my name finally rang a few bells in her brain, her face transformed from stormy menace into a beatific grin.

"Oh my goodness, you're Death's Daughter."

It was a statement, not a question. Still, I felt that I had to acknowledge her somehow, so I just nodded, strangely embarrassed by the look of reverence she was beaming in my direction.

"Uhm, yeah. That's me, I guess."

"You saved your father *and* fought the demon Vritra *and* found the Cup of Jamshid . . ."

Suri started to rattle off my various accomplishments in backwards order, which only made me feel *more* embarrassed than I already was. I had never seen hero worship alive and well in someone's face before, but there it was, stamped on Suri's visage for the whole world to see. It was a totally new and weird experience for me, one that I wasn't completely sure I liked.

"Yes," Jarvis said, interrupting Suri as she continued to extol my virtues for the assemblage. "This is the same Calliope Reaper-Jones. Now, quit squawking and order your knights to step aside so that she may deal with the Shade."

I wanted to kiss Jarvis for being so amazing.

"But I can't allow a civilian to deal with—" she began, but Jarvis held up his Fran Drescher hand.

"We both know that the one defense this guard is lacking in is"—he gestured to the armored knights, who stood in an unmoving circle around the table where Daniel's Shade was still standing—"their ability to deal with noncorporeal entities."

Suri looked shamefacedly at the ground, then gave a meek nod of acquiescence.

"This is true, but there was good cause to fire the witch doctors, as you know already . . ."

Jarvis didn't let her off the hook so easily.

"This is something that our President and CEO has commented on in the past, but that you and your retinue were unwilling to deal with in a timely fashion."

Suri continued to look down at her feet.

"But we *do* have plans to bring in another—"

Jarvis abruptly cleared his throat, cutting her off.

"When you released those Senegalese witch doctors from your employ, you should've hired someone to fill their place at once," Jarvis said tersely. You could tell this was a subject that he and my dad had talked about at length, but hadn't been able to induce Suri and her team to act on yet.

Suri looked up at Jarvis, chagrined.

"I swear that we'll get someone in here immediately."

"Until then," Jarvis said, his tone chiding, "you have a disruptive Shade in the Hall of Death—which is supposed to be one of the most heavily defended places in all of Purgatory, but apparently is *not*, as you have just proven by this spectacle."

Suri nodded, red-faced, as Jarvis continued his gentle, yet firm, dressing-down. I could tell by the way Jarvis was trying not to smile that this was exactly where he wanted our guide: ashamed and vulnerable; i.e., *easily manipulated*.

"I suggest you let Miss Calliope deal with your Shade," Jarvis said breezily. "As you already know, she is a professional when it comes to things of this nature."

Jarvis was quickly becoming my new hero.

It was funny, but until now, I'd had no idea what a master at the art of deception my dad's Executive Assistant was. Right before my eyes, he'd twisted our little guide into such an emotional pretzel of embarrassment that she didn't know whether she was coming or going—and of course, Jarvis was right there, ready to lead her in whichever direction he deemed best.

Hopefully, it was the direction that would allow me complete and unfettered access to Daniel's Shade.

"I don't know," Suri said, but Jarvis was having none of it.

"Then I'm afraid I'll have to call in the Jackal Brothers. Hopefully, they can instill a little order in the Hall of Death—"

"No!" Suri yelped, fear in her eyes. "Please, not the Jackal Brothers."

She looked so freaked-out that I almost felt sorry for her.

"But if you can't take care of your own—"

Suri blanched, all the blood draining from her creamy, golden skin.

"We can. We will! I swear it," she offered, her voice a shrill whine in my ear. Jarvis was unmoved by her outburst.

"As the Day Manager of the Hall of Death," Suri said, turning to me, "I beg of you. Please help us contain the Shade."

I could tell that it pained her to do what Jarvis wanted, but the threat of the Jackal Brothers taking over her domain was a very real thing to her.

"Thank you for being reasonable," Jarvis said pithily, then turned to me, bowing low.

"Mistress Calliope, the floor is yours."

I felt weird telling Suri thank you because it was so obvious that she really didn't want my help and was being forced to let me take a shot at the Shade, but I gave her a quick smile anyway.

"I'll do my best," I said, hoping that this was compromise enough, then I winked at Jarvis as I stepped past the archway and into the room.

"Why don't you guys go back out in the hall," I said to the knights. "That way no one gets hurt."

I waited, but after a few moments it was apparent that none of the dum-dums was gonna do what I said. I looked back at Suri, who sighed.

"Out here, guys!"

At Suri's command, the knights instantly moved out of defensive position, falling into one single-file line that quickly shuffled out of the room, battle-axes and swords clanging as they went. It was like watching a group of high school football players leaving a locker room. As they passed me by, I got a whiff of some of the gnarliest body odor I'd ever encountered, giving me the distinct impression that whatever creature lay hidden beneath that armor did not have a good relationship with its shower.

Well, that sure got their butts in gear, I thought grumpily as I waited for them to clear the room.

Once they were gone, I walked up to the edge of the table, my heart hammering like an out-of-control jackhammer. I felt my mind whirl at the prospect of talking to Daniel again. It wasn't like I was the greatest at talking to men I was attracted to anyway, but add in a case of the heebie-jeebies and you could forget it. On more than one occasion, my brain had decided to shut down, leaving me gawping like an imbecilic cod fish at whatever hunk of manhood I'd been about to chat up.

I just prayed that was not gonna be the case in this situation.

I took a deep breath as I came to stand in front of the Shade. I tried to see some kind of resemblance to the Daniel I knew, but there really wasn't any.

"Well now, fancy meeting you here," I said, clasping my hands together behind my back nervously. "Long time, no see."

I couldn't believe that *this* was how it was going to go down! Was I really just gonna stand there and babble at him like an idiot? Apparently that was *exactly* what I was going to do.

"You look well. I mean for a Shade, that is."

I offered up that little bon mot like it was the holy grail of repartee. Boy, was I on a roll or what?

Any more witty dialogue and it'd be a regular Preston Sturges movie around here, I thought miserably.

Daniel's Shade stared down at me from its table perch and I wondered if this was what *my* Shade looked like. Had I run into anyone while I was doing my whole "out of body" floating spectacle through the Hall of Death, was this what they would have seen?

God, I hoped not. Because Daniel's Shade was a pretty crazy-looking character.

I guess the best way to describe a Shade is to compare its

composition to the fuzz you see on a television set when the cable has gone out. Only, a Shade is much, much, *much* more transparent than any TV fuzz. In fact, if you didn't look directly at it, the Shade kind of blended in with whatever its surroundings were, almost like it wasn't there at all.

Its only discernible human feature was its eyes, which were so cold and piercing that they gave you the shivers every time you looked into their depths. The Shade possessed no nose, no mouth, and no ears; so I guess you could barely call its face a *face*, even. It had arms and legs, but they were so mottled— like the rest of its fuzzlike body—that unless they were in motion, you wouldn't have known it had any appendages.

Help me.

The words startled me and I looked around to make sure that I was really hearing them in my head, not in reality. Satisfied that there was no one else in the room, I said:

"How?"

Daniel slipped into radio silence and I tried not to stare too deeply into what passed as his eyes while I waited for his reply.

We're connected, you and I.

I nodded. Madame Papillon had told me this very same thing not even twenty-four hours before.

I didn't mean for that to happen, Daniel's voice said wearily. *I'm sorry.*

I shrugged.

"No worries. It happens," I offered, even though it was the *understatement* of the century.

But maybe we can use it to our advantage.

"Okay," I said.

I loved how Daniel was using the all-powerful pronoun "we." It's lovely to be a "we" when the guy you dig is standing right in front of you, all hot-blooded and alive, but quite another thing when he's nothing but a monstrous outline of himself.

"What do you propose?" I asked as I looked back over my shoulder and saw Suri and her minions waiting impatiently out

in the hallway. It only served to remind me that I was under a
deadline, both here in the moment *and* in the greater scheme
of things.

Let me come inside you.

I nearly choked on my own saliva.

"Excuse me?" I squeaked, all the blood in my body quickly
pooling to my lower extremities.

If I slip inside of you, they'll think you've banished me,
Daniel's voice said.

I could feel the heat in my face—and in between my legs—
and I wondered suspiciously if Daniel was choosing those
words on purpose just to screw with my head.

"Let's not use the words 'come' and 'slip' and 'inside' in
the same sentence again, okay?" I said, brushing my hair back
off my face with my hand nervously.

Oh, the voice said, followed by an embarrassed silence.

"Yeah. Uh-huh," I replied, sort of pleased to have made *him*
feel as uncomfortable as he'd made me.

All right, then, he said. *Let's try that again. I will go in you—*

Jesus, this was no better than all the "slipping" and "coming." I guess there was nothing I could do but give the Shade a
tight smile and hope that my legs would continue to hold me
up during the sexually charged hot flash I was in the middle of
having.

"Just do whatever you're gonna do," I said through gritted
teeth.

Thank you, Callie.

That was all it took to melt my heart. I just wanted to put
my Humpty-Dumpty Daniel back together, then find a nice
private place where I could shatter him into a million pieces
over and over again—and I did *not* mean by pushing him off
some stupid wall.

I looked up at Daniel's Shade, allowing my brain to enmesh
itself in his mesmerizing stare, becoming the humble prey to
his seductive snake charmer. I was so entranced by him that I
barely even noticed when I felt that now-familiar tug on my soul
and a searing pain split my head apart, sending me spiraling

toward unconsciousness. I fought the encroaching blackness, not wanting to alarm Jarvis or Suri by passing out, afraid of what would happen if they realized I was no longer in control of the situation.

Suddenly, the pain lifted and I whimpered, relieved that the horrible experience was finally over—but my relief was short-lived as the feeling of agony slammed back into me, increasing threefold as the pressure overwhelmed my brain and quickly began to subsume my body. I bit my lip and I felt a trickle of hot, salty blood on my tongue. I desperately choked back the sensation of nausea brought on by the taste. The pain consuming me was so exquisite that it nearly drove me out of my head, but then as it finally subsided, I realized that Daniel had done exactly what he had promised he would do:

He had come inside me.

fourteen

When I opened my eyes, Daniel's Shade was gone and I was alone. I immediately expected to feel some kind of weight inside me, reminding me that another soul was now sharing head space with me, but as I mentally checked my body, I felt no sign of Daniel's presence at all.

That's so weird, I thought to myself. *Shouldn't I be able to feel someone else kicking around inside me?*

The realization that I couldn't totally freaked me out. It meant that *anyone* could inhabit part of my body and I might never even know they were there.

What a totally frightening thought!

Suddenly, I heard a *creaking* noise behind me that made my heart drop down into my stomach. I quickly spun around, ready to defend myself from whatever badass was about to attack me, only to find that there wasn't just *one* bad guy ready to take aim at me, but a whole *battalion* of them.

It seemed that while I was otherwise engaged, the armored knights I'd shooed out of the room earlier had decided to surround me, their battle-axes and swords at the ready. I cringed, waiting for the blow that I knew would separate my head from my body, making the whole immortality thing an even *more* thrilling adventure.

Not!

But when no blow was immediately forthcoming, I slowly opened my eyes. Still expecting the worst—I had no idea *what* might be worse than spending immortality trying to reattach your head to your body—I peeked out at the armored knights through half-lowered eyelashes.

Yup, still armed and ready to destroy.

This totally bites, I thought disgustedly.

I realized that the more time I spent in Purgatory, the more I came to appreciate what a jerk Cerberus was and how reprehensible the whole stupid deal I'd made with him had been. I hadn't bargained for all this crap when I'd signed up for the job. I mean, decapitation was pretty high on my list of "not so much fun things to do with your weekend"—yet here I was, actually having to deal with a possible decapitation scenario on what *should* have been a day of rest and recuperation from a very hectic workweek.

No, this doesn't totally bite, I thought sarcastically.

"This sucks," I said out loud.

At the sound of my voice, I noticed a few of the knights surrounding me nervously fidgeting in their places—which seemed totally odd. I mean, if these guys were *so* itching to destroy, why hadn't they just bitten the bullet and chopped me up into little bits already?

That was when it hit me.

I wasn't the object of their bloodthirstiness.

My mind, which had been so busy floating around unhinged from my body all day, clicked into gear, putting all the contextual pieces of information I had gleaned together. From their aggressive stance, I'd just *assumed* that the knights were in attack mode, but when I really took the time to study their formation, I discovered that my little buddies were *actually* in some kind of defensive stance, the intent to kill radiating *away* from me, not toward me.

Oh my God, I thought to myself. *They're protecting me!*

"Miss Calliope?" I heard Jarvis say behind me. I turned to find Suri and my dad's Executive Assistant standing in the archway, looking utterly confused by this turn of events.

"Uh-huh?" I replied tentatively. I was afraid any sudden moves on my part might destroy the tenuous arrangement the knights and I had unconsciously come to—and I had absolutely no interest in getting my armored retinue all hot and bothered again.

"They won't let us in," Jarvis said. "They seem to be defending you for some reason."

I gave him a tight smile.

"Yeah, they're probably just smitten with my gorgeous face and tight ass," I joked glibly, which garnered only a return roll of the eyes from Jarvis.

"Uhm, well, anyone have any ideas?" I continued, since no one seemed amused by my little joke.

Jarvis shook his head, but Suri's eyes nervously darted around the room, lost in thought. When they finally settled on me, I could tell that she was pretty annoyed about not being able to control her knights, but since she was no longer the master of the "Hall of Death" universe, she was just gonna have to go with the flow like the rest of us.

"I know why they're not listening to me," she said, indicating the defensive line the knights had created.

"Well, you wanna let us in on the secret, then?" I asked, really hoping that whatever she was gonna say, it had nothing to do with body swapping, body sharing, or anything else of that particular nature.

"It's because of your lineage. You are one of the chosen," Suri said. "You might be their boss one day, so maybe it's, like, they're kissing up to you?"

Well, I thought to myself, *at least they're only brownnosing, not chopping me up into little bite-sized pieces.*

"Besides, the knights have always been partial to the witch doctors we employ to deal with the noncorporeal clients we work with," Suri continued. "I guess you banished the Shade, so they're rather impressed with you at the moment."

"Great," I said. "Nice to see a little appreciation for a job well-done."

"The knights killed the last witch doctor we had here in the Hall of Death," Suri said suddenly. "But he was pilfering Death Records, so I'm sure you'll be fine."

I gulped, not liking where this was going at all.

Up until that moment, I hadn't felt Daniel's presence inside me, but suddenly I was filled with the urge to hit the bathroom so badly that I nearly started doing the pee-pee dance right there on the floor.

Leave it to Daniel's Shade to take up residence in my urinary tract, I mused.

"Are you all right?" Jarvis said, his talent for observation quickly discerning my need for the toilet.

"Bathroom," I replied through clenched teeth. I didn't think I really had to pee or anything, but I didn't want to take the chance. Whether it was a real need for release, or just Daniel trying to be cute, I decided that I needed to find the bathroom, wherever in the Hall of Death it might reside.

Jarvis turned to Suri, who merely shrugged.

"We don't usually get that kind of request . . ." she began, but I wasn't having any of it.

"I don't care if no other living soul in the whole history of Purgatory ever answered the call of nature while visiting the Hall of Death," I said. "I *need* to pee."

Suri stared at me for a moment, then nodded.

"Okay, fine. There's an employee bathroom behind the entrance to the Death Records."

"Thank you," I said exasperatedly.

I started to take a step forward, the need to be alone becoming extremely necessary, but then I stopped, remembering just in time that a ring of very lethally armed knights was still surrounding me.

"Uhm, hey, guys," I said tentatively. "What do you think about me maybe just slipping right by that battle-ax and going—"

I was interrupted by said battle-ax dropping down in front of my face, blocking any thoughts of exit I might've had.

"Okay, I guess that answers that question," I surmised. The guard, its helmet blocking any view I might've had of its face, lifted the battle-ax away from my head, its point well made.

"Now what?" I asked Jarvis.

"I believe they say that the best offense is a good defense," the faun replied.

I glared at him.

"*Who* says that? Stop being obtuse, Jarvis!" I blurted out, my words infused with more acid than I'd intended. I didn't want to alienate the only person that was in my corner—especially when I was surrounded on all sides by weapon-wielding Death acolytes—so I apologized.

"Sorry. Didn't mean to be such a bitch."

Jarvis seemed thoroughly suspicious of my apology but, like the friend he was, grudgingly accepted it before elucidating upon the "good offense" statement.

"I believe it's a football term—"

I rolled my eyes.

"If you don't want me to continue," Jarvis said, interrupting himself.

"No, no, no," I said. "Please, I really want to know how you're gonna spin this."

Suri stared at Jarvis, then at me. The look on her face implied that we were both nutso—which was probably closer to the truth than I cared to admit.

"As I was saying," Jarvis began again, "I believe that if you do as you wish, rather than ask for permission, the knights will be forced to follow you."

"Maybe," I said, trying to appear doubtful of his suggestion even though I had a feeling it was on the money.

Usually, I would do anything *not* to give Jarvis the satisfaction of being right—he just *loved* to gloat, which made it really difficult to deal with him for days afterward—but in this scenario, I saw only one option: *his.*

"Here goes nothing," I said and took a step forward.

There was a moment of confusion when the knights didn't know if they should try to stop me or move with me, but ultimately they decided to just follow my lead. Each step I took, they were right there with me, weapons at the ready, armor clanking like the collar bells old ladies sometimes put on their critter-murdering cats to thwart them from their misdeeds.

Jarvis and Suri quickly moved out of sword's reach as my retinue and I crossed the threshold of the archway and stepped into the hall. I felt a little stupid as I looked down the length of the hall and saw that every person or creature who'd been working quietly inside one of the study rooms was now standing in the hallway, watching my progress. It really was like being in one of those dreams where you show up at work, or school, buck naked and everyone stares at you and you feel like a complete and total idiot—only *that* was a dream and *this* was reality.

"Okay, everyone," I said loudly, "move along. There's nothing to see here."

Of course, there was *lots* to see, so no one moved an inch.

Since they weren't going to listen to me anyway, I just decided to ignore them and let them enjoy the show. I'm sure nothing as interesting as a twentysomething immortal and her band of merry armor-clad men slowly clanking their way to the bathroom had ever happened in the Hall of Death before.

We moved slowly, the knights not really wanting to come with me, but doing it anyway. As we continued down the hall, we came upon a couple of brown-robed men in their late sixties standing inside one of the arched doorways watching us. I was pretty sure they were Christian monks, but I received no Christian charity from them as we went past. They gave us a wide berth, almost stepping back into their study room, then made the sign of the cross, insinuating I was some kind of Hell spawn or something invading their turf.

"Sorry about the interruption, boys," I murmured snarkily. "Hope we didn't scare you into wetting your vestments or anything."

The two monks weren't the only bad apples we encountered on our search for the bathroom. No, we were pretty much treated like pariahs by everyone and everything we passed on our march to the toilet.

At the end of the hall, not far from the tapestry of the knight, the cat, and the unicorn that I had encountered in my astral wanderings, I spied a small Abyssinian cat sitting in one of the rooms, its hind legs perched on a chair, its front paws delicately balanced on one of the long reading-table tops, a large calfskin-bound book opened before it. As I passed by, my knights still flanking me, the cat looked up from its book, its amber eyes locking onto mine. I took a step back, nearly knocking into one of my new guards, but I could not tear my gaze away from the cat.

The cat seemed just as interested in me as I was in it. It jumped off its chair and slowly started to weave toward me, its long tail trailing rakishly behind its body. Terrified, I took another step back, this time managing to poke myself in the shoulder with one of my guards' broadswords.

"Ow!" I yelped, taking a step back toward the cat—totally not the direction I wanted to be going, but since I didn't want to get poked again, I was kind of out of options.

"Please," I cried, "please stay away from me."

The cat didn't seem at all swayed by my entreaties; instead it continued to glide steadily closer, its body a sleek, fur missile heading unwaveringly toward my destruction.

"Do something!" I yelled at the knights. If they were really going to protect me, then now was the time to get their butts in gear. The closer that cat got to my person, the less chance I had of getting out of Purgatory with my life intact.

"Please!" I implored the cat. "You don't understand . . ."

The cat stopped just outside the line of scrimmage, and still my knights made no move to stop it. The cat sat back on its haunches and started licking its pale gold coat.

"Look," I said, "I'm sure you're a very nice kitty—"

And that was when I sneezed.

This was *not* an ordinary sneeze. This was the monster of all sneezes, or at least the monster of all sneezes that *I* had ever

endured. It was so intense, so full of energy, it rocked me
bodily forward, making me stumble onto my knees in front of
the cat. I felt a tiny pop inside my brain and then watched, horrified, as a thin stream of translucent ether slipped out of my
nose. I reached out, trying to contain what I knew was Daniel's
Shade, but I wasn't fast enough. Before I realized what was
happening, the cat had pounced, drawing the fragile Shade
substance into its own nostrils.

Being in such close proximity to the feline made me sneeze
again, but this time there was nothing surreal about it—or the
other three sneezes that followed. I stared at the cat, my breath
coming in ragged, wheezing fits. My chest felt so heavy I
thought it was going to collapse and crush every internal organ
I owned into mushy offal.

I realized with abject certainty that I was gonna die right
here in the Hall of Death, only fifty feet from where my own
Death Record was probably sitting, waiting to record all the
intimate details of my fast-approaching demise. I wondered if
I could hold out long enough to find my own Death Record and
stop it from documenting my death.

I was beginning to die. I could feel the power of the cat
bleeding into my soul, as it became harder and harder to
breathe. A drape of all-consuming blackness slipped across my
eyes and I fell forward onto my stomach, the scratchy warmth
of the Oriental carpet biting into my cheek as I wheezed my
final breath and—

"Miss Calliope?"

I heard Jarvis, but still in my death throes, I could not answer him.

"Mistress Calliope, stop being a drama queen and get up."

Has Jarvis no respect for the recently deceased? I thought
angrily. *Here I am lying dead on the floor and all he can do is
call me names?*

I felt something cold and metal prod my hip, but I didn't
move. I had just exerted a lot of energy dying, and frankly, I
just wanted to be left in peace for a few minutes.

Since I had no memory of my past deaths, I wasn't sure if

this was how the whole thing usually went down, but I really, really hoped that they just let you molder in your body for a few hours before the harvesters came along to collect you for the Afterlife.

Suddenly, I felt something warm and scratchy lick the side of my check and I instantly opened my eyes.

"What the hell—" I started to say, but was interrupted by another giant sneeze that sent the cat, who up until that moment had been pressed up against my face, backtracking. It sat hard on its haunches, but didn't move again as I was assailed by two sneezes in quick succession.

"They should outlaw sneezing when you're dead," I said to no one in particular. I was dead, after all, so no one I knew could see me anymore—well, at least not the soul part of myself.

"And who said you were dead?" Jarvis answered.

Obviously he missed the memo about me dying.

I looked up and saw the faun standing beside Suri, still a few feet away from the knights, but well within talking distance.

"Cats are my weakness . . ." I began, but stopped when I heard Jarvis tut-tutting. "They are! Madame Papillon told me so."

Jarvis merely shook his head.

"I know all your family's weaknesses—even yours," Jarvis replied, switching his weight from one hip to the other. "And felines ain't it, my dear."

"How can you be so sure?" I said, sitting up so that I could get a better look at him *and* keep my eye on the cat at the same time.

"When an immortal is born—not made, mind you—their weakness is foretold at birth," Jarvis countered. "That's how."

"But I thought I was dead—"

This time the cat answered me, its pale gold eyes full of amusement.

"You thought wrong," the cat said, its voice smooth as silk. It blinked as it stood up and lazily slipped between the ranks of my armored guard. The knights didn't move a muscle as the cat sat down beside me.

"Tell them to go," the cat said before bending its head forward to lick one of its paws.

Without hesitation, I said: "Go away, knights."

They did as I asked, breaking rank as they fell in step behind each other and marched back down the hall, eager to return to their individual posts. Now that I wasn't in possession of the Shade anymore, I wasn't so interesting to the knights.

"Well, that was easy," I said to the cat before my body was overtaken by another sneezing fit.

"You're just allergic," the cat said softly. "It's not fatal. I swear it."

Once the knights had completely disappeared, Jarvis came over and kneeled down before the cat.

"Miss Calliope," Jarvis said, his voice low. "I want you to meet someone very special."

He inclined his head toward the cat, who began to purr greedily.

"This is Bast, ex–Egyptian Goddess and Queen of the Cats."

I gave her a quick smile.

"Hey, as long as you're not out to kill me, it's very nice to meet you," I said, trying to decide if it was appropriate to extend my hand for a shake or not.

"You don't understand," Jarvis said, agitated. "*This* is not just some arbitrary creature that you are meeting, Miss Calliope."

"Okay?" I said, not really understanding what Jarvis was getting at. He sighed and tried another tack.

"*This,*" Jarvis intoned, "*is your father's spirit guide.*"

fifteen

"Spirit guide?" I repeated after I had sneezed one last time. "How namby-pamby can you get?"

Now, as far as spirit guides go . . . Okay, I know that the Afterlife is full of all kinds of strange and unique creatures, but did they have to get so clichéd about it? I mean, *come on*. I could handle Executive Assistants and Devil's protégés galore, but an anthropomorphic cat that guided you through the spirit world was so New Agey it was ridiculous.

"Spirit guides are an integral part of the Afterlife and the supernatural world," Jarvis said, his voice coming out all snippy.

I could tell he was annoyed with me for being so obnoxious, but seriously, I was allergic to the damned cat, and while I was in such close proximity to it, how dared he expect me to be chipper about my situation—my head hurt, my nose wouldn't stop running, and my eyes were turning into mini waterfalls.

Madame Papillon may have been wrong about cats being my weakness, but at least I could hold on to the fact that I was still highly, *highly* allergic to the furry little monsters.

"Look, I don't mean to be rude, but I really need to get about twenty feet away from you," I said to the cat as I pushed myself up onto my hands and knees, my ankles *popping* loudly as I stood up.

Ow!

Great, not only was my face a red, blotchy mess, but now I was turning into an arthritic cripple, too. Boy, this was fast becoming so *not* my day.

As soon as I was back on my feet, I brushed the dirt and lint off my clothes and moved as far away from Bast as I could—not that it mattered anymore whether or not there was any crud on my "going to the Goodwill as soon as I get home" Missoni sweater.

Looking around me for the first time since I had awakened from my mock death, I noticed that the party had finally ended and "the neighbors" had returned to their homes again. I sighed, happy not to be the center of attention anymore, but I did wonder exactly what the people who had watched my little meltdown had thought about the whole thing.

The two monks were long gone, as well as the other people I'd spied lurking farther down the hallway. They'd been too far away, so I hadn't been able to see who or what they were, but I knew they'd probably made a few mental connections concerning my identity.

Had they all thought I was some crazy loon who'd accidentally been let into the Hall of Death, or did they know precisely what I was? That I was the Grim Reaper's Daughter?

I had never really given much thought before to the fact that I was a flesh-and-bone representative of my father and his administration. I'd always assumed that it didn't matter what people thought of me, that I was my own person who could do exactly *what* I wanted, *when* I wanted, and it affected no one. But now I was starting to think otherwise, that maybe I had more of an impact on how my father was perceived here in the Afterlife than I realized.

"Uhm, Jarvis," I asked curiously, "does everyone in here know who I am?"

Jarvis didn't even deign to reply. He just snorted and smoothed his mustache down against his upper lip. Bast, the

Queen of the Cats, continued to stare at me, her molten yellow eyes following my every move, but I wasn't too worried about her. She and I shared a secret—she was still in possession of Daniel's Shade—and *she* knew that *I* knew that *she* knew what the deal was. If she had really wanted to get me in trouble, she would've done it already.

No, she had other plans for me, and I was just going to have to wait and see what they were.

"We keep records of who comes and goes, so I'm sure if someone didn't know your name before, they would after today," Suri piped in helpfully.

The young Day Manager of the Hall of Death seemed to be in much better spirits now that the Shade was gone and the knights were back at their individual stations. I got the impression Suri was one of those people who loved to deny they had any problems—except a battalion of knights following around one of your patrons was a problem too obvious to ignore.

"Since everything seems to be in order again," Suri said happily, "how may we at the Hall of Death help you, Death's Daughter?"

The name made me cringe. If there was anything in this world that made me want to gnaw my own arm off, it was someone using an appellation that denoted I was not my own person . . . but some kind of derivative of my father.

"Just call me Callie," I said to Suri, "and we'll be just fine."

The girl smiled at me and nodded.

"Callie it is, then, but only if you call me Suri."

"Sure, okay, whatever you like," I replied. Apparently, now that things had returned to normal, Suri was going to try to be my new best friend—yay!

Not.

"We have a letter from Death himself, requesting the Death Record of a particular individual," Jarvis said, interrupting the pleasantries between Suri and me and producing a small, cream-colored envelope with the Death, Inc., seal on it.

I mouthed the words "thank you," but Jarvis shook his head.

"Follow me, then . . . *Callie*," Suri said, taking off down the hall toward the main desk. "By the way, you still need that bathroom?"

I looked over at Bast, who had apparently decided to join us for the duration, before shaking my head.

"Nope, I think having the death scared out of me kinda sent my bladder into shock," I replied.

This seemed to put a kibosh on any more conversation and we finished our walk to the main desk in silence.

when we got there, we found a man sitting behind the desk, waiting for us. I did a double take because I hadn't noticed him before—but here he sat, his chin in his hand, watching our ragged procession with not even the hint of a smile on his buttery, round face.

He was a pudgy man who appeared to be in his late thirties, but with the weird way time ran in the Afterlife, he could've been any age. The first thing that came to my mind when I looked at him was that he resembled a less flour-y, more Sumo Wrestler-y version of the Pillsbury Doughboy.

Upon our arrival, he dropped his hand from his chin so that both arms were now folded on top of the long desk, his puffy body stuffed into one of those ergonomic office chairs like a perennial breakfast favorite of mine: pigs in a blanket. The desk Pudge Boy sat behind came to my waist. It was made of warm, cherry wood and boasted lots of nicks and scratches on its scarred surface. There was a computer on the desk to the man's right, but it didn't look as if it was much employed. In counterpoint, the large apothecary's cabinet standing behind the desk like an enormous green-painted sentinel seemed well-worn with age and use.

Suddenly, the man's face broke into a wide grin and he began to laugh, his tummy rolling up and down with waves of mirth.

"Tanuki, this is—"

"I know who she is," he said, and this only seemed to amuse him more.

"They need a Death Record, please," Suri said, oblivious to Tanuki's massive sense of good humor.

"Is *this* the one you want?" Tanuki said, his mirth instantly replaced with a mischievous grin as he whipped a bright pink folder right out of the very air. "Or is *this* the one you seek?"

Now the pink folder was gone, disappearing right before our eyes, only to be replaced by an even brighter orange one. I stared at him, uncertain as to what he was playing at. We were supposed to get the stupid Death Record and then get the hell out of Dodge. This wasn't supposed to be some kind of bloody magic show.

"Neither," I said, grabbing the orange folder right out of the man's hand and holding it up for all to see.

There was a shocked silence as everyone looked at me, their eyes glued to the orange folder I clutched in my hand. Even poor Tanuki looked up at me with shock and maybe a little bit of awe. I don't think he—or anyone else for that matter— thought I had the hand-eye reflexes necessary to pull off that kind of sleight of hand. Little did they know the bizarro things I'd had to do since I'd started my job over at House and Yard. My boss, Hy, was a tricky bitch, so that meant in order to stay employed, I'd had to learn a few tricks of my own.

"You seem like a very sweet guy, whatever your name is, but I'm in no mood to play any games with you right now," I said, my voice loud enough to carry down the hall. "Now, here's your folder back."

I put the orange folder back into his hand. He looked down at it, then started to giggle.

"I like this one," he said to Suri. "She means business."

"I try," I said helpfully. "Hey, Jarvis, pass my friend here the note from Pop."

Jarvis bristled at my calling my dad "Pop," but he forked over the letter without further hesitation.

"Here," I said, passing it across the desk to Tanuki, "this oughta do it."

Tanuki unfolded the envelope and pulled the letter Jarvis had forged out of its cream binding. He scanned it quickly, then nodded.

"It's a red folder, Suri," Tanuki said, looking nervously over at his boss.

Suri only shrugged.

"So be it," she said.

"But—" he started to say before Suri cut him off.

"Just call it up, Tanuki."

Tanuki sighed unhappily and turned around in his rolling chair. He used his tiny legs to scoot himself across the carpeted floor and over to the apothecary's cabinet. He opened one of the little drawers, closed it, then opened it again. He scooted all the way down to the far side of the cabinet and repeated the process with another drawer. This time, before he closed it, he whispered the name "Senenmut" into the drawer.

Somewhere up above us, I knew that a cascade of folders was flipping its little guts out, as it searched for the Death Record that we wanted. Almost immediately, the last drawer that Tanuki had closed flew open and a bright red folder popped out of it. Tanuki moved so quickly that I barely registered he'd even caught the folder, let alone that he was now holding it out for me to take. I reached for it and Tanuki caught hold of my wrist.

"Be careful. The red files are always bad news," he whispered in my ear, before he released my arm. I took the file folder he pressed into my hands, holding it to my chest.

Part of me didn't want to deal with what was in that file, but the other, more intrepid side of myself was itching to find out where Cerberus's lost charge might be.

"Open it," I heard a soft, reedy voice say.

I looked over and saw that Bast had taken the opportunity to jump up onto the desktop and was now sitting on her haunches beside me, waiting for me to proceed with the opening of the folder.

"Is that an official spirit guide request?" I asked as I covered my nose with the back of my sleeve, hoping to ward off another sneezing fit.

Bast purred and rubbed her head against my arm.

"I'll take that as a yes," I said, answering my own question. Slowly, I eased the folder open, and a thin slip of paper fell out onto the desk.

"What does it say?" Jarvis asked, squeezing past Suri to get a better look.

"I don't know," I said. "I have to flip the page over."

"Do it," Bast urged, her tail flicking dangerously close to my nose as she stood up.

"All righty, then," I said. "Here goes nothing."

I reached out to pick up the flimsy piece of paper, but just as I grasped its razor-thin edge, a giant sneeze I didn't even know was inside me escaped my sinuses and sent the piece of paper wafting off the desk and onto Tanuki's side of the floor.

Tanuki, the mischievous grin back on his moon face, bent down and picked up the piece of paper and put it, right side up this time, on the desk.

"Told you red folders were bad news," he said with a twinkle in his eye. I returned his grin before looking down at the paper.

"That makes absolutely no sense, Suri," Jarvis said as I let my eyes scan over the words that he had already speed-read ahead of me. I had no idea what Jarvis was talking about. What was written on the paper seemed pretty straightforward to me.

"What makes no sense?" Suri asked as she, too, stepped up to the desk. I moved out of her way—and out of Bast range—so that she could see the paper better.

"Oh, but that can't be," she said after a few moments of consideration. "There must be some mistake."

She went around to the other side of the desk, so that she stood beside Tanuki, and started haphazardly opening every drawer in the apothecary cabinet.

"Tanuki, help me, please," she said as she yanked one of the drawers out of its slot.

"I can't help if I can't read it," he said, another broad smile on his face.

Suri sighed, looking heavenward.

"You have my permission."

Tanuki greedily reached for the paper, almost inhaling the words that were inscribed on it. Satisfied, he sat back in his chair, as unhelpful as he had been before he'd read what was on the paper.

"Well?" Suri said. "What do you make of it?"

"Is it a mistake?" Jarvis chimed in.

I was starting to feel totally left out of the loop here.

"Is *what* a mistake?" I asked, but my request was greeted only by silence. Annoyed by everyone's lack of explanation, I picked up the paper and started walking back down the hallway.

"Hey, does anyone here know where I can find the Jackal Brothers?"

"Calliope Reaper-Jones!"

Jarvis's stern tone followed me down the hallway, but I ignored it, just like he and everyone else had ignored me earlier. I know I was acting like a petulant child, but sometimes I've found that the louder the fuss, the more people do what you want them to do.

"I'm looking for the Jackal Brothers," I continued. "Any takers?"

I felt something small yet sturdy pressing up against my leg, and I looked down to find Bast rubbing herself against me.

"Please don't do that," I asked as nicely as I could muster. "You're gonna give me a respiratory attack or something."

Bast ceased her rubbing and sat back on the Oriental carpet, waiting.

"I can take you to them, if you would like," she said.

It was really strange to see the English language spoken via a cat's mouth, but I supposed it was good practice for when Runt started talking.

"I would like that," I murmured, looking down the hall where Jarvis and Suri were steadily gaining ground on us, Jarvis moving as quickly as his little faun legs would carry him. I thought my dad's Executive Assistant looked pretty pissed off, but since I didn't know Suri that well, I couldn't *imagine* how she was taking all this.

"They can't come with us," Bast said, her tail twitching excitedly as she spoke, her eyes ratcheted to mine.

I'd had a feeling that that one was coming.

"Okay," I said.

"Good," she purred. "I'm glad you agree. It's so much easier when you do what I want."

It's not like you gave me much choice, I thought to myself.

"Follow me," she said as she got up off her haunches and started sashaying toward the knight, cat, and unicorn tapestry that was fast becoming a favorite of mine.

As I stared at the tapestry, something niggled at the back of my brain. When I realized what was bothering me, I almost choked. The small golden cat that had been in the tapestry when I'd first encountered it was missing. I gave Bast a questioning glance, but she stared back at me, mute. I wanted to ask if she was the cat I'd just seen hanging in the woven panel, but before I could form the words, Bast picked up her gait and disappeared into the tapestry. Let me repeat: She disappeared *into* the tapestry, not through it, not around it, but *into* it.

I stopped, shocked as I watched the image of a cat begin to weave itself into the fabric.

I guess that answers my question.

I knew that I was supposed to follow her, but it seemed like such an alien thing to do that I was having a hard time making myself do it.

This is craziness, I thought to myself. *Who follows a cat into a medieval tapestry without the proper vaccinations and visas? Anyone ever hear of the bubonic plague? Anyone?*

I swallowed hard, fear tiptoeing up my spine as I finally made my decision. It was now or never—and I wanted Runt as a permanent member of my family, so I was left with no other choice. I took one step, then another and another, until I was mere inches from the tapestry.

"Here goes nothing," I said, closing my eyes and trying to make my fear disappear. I took a long, deep breath, letting it out slowly, then lifted my leg and took a final step forward, half expecting to run into the cool limestone wall that I knew *intellectually* was waiting only a foot or so in front of me. But instead of slamming headfirst into the wall, I felt only calm and the sense that my body was being enveloped in a welcoming warmth.

I wonder what I look like as a tapestry princess? I thought curiously as the warmth overwhelmed my senses and I felt my body disintegrate into nothingness.

sixteen

I opened my eyes to find myself in what I can only call a medieval torture chamber.

I knew that it was a torture chamber primarily because there was a stretching rack in one corner of the cold, stone room; a Catherine wheel directly across from that; and a big bronze pot—which I assumed was used to dunk people in boiling oil—making up the vertex of what could only be termed a "torture triangle."

To add to that, there were heavy iron manacles roughly embedded into the walls, a rusty shackle affixed to each long dendrite of chain. Oh, and let's not forget the pièce de résistance—the occasional human being tethered to said manacles like a rabbit's foot dangling at the end of a lucky key chain.

There were no windows in the room. The only light in the place came from a half dozen torches set into the walls, each one emitting such a paltry glow that it barely illuminated what was directly beneath it. As they burned, they gave off an overpoweringly noxious stench that made my throat burn and my sinuses sting. I decided that even if they Cloroxed the whole place, whitewashed the walls, and let the prisoners out for good behavior, there was no way in Hell this place was gonna ever be up to EPA standards. I actually had half a mind to call my local environmental protection agent and complain—until I remembered that even if the EPA *wanted* to shut this place down, they wouldn't have any jurisdiction to do it because we were in the Afterlife.

I did take note of the *one* door in the place—a big wooden monstrosity that appeared to have what looked like bloodstains splashed across its oaken mass—but the large iron lock wedged below the keyhole was more than enough to deter any burgeoning escape plan.

It was oddly silent for a place so full of human misery, I decided. I mean, I expected to hear *at least* a few moans of agony, but there was nothing, not even a snore.

I had been crouched down in my hiding place, behind the big bronze pot, for almost twenty minutes, and nothing was happening, aside from a really nasty-ass leg cramp in my right calf. I decided that if I wanted to get anywhere anytime soon, I was gonna have to make the first move.

I had expected to meet back up with Bast once we'd gotten to where we'd been going, but from the moment I'd opened my eyes and discovered all the exciting amenities my new environs held—*not*—I'd known in my gut that I was alone here in Jackal Brother land.

It was probably all my own fault anyway. I'd just *had* to be a smart-ass about the whole "spirit guide" thing, so I shouldn't have been so surprised to find myself on the wrong end of a passive-aggressive payback from the überspirit guide Bast, ex–Egyptian Goddess and Queen of the Cats. I whispered a silent apology to my missing feline companion in hopes that she'd somehow magically appear beside me and tell me what to do next, but after a few tense moments of expectation, I realized she was *not* gonna be coming to my aid.

I pulled out my rubidium clock.

"How much time now?" I asked, waiting for the ticker tape of flashing numbers to stop.

"Only fifteen hours?" I said, incredulously as I read the string of numbers on the clock front. "That's not fair!"

Well, at least I still have Senenmut's Death Record, I mused thoughtfully as I pulled out the paper I'd stolen from the Hall of Death.

I looked down at the almost-translucent sheet of stationary—my guess was that it was made out of rice paper, but I wasn't an expert—and saw the same words I remembered from my last view still embossed across the page.

It read simply: *Under the remand of the Jackal Brothers until further notice.*

I thought about what that meant and decided that having to hang out in this torture chamber for more than a few hours probably wasn't a very nice fate. I'd spent some time in the company of the Jackal Brothers—and were they a laugh a minute or what?

Uhm, let's go for the "or what."

Seriously, they were two of the most stone-faced—and not just because of their stonelike Jackal heads—unresponsive, and lacking in any kind of a sense of humor fellows that I'd come across in a long, long time. Usually, even if someone was a total stick in the mud, they would have at least *some* sense of humor, but the Jackal Brothers were entirely devoid of wit or charm. Frankly, they wouldn't have known a joke if it had bitten them on the butt and caused a boil on one of their cheeks. Of course, by the type of surroundings I now found myself in, it appeared my little observation about them was more than valid.

I stood up, leaving the relative security of my boiling oil pot, and stretched my legs, shaking out my right calf in hopes of getting rid of the cramp—but no luck there. I expected to get a few gasps and/or moans of interest from the peanut gallery, but of the five prisoners I counted, only one of them actually had his eyes open. The others all seemed to be in a state of heightened doze.

The one conscious fellow in the room was staring at his feet with a look of intense concentration on his face. From the way his body was splayed out on the floor, both arms stretched far above his head and cuffed to the wall, I surmised that the only freedom he had was the freedom to move his toes around.

"Excuse me," I said tentatively as I watched him slowly move one big toe, then the other.

Feeling my stare, he casually looked over in my direction. He had a shock of white hair that pooled around him on the floor and the palest yellow eyes I'd seen outside the Big Cat House at the zoo. A long, scraggly beard went past his waist, reconnecting with the hair from his head somewhere around his hips. He blinked, his eyes more alive than anything else in that Hellhole, but he didn't say a word in response to my question.

Finally, having sized me up—and found me wanting—he returned to his toes.

Okay, maybe he's deaf, I thought to myself.

I was pretty sure it couldn't get any worse than trying to get information from a deaf prisoner while stuck in a medieval torture chamber with no means of escape.

I decided that the best course of action would be to start yelling at the deaf guy and see if I could wake anyone else up in the process.

"Excuse me!" I said much more loudly this time, my voice echoing like buckshot around the chamber.

The only response my yelling garnered was a full-on, nasty glare from my new prison buddy. I gave him an apologetic smile, but he only shook his head, his butter yellow eyes flashing like fire, and returned to examining his toes.

Great, I had just been reprimanded by a deaf-mute.

Feeling totally rejected, I leaned against the large bronze pot and rested my chin in my hands. Since no one was gonna offer up any useful information, I decided to ignore my torture-chamber mates for the time being and gingerly pick my way across the low-lying chains and exposed body parts so I could try my hand at unlocking the massive oak door.

Just as I had resolved to put my plan into action, I felt the bronze pot I was leaning on suddenly give way, letting out a long *screech* as it slowly began to tip forward. I grasped the edge of the pot, trying to set it upright again, but it was too heavy. The only thing I got for my trouble was a load of partly coagulated grease down the front of my sweater. Once again, my fashion forward sense had been thwarted by the Afterlife and another beautiful designer creation would now, without a doubt, be resigned to the rag pile.

Sometimes I hated my life.

There was an eardrum-shattering *ring* as the pot fell forward, spilling its contents out onto the cold stone floor. The sound of metal on stone was so intensely painful that I tried to cover my ears with my hands, totally forgetting that they were coated in torture grease. So, not only did I *not* protect my hearing, but I also got rank-smelling grease in my hair.

Yummy!

"Ew!" I shrieked as I tried to wipe the remains of the grease onto my sweater, but the stuff was pretty caustic and wouldn't come off. I was going to need way more than just a shower when I got home; I was gonna need some hard-core decontaminating.

I suppose the sound of the oil pot slamming into the floor was loud enough to get the attention of the Jackal Brothers, but I like to think that they were already coming down to the torture chamber to check on their prisoners anyway, regardless of what I had just done.

Needless to say, I was still standing in the middle of the room, rubbing my hands across my chest like an amateur You-Tube porn star, when the lock clicked and the big wooden door flew open. Immediately, the other prisoners in the room started moaning and screaming in agony—including Mr. Golden Eyes, that traitor. I had no idea what had set them off, other than the door opening, but the intensity of their howls was enough to send shivers up my back.

"Who goes there?" sounded a deep voice from across the room. I looked up to find one of the Jackal Brothers standing in the doorway, his cold, dark eyes fixed on me.

"Oh, hello there," I said. "You remember me, don't you? Calliope Reaper-Jones? You took me to meet with the Board of Death a few months ago . . . ? Uhm, I think you know my father."

I finished my babbling, only to be greeted by silence—and the intermittent moans and screams from the peanut gallery.

"Oh, be quiet," I snipped at the prisoners. "You know you're only doing it for the attention."

There were a couple of boos—and a hiss or two—but it seemed to shut them up for the moment.

"I don't know why you've got all these people held prisoner in here with all this medieval torture crap, but it's pretty creepy," I said to the Jackal Brother, who stood stock-still in the doorway, his very muscular body clad in only a modest cotton loincloth.

"I mean, sure, you're all badass in your loincloth, but what do you think you're gonna accomplish by being so aggressive and violent with these men—and when I say *men*, I'm really only being polite. They're barely even human anymore, the way you've emotionally castrated them like this."

Did I ever mention that when I'm extremely nervous, I like to talk? Actually, it's less that I like to talk and more that I just can't make myself shut up.

The Jackal Brother continued to stare at me, then, finally, he spoke:

"Castration is a good idea."

This only garnered another round of boos and hisses from my torture-chamber mates. Some inventive fellow even figured out how to lob an old, gnawed-on bone in my direction with his foot.

"Wait a minute. You totally took that out of context. That is *not* what I was talking about," I said, my voice inching up an octave as I spoke. "Look, all of this is beside the point. I'm here for one thing and one thing only!"

Now the catcalls started. Of course, these poor guys hadn't gotten laid in, like, a zillion years, so anything I said was gonna get turned into sexual innuendo.

"That's so not what I meant, either, you guys, so get your mind out of the gutter," I said loudly, over the whistles.

"And what is that one thing?" the Jackal Brother asked me—and I thought I detected a note of curiosity in his voice.

"I'm here to collect a guy for a friend," I said, trying to sound as official as I could. "His name is Senenmut."

Silence. Seriously, you could've literally heard a pin drop. I looked around the room, but all the prisoners had become very interested in the ceiling or the floor or the backs of their eyelids.

The Jackal Brother began to laugh and the sound was so horrible that it filled me—and seemingly the rest of the chamber, too—with dread.

"What does that mean?" I demanded, trying to combat the hideous laughter.

"It means," said the Jackal Brother, "that it is upon a fool's errand you have come."

"It is not," I said haughtily, thinking of Runt and how much I would miss not getting to see her anymore if I failed before I'd even started.

"But you ask for our most treasured possession," he replied.

"So?" I replied. "I want him."

The Jackal Brother took a moment to consider what I had just said—then he smiled.

The only other time I'd spent in the company of the Jackal Brothers, there had been absolutely *no* smiling—and let me just add that that had been a blessing, because the smile that crossed this Jackal Brother's face was so foul, so *horrid*, that it made me want to start praying.

I tried to make myself avert my eyes from the two rows of sharp—I mean, filed down to a point *sharp*—teeth, but I couldn't. All I could do was stare at the bits of ragged meat stuck in between its incisors and what I assumed must be its molars.

"If he is so important to you, then you would be willing to wager your own soul for his, would you not?" the Jackal Brother said, finally shutting his mouth and making me sigh in relief.

Uh-oh, this is so not where I wanted this scenario to be going, I thought to myself.

"Sure, a little wager? Why not?" I replied, ignoring my brain's pleas for me to shut up.

My response brought on another bout of smiling from Jackal Head. He seemed inordinately pleased with my answer, which only made me more worried about what I'd gotten myself into.

"So, if I win, I get Senenmut *and* I get to keep my soul?" I said, my hands starting to shake as I took in the magnitude of what I was agreeing to.

The Jackal Brother nodded.

"And if you lose, we will possess Death's Daughter's soul for all of eternity," he cackled.

"Sure, fine. Whatever," I said, just wanting to get the whole thing over with. "Now, I want to see Senenmut and make sure that he's still all in one piece. Otherwise, it's no deal."

Without hesitation the Jackal Brother inclined his head toward the utterly silent—possibly deaf—guy with the yellow eyes.

"That's him?" I blurted out before I could stop myself.

The Jackal Brother nodded.

"Crap. Are you sure?" I asked, even though I knew with my luck being what it was, that this was *exactly* how it was gonna go down.

I turned and looked at my "new friend," but he was back to his toe-training exercises.

This is the schmuck I am wagering my soul for? I thought miserably.

"Are you satisfied?" the Jackal Brother said as he moved toward me. I wanted to take a step back and away from him, but the burning oil pot was hemming me in.

So, instead, I just nodded my agreement.

"I *guess* I'll have to be."

"Now," the Jackal Brother said as he closed the gap between us and invaded my space, "I will explain the terms of the wager."

"Go for it," I said gamely, trying not to stare into his massive jaws again.

"We will measure the weight of your heart against the feather of Ma'at, Death's Daughter, and if it is judged to be too heavy with sin and greed, we will own you, body and soul," he finished.

Suddenly, he raised his hand and the room around us went dark. I felt my stomach clench as the floor dropped out from beneath my feet, the walls disappearing right along with it.

I got the impression that we were in some kind of anti-space—and if I failed this test, then I would be lost here, in this world of nothingness, for all time—and just the *idea* of what "all time" entailed made me shiver involuntarily.

I looked over at the Jackal Brother and he smiled at me again.

"Bring the scale!" he called into the nothingness.

I blinked and suddenly we were no longer alone—the Jackal Brother's twin was now standing next to him, holding a set of large golden scales in the palm of one hand and a tiny golden ankh in the other. Beside him sat an incredibly strange-looking creature with the head of a crocodile and the body of a lion, its silvery blue eyes telegraphing intense hunger. Wrapped around its throat was a heavy silver chain, the end attached to the waist of the newly arrived Jackal Brother.

I instantly felt sorry for the poor half-breed thing. I mean, what kind of a life could this disparately crafted creature really have? Then the nasty croco-monster abruptly snapped its massive jaws in my direction and that ended the pity party right there.

"Why don't you watch where you're pointing that thing?" I said, glaring at the giant croco-monster, but only getting another round of maw chomping for my trouble.

"Fine. *Whatever*," I said as I shrugged and shifted my gaze to a more pleasant subject: the set of shining scales the Jackal Brother was holding in his hand.

The scales were truly a thing of beauty, with intricate hiero-glyphs lovingly etched into its golden body. At the apex stood a sculpture of a tiny, nude woman, one golden ostrich feather woven into her long, metallic hair. The rest of it was covered in more glyphs—none of which I could read, but a few of which I *did* remember seeing in the Hall of Death.

"Are you ready to be judged?" the Jackal Brother holding the scales said, interrupting my thoughts.

I nodded.

"Close your eyes," he said, "and it will only hurt for a moment."

I did as he said, shutting my eyes and swallowing hard as I waited.

"Hey!" I said as I felt a sharp pain blossom in my chest that slowly—very slowly—began to turn into a dull ache between my ribs. I looked down, my eyes nearly popping out of my head.

My heart was gone!

"What did you just do to me?!" I cried, starting to freak out as I stared down at the great, gaping hole in my chest where my heart used to be.

I looked over and found the first Jackal Brother holding my still-beating heart in his hand.

"Whoa," I said, watching my heart drip its lifeblood onto the ground. "Can I have that back now, please?"

The two Jackal Brothers ignored me as they set my heart on one side of the scales and gingerly placed a single silken ostrich feather on the other. For a moment the two sides were totally balanced, but then the side with my heart on it began to dip lower than the feather. I held my breath, fear curdling my blood.

I noticed the look of excitement that passed between the two brothers—of course, they were being *totally* obvious about the whole thing—and my stomach began to burn.

Had I really just screwed myself out of the rest of my immortal existence?

Please, God, I found myself praying, *please just let me scrape by this one time. I promise to be a good sister and friend and daughter for the rest of my immortality, if you'll just not let the Jackal Brothers get me.*

When I opened my eyes, I saw that the scales had stopped dipping, and instead, the two sides were slowly moving back into a state of balance. We all waited with bated breath, me willing the scales to go one way and the Jackal Brothers willing them to go the other.

Suddenly, I felt a cool breeze envelop my body, toying with the grisly hole that had been left between my ribs.

"Where did that come from—" I started to say, but clamped my mouth shut when I realized the breeze had blown past me and was now eddying around the single ostrich feather.

"No!" the Jackal Brothers screamed in unison, but it was too late. The breeze swirled around, lifting the feather high up in the air, then suddenly dying away as it dropped the feather *right into the open jaws of the croco-monster.*

I heard a sharp intake of breath—I was pretty sure it came from me—and a feeling of intense relief overwhelmed me.

"That's not fair!" one of the Jackal Brothers wailed—and it took everything I had inside me not to jump for joy and scream, *Yes, it is fair, you little shits!!*

"So, what does it mean again when the scales are all balanced like that?" I asked innocently.

"It means that you win," the two brothers said as, together, we watched my heart disappear from its place on the scales. Instantly, I felt it beating in my chest again, making me nearly cry out with joy.

It was a miracle! My heart had been judged and it had been found . . . *not* lacking!

Of course, the Jackal Brothers weren't the only ones depressed by the outcome. The croco-monster didn't seem at all satisfied by its ostrich feather meal. It just kept snapping its huge jaws at me in frustration. I *wasn't* 100 percent certain, but I kind of thought if my heart had been deemed unworthy, the croco-monster might've gotten to eat it up as some kind of creepy parting gift.

Yuck!

"The judgment is complete," the Jackal Brothers said as one. "We shall record that the half human, Calliope Reaper-Jones, is possessed of a truthful, just heart."

There was a clap of thunder that shook the very ether, and as the sound faded away, I found that I had left the nothingness behind me, so that, once again, I was back in the Jackal Brothers' medieval torture chamber.

The man with the yellow eyes was waiting for me, unchained now, in the middle of the room. He stared at me as he rubbed his bruised wrists uncertainly.

"Let's get out of here," I said as I reached out and took his unwilling hand, keeping him as close as possible just in case the Jackal Brothers decided to change their minds at the last minute.

Suddenly, from below me, I heard a voice say:

"You've done well."

I looked down to find Bast sitting at my feet. Immediately, my nose started running and I let out an ungodly sneeze.

"You totally ditched me—" I started to say just as another sneeze shook my sinuses, but Bast ignored me, turning to the Jackal Brothers instead.

"Please open a wormhole home for us, sons of Nephthys," Bast said pleasantly, and one of the brothers—don't even *ask* me to tell them apart when they aren't holding any accessories to help me—lifted his hand. Without so much as speaking a word of magic, he opened up a wormhole right there in the middle of the torture chamber.

I watched as the other prisoners stared greedily at the wormhole, its pitch-black swirling vortex beckoning them toward it. It was probably the closest thing to the outside world most of them had seen in millennia.

Watching the Jackal Brother call up that stupid wormhole with such ease made me feel really inadequate. It wasn't fair that *even* the bad guys could work magic without breaking a sweat. I decided that I really needed to hook Senenmut back up with Cerberus, so I could go home and take that stupid wormhole-summoning lesson Madame Papillon had promised me.

"After you," Bast said, indicating the swirling wormhole.

I grasped Senenmut by the hand and attempted to lead him forward, but the dumb jerk just kept trying to pry my hand off his. The poor guy had been out of commission for way longer than he realized because I was easily able to maintain my grip *and* keep him moving at the same time.

"Come on!" I said, inching him bodily toward the wormhole as he continued to fight our every step.

Seriously, I had never met a guy who had been so difficult to deal with in all my life. It was totally obvious that he did *not* enjoy having a girl boss him around—even though he *should've* been thanking his lucky stars that I'd come along and released him from eternal bondage—but *whatever.*

"Uhm, one last question," I said, looking back at the Jackal Brothers as I dragged my "new friend" closer to the wormhole.

"Is this guy deaf and dumb . . . *or just a prick?*"

And without waiting for an answer, I threw myself—and Senenmut—into the wormhole and disappeared.

seventeen

When Bast had used the word "home," I had just assumed she *really* meant that we were going back to the Hall of Death. I guess you should always take things other people say at face value, because instead of finding myself face-to-face with an irate Jarvis, I found myself getting licked on the face by an unruly hellhound pup.

Somehow, the wormhole had transported us back to Sea Verge—to the *kitchen* at Sea Verge, to be exact—where I found Clio, Runt at her side, in the middle of making Gruyère and spinach croquettes under the watchful eye of my mother's chef, Declan.

As I said earlier, Declan is a man of vast emotion and he loved to impart that emotion—whichever one he happened to be experiencing at the time—into his cooking.

As big around as he was tall—and at five feet eight inches tall, that made him a pretty large fellow—Declan was a mainstay of the Reaper-Jones household. With his lively brown eyes, the biggest, roly-poly belly that ever existed on a human being, and a well-pruned red beard that was never farther than two inches from his face, he'd been a childhood hero of mine. Having grown up in Glasgow, he possessed an incredibly thick Scottish brogue that made it really hard to understand what he was saying when he got all worked up. Once, when I was a little kid, I had heard him call a stockpot he was using a "dunderheid," so after that, I called everyone *I* met a "dunderheid."

Of course, my mother was just *thrilled* with that one.

For as long as I could remember, Declan had worn the same outfit: chef's whites, topped by a big, pearl-colored chef's hat that made him look like a Scottish version of Chef Boyardee. I'm pretty sure if I ever saw the man in street clothes, I wouldn't even recognize him—the "chef look" was that ingrained in my brain. He had been a part of my life for so long that no matter whether he was in a good mood or a crappy one, I was always glad to see him.

And of course, since he had run a number of very famous four-star kitchens in Europe before my mother had hired him away into the private sector, he was an incredible chef. Because of him, I *adored* snails as a child—and I don't mean the kind you find out in the backyard. I had very distinct memories of being the only kid *I* knew of who ate foie gras, shaved tuna hearts, boudain, and on very special holiday occasions when Declan got into cooking overdrive, haggis.

In fact, it wasn't until I was about thirteen that I realized *exactly* what haggis was made out of and decided that maybe it wasn't the most well suited of dishes to accompany eggnog and fruitcake.

"Who are you?" Clio said to Senenmut, holding up a beautifully bronzed and delectable-looking minisandwich. Before I could stop him, he had reached out his grubby hand and stolen the croquette right off Clio's plate.

"Hey," I said, grabbing him by the collar and yanking him away from my sister, but not before he'd stuffed the entire croquette into his mouth.

"Uhm, this is Senenmut, a friend of mine," I said cagily as Declan frowned at my guest's rudeness. "He probably hasn't eaten in . . . oh, I don't know . . . about five thousand years—whenever they built the pyramids give or take a millennia or two."

Before I could say anything else damning, Senenmut pinched my arm.

"Ow!" I yelped as he used the distraction to escape my grasp and run and hide over in the corner, so he could presumably continue to chew his food in relative privacy.

"He smells funny—" Clio started to say, but was interrupted when Bast hopped up onto the counter and nuzzled against her. "Hey, who's this pretty girl?"

I bit my lip.

"Uhm, 'that pretty girl' is Dad's spirit guide, Bast, Queen of the Cats," I said uncomfortably as Clio stopped scratching Bast's head.

"Oh, I'm sorry," she said to Bast. "I didn't know you weren't a regular old cat."

Bast only purred in response.

"She *does* talk," I said lamely. "I mean, she can if she wants to."

"Ah dunnae care if she be Queen of the bloody Universe," Declan said testily. "There's nae supposed to be animals on my counters! Do ye understand?"

Clio quickly scooped Bast up in her arms and moved away from the food prep counter.

"Thank ye much," Declan said as he picked up the dirty pan and plates. "Aye, to the washin' up."

I had always loved how nonchalant Declan was about all the weird happenings in the Reaper-Jones household. Of course, he had no idea what my father *actually* did for a living— he only knew that my dad was the CEO of some multinational company—but he must've suspected that there was a lot more going on than he was privy to. I was pretty sure my dad had put some kind of glamour on Sea Verge, so that the nonmagical and non-Afterlife-bound beings wouldn't see all the really weird stuff: like the fact that Jarvis was a faun and not just a height-challenged human being.

Still, more than any glamour, I think the real reason Declan didn't run out of the house screaming was because he was so well paid by my father and so devoted to my mother. He'd probably recognized a long time ago that the "keep your mouth shut" policy was the best one to adhere to while employed at our house.

Still, when *my* loose lips spilled the beans on stuff like spirit guide cats and Egyptian prisoners of war, well, I'm sure his curiosity *must've* been piqued—even if he didn't show it.

"Calliope-Reaper Jones!"

Jarvis's resounding voice filled the room as he stepped out of the hallway and into the kitchen. The glare he shot in my direction was filled with so much venom, it actually made me feel woozy.

"Well, well, well," Jarvis continued. "I see you made it home without too much trouble. The same cannot be said for myself, as I was attacked by a phalanx of armored knights directly upon your exit."

"Oh, Jarvis," I said, feeling sick, "I'm so sorry. I didn't mean to get you in trouble."

I started to walk over to the little faun, but he held up his hand for me to stop.

"There's no point in dredging up an apology, Mistress Calliope," he said, his mustache trembling in time with his upper lip as he used his eyes to shoot daggers at Bast. "I can see that my help was . . . *unnecessary*."

And with that, he turned on his hoof and strode out of the room.

"What did you do to Jarvis?" Clio asked, still holding Bast in her arms. "He looked like he was about to cry. Did you see his mustache trembling?"

Duh, of course I saw his mustache trembling, I thought, but instead I said:

"Bast made it very clear that the only way I was gonna get Senenmut was to do it myself," I offered. "So, I had to leave Jarvis out of the game plan."

"That was cold," Clio said.

Sometimes my younger sister could be completely unhelpful.

"Really?" I shot back. "You really think that was cold, Clio?"

"You don't have to be a bitch," she said, raising an eyebrow.

Runt, sensing my mood, sidled up to me for a pat—probably hoping to diffuse the situation—but I wasn't in the mood to play and shooed her away. Clio was right, of course. I didn't *have* to be a bitch, but I felt so bad about making Jarvis almost cry that I had to let it out somehow.

"Okay, dirty man," I said, transferring my gaze to Senenmut, who was still crouched in the corner licking his fingers. "It's time for a bath and a shave . . . *and then we go to Hell.*"

i had never seen a dirt ring around the inside of the tub before. I'd had some dirty—and I mean as in the kind of dirt you find on the ground—moments before, but this was ridiculous.

At first, Senenmut had refused to get into the bathtub.

I think he must've associated anything large and liquid-retaining with the big bronze oil pot I'd knocked over back in the Jackal Brothers' torture chamber, but after I filled it up and put my own hand into the lukewarm, bubble-filled water, he seemed to accept bathing in the tub as a safe endeavor.

The shampoo was another matter entirely.

I had originally decided that using Clio's bathroom upstairs made the most sense, but when she realized what I intended, my sister strictly barred me from befouling her tub. So, instead, we ended up in one of the guest baths downstairs. Which wasn't so bad, as far as bathtubs—and bathrooms—went. The floor and walls were made out of beige tumbled marble tile and the tub was one of those giant Kohler soaking tubs you could fill to the brim and watch the water drain out over the top.

Totally chic, but kind of intimidating when the last time you took a bath, your tub was a river.

All the sweet-smelling Bumble and Bumble bath products crowding the edge of the tub immediately intrigued Senenmut. Shampoos, conditioners, bath bombs, and salts—you name it and my mother'd already put it in the guest bathroom. It was everything I could do to stop my charge from opening all the bottles at once and dumping them into the already soapy water.

I had just eased my new friend into the tub—averting my eyes from his naked parts—when he sat back and slid under the water. I thought maybe he was playing with me, trying to get me to jump in and save him or something, so I didn't do anything.

"Not funny," I said. "*Really* not funny."

After I'd counted to ten and still no Senenmut, I started to get worried. I stuck my hands into the bubble bath–filled tub and reached around in the muck, trying to get a good grip on my Egyptian friend. Finally, I found a hank of hair—or it could've been beard, for all I knew—and dredged the half-drowned man out of the water.

It was amazing how wracked with guilt you can feel when you've almost let someone drown.

Seriously, I was like some kind of errant new mother who'd almost let her infant die while giving him his first bath. I made a New Year's resolution right then and there (even though I was quite aware of the fact that New Year's was a number of months away) not *ever* to have children because I was completely unfit to be a mother. Hell, if I couldn't even manage a five-thousand-year-old Egyptian man, what dastardly things would I do to a baby?

I was a wreck, but Senenmut seemed unfazed by the adventure. He sat back in the tub and watched his beard float to the surface. Then he stared at his toes in exactly the same way he'd stared at them back at the Jackal Brothers' torture chamber.

Finally, I got bored with watching him watching his toes, so I picked up a bottle of coconut-flavored shampoo and put some in my hand. It was only then, as I began to contemplate washing the tangled rat's nest that was Senenmut's hair, that I realized it would've been much smarter if I'd cut his hair before attempting to shampoo it. Annoyed with myself, but knowing there was no point now in pulling out some scissors and probably scaring the shit out of my bathing charge, I plopped the shampoo on Senenmut's head—totally *not* expecting what happened next.

Senenmut started sniffing the air, his nostrils flaring as he grabbed my wrist and stuck his nose directly into the remains of the shampoo I had in my palm.

"Ew," I said, yanking my arm out of his grasp. "Stop that!"

He stared at me, then his eyes quickly darted over to the bottle of shampoo. Before I could stop him, he had the bottle in his hand and was squeezing its contents into his open mouth.

"Oh my God!" I screamed, wrestling the bottle away from him as he started gagging. "That's shampoo, not food, you idiot."

"I'm not an idiot," he said, his words garbled by shampoo bubbles, but still distinct. I stared, shocked that he could speak—I had only been half joking about that deaf-and-dumb thing earlier.

"You can talk?" I said.

Senenmut nodded.

"Why didn't you talk to me before?" I said, annoyed.

"You didn't look like you were worth talking to."

I sat back on my heels next to the side of the tub and pushed a few errant strands of hair out of my face.

"Oh, okay."

I didn't know quite what to say. I had saved this guy's life, like, twice now and *he* didn't think I looked like I was worth talking to?

"Okay," I repeated as I stood up and headed for bathroom door.

At that moment, I didn't care *whom* I owed. If Cerberus wanted the prick in the tub, he could just come and get him himself.

"Wait!" Senenmut said.

I was half-ready to ignore him, but something in the tone of his voice made me stop.

"The spirit in the cat. You love him?"

Well, that definitely froze me on the spot. I had *totally* forgotten that poor Daniel was still trapped inside Bast.

"How do you know about him?" I said, turning back around.

Senenmut shrugged.

"He is your great love?"

It was my turn to shrug now.

"I don't know."

But even as I said the words, I knew I was full of it. My heart got all jumpy just thinking about Daniel. If he wasn't my *great* love, he was at least something *close* to it.

I sat down on the lid of the bone white Toto toilet and sighed.

"Okay, he *might* be my great love . . . and he might not. I just don't completely know how I feel about him at the moment," I said, resting my chin in my hands.

"When he made love to you—"

"Stop right there," I said, getting all depressed. I so did *not* want to say what I was going to *have* to say next.

"Up until this very moment, no love has been made."

Senenmut's eyes went wide.

"He has not made love to you? I don't understand. Love is a gift from the Gods. A man must make good use of it."

"Yeah, well, he hasn't." I sighed. "At least not yet."

Senenmut shook his head, a look of pity crossing his gaunt face.

"You are unloved. How sad for you."

"Shut up and wash your stupid hair," I said, frustrated by the situation I now found myself in. "And by the way, I don't *need* your pity. I'm not unloved. That is, I've been loved before."

Ha, I thought to myself, *I can count all that loving on one hand—four fingers to be precise and one of them doesn't even really count!*

Okay, when I was eighteen, I *tried* to have sex with a guy in my Introduction to Nineteenth-Century Literature class— and "tried" is definitely the operative word here.

His name was Samuel and he was absolutely adorable. Originally, he was from England—he had this amazing British accent that I just drooled over—but he'd lived in California since he was fourteen, so he wasn't a total foreign-exchange type.

Thinking back, I could still see his dark brown puppy dog eyes, long eyelashes, and delicate bone structure. God, he really was a gorgeous specimen of a man. And to this day, I really don't think I've ever dated anyone prettier. In fact, he actually kind of looked like a more girly/sensitive version of James McAvoy—that Scottish actor whom I think is just delicious!

And the beauty of the whole thing was that I didn't even have to lift a finger to make the hookup happen. I was just sitting in class, going over my notes, when he came up to *me* and asked *me* out for coffee. All I had to do was nod my head yes. It couldn't have been any easier.

So, our coffee date went reasonably well—I only spilled my cup of coffee on *myself*—and we ended up dating in earnest for, like, two weeks.

Now, at that point in my life, I had never had sex with another person—and barely even myself—so this thing with Samuel was new territory for me. I mean, I'd fooled around with people and stuff, but actual "penetration" hadn't really been on the table yet.

Well, the more time I spent with Samuel, and his sexy accent, the more I wanted to get some "penetrating" action going on, but the funny thing about Samuel was that the more I insisted that I was ready to give it up to him, the more *he* kept insisting that it wasn't a big deal and we should just wait.

At first, I thought it was supersweet that he wanted my first time to be special, but then as the weeks wore on—we were coming on three weeks now, which was like an eternity in college—I started to get kind of antsy about all the waiting I was having to do. Heck, I was a red-blooded American girl who was more than ready to make love to the handsome British man of my dreams—and the handsome British man was so *not* cooperating. This was *not* the way this sex thing was supposed to go down. *I* was the one who was supposed to be fending off *his* advances, not the other way around.

Finally, after I couldn't take it anymore, I called my best friend, Noh, in Rome to ask her for some advice. She had deferred her first year of college in order to spend time in Italy with her aunt Sarah, volunteering on an archeological dig outside the city. They were helping to excavate and catalog an ancient Roman cemetery before the city planners razed it to make room for a new road.

Anyway, when I finally got ahold of Noh—time difference and odd working hours making the call much harder to put through than one would've expected—she had one piece of advice for me, and one piece only.

Seduce him.

So, on an evening I knew my roommate would be out partying all night—and hopefully puking her guts out in someone *else's* bathroom for a change—I invited Samuel over to "hang out."

At least, that was the plan . . . but I had other ideas in mind.

I opened the door wearing a silk kimono with a dragon embroidered on the back that my mother had given me for my last birthday—and nothing on underneath it.

After shutting the door and locking it behind him, I whispered this fact into Samuel's ear. I expected him to kiss me, or hold me *or something*, but he just nodded, a little frown creasing his sensitive face.

Even though my room was just a typical mouse hole of a dorm room—with two twin beds, two desks, and two chairs—I had put sandalwood candles on every available space in the place and it looked and smelled incredible. There was even an open bottle of red wine that I'd bought off a guy down the hall and two wineglasses waiting expectantly on my desk while soft, sexy music—a little Jeff Buckley, actually—played in the background.

I took Samuel's coat and dropped it on my desk chair, then

took his hand and maneuvered him toward my tiny twin bed. He sat down beside me and I handed him a glass of red wine. We sat like that for a few minutes, each of us sipping wine and looking uncomfortable. After two glasses, I had a little Dutch courage, so I leaned forward and kissed him—which he seemed pretty all right with—so I took that as a sign that it was time to move forward with my plan.

I started unbuttoning his pants.

Once again, let me state for the record that he seemed perfectly okay with the whole thing. I mean, it wasn't like he didn't know where all this was going, right? Candles, wine . . . naked Callie? Pretty self-explanatory, *I* think.

After a few more minutes of kissing, I pushed him back on the bed and straddled him. He tensed and stopped kissing me back, but I was too hot and bothered by now to really notice.

"Do it," I moaned in his ear. "Put it inside me."

I reached down and grabbed his penis—which was erect, so there had to be a little reciprocation going on—and pulled it toward me. All that was left for me to do was climb on top of him and—

Suddenly, Samuel started squirming like an eel beneath me, shoving me so hard that I went flying off him and landed hard on the floor, slamming my tailbone against the bottom of my desk.

"Rape!" Samuel screamed, cuddling his now-limp penis in his hand like it was a wounded animal.

"No! No rape!" I yelled back at him, terrified someone in my hall would hear all the commotion and call our RA. "There were candles, for God's sake!"

He glared at me, wild-eyed.

"You took advantage of me!"

"No, I didn't," I pleaded, crawling over to him and grabbing his leg.

"Rapist!" he hissed as he pried me off his leg.

"Please don't go . . ." I cried, but he just shook his head, slamming the door resoundingly behind him as he went.

I was too upset and shocked to even cry, so I just sat there on the floor, kimono askew, wondering what I had done wrong.

I spent the next two hours—and two hundred dollars in long distance—on the phone, rehashing the whole story for Noh. After laughing so hard that she started snorting, the only thing my friend could come up with was that Samuel was either gay or just highly allergic . . . *to me.*

In the end, it turned out he was just gay. A few weeks later he started dating this really hot guy in our literature class, and after that I didn't feel so wretched about the whole experience.

Needless to say, it was a *long* time before I tried my hand at the "penetration" game again.

"Okay, I know that you are a gambling woman," Senenmut said, startling me out of my thoughts, "so I will offer you an exchange."

"Excuse me?" I asked, wondering what I'd missed while my mind was ruminating over my old "sex gone wrong" memories.

"You help me find my great love and I will help you acquire yours," he said, sniffing the bottle of shampoo again. "Bast is a jealous one. She will keep you from your man just because she might."

I narrowed my eyes, wondering what the catch was.

"I know that you have promised to take me to Hell, but before you do, allow me one last folly . . . and I will help you steal your love away from the Queen of the Cats."

This was an enticing offer, but I really didn't think we had the time to piss around looking for Senenmut's lost love. Still, I pulled out the little rubidium clock so I could check to see how much time was left before we had to get our asses down to Hell.

"We only have, like, twelve hours," I said. "I don't think this is such a good—"

"I beg of you," Senenmut cried, scrambling out of the water and grasping my arm, getting me even wetter than I already was.

I tried to ignore the fact that a naked man was holding my

arm and focus on the situation at hand, but as the bubbles started sliding down his wet torso, I found myself getting pretty darn distracted—and unbelievably embarrassed at the same time.

"Help me find my great love, then I will go with you willingly," Senenmut said, squeezing the fatty part of my upper arm. "Otherwise, I will be forced to find a way to escape and search for her on my own . . . and Bast will make a prisoner of your lover's spirit forever."

"Is that a threat?" I asked incredulously.

Was this guy *really* sitting in my parents' tub, eating their shampoo, and threatening me?

Yup.

"It is a promise." He sighed.

"Let me think about it," I said.

I decided that the first thing I needed to do was find Bast and make sure Senenmut wasn't full of crap. Then I could make a more informed decision.

"Hurry and make up your mind, Calliope Reaper-Jones," Senenmut said as he sat back down and reached for the lemon verbena bar of soap sitting on the side of the tub. "Time slows for no one."

I glared at him as he started scrubbing his pits with an expensive-looking loofah.

What the hell does he know about time? I thought angrily, but little did I know then how very right he was.

eighteen

Bast looked at me like I was crazy.

"Of course he belongs to me now," she said in between licks while grooming her honeyed coat. "Finders, keepers."

I stared at her. I couldn't believe she was being serious. *Finders, keepers?* That was *so* elementary school. Yet there it was, rearing its ugly head again. I'd always thought that getting older meant dealing with a whole new caliber of problems, yet more often than not these days, I found myself confronted with the same old business over and over again.

"Fine," I said. "Be a bitch."

"Can you call a female cat a bitch or is that just for dogs?" my sister said offhandedly as she flipped through the channels on the television set.

I could tell that she wasn't really paying attention to what she was watching because she passed her favorite show, *Cities of the Underworld*, twice and didn't stop either time.

"Just for dogs," Bast said, looking over at Runt, who was splayed on her back on the floor in front of the television. She was snoring softly, unaware that she was now the topic of our conversation.

We were in Clio's utilitarian bedroom, where the girls had

decamped after I took Senenmut to the guest bathroom for his bath. Clio was on her bed, a bottle of pink toenail polish on the floor beside her. I had never known Clio to have *any* interest in makeup or clothes, so watching her paint her toenails with such practiced dexterity was kind of shocking.

Bast was curled up at the foot of Clio's bed, looking for all intents and purposes like she owned the place. I stared at Clio, hoping she would intercede on my behalf, but she was more interested in messing with her remote control than helping me.

"Clio, can you explain to the Queen of the Cats here that Daniel belongs to me?" I said.

Clio put her remote down and cocked her head, thinking.

"I thought you were mad at him for pretending to be dead," she offered finally.

"Well, I *was*—" I began, but she interrupted me.

"Then why do you care what happens to him now? Good riddance and all that, right?"

I narrowed my eyes, trying to think of a witty comeback, but nothing came to mind.

"No, *not* good riddance," I said. "I don't understand how someone can call finders, keepers on another human being."

Bast looked up, midlick.

"Who says that he's a human being?"

Well, that stopped me in my tracks. The cat was right about that. I was just *assuming* that Daniel was a human being, but I'd never even asked him about his past before. I'd been much more interested in myself and what was happening to me than in what Daniel's deal was. I guess that made me a pretty cruddy friend . . . and an even less appealing possible lover.

Argh.

"Look, human being or not, he doesn't belong to you, Bast," I said.

The cat lazily blinked her golden eyes twice, then went back to licking one of her back legs.

"Callie, you just said that Daniel belonged to you," my sister said instead. "So, I don't know how you can accuse Bast of treating Daniel like an object when you're doing exactly the same thing."

"You're my sister. You're supposed to me on my side," I whined at Clio, who only shrugged.

"Just pointing out the obvious."

And with that, she went back to futzing with her remote control, leaving me to stew in my own thoughts.

Okay, Clio was *kind of* right. I *had* just treated Daniel like a piece of meat, but that didn't mean that I didn't have his best interests at heart. Once I got Daniel back to normal—and asked him a few pertinent questions—I was going to let him go on about his business, no strings attached. Bast, on the other hand, might have other plans for him, plans that involved indentured servitude or the relinquishing of his firstborn. She was a wily feline, I would give her that, but that wiliness served only to increase my mistrust of her. After all, she had lured me into the Jackal Brothers' torture chamber and then completely left me on my own to fend for myself—and if *that* wasn't an indicator of her sensibility, then I didn't know what was.

"I'm just gonna lay this out there once, so you guys had better pay attention," I said firmly. "If you don't release Daniel right this instant, I will not be responsible for what I'm gonna have to do to you."

Bast blinked, but didn't respond. My sister shrugged.

If I didn't know better, I would think that Bast had Clio in some kind of thrall because Clio was being just as obstinate as the cat.

"Clio, help me out here," I said.

"I think you need to focus on Senenmut and then we'll worry about finders, keepers after you've taken him to Cerberus."

I threw up my arms in frustration.

"I just said that if Bast didn't produce Daniel's Shade, I was gonna have to do something that I don't want to have to do and it *will* directly affect you guys. Why are all my threats just considered 'idle'? Am I that pathetic?"

"Runt's future is at stake here," Clio said. "And Bast isn't gonna hurt Daniel in the interim—"

"This is absurd!" I almost yelled at Clio. "You're taking the dumb cat's side over mine? What's wrong with this picture?"

Clio set her remote down on the bed and crawled over to the edge so that we were only a few feet away from each other now.

"I think that you need to go take Senenmut back to Cerberus before you screw everything up for Runt," Clio said. "That's what I think."

I stared at her, my mouth hanging open so wide that I would've caught flies if there'd been any around to catch.

"I can't believe you just said that. I *so* do not screw things up . . . very much, that is."

Clio crawled back over to the head of the bed and picked up her remote, turning up the volume on the television just as Paris Hilton's bulbous bleached blond head filled the screen. I gawked at the television, in shock that my superintelligent sister would be watching a Paris Hilton reality show—especially after how many times she'd made fun of me for watching shows that were just as inane.

I opened my mouth to comment on her choice of show, but then shut it again. Bast was watching me intently, waiting for me to say something that would push my younger sister even further away from me than she already was.

Well, I thought, *I will not give her the satisfaction.*

"Okay, Clio, you're right," I said, letting the lie flow out of my mouth with as much confidence as I could muster. "I'll just take Senenmut back to Cerberus like you said and then we'll figure out the Daniel thing later."

Clio appeared pleased with my answer.

"I'm glad you're doing the right thing, Cal," she said, her gaze still on Paris Hilton's face. "Bast said you were impetuous and wouldn't listen, but I knew you'd see the light of reason."

"Thanks for the vote of confidence, Clio."

I gave her a wide, mocking smile, but she ignored the sarcasm and smiled back. I turned to Bast, who was quickly sashaying her way up my shit list. She was looking at me through narrowed amber eyes.

Trying to size me up, huh? I thought. *Well, you can just try all you want, kitty cat, but don't expect to get one over on me anytime soon.*

I pointed to my eyes, then pointed back to Bast.

"I'm watching you," I mouthed as I stood up and walked to the bedroom door.

Bast was definitely trying to dominate my sister's mind, but standing there arguing with her wasn't going to win me any friends. I was gonna have to align myself with Senenmut and hope that he was as good as his word. Otherwise, I was going to have one hell of a time disentangling my sister's mind from Bast's malicious machinations.

"See you guys later," I said, trying to be as cheerful as I could as I gave my sister one last lingering look and let myself out.

I stood in the hallway next to Clio's door and took out the rubidium clock. I decided that if I had more than eleven hours and forty-five minutes left on the clock, then I would take Senenmut up on his offer.

"How much time do I have?" I asked.

The numbers slowed to a crawl.

"Shit," I said under my breath.

I had exactly eleven hours and forty-six minutes, eleven seconds, and 3.4×10^{-44} s left.

"I'm in!" I nearly yelled as I threw open the bathroom door and found myself standing face-to-face with an intoxicatingly handsome man whom I had never seen before. He had large, almond-shaped eyes, an aquiline nose, a wide, sensuous mouth, and a clean-shaven, honeyed complexion.

"Oh, sorry," I said as I started to turn back around and close the door.

"It's me," the man said, grabbing my arm to stop me. "Senenmut."

I stared at him.

"Where's your beard? And your hair?"

This was all I could manage to say as I took in the man that stood before me. He was so unlike the Senenmut I'd first met that I had a really hard time reconciling that this was the same person. Where the Senenmut I knew looked like an escapee from a prison camp—which he was—*this* guy looked like an Armani model.

"I found a razor."

The only razor I'd seen in the guest bathroom was of the ladies' disposable variety.

"Oh. That was a lot of work, then," I mumbled, trying not to stare at his naked torso.

He shrugged and once again I couldn't help noticing the muscle definition in his chest and abs. Of course, he had a towel chastely wrapped around his waist, so I couldn't see if the rest of him matched his chest muscles, but I had a funny feeling that they did.

"You look so different," I said meekly. Seriously, he was like a different man. I thought back to when I'd last seen him. He was standing in the bath, pleading for me to help him find his lost love, and I was pretty sure that those muscles hadn't been there then.

"My body is renewing itself now," he said. "I made an offering to Osiris with my blood and he has answered me."

"What kind of offering?" I asked as we stood in the bathroom doorway, looking at each other.

He held up his arm and I saw a deep gash in his side. It still looked pretty nasty, but I could see that the wound was already starting to scab over.

"You did that with a ladies' disposable razor?" I asked.

He shrugged. "Yes, I think so. It was all I had to make my offering with."

Well, I couldn't argue with *that* logic.

"You said that you were 'in'?" Senenmut continued, looking up at me through long, dark lashes.

I nodded, trying not to let the fact that my body found him thoroughly attractive affect my ability to speak.

"Uhm, well, you were right about Bast. She won't let Daniel go."

Senenmut, looking grave now, nodded.

"Yes, she will hold on to him as long as she can. He is the way to controlling you and she knows that," Senenmut said, running his hand across his now-bald pate. "She is a collector, Calliope Reaper-Jones. And the Daughter of Death would be a rather unique addition to her collection."

"But Jarvis said that she was my dad's spirit guide," I said, confused. "How can she do anything against someone in his family?"

"I can only say that Bast would not become *anyone's* spirit guide willingly," Senenmut said. "That I know for truth."

"Oh my God, you think he tricked her into it?" I asked.

It wouldn't be the first time my dad had done something like that and it *would* offer an explanation as to why the cat seemed so hell-bent on making my life difficult.

Maybe using my sister and me to get to my dad *was* her ultimate goal.

"Well, whatever her reasoning, you were right," I said, trying not to stare at the trail of downy black hair that started between his nipples, wandered down his flat belly, and disappeared beneath the towel.

"Then you will help me find Hatshepsut?" he said, grasping my hand and squeezing it in his much larger one.

"Uh-huh," I almost moaned. "Whatever you want."

"Thank you, Calliope Reaper-Jones. Thank you," he said as he pulled me close and kissed first one cheek, then the other.

"Anytime," I replied, dazed by his nearness.

"So, next we will make an offering to Nephthys, the Goddess of Hidden Things," Senenmut said as he released me, "and she will tell me where I will find my lost love."

I nodded, but something he said didn't sit right with me. It took me a second to access the memory, but then I knew exactly where I'd heard the name "Nephthys" before.

"Wait a minute," I said, trying to remember the exact words Bast had used back at the Jackal Brothers' torture chamber.

"Didn't I hear Bast say that the Jackal Brothers were the sons of this Nephthys lady?"

Senenmut nodded. "Of course."

"Well then, offering or not, why would she want to help you?" I asked incredulously. "I mean, you just escaped from her sons' clutches. It kind of seems like a conflict of interest to me."

Senenmut looked at me curiously.

"There will be no conflict of interest, as you say. She will help me because I ask. That is the way of the Gods."

I wasn't buying it. I knew that a mother's love could be the most dangerous kind of love out there—and when you messed around with one of her kids, well, you could just forget about getting any kind of leniency from her at all.

"Are you sure about that?" I asked. "Women can get pretty squirrelly when you start screwing with their kids, Senenmut."

He just shook his head like I was being ridiculous.

"In Egypt, it does not work that way."

"Whatever you say," I replied, knowing that *I* wasn't going to be the one to change his mind. "Let's just go make this stupid offering and see what she says."

Senenmut nodded happily.

"But first, let's get you some clothes so you don't have to go around in that towel all day," I said, stepping out of the doorway.

"Agreed," Senenmut said as he dropped the towel and followed me into the hall.

it took every ounce of willpower that I possessed not to look at Senenmut's junk as he followed me up to my dad's bedroom and I pulled out a dark pair of slacks, boxers, and a men's undershirt for him to wear. I tried to move as quickly as I could through the house, so that no one was exposed (no joke intended) to Senenmut's nudity. From what I could see, if Senenmut was any indication, the Egyptians' relationship with clothing was pretty laissez-faire. That is, they seemed to have no problem whatsoever with going around stark naked.

Once he was properly attired, we went back downstairs and out into the backyard. Senenmut's idea of the perfect offering to Nephthys included burning some of his hair and then throwing the ashes into the ocean. Since it all seemed pretty benign to me, I just sat back—after I found him some matches to use—and let him do his thing.

We walked across the back lawn until we were at the very edge of the cliff, where the three stone benches that had creeped out my sister and me as children stood. Trying not to feel uncomfortable about the impending visit from Nephthys, I sat down on the middle bench and watched as Senenmut pulled some of his hair from his pocket and set it alight.

"O great Goddess Nephthys, hear my prayer!" he yelled into the furiously blowing wind as it whipped at my hair and made me shiver. I hadn't realized how cold it had gotten recently, but now I felt the chill deep down in my bones.

Luckily, I had been able to make a quick clothing change while Senenmut was getting dressed. I had slipped into my old room and found a pair of thick corduroy trousers and a hot pink mohair sweater. I hadn't had time to shower, but just slipping out of the nasty old Missoni sweater made me feel like a brand-new human being.

Once I was dressed, I'd snuck into my mother's bathroom and sprayed a little Chanel No. 5 on my pulse points. If I could've bathed in the stuff, I probably would've—that's how much I loved it. It was hands down my favorite perfume and I just adored the way the scent lingered on my skin and clothing long after I'd put it on.

"It's not working."

I looked over at Senenmut, my nose still filled with the scent of Chanel No. 5, and saw him pacing angrily up and down the edge of the cliff.

"I hate to say I told you so," I offered, but he was too lost in his own head to hear me.

"I will have to try something darker, then," he mumbled to himself.

I watched as he pulled the disposable pink razor out of his pocket—where the hell had he been hiding that thing when he was running around without the towel on?—and raked the blade across the top of his shaved head. Instantly, a pool of blood began to well up where the blade had crossed it, spilling down the side of his head and into his ear. The image was so gross that I had to avert my eyes.

"Nephthys, Goddess of Hidden Things, take this offering of my blood as payment for my answer!" he screamed.

I opened my eyes, shocked to see a large red bird with a curved midnight-colored bill swoop down from the empty blue sky and land right on Senenmut's shoulder, where it quickly began to lap up the blood that was spilling from his scalp. Once the bird had had its fill, it lowered its coal black beak to Senenmut's ear and began to whisper something to him. I was too far away to hear what it was saying, but from the look of exaltation on his face, I knew it had to be good news.

As suddenly as it had appeared, the bird took wing and disappeared back into the cloudless sky. Senenmut turned to me, a wide smile on his handsome, bloodied face.

"It is done. By Nephthys, I know where my lost love's present incarnation resides!" he said wildly, his arms lifted in victory. Then, as the blood from his scalp began to gush in time with his heartbeat, he keeled forward and passed out at my feet.

I didn't know if it was from sheer happiness or just a side effect of all the blood loss—but my bet was on the happiness.

nineteen

"Damn," I moaned under my breath as I squatted down beside the unconscious Egyptian, unsure how to help him. "I wish I had a frickin' towel."

Instantly, a clean, white, fluffy bathroom towel appeared in my hands. I was so surprised that I nearly dropped it on the ground. This "ask and you shall receive" stuff had happened to me a few times in the past, usually when I was in a high-stress situation, but it still made me feel weird. It was one thing when I could *make* magic happen of my own accord, another still when my body did it without my knowledge.

"Thank you," I said to whatever magic had provided the towel before pressing it against Senenmut's scalp.

I get a little squeamish when it comes to blood—okay, just the sight of the stuff makes me grit my teeth and want to scream—but since I was the only one available to help him, I sucked up the queasiness I felt as best I could and tried not to watch as the towel in my hands went from white to scarlet to brown as the blood soaked in, then dried.

The stench of iron assailed my nostrils, drowning out the spicy tones of my Chanel No. 5, and it became very hard not to pass out myself. I tried to think about something else as I applied pressure to the wound, but the only thing that kept popping into my head was how bizarre it would be for someone to die by ladies' disposable razor.

I'd had a few run-ins with a disposable razor in my time, so I knew how painful a cut from the little buggers could be, but I'd never thought of them as dangerous weapons before. I couldn't help imagining what it would be like to accidentally exsanguinate by razor as the water in the bathtub slowly turned ice-cold around you.

Ew! I thought to myself. *This is so not helping the situation.*

Finally, after what seemed like eons, Senenmut opened his eyes and looked up at me. He still had that stupid exalted look on his face—up close it was more lovesick than exalted—but his pupils were dilated and he kept opening and closing his mouth like he wanted to speak but couldn't find the right words. If Jarvis had been there, he would've gone all Mary Poppins on the Egyptian and told him to shut his mouth *spit spot on the double now* before he ate a bug.

Just the thought of Jarvis standing there, intoning lines out of a Disney musical, made me giggle. Then I started to feel bad. I had obviously hurt Jarvis's feelings by following Bast into the tapestry—and the suckiest part of the whole thing was that he had been totally right. I should never have gone without him. I knew deep down that the little faun had my best interests at heart, which was not something I could claim about the cat.

I decided that after I got back from helping Senenmut, I was going to go find Jarvis and apologize to him—then I was going to do what I had promised and somehow, Lord knew how, hook him up with my corpulent beauty of a boss, Hyacinth.

"Why do you laugh?" Senenmut said groggily as I helped him to sit up.

"Oh, no reason really," I mumbled, feeling silly. "Just thinking about something funny."

"Would you tell me what this funny thing is?" Senenmut said as he pulled the towel from his head and probed the wound with his fingers.

"I was just thinking about what my friend Jarvis would say if he'd been here," I said, faltering as I realized that without the proper context, i.e., knowing Jarvis as well as I did, there was no way Senenmut was gonna find any of this funny.

"You know what? Forget it," I said, interrupting myself. "It really wouldn't be all that funny to anyone but me."

Senenmut nodded, as if he saw the wisdom in what I was saying.

"So, where is she? Your special lady friend?"

Senenmut got that silly lovesick look on his face again, and the saccharine-ness of the whole thing totally made me want to gag. I decided that it was one thing to talk about helping someone find their true love; it was another thing entirely to actually help them do it—particularly when it got you no closer to finding the same thing for yourself.

"She is in a place called Target," he said.

I sighed.

"Did the little birdie happen to mention which one?"

Senenmut nodded excitedly.

"The ibis told me that this place is not far from here. It even gave me directions."

He paused, trying to remember the bird's exact words.

"Yes, I remember," he began excitedly. "I am to take a thing called Highway 80 all the way to a place called Las Vegas. This Target resides there."

Oh, brother.

there were eleven Target stores in the greater Las Vegas area. This I gleaned from a quick web check on my PDA.

I usually neglected to bring my dippy BlackBerry wannabe with me whenever I went home because it never got reception there—in fact, from what I could tell, *no* cell phones worked within the vicinity of Sea Verge. I knew from experience that if you wanted to make a private call, you had to take a walk off the property. If you were a teenager home from school for the summer, trying to have long, meaningful gossip sessions with your best friends, using your cell phone was a losing endeavor. Let's just say that the battery on my phone died long before I was ready to stop talking.

Of course, you could always use the house's landline, but who knew if there was someone listening in or not? That was one of the *nonperks* of being the Grim Reaper's kid: no real privacy to speak of. There was always someone, somewhere, watching.

As I had absolutely no interest in, nor did I have the time for, taking a prolonged road trip with my new Egyptian pal, I knew that I was going to have to up my time frame for apologizing to Jarvis. He was the only person, other than Clio (who was under Bast's spell and not an option), who could pull a wormhole out of his hat and get me where I needed to go in a timely fashion.

I left Senenmut sitting on the bench by the cliff's edge, staring out at the ocean, towel pressed to his rapidly healing head wound, and walked back to the house to make my peace with Jarvis. I kept looking over my shoulder as I crossed the yard, feeling kind of bad for my new Egyptian friend. At first, Senenmut hadn't seemed to notice the humongous body of water that surrounded us, but once he'd gotten Nephthys to give him the info on his lost lady love, he'd stopped being so one-track-minded and actually started paying attention to his surroundings.

"I loved the sea as a boy. My father would take my brother and me to Kem-Ver—the Black Sea in your tongue—and we would watch the slaves building the ships," Senenmut said wistfully. "Those were some of the happiest times in my life."

I could empathize with the guy—minus the slaves. There was something about remembering your childhood that made you feel all old and sad inside. Of course, for me, I had only twenty-some years to reflect back on. For Senenmut, his memories straddled thousands of years and the death of his whole world.

Maybe empathy was overrated.

Damn, he just looked so out of place at Sea Verge. He didn't belong here in this time. He was from a whole other period in history where magic and an open dialogue with one's Gods still existed. The world was different now, and I had the distinct impression that once the novelty of being free again after thousands of years of bondage wore off, Senenmut would become disillusioned and depressed. This realization made me understand that the kindest thing I could do for the guy was to deliver him to Cerberus—whether we found his lost love or not—and get him into the system of rebirth and death again, so he could let go of his old self for good.

It really is for the best, I decided gloomily as I reached for the knob on the back door of the main house. Before I could even turn the dumb thing, the door swung open and I nearly fell face-first into the house.

"Hey!" I said as I grabbed onto the nearest thing I could find to steady myself—which just happened to be Jarvis and the doorjamb. "*Hey*, I was just coming to look for you."

Jarvis stiffened, but continued to let me use his shoulder to steady myself inside the doorway.

"Yes?" he said once I was finally back to a full upright position.

"Just a minute," I said as I checked to make sure that one of the heels on my boots hadn't come loose. "All right, sorry about that."

I reached out and tried to brush some pretend lint off the lapels of Jarvis's shirt, but he shooed me away.

"Stop that!" he said, looking down at his shirt just to make sure there *wasn't* really anything on it.

"Look, Jarvis," I said, hanging my head and looking down at my feet in contrition. "I'm really, really, really sorry that I left you in the Hall of Death and went with Bast all by myself."

I peeked through my lashes to see if he was buying my apology—which he wasn't. Instead, he was using the edge of his pince-nez to pick some dirt out from under his nails, barely even deigning to pay attention to me.

"You want a manicure, I'll get you a manicure," I said, putting my hands on my hips. "But right now just listen to me for a minute, okay?"

Jarvis sighed and looked up, slipping the pince-nez into his jacket pocket.

"Fine. I suppose I can spare a few moments."

I gave him a wobbly smile.

"Thank you, Jarvis."

He shrugged, but at least he was listening finally.

"I want to apologize. It was straight up all my fault. You were helping me out and I totally blew you off," I said. "And I'm just . . . really, really sorry. I know that saying I won't do it again means nothing, but I promise you before I do something stupid again, I'm gonna stop, take a minute, and ask myself: What Would Jarvis Do?"

Jarvis cleared his throat.

"You pinched that off the Jesus freaks, didn't you."

I nodded.

"Yup, I saw WWJD on a rubber bracelet, and for, like, two seconds I actually thought it *did* stand for 'What Would Jarvis Do?'—I swear to God I'm not lying."

I could see the edges of Jarvis's mouth trying to draw up into a smile, but the little faun was doing everything in his power not to give in and accept my apology.

"Please forgive me?" I begged, but still, Jarvis wouldn't relent.

"You're really gonna make me do this, aren't you?" I sighed.

Jarvis nodded.

"Okay," I said as I got down on my knee in the doorway and put my hands together in mock prayer. "Please, Jarvis. Please, please, *please* forgive me."

"This is ridiculous," Jarvis said, grasping my arm and hauling me back onto my feet. "Stand up."

"Forgiven?" I asked.

"How can I say no when you're blocking the doorway like this?" Jarvis said dryly.

"I thought you'd see it my way," I said. "Now that we're all made up, I need another favor."

Jarvis rolled his eyes heavenward.

"Of course you do, my dear. As they say in the animal kingdom: A leopard *never* changes its spots."

I took the dig willingly. At least I knew Jarvis was back on my side again, thank God.

"I need you to take Senenmut and me to Target."

"Oh, you *are* slumming it, aren't you?" Jarvis said, snickering. "Calliope Reaper-Jones shopping the Jaclyn Smith Collection at Target? *This* I have to see. I'll go get the car."

He started to head toward the garage, but I stopped him.

"Actually," I said, loving the fact that Jarvis was wrong about something for a change. "I *think* you mean Kmart when you're talking Jaclyn Smith, Mr. Smarty-pants. And we're gonna be needing a wormhole, not a car, so you better get cracking."

originally, jarvis had wanted to come with us on our long-lost-love search, but after I told him about my last run-in with Bast, he changed his mind.

"She's a piece of work, that cat," Jarvis said as he opened the wormhole for us. "She hates working with your father, even though he does *nothing* but treat her with respect."

"Maybe she just doesn't like being controlled," I offered, but Jarvis only shook his head.

"I think it's more than that. I think it has nothing to do with being controlled and *everything* to do with power."

I wasn't sure what he meant.

"For centuries, humanity worshipped her, made offerings in her name, sacrificed for her blessings," Jarvis said in explanation. "Now the cult of the cat is over. She has lost most of her power and she blames your father for it. Totally irrational, I know, since he had nothing to do with the death of the Egyptian culture."

"So why is she working for him, then?" I asked curiously.

"As Death's spirit guide, she retains some of her previous powers," Jarvis replied. "Powers that she would've lost otherwise."

"You think she's gonna use those powers on Daniel?"

Jarvis only shook his head.

"I don't know," he said finally. "But one of us must remain behind to make sure that cat doesn't get into too much mischief here at Sea Verge while your parents are away."

"I think she's turned Clio's head," I said. "She's got her watching reality TV and painting her toenails."

Jarvis sighed and shook his head.

"I don't think that's Bast's doing. Your sister has been behaving very strangely as of late."

"What do you mean?" I said, even though I already had an inkling as to what he was talking about.

"Your father and I believe that she has been secretly seeing your friend Indra."

"What?" I squeaked. "And by the way, he is so *not* my friend."

Okay, let me just preface this by saying that the only experiences I've had with Indra were when he was being a total egocentric prick. In fact, during the whole "dad kidnapping" fiasco, he had been a *real* pain in my ass, causing me nothing but strife. He'd been the proud owner of one of the items that the Board of Death had wanted me to retrieve in order to fulfill my tasks and take over my dad's job. Needless to say, Indra had been anything *but* forthcoming at the time. It wasn't until *after* I'd saved his butt from the demon Vritra that he'd changed his attitude and gotten a whole lot nicer to be around.

He was one of the few Gods I knew who still liked to keep his hands in the world of human affairs. He had taken on the persona of a noted Bollywood actor and director, winning more acclaim and accord with each new film he conceived. The human world might not have known he was a *real* God, but there were plenty of ladies out there who thought he was the human equivalent.

After we—Daniel, Jarvis, Kali, Runt, Clio, and me—vanquished the demon Vritra, Indra had invited everyone to the premiere of his latest Bollywood spectacular. I hadn't *seen* Clio talking to him that night, but I'd been pretty preoccupied with the Gopi—Indra's hard-core female bodyguards, whom I'd resurrected from the dead after Vritra had decimated them—so I wouldn't have been surprised to find that I'd missed their flirtation.

"Wow, okay," I said calmly. "Well, you could've knocked me over with a feather on that one."

Jarvis merely pursed his lips and nodded.

"Your father doesn't think the relationship is appropriate, but he has chosen to remain silent—he doesn't want to lose another one of his daughters by speaking up."

Well, that hit me right in the heart. With Thalia in Purgatorial jail and me hiding out in New York, I guess I couldn't blame my dad for not wanting to alienate Clio.

"Boyfriend or not, I think you'd better keep your eye on her," I said. "Bast has something up her sleeve and I don't think it's gonna be pretty."

Jarvis nodded his agreement.

And with that, I left my dad's more-than-capable Executive Assistant to watch Sea Verge . . . and I led Senenmut into the wormhole.

my feelings about wormholes notwithstanding, the trip to Vegas wasn't too torturous. That is, no one got queasy or lost or dead, so I considered it pretty much a success.

Jarvis had sent us to the first Target on the list—but had missed by a shrub, the length of one humongous casino, and three plain old city blocks. My new Egyptian friend seemed immediately impressed by all the neon signs that surrounded the casino—especially one sign in particular, which held his attention even when I tapped his arm and tried to get him to follow me down the sidewalk. It advertised "An Evening with Wayne Newton" and showed a picture of the man himself, his wide-

lipped smile exposing some of the largest teeth I'd ever seen in
a picture—*or* in person, for that matter.

"I know that smile," Senenmut said, staring at the gaudy
signage that blinked on and off like some tentative, silent
heartbeat.

"Yeah?" I said.

He took a few steps forward, getting as close to the sign as
the sidewalk, and an encircling gate, would let him.

"Yes," he said, his eyes narrowed. "Teeth like a crocodile."

"Was that his name in a past life?"

Senenmut shook his head.

"No, that's just what his teeth looked like."

"Okay," I said, not wanting to dredge up bad memories.
"Look, we don't have a ton of time and there are, like, eleven
possible Targets in the greater Las Vegas area, so we need to
get a move on."

Senenmut nodded, not wanting to drag his gaze away from
Wayne but gently letting me lead him down the sidewalk toward our first destination.

senenmut was adamant that he would know Hatshepsut when he saw her—regardless of what body she was sporting these days. I was a little skeptical of his ability, but since
this was his show, I just kept my mouth shut.

My bald-headed Egyptian friend walked the length of the
first Target we entered, his eyes wide with wonder, but nothing
love-interest oriented caught his eye.

Now, the store itself was *another* story entirely. It dawned
on me as Senenmut stalked the bright red and white aisles of
domestic goods and foodstuffs that the man had never seen
anything of this conspicuous consumption magnitude before
in his life.

Ancient Egypt might've had the pyramids, but *we* had strip
malls and casinos.

The refrigerated aisles held the most interest for my friend.

I vaguely remembered Cerberus saying that Senenmut had been an architect once upon a time, so it only made sense that something all technical and engineering-based would grab his attention. He kept asking me how they made the cold air that circulated inside the cases, but *I* had no idea how refrigeration worked. I promised to get him a book or something on the subject, which only seemed to spark his curiosity, not assuage it.

"She is not here," he said finally after he'd walked the entire length of the store three times and inhaled the two Butterfingers and one Kit Kat bar I'd bought him at the self-serve checkout stand. Needless to say, he was overjoyed when I introduced him to the water fountain over by the toilets. I almost couldn't get him to leave it behind. He kept examining how it was connected to the wall, trying to gauge how he could get it off its moorings and take it with him.

And thus it went with the next six Targets we attacked.

Luckily, I'd brought my purse with me, so we didn't have to hoof it all over town. Senenmut was terribly intrigued by the taxis we trooped in and out of, which made me realize just how foreign my world must seem to him. He'd actually climbed on top of the first taxi that picked us up and I had to gently, yet firmly, yank him off the car's roof.

Like an irate child, he "not so" gently protested my being hands-on with him—and at one point, he might have even been having what I think parents like to term a "temper tantrum." In retrospect, I guess it *had* been a while since he'd been man-handled by a girl, but that was still no excuse for his trying to bite me as I settled him into the interior of the taxi and threw a wad of bills in the taxi driver's direction.

"Drive!"

The whole experience made me even more certain that having children was going to be a low priority on my "things to do before I die" list.

At the seventh Target—and after Senenmut had gotten completely bored with driving around in "horseless chariot" after "horseless chariot," as he called the taxis—we finally hit pay dirt.

she was standing in one of the checkout aisles, her short, dyed-black hair pulled back in a silver bandanna. She had on a pair of fitted black leggings that made her twiggy legs look even more emaciated than they were, a wifebeater that was two sizes too big for her—it was really more of a dress than a shirt—and a wide silver belt that kept the wifebeater cinched at her waist.

"That's her?" I asked incredulously as Senenmut pointed at her.

She was unloading the last items out of her shopping cart and appeared to be having trouble lifting a twenty-four-pack of bottled water from the cart's bottom rack.

"I feel a connection to her," Senenmut said, still pointing. I pushed his hand down so people would stop staring at us.

"So what do we do now?" I asked uncertainly.

Senenmut didn't even bother to answer my question.

Seeing his opening, he took it. Like a proud parent, I watched him saunter over to the struggling girl—she couldn't have been more than eighteen—and offer to help her. She looked around suspiciously, sensing some kind of trick, but when no cameramen leapt out of the shadows to yell *Punk'd* at her, she relented and let him lift the water out of the cart for her.

Once the water was on the conveyor belt, Senenmut leaned on the cart, trying to engage the girl in conversation. She looked around worriedly, wondering why no one from Target upper management was calling security on the weird terrorist-looking guy who wouldn't leave her alone.

I stood on the sidelines, watching and waiting for a sign—or better yet a frantic 911 call on the girl's cell—that signaled a need for me to intercede, but after a few more minutes of talking at the girl, Senenmut frowned and walked back over to where I had nonchalantly hidden behind a glass case of revolving soft pretzels.

"What's wrong?"

Senenmut merely shook his head, unable to speak.

"What happened?" I pestered him.

Senenmut shook his head again, and as I watched, one single, solitary tear slipped down his cheek.

"She doesn't know me," came the dejected answer.

And then the big strong man standing before me began to cry.

twenty

As the tears began to trickle down his cheeks, I found myself pulling him toward me into a giant bear hug. Even though I now felt more like his mother than a single female in close proximity to a hunka, hunka burning manhood, I had to admit that it was really nice to have a firm pair of man-arms wrapped around me. Needless to say, it had been a while since I'd had any kind of physical contact with someone I wasn't related to.

"Hey, don't cry," I said, patting his back in the best approximation of parental support that I could muster. It felt awkward and uncomfortable, but it seemed to make Senenmut less miserable, so I just kept patting.

Now, I had *never* been one of those girls who adored babies and small children. I *liked* them—don't get me wrong—but was I interested in getting drool and baby food all over myself just for, like, *fun*?

Nope.

I'd never done any babysitting, never been a camp counselor or even a card-carrying member of Big Brothers Big Sisters of America. I didn't plan elaborate baby showers for my pregnant friends, nor had I *ever* gone specifically to visit a friend because she'd just—*ouch*—given birth to a newborn.

I was one of the large but mostly silent group of women out there who just didn't get the whole "baby" thing. I understood that having children fulfilled some kind of biological imperative, but that still didn't mean I *had* to listen to my biological clock. I didn't want to deal with motherhood until it was (1) thrust upon me, and (2) someone had found a way to put a stop to all that pesky weight gain that went along with it.

Yes, I was being shallow, but it was my body, so bug off.

Besides, I had, like, a zillion years in which to change my mind. Unlike pretty much 95 percent of other women on the planet, I was immortal. I could take my time making important decisions like whether or not to pop out a screaming bundle of joy that I would have to be responsible for until the end of time.

Speaking of immortality, I suppose since we're already on the topic, now would be as good a time as any to explain how it works. You see, there are two ways to live forever. The first—and best—is to be born that way. You lead a pretty normal existence for your first eighteen or so years, but then at the point when a normal person's body stops growing and starts dying, an immortal's body diverges from the pattern and just kind of goes into a state of suspended animation—your cells don't die; your body doesn't age . . . You basically stay exactly the same forever and ever.

Now, the second—and not as good—way to get on the immortality gravy train is to be *granted* immortality by some supernatural entity. That's the path that both of my parents took. When you're *made* immortal, the same suspended animation thing happens to your body, but you stay whatever age you were when you were granted immortality. So, instead of looking all young and beautiful forever, you *might* look like an old, wrinkly grandma—if that's what you were when you got your "gift."

Craziness, huh?

"What can I do to help you?" I asked Senenmut as I ceased my incessant patting and took a step away from him. I was hoping that he'd say, "Just take me down to Hell and hand me over to your buddy Cerberus and be done with it," but of course, *that* didn't happen.

"I want to go back to Egypt," he said in between sniffles.

"Yeah," I said. "I can see why that would sound like a good idea to you, but trust me when I say it's not the same place you knew anymore."

Until that moment there'd been only a few weird looks from our fellow shoppers as Senenmut blubbered against my shoulder, but now a security guard I hadn't noticed before was slowly sneaking toward the little deli/restaurant area where we were standing, a crackling walkie-talkie in his hand.

Finally, it seemed we had started to wear out our Target welcome.

"I think we should talk about this outside," I said, taking his hand and leading him toward the exit—with a quick pause so that Senenmut could watch the automatic doors open and close twice before we went outside.

Once we were standing out in front of the store, I thought we were home free, but before I could explain to Senenmut *why* the Egypt of today was so very different from the Egypt that he had known, the dumb girl who was the reincarnation of his lost love pushed her stupid cart through the automatic doors.

Senenmut's head instantly went up, and suddenly, like an overexcited dog, he was dragging me over to the girl. She saw us coming and began to pick up speed. I think she was trying to outrun us, but there was no hope of that happening now that Senenmut had regained most of his old agility and speed.

"Senenmut, stop!" I commanded as I was pulled bodily forward, my feet barely touching the ground as he gave chase to the frightened shopping cart–wielding girl.

I realized that it didn't matter what I said because he was hell-bent on catching her. The best I could do, given the situation, was to try to ease the awkwardness of the whole thing once he caught her—so I was totally unprepared for what happened next.

"Eat shit and die!" the girl screamed as she let go of her

cart and held up her key chain, spraying Senenmut right in the eyes with a liberal dose of pepper spray. The Egyptian let go of my hand and began clawing at his eyes, tears of anger and pain running down his face.

"Hey, why'd you do *that*?" I screamed at the girl as she chased after her cart.

"You want some of this, bitch!" she called back at me as her hands grasped the cart's handle and she started to roll her groceries toward a green Honda Element parked about three cars away.

"He just wanted to ask you a few questions," I yelled, keeping my distance because I so did *not* want to get splashed with any pepper spray.

"Questions, my ass!" she yelled back at me. "If you don't back off, I'm calling the police!"

She held up her cute pink RAZR phone like a weapon as she fumbled with the lock on the driver's-side door.

"It's just that you really look like someone he used to know," I said, trying a different tack, but the girl was having none of it as she threw open the car door and began shoveling her groceries inside.

"Yeah, a dead Queen," the girl said angrily, "*from ancient Egypt.* Now, why don't you two just go back to whatever mental institution you escaped from and leave me alone!"

Well, I couldn't argue with her. Madame Papillon had told me that it was rare for a soul to remember its past lives, so if this girl didn't know that once upon a time she was an ancient Egyptian Queen, then there was nothing Senenmut or I could do about it.

"Okay, you win," I said. "We'll get out of your hair."

I turned around, not bothering to listen to her obscenity-laden response.

I found Senenmut lying in the fetal position right in the middle of the parking lot, his arms wrapped around his legs as if he had returned to the womb. I squatted down beside him.

"You all right?" I asked, reaching out to stroke the small of his back with my hand.

I ignored the fearful looks we were getting from shoppers as they wheeled their carts around us to get to their cars and focused my attention on getting Senenmut out of the parking lot before the police arrived. I had absolutely *no* doubt that they were already on their way because out of the corner of my eye, I had spotted three Target security guards moving stealthily toward us.

"My eyes burn like they are on fire," Senenmut moaned as he rubbed at them—probably making himself worse in the process.

"Well, don't rub 'em anymore," I said helpfully. "It's just pepper spray. You'll be fine . . . I think."

I looked over at the entrance to the Target and saw that the guards had gained ground on us. If we didn't get our butts in gear soon, we were gonna be singing for our supper in jail—and how much fun would *that* be, explaining to the Las Vegas PD that they wouldn't find my new Egyptian friend in their database because he'd been cooped up in a medieval torture chamber for the last couple thousand years.

"Okay, I know your eyes hurt, but we have to get out of here," I said, trying to be as calm and soothing as possible.

"I don't want to go," he whined. "My eyes hurt."

"Well, guess what? I don't care *what* you want," I sniped back at him. "You're just gonna have to trust me on this one."

I grasped him around the middle and tried to lift him onto his feet, but he was *way* heavier than I had anticipated.

"Get up!" I hissed in his ear. He wrapped his arms around my middle and together we got him back on his feet. He leaned his head—and most of his weight—against me, causing me to almost lose my footing.

"Stop it," I said as I braced myself against a nearby car. "I can't do this if you're gonna be a baby about it."

Being called a baby seemed to be the kick in the pants that Senenmut needed. He stood up straighter, relieving me of the weight that had been so incapacitating.

"Now, just follow where I lead," I said, holding on to his

arm as I began to snake through the aisles of parked cars, trying to keep the Target security brigade at bay.

"Ow!" Senenmut said as his knee slammed into the bumper of a Buick Skylark because of my poor maneuvering skills.

"Sorry," I murmured as I wiped away the thick bead of sweat that had accumulated on my upper lip. I looked up at the brilliant blue sky and cursed the disgustingly hot weather.

Damn desert climes, I thought angrily. *It's, like, bloody sweat city around here! If only we could have a torrential rainstorm and swim our way out of this mess.*

As soon as that thought crossed my mind, I realized it for the epiphany that it was. Immediately I began to wish for a bunch of nasty thunderheads to roll in and cause a flash flood that would wash away our quickly gaining pursuers and float us to safety.

"C'mon," I begged the sky, "help me out here. Can't we have, like, *one* cumulonimbus cloud? Please?"

I got nothing from the heavens, not even a gust of wind. The sound of Senenmut's ragged breathing filled my ear as I mercilessly pushed him farther and farther into the maze of cars. The closer we got to the heart of the parking lot, the more frustrated by the situation I became. Finally, I'd had enough. I was tired of things *just happening* to me. For once in my life *I* was gonna make something happen for myself.

"Give me a goddamned thunderstorm!" I screamed up at the sky with every ounce of energy I possessed in my body. Senenmut realized what I was doing and grabbed my hand, squeezing it hard as he funneled his own magical power into my effort.

Instantly, the air was rent by a jagged flash of lightning that split the sky; the rumble of approaching thunder filled my ears.

"Yes!" I screamed, giddy with my own power—and sent a silent thank-you heavenward.

The first splash of rain hit my cheek, the coolness of it shocking on my hot skin. A few more drops closely followed and then, like a gift from God, the heavens opened up, spilling their bounty onto the sizzling asphalt.

It was a deluge, collecting dirt and garbage in its slipstream as it pounded the earth. People around us shrieked and ran for cover inside cars and underneath the wide front lip of the Target store. A few daring souls braved the downpour, holding purses and newspapers over their heads as they ran through the parking lot.

Senenmut released my hand and stopped beside an SUV. He leaned backward against the car, raising his ruined face to the sky. I had a feeling that water was probably the best thing we could've asked for to dilute the effects of the pepper spray. I looked back to see what our stalkers—the security guards—were up to, only to find that they had turned back in the face of the unexpected storm. All I could see of them as they ran higgledy-piggledy toward the safety of the building were their sopping, blue security–uniformed butts.

"Let's get out of here," I said after a few moments, my pink sweater waterlogged and my boots as heavy as snowshoes. I felt like a drowned rat and I was pretty sure that I looked like one, too. I hefted my soaking leather purse over my shoulder and took Senenmut's arm.

"I think we are in desperate need of a ride."

Ignoring the rain, I took out my phone and dialed the only number I knew by heart.

"Hi, Information? I need the number for a local cab company. I don't care which one . . . Fine, why don't you just give me *all* of them?"

As I dialed the first number that Information gave me, I took out my trusty rubidium clock from where I'd stashed it in my back pocket.

"How much time?" I whispered.

Nine hours.

More than enough time to have a bath before we went to Hell.

Senenmut *said* he wanted to go back to Egypt. But since that wasn't really an option, I did the next best thing.

I booked us a room at the Luxor Hotel.

With the need for a shower and something to eat ingrained in my brain, I couldn't help myself. I mean, how often does a person get to stay in a fake Egyptian pyramid with one of the guys who probably helped invent the architectural style in the first place?

When the taxi pulled up to the front of the hotel, I could barely keep Senenmut in the car. His face was still a red, puffy mess, but the water and time had helped wash away most of the pepper spray's effects so that he could at least see again.

With its clean steel and glass lines, the hotel may have resembled a deconstructionist's vision of what an ancient Egyptian pyramid looked like, but that didn't seem to faze Senenmut at all. As soon as the doorman (a handsome young guy in a well-fitting beige costume) opened the car door for us, Senenmut was out like a shot. He bounded past the doorman—nearly knocking the poor guy over in the process—and made a beeline for the automatic front doors.

"Wait for me," I said as I paid the driver and tipped the doorman so he wouldn't sue us.

Boy, this guy is expensive, I thought as I looked down at the fast-dwindling wad of twenties I'd pulled out of a 7-Eleven ATM only a few minutes earlier. The taxi driver hadn't *wanted* to make a pit stop at the 7-Eleven, but when I told him it was the only way he was gonna get paid for services rendered, he quickly obliged me.

I caught sight of Senenmut blocking one of the automatic doors as he stepped in and out of range of the door's sensor. Lucky me that my new best friend was so obsessed with modern conveniences—or else I'd have probably lost him to the call of the casino already. I hastily made my way down the graded entranceway, bypassing a horde of German tourists who were watching Senenmut's battle of the automatic doors with unabashed curiosity, and took my friend by the arm.

"Enough playing with the door. Let's go inside."

He didn't seem to like the sound of my plan very much, but he reluctantly let me lead him away, looking back only *once* with longing as the automatic doors closed behind us. Inside the casino, we were immediately greeted by a blast of cold air that made me shiver. I had forgotten from my one and only trip to Las Vegas that the casinos were notorious for freezing your ass off 24/7, so you wouldn't get sleepy while you were throwing all your money at the craps table like an automaton—something I'd had some personal experience with and didn't like to discuss (a bachelorette party in Atlantic City gone wrong) because it made my pocketbook hurt just thinking about it.

The hotel was dressed in varying shades of gold, beige, and brown—all of which I decided were on the tasteful side of the color spectrum. In fact, I would've said that the place was well-appointed and imposing if it weren't for the fake Egyptian statuary and hieroglyphic-inspired scenes painted all along the walls and the fake mud brick and palm tree motif (not my favorite) that overwhelmed most of the interior design, making the place look vaguely cheesy in a way that was particular to Las Vegas.

"What is this place?" Senenmut said as we left the confines of the lobby and headed toward the front desk.

My plan *was* to grab our key, head to the shopping area, buy some dry clothes, take a shower, order room service, and, while we ate, call Jarvis to come and pick us up via wormhole. I thought it was a pretty great plan and I was more than ready to put it into action.

"It's called a casino," I said, stepping in line behind a tall man with long, wavy gray hair and glasses.

He gave us a cursory look then made one of those haughty sniffing sounds. Before I could give him a nasty look in reply, he was called up to the front desk and I was left fuming quietly to myself.

Senenmut, on the other hand, didn't seem at all fazed by the man's bad attitude. Instead, he was too busy goggling at the wide-open expanse of gaming tables and slot machines to care what anyone thought about us.

"This is unlike any pyramid that I have ever seen," Senenmut said in hushed tones. "Where is the burial chamber?"

When Senenmut said the words "burial chamber," I didn't think for a minute that my Egyptian friend was referring to the basement vault where the casino kept all their cash. No, he was talking about a real-deal burial chamber where the real pyramids kept their mummies and funerary finery.

"Uhm, *this* isn't a real pyramid," I said, trying to explain.

The old guy who'd sniffed at us earlier had gotten into some kind of argument with the lady behind the front desk, and it did not seem to be coming to a quick resolution. I was pretty sure we were gonna be standing in line for a while, so I decided to elaborate.

"You see," I began, "Las Vegas is a city unlike pretty much any other city in all of America—not including Atlantic City, New Jersey, of course. It's actually called Sin City by those in the know because it was built on a love of gambling and sex and really tacky clothing."

"I don't understand," Senenmut said, frowning.

"Okay, let me try this a different way."

"Please do," Senenmut said as the line behind us only seemed to grow.

"Well, this place we're in is called the Luxor—"

"We are in Egypt?" Senenmut said, surprised.

I shook my head.

"No, we are in a building *called* the Luxor, but it's nowhere near Egypt. It's actually in America and it was built to *resemble* an Egyptian pyramid on the outside, but on the inside, it's used for something totally different."

"Then there are no Kings buried here?" Senenmut asked suspiciously.

"Nope," I said. "Not a one."

Senenmut narrowed his eyes.

"Then what is that?"

He was pointing to a sign hanging from the ceiling. It read KING TUT MUSEUM and had an arrow pointing directly ahead.

"Uhm, well, *that* is—"

"You have lied to me, Calliope Reaper-Jones," Senenmut said evenly, the complete austerity of his words at odds with his puffy red face. "And for that, we are no longer compatriots."

"Hey, that's not true—" I started to say, but Senenmut wasn't listening to me anymore. His focus was now on the sign and wherever it would lead him.

"Until we meet again under better auspices," Senenmut said, then turned around and walked away, leaving me standing in the line at the front desk of the Luxor Hotel all by myself.

twenty-one

Just as Senenmut made his untimely exit, two hotel security guards—how many damn security guards was I gonna have to deal with in one day?—came striding toward me. Panicked, I left my place in line and started fast-walking in the same direction I'd just seen Senenmut take. As I made my way into the casino proper, I looked back to see what kind of lead I had on the security guys, but to my surprise, I found that they weren't anywhere in my vicinity. In fact, *I* wasn't the person they'd been gunning for at all. It was the snooty older man with the wavy gray hair that they'd been after.

I watched, feeling vindicated, as the older man was led away, his mouth set in an angry *O*, both hands held behind his back by the two security guards.

Yes! Finally, the real jerk gets in trouble, I thought happily as the old man and his entourage disappeared into the crowd, his indignant protests swallowed up by the madcap chiming of slot machines paying out their winnings.

Safe now, I looked around the casino for another sign that would direct me to the King Tut Museum. I spotted one across the floor, the museum's name printed in big, bold letters with the universal sign for "elevator" (the little square box) beside it. I made my way back across the sea of gamblers—old blue-haired dowagers; middle-aged, potbellied married couples; and clumps of tackily dressed twentysomethings looking for a little action to get them through the night—and wasn't even tempted *once* to stop and put a quarter in a slot.

I got to the elevator (or *inclinator*, as they called it at the Luxor, built on an incline to match the angled interior walls of the pyramid) right when a family with three little angelic-faced kids walked up. The littlest kid, a boy of about three with white-blond hair, a booger-infested nose, and the remains of a chocolate candy bar on his face, reached out his grubby hand and pressed the call button, smearing chocolate all over it.

"Sorry about that," the father said, looking sheepishly down at his child and ruffling his hair.

He was so laissez-faire about his kid sliming the elevator control button that there was no way he could be one of those anal, yuppie dads that planned out their family's vacations down to the last potty break. This guy seemed more like the cool dad. You know, the one who smoked pot with you and told you stories about the girls he banged when he was a teenager.

"No problem," I replied with a smile.

It wasn't my elevator. Besides, while his kids *may* have been messy, they were obviously well loved.

While we stood there waiting for our inclinator, the same little boy dropped to his knees, crawled over to where I was standing, and poked my boot.

"King Poot," he said as he poked the tip of my shoe again, getting chocolate on it.

"Ansel!" the father said, bending down and scooping the small child up in his arms.

No wonder the kid has issues, I thought. *With a name like Ansel, who wouldn't?*

"He's usually not so forward," the mother said, taking the other boys by the hands—both were older than Ansel, but with the same white-blond hair—and reining them in close to her sides. "I think he likes you."

The woman was slim, with feathery blond hair, blue eyes, and a warm smile that was genuinely welcoming. She had a nice figure—especially for someone who'd popped out three kids—but she wasn't what you would call a beautiful woman. There was a sharpness to her chin and nose that kept her from being truly striking.

We aren't really that different, I thought to myself as I watched the woman struggling to keep the two older boys from slipping out of her grasp. *This could be my fate, too, someday . . . if I want it to be.*

"C'mon, Walker, stop pulling on Mommy's shirt," the woman said, taking her kids' exuberance good-naturedly. Still, *I* could tell—call it women's intuition here—that all she wanted to do was find a black hole to drop her family into for a couple of hours, so she could hit the spa without feeling guilty about it.

Not that I blamed her. She looked like she very much deserved a couple of undisturbed hours roasting in a seaweed and black mud wrap.

The inclinator doors opened and the evacuating tourists swarmed us like a horde of agitated, foreign-tongued wasps. The tourists, while loud and obnoxious, were very slow moving, taking so much time to disembark that the family and I almost didn't make it inside before the doors closed in our faces.

"Well, that was intense," I said as I moved to press the button that would take me to the atrium.

I paused, my finger hovering over the button, when I caught sight of my little buddy, Ansel, staring at me with a look of utter defeat on his cherubic face. I realized that *he* wanted to press the button, but since he was trapped in his father's arms, he was stuck. I knew that I didn't owe the kid a thing—he'd slimed my boot, for God's sake—that all I had to do to get to the King Tut Museum and find Senenmut was to just finish my action and press the button.

I looked over at Ansel, his sad puppy dog eyes piercing my very soul.

I couldn't do it. I couldn't press the button.

I dropped my hand and cocked my head in Ansel's direction.

"You wanna press the button?" I asked brightly.

The little kid stuck his fingers coyly in his mouth and nodded.

"Hey, Ans, wow," the dad said, squeezing the little boy. "What do you say to the nice lady?"

Ansel dipped his head into the crook of his dad's arm, hiding his face.

"Phank ewe," came the muffled reply.

"Press the one that says 'twenty-seven,'" his dad said, leaning forward so that Ansel could reach the buttons.

"Then press the one that says 'Atrium,'" I added quickly because I had *no* intention of going up to the top of the hotel with them.

Ansel gave me a shy smile before turning his attention back to the numbered buttons. I watched, fascinated, as the kid stared down at the heavy brass panel, weighing his options with such intensity that I wondered if he was actually deciding whether to bomb Russia or not.

Then, to my utter horror, the kid did the unexpected.

He slammed both hands across the panel, hitting as many buttons as possible in one whack. The inclinator made a funny clicking noise, then took off. I stared, in shock, at the one button Ansel *hadn't* pressed: the atrium-level button. Too late, I smacked the brass button just as we sailed past it.

"Crap!" I said, glaring at the demon child, who was wearing the biggest, teeth-baring smile I'd ever seen. Senenmut probably would've called him "crocodile boy" in honor of Wayne Newton.

"I'm so sorry," the dad said as the inclinator came to a stop and the doors opened. "I don't know what he was thinking."

I was speechless. If my count was correct, I had, like, a zillion floors to go before I even *started* to descend again.

"Hey, it happens," I said through gritted teeth as I clutched my hands into fists, hoping that the pain of nails against fleshy palm would ease my agitation.

Totally didn't work.

The inclinator doors opened on the third floor, then shut again when no one got on. As we started for the next floor, I fumed while Ansel just enjoyed the ride.

This went on for, like, *twenty* more floors. I knew I could've just gotten out and hoofed it on the stairs or waited for another inclinator—which could've taken even longer—but I was determined not to let the little snot muffin know he had gotten my goat.

I have to say that it was to my credit that I didn't reach out and flog the poor kid each time the elevator doors opened and closed. I had obviously decided to take the high road, so I was determined to close my eyes and "enjoy" the ride as much as my three-year-old counterpart.

I could feel five sets of eyes watching my reflection in the mirrored inclinator walls as we ascended ever higher, but I ignored them. I wasn't going to engage; I was just going to mind my own business and hope that they got off the inclinator sooner rather than later. Finally, after an eternity, we reached the twenty-seventh floor and the family quietly shuffled out.

As the doors began to close on my toddler-sized nemesis and his family, Ansel and I locked eyes. I knew that we were both thinking the exact same thing: It had been a battle of wills . . . and *I* had been bested by a baby in Pull-Ups.

"Bye-bye!" Ansel said loudly, his chubby, chocolate—God, I *hoped* it was chocolate—stained hand waving up and down at me with limp-wristed abandon.

The doors eased shut with a quiet *whoosh* very much like what I suspected the first shovelful of dirt being thrown onto your coffin might sound like. I felt a shiver run up my spine at the thought. It was weird, but no matter what I did, I just couldn't shake the feeling that something not so nice was about to happen.

Alone in the inclinator now, I leaned back against the mirrored wall and closed my eyes. I realized I had absolutely no idea what to do when I actually found Senenmut. Hopefully, he would still be at the King Tut Museum when I got there, but after that I had zero ideas about what should happen next—other than that eventually I was gonna have to get on a stick and take Senenmut down to Hell.

I supposed I could just call Jarvis and get him to meet me at the King Tut Museum. Together, we could probably trick Senenmut into entering a wormhole that would take him down to Cerberus, but then, if I did that, I was gonna have to deal with Bast, the Queen of the Cats, all by myself. She would keep Daniel, and I would be forced to fight her for him—and that was somehow *not* a task I thought I was up for at the moment.

I *needed* Senenmut's help, and for that, I was gonna have to help him first.

the inclinator ride *down* went a lot more quickly than the ride up, the doors remaining firmly shut as we bypassed floor after floor until we hit the atrium level and the inclinator eased to a gentle stop. The doors slid open and I stepped out onto the carpet, the sounds from the casino a floor below like a ghostly echo all around me.

I followed the signs that led to the museum, pausing at a nearby ticket booth to pay my nine-dollar-and-ninety-nine-cent entrance fee. I scanned the surrounding crowd before I went in, hoping to spot Senenmut, but he was nowhere to be seen. That meant that he was either inside the museum or he was long gone, never to be found again. I didn't know why, but had I been a gambling woman—which I wasn't anymore—I would've put my money on finding Senenmut in that museum.

Either way, it looked like my only option was to go inside and see what I could see, so I pushed my way past the throng of people at the front who were waiting for the self-guided tour headsets and slipped inside.

I bypassed a video presentation on King Tut's tomb and its discovery by archeologist Howard Carter—not something I would've sat through even if I hadn't been under the gun. The next part of the museum was divided into rooms that were exact re-creations of the actual tomb located in the Valley of the Kings in Egypt. There was a room just for King Tut's golden sarcophagus, funerary jars packed with the guy's internal organs, and assorted amphora full of rotten food and drink. The other rooms held golden statues, jewelry, pottery, and baskets: all the goodies a pharaoh needed when his soul transmigrated into the Afterlife. All in all, it wasn't a bad little setup, if you ignored the hordes of tourists and the copious amounts of track lighting overwhelming the place—neither of which one expected to see in the great Tutankhamen's *real* burial chamber.

Being a weekend, the place was pretty packed, but the stupid self-guided tour headsets only made the gridlock worse. For some reason, the moment a human being puts on a headset, it's like they're transported into another world. In this other world, they are given license to just stop randomly wherever they are and stand there, blocking traffic, so they can read a little tiny sign next to an exhibit and hear the tour commentary at the same time. I was already flustered, worried that I had major-league screwed up with Cerberus, and now I had some dumb pedestrian planted in front of me like a grazing cow. It was ridiculous.

"Excuse me," I said, elbowing my way past the guy, but stopping short when I realized I had reached the end of the museum and I hadn't seen hide nor hair of Senenmut.

"Damn it," I said under my breath, engendering a nasty look from the two older women standing beside me. I didn't know how they heard me curse with their stupid headsets on, but I gave them an apologetic smile.

"Don't you wish it was a little bigger?" I said thoughtfully, but they ignored me. Sometimes, I think people only hear what they want to hear.

By now, I had started to give up any hope of finding Senenmut in the museum. He obviously would've realized immediately that the place wasn't a real tomb, just a tourist trap installed in a hotel to make some extra cash.

"Look, Denise! Look at that man!"

The alert had come from one of the old ladies beside me

who'd given me a nasty look. The woman's voice was so insistent and shrill that I turned around to see what had set her off. To my surprise, I discovered that she was pointing into the next room, where a man was crouched beside King Tut's golden sarcophagus, trying to jimmy the lid off.

And that man was Senenmut.

I pushed past the two old ladies and made a run for the sarcophagus. I got there just as Senenmut picked up a nearby statue and slammed it into the heavy sarcophagus lid with a resounding *thunk* that made everyone in the place look in our direction.

"What're you doing?" I hissed at him, grabbing his arm and trying to drag him away.

"I am going home," he said, pulling away from me.

"Going home?"

I had no idea what he was talking about.

"I have made an offering to Amun-Ra."

I hated how the man would just not explain a goddamned *thing*. He made an offering to Amun-Ra—whoopee for him, but what did that *really* mean? The last time we'd done the whole "offering" thing, we'd ended up traipsing through about a zillion random Target stores and *still* coming out of the experience empty-handed.

"Look, I know it was a low blow, your lady friend not recognizing you, but I think if we just go back to Sea Verge and *talk* about this—" I began, but Senenmut shook his head.

"No, the time for talk is through."

I didn't know what to do. Everyone in the place was staring at us, I'm sure someone had already called security, and if we didn't get our exit strategy planned, like, *right now*, we were gonna be totally screwed.

"Okay, fine. We won't talk anymore," I said, "but let's just go before security gets here. I don't think my heart can take another police chase scenario."

I really thought my last words had gotten through to the Egyptian because I could feel the muscles in his arms relax, but before I could congratulate myself on a job well-done, Senenmut let out a loud yowl and ripped himself out of my grasp, slamming himself bodily into the sarcophagus. The thing toppled forward with enough velocity to hit the wall and break some of the surrounding statuary. This caused some random screaming, followed by the mass exodus of all the tourists. Within seconds, we were the only ones left in the room.

I wonder what the self-guided tour headsets had to say about all that, I thought wickedly as I picked up a broken piece of pottery and examined it curiously.

"We're screwed, you know," I said to Senenmut, who was still busy trying to get the lid off the stupid sarcophagus.

The giant thing had landed on its side, but the lid had remained firmly in place. I didn't have the heart to tell Senenmut that no matter what he did, the lid probably wasn't going to come off. I mean, there couldn't be anything inside it—it was just for show—so why would they need it to open, right?

He ignored my negative comment and picked up what looked like an effigy of one of the Jackal Brothers. He measured the weight of the thing in his hands, then grabbed it by its jackal head and began to hammer away at the lid with it.

Now I knew for sure that security *had* to be on their way. You didn't just destroy casino property, cause a stampede, and hang around afterward to break more stuff without *someone* coming after you. There wasn't an exit strategy in the world that could get us out of the mess we were in. Resigned to spending the night in jail—which would seal my fate as the next Guardian of the North Gate of Hell *and* make me lose Daniel and Runt at the same time—I sat back on my butt and waited for whatever was gonna happen to happen.

The whole thing was my own fault. I'd caused everything to get all screwed up and now there was no one to blame but myself. Who was the idiot who had made the deal with Cerberus in the first place? Me. Who was the nincompoop who tried to help Daniel, only to have his Shade stolen by the Queen of the Cats? Me. Who was the dumbo who'd taken pity on Senenmut and gone to Las Vegas only to find that the guy's lost love didn't even remember him anymore? Yours truly. That's who.

I began to feel the stirrings of a pity party coming on—and from what I could tell, it was gonna be a big one, a frickin' *block* party–sized one. Rage at my own stupidity overwhelmed me, and before I even realized what I was doing, I had picked up a piece of broken pottery and was throwing it as hard as I could at Senenmut's head. He must've sensed the pot coming because he dodged my throw, letting the potshard explode into a million pieces as it hit the sarcophagus.

That was when I heard a *pop* . . . and then the lid to the damn thing fell off.

twenty-two

There was a blinding flash of light as the lid hit the ground. I covered my eyes with my hands, trying to block out the brightness, but the aftereffect lingered behind my eyelids. There was a rush of dry, hot wind that ruffled my hair and made my body start to sweat. This was followed by a barrage of small, sharp particles that stung every available piece of flesh on my person. The stinging lasted only a few minutes, but I felt as if my skin had been sandpapered off when it was over.

The wind began to die down, blowing with less intensity now that the stinging particles had ceased attacking me. Still worried that the wind might pick up again at any moment, but curious to see where the hell I was, I cracked open one eyelid. Nothing happened, so I opened the other eye, too. To my surprise, I found myself sitting in the middle of a desert, my body draped in the finest of white linens, leather thong sandals on my feet. I looked down at my arms, terrified that I would find the topmost layer of skin stripped away, but happily my skin was all in one unscathed piece.

"Welcome to Egypt."

A long shadow cut across the sand and I looked up to find Senenmut standing above me, clad in the same white linen getup

I was wearing—but this Senenmut was another man completely. He was so tan that his skin was the color of toasted almonds, and dark hair coiled thick and luxurious to his shoulders. The biggest change was how relaxed and rested he looked.

"This isn't Egypt now, in my time, is it?" I asked as I stood up and brushed the sand off my butt. I noticed that the piece of linen I was wearing was cut *exactly* like one of my all-time favorite dresses: a silk Givenchy sheath that my mother had given me for my seventeenth birthday. I'd loved that dress so much I'd worn it until it disintegrated. Needless to say, I was superexcited to find myself wearing an ancient re-creation of it.

"And by the way, who makes these things?" I continued, indicating my new favorite dress.

Senenmut stared at me, then shrugged. I guess it was an ancient Egyptian fashion faux pas to ask who had designed one's dress. I could just imagine Joan Rivers asking Cleopatra what designer she was wearing and getting an asp in her face for her trouble.

"Forget it," I said. It wasn't like I was gonna be here long enough to track the seamstress down anyway.

"I asked Amun-Ra to return me to the day that I died," Senenmut said evenly. "We are in the Valley of the Kings."

"Are you *crazy*?" I yelled at him, then quickly lowered my voice. "Why would you do that?"

We may have *looked* alone out here in the desert, but I didn't believe for one second that we really were. Maybe it was because the Valley of the Kings had all those mummified bodies hidden in tombs beneath its sands—or maybe it was just me being paranoid, but I got the distinct feeling that someone, somewhere, was watching our every move with great intent.

I scanned the hills around us, noting that we weren't just surrounded by sand. Here and there were eroded outcroppings of man-made brick—each one probably marked the entrance-way to a sacred King or Queen's burial place.

Creepy!

"I will find Hatshepsut and tell her of my journey. I will explain everything, and my ending will not be repeated," Senenmut said, his words precise as bullets.

Wait just one little minute there, buddy! I thought angrily. *Something smells pretty damn fishy in the State of Denmark and I think it's you!*

I realized for the first time that I had just been taking what Senenmut told me at face value. I had just assumed that he wanted to see his lost love because he missed her and loved her, but now, from the rigid set of his jawline, I understood that what he had led me to believe might not be the *exact* truth.

This man was on a mission, but not what I would call a *love mission* by any stretch of the imagination.

"Hold it right there," I said as Senenmut began to trudge through the sand toward one of the outcroppings of brick. He stopped, his shoulders taut as a rubber band someone was just about to flick. He sighed and turned back around to face me.

"You're a liar," I said plainly, since there was no use beating around the bush. "You conned me, under false pretences, into letting you drag us all over Hell and high water looking for some woman who—for all I know—you might've made up to manipulate me into doing your bidding in the first place!"

"Calliope—" Senenmut tried to interject, but I poked him in the chest with my finger.

"You used my problems in the romance department to sucker me into buying something completely different than what I thought you were selling!"

Ashamed, Senenmut hung his head. He didn't argue with me or tell me that I was totally off base with my assumptions. All he said was:

"She does exist."

No offer of explanation, no begging for my forgiveness, just a three-word sentence that didn't even go *halfway* toward an apology—which was exactly what I thought my little Egyptian friend totally owed me.

"Go on," I said, glaring at him.

He sighed again and I could see that he was mulling over in his brain how much he *really* needed to reveal to me.

"All of it!" I yelled, not caring who was listening—dead people be damned!

"As you wish," Senenmut said resignedly.

"Damn straight I wish it," I hissed at him.

"It is a long story and we do not have much time, so I will try to be precise," Senenmut said.

I wanted to interrupt him with another snarky comment, but I decided that the best thing I could do given the situation was to just keep my mouth shut.

"You see," Senenmut continued, "I fell out of favor with my one true love, the Queen Hatshepsut, and she condemned me to death. She was a wildly jealous woman, and I can imagine some members of her retinue whispering my imagined misdeeds into her ear to gain her favor."

"So, you were a good boy and kept it in your pants, then?" I asked, expecting him to get all defensive on me.

"Why would I need another woman when she fulfilled every part of me?" he replied in all seriousness. "She was my best friend and my partner in both the literal and physical sense."

I nodded. Obviously, this woman had it going on if she could keep a man like Senenmut madly in love with her for thousands of years.

"As the living consort of the all-powerful creator, Amun-Ra," Senenmut continued, "Hatshepsut had ultimate power. With her hatred for me overflowing, she ordered me to be mummified while I was still alive and placed in the tomb of her beloved daughter, Neferura, for all eternity. This is how I know that she had not fully forsaken our love. Otherwise, she would not have placed me so close to the one she loved best, so that we all might meet again in the Afterlife."

"Oh," I said, not really sure what to make of Senenmut's story. I didn't think a girl who was still in love with a guy would have him mummified alive like that. Maybe castrated if she thought she was being cuckolded, but the murdering part didn't sit quite right with me.

"There is more," he continued, his eyes wide with remembered pain. "When my earthly body finally succumbed to starvation, I was greeted by Anubis and his twin, Bata—"

"I've always just called them the Jackal Brothers," I interrupted. "I didn't know they had different names."

"They are so alike that there is none who can tell them apart," Senenmut said. "But while they both represent Death, each one embodies a different aspect: Anubis sits in judgment, while Bata enforces that judgment."

"Okay," I said, shaking my head. "So, what happened when Anubis and his brother came to get you after you died?"

"The brothers told me that I had not respected Hatshepsut, Amun-Ra's earthly consort, and for that they would punish me themselves. They refused to judge my heart and discover its worthiness. They knew if they did, they would be forced to let me pass into the Afterlife because all I had in my heart was my love for Hatshepsut. And that would be my redemption."

"I knew those guys were just two jerkoids," I said angrily.

Senenmut smiled wearily at me.

"But then you came to rescue me, and for that I thank the Gods," he said. "Now I am free to find Hatshepsut, discover what I did to displease her, and save my past self from the horrible fate he will be forced to endure upon this day."

"Look, I would love to help you out, Senenmut," I said, "but I don't think we really have time for this. If I had known that you were doing all this under false pretenses . . ."

I trailed off. It didn't matter what I *would* or *wouldn't* have done anymore—all of that was in the past now. And you can't change the past, no matter how hard you try. That was what Senenmut didn't understand. *This* was our future—albeit in the guise of the past—and all we could do was make smarter decisions from here on out.

I found the rubidium clock in a small pocket at the side of my sheath dress. Since it was a magical device, I wasn't surprised to see that it had followed me through time.

"This clock tells me how long I have before I have to get you to Cerberus," I said. "If I don't get you there before it runs out, we will be in serious three-headed doggie doo-doo."

Senenmut watched as I held up the clock and whispered to it:

"How much time is left?"

The numbers came to a stop and the tiny screen went black.

"That's weird," I said, shaking it. "Must've gotten messed up when we went back in time."

Suddenly, a string of numbers flashed in front of me. I still had over six hours until Senenmut was due in Hell.

"What does it say?" Senenmut asked.

I looked up and smiled at him. I didn't have the heart to begrudge him a few more hours in Egypt. Besides, what harm could it do? If things started to get out of hand, I'd just grab Senenmut and tell the little clock to take us to Cerberus.

"We have time," I said. "So if you want to look for Hatshepsut for a few hours, I'm okay with it."

Like I said, it was gonna be all about the decisions we made from here on in. Senenmut let out a whoop and grabbed me in a hug, swinging me around like a rag doll.

"I could kiss you," Senenmut said, grinning like an idiot as he set me down, making me blush.

"Why don't you save it for your lady love?" I replied, but his positive attitude was rubbing off on me.

"All right, just plant one right here," I said, indicating my cheek. As Senenmut leaned forward to give my cheek a thank-you kiss, I saw a flash of white streak across the sand a few hundred feet away from us.

"Wait a minute," I said, stopping Senenmut. "I just saw something over by those bricks."

Instantly, Senenmut was on the alert. His swiveled his head around to see what I was pointing to, but there was nothing there.

"Are you sure you saw something?" he asked me. "Maybe you only imagined—"

He was interrupted by the whoosh of an arrow as it sliced the air between us, embedding itself in the sand at my feet.

"Damn it, I didn't imagine *that*," I yelped as Senenmut grabbed my hand and we began to race toward the place where the arrow had come from.

Wait a minute, I thought to myself, *this doesn't feel right. Why the hell are we running* toward *the bad guys?*

"Shouldn't we be going the other way?" I screeched at Senenmut, but my query was ignored as I was suddenly shoved down behind an outcropping of brickwork.

"Stay here," Senenmut whispered to me before disappearing around the other side, leaving me to my own devices should the bad guys decide to circle back around to where I was hiding and get me.

"I am not sitting here like a goddamned duck," I whispered to myself, noticing a small opening between the bricks. It looked dark and totally uninviting, but I decided that I would be safer inside it than hanging around out in the open.

Here goes nothing, I thought before dropping on my hands and knees and crawling into the hole.

It wasn't what I'd thought it would be like inside the hole because it wasn't actually a hole.

Yep, yours truly had crawled into the opening of a tomb.

"Hello?" I said, expecting my words to echo inside the cavernous entrance chamber, but the sound was absorbed into the emptiness without repeat.

Okay, I thought, *it could be a lot worse. You could be in utter darkness. Luckily, someone has been here recently and left behind a couple of burning torches to keep you company.*

I stepped farther into the entrance chamber, my eyes dazzled by all the beautiful hieroglyphic writing that'd been painted onto the walls, even extending onto parts of the ceiling as well. I liked how the hieroglyphics weren't just abstract images, but actually pictorial representations of the words they represented. I tried to deduce whom the tomb belonged to by the images that surrounded me, but the only thing that gave any kind of hint as to who was buried here was a small black stone statue pushed far back into the corner of the room. It was of a man in a headdress, holding a young girl in his arms. The man's face looked sad, like maybe the girl in his arms had died or something—

"Who dares trespass against my daughter's burial place?" a voice called, interrupting me.

It was a woman's voice, but when I turned around, I found a man standing in the doorway that led to the next room.

"Uhm, look, I don't mean to trespass against anyone or anything," I said, but the man only glared at me.

I stared at him, something about the guy's face striking me as familiar. I took in his white linen sheath, the thick beard on his chin—wait a minute. There was something wrong with the beard.

"Hey, you're not a man," I said. "That's a fake beard."

I walked over and pulled on the man's beard. It easily fell away in my hands. The man/woman was so shocked by my forwardness, that he/she did nothing to stop me when I yanked off its headdress to reveal a topknot of thick, dark, *womanly* hair.

"How dare you!" the woman said—I was sure she was a woman now—as she shoved me away from her, scooping up her golden headdress and ramming it back down on her head. "You will pay sorely for your misdeeds!"

"Oh Jesus," I said, holding out her fake beard. "Just take your stupid beard and put it back on already."

She stared at me and I could tell that she was not at *all* used to being talked to this way. Reluctantly, she took the beard and slipped it into her pocket.

"What? No thank-you?" I asked, but my sarcasm was lost on her.

"Hey, I know you," I said, recognition slowly dawning on me as I gazed at her beardless face.

It was Madame Papillon—only, like, a zillion years younger and prettier.

"It's Calliope Reaper-Jones. Remember? You said you were gonna teach me how to call up wormholes . . . ?"

The woman had no idea what I was talking about. She pursed her lips and frowned, perplexed.

"I do not know of what you speak," she said, cocking her head as she tried to size me up. "What is this Papillon you talk of?"

I didn't know where to start.

"Uhm, well—" I began, but was interrupted by a ray of sunlight that slit the semidarkness and slammed into my face, nearly blinding me. I could hear someone shifting the bricks away from the entranceway, so that more and more light began to spill into the burial chamber.

"My King! I have seen something terrible!"

The voice was low and mellifluous, more masculine than feminine, but this time I didn't let any gender assumptions throw me. I knew that voice and I could picture exactly whom it belonged to.

It was Madame Papillon's Minx, Muna.

Only, the creature that stepped out of the light and into the dimness of the chamber wasn't the Muna that I remembered. This Muna was tall, dark-skinned, and decidedly male. He was wearing a short black leather tunic, a black headdress, and carrying a quiver of arrows and a bow on his back. Behind him were three other men, dressed similarly, but with gray tunics, not black.

"Mustafa, take this woman away from me," the young Madame Papillon said, pointing at me.

Mustafa signaled the other guards forward and they instantly surrounded me.

I wondered if the *Guinness Book of World Records* had an entry for the most time spent under armed guard. If they did, I thought I might actually have a chance at beating the record because the last—almost—twenty-four hours had to have set one of *some* kind.

A guard grabbed my wrists and bound them really tightly behind my back with a piece of twine.

"Ow!" I said. "That hurts."

The guards seemed mystified by what I was saying, so I repeated myself again, only slower.

"Ow. That. *Hurt*. Loosen them, please!"

Once again, all I got was a mystified look from the three guard boys. It took me a moment to understand what was going on, but when I got it, it made total sense. These guys didn't understand a word I was saying. In fact, my English probably sounded like gibberish to them, the ravings of a mad woman, even.

Oblivious old me hadn't thought twice about the fact that Senenmut—and the younger Madame Papillon and Muna/Mustafa—could understand me. I mean, we were in Ancient Egypt, where I bet pretty much *no one* spoke English—if the language had even been invented yet, which I doubted—so why were the four of us able to understand each other? It didn't seem possible, yet it was happening.

It didn't take a big leap to figure it out: *We all possessed magical abilities.*

"Hey, as one magic user to another—" I began, but one of the guards slammed his fist into the small of my back, knocking the wind out of my lungs and sending me to my knees.

"What is this terrible thing that you have seen, Mustafa?" the younger Madame Papillon said impatiently, ignoring me as I tried to catch my breath from my place on the floor.

Mustafa looked over at me, his eyes full of fire and piss.

"O great King Hatshepsut, this wretched creature was seen consorting with the architect Senenmut."

Oh Jesus, I thought miserably, my heart in my throat. *This is Senenmut's true love? Madame Papillon?*

"What do you mean?" Hatshepsut, a.k.a. Madame Papillion, said, a catch in her voice. She looked down at me, her beautiful eyes stricken.

"We chased the architect away, but not before we saw with our own eyes his indiscretion," Mustafa said.

"What do you mean?!" Hatshepsut screamed, clutching her fist to her breast. *"What do you mean?"*

Mustafa had a gleeful look in his eye that I did not like one little bit. I watched, shocked, as the man opened his mouth and bald-faced *lied* to Hatshepsut's face.

"We caught them fornicating upon this very spot where your daughter, Neferura, lies interred."

"That's not true. It was totally benign—" I yelled out, but a kick from one of the guards to my right kidney made sure no more words came out of my mouth.

Seriously, the pain was so intense I really thought I was going to be sick right there on the floor. I could just imagine some modern-day archeologist scratching his head over why there were cupcake remains in what was supposed to be an ancient Egyptian's upchuck.

I was ripped out of my pain-induced fantasies by the most bloodcurdling scream I had ever heard escape from the lips of a human being. I looked up to see Hatshepsut's face contorted in rage.

"You will die for this!" she screamed again, her voice like nails on a chalkboard.

I wanted to say something pithy in response, but before I could draw together my strength, she pounced, attacking me with every ounce of rage she possessed. She raked her nails across my face, then grabbed me by the hair and started slamming my head into the compacted mud brick floor. Of course, with my hands tied behind my back, I was helpless to defend myself. I could feel the blood spurt out of my broken nose, tasting it on my tongue as it dripped down and mingled with the blood from my split lip.

As the pain overwhelmed me and my brain began to cease functioning properly, one thought floated in and out of my consciousness:

I was the reason that Senenmut was put to death.
I had been here before.

twenty-three

I woke up with a headache so terrible, so awful . . . so *all-powerful*, that I was convinced I had drunk my way through an entire bar, starting with Captain Morgan and working my way down the alphabet.

"Oh God," I moaned involuntarily as I tried to turn my head.

A shot of raw, white-hot pain ran up my spinal column and into my brain, making me decide that if I needed to move my head again, I was going to hire someone else to do it for me.

I tried to open my eyes, but they were caked in what I *hoped* were dried tears—not blood. I wanted to reach up and rub away whatever was in them, but I was too scared to try to lift my arm. I was *not* interested in encountering another shot of pain like the one I'd just experienced.

With a little work, I was able to crack my right eyelid open a little bit so I could see where the hell I'd been stashed. The light was very low, but I could just make out the shadow of a statue before me. I cracked the other eye open, and together, my eyeballs were able to discern that the statue was the one I had seen earlier in Hatshepsut's daughter's tomb. Which meant that they hadn't stashed me anywhere; I was in the exact same position and place I'd been in when I'd fainted.

I had to get up. I didn't want to, but in my heart I knew that I had to make myself do it. Being immortal might've had its perks, but getting trapped in a tomb with a bunch of mummies until Howard Carter—or someone of his ilk—stumbled on me thousands of years later sounded about as appealing as getting myself defingernailed.

I gritted my teeth, glad to see they all seemed to be where they were supposed to be, and lifted my head off the ground. There was more horrible pain in my head, but I sucked it up as best I could and used my elbows and hands to bring myself into a sitting position. The room spun around like a carousel, only there were no pretty horses in brightly painted colors on *this* ride. Instead, the hieroglyphics on the wall were my companions, weaving in and out of my peripheral vision as I tried to keep my eyes open and the encroaching blackness at bay.

"Oh God," I moaned again, raising my hand to my head to steady the spinning—which *so* didn't work.

I probed around my skull, feeling for bumps or lacerations, but couldn't find any. Next came the nose check and I immediately knew the bitch had broken it. Even worse than that, when I pulled my hand away, there was blood all over my fingers—and not the dried stuff, either. I'm talking fresh, newly exposed blood with lots of clots and crap in it.

I almost lost it right there. I don't like blood. It makes me nauseous and unable to think straight. It's better when it's someone else's blood, but not much.

"Oh God, Oh God, Oh God . . ."

I was starting to get a little hysterical, and if I didn't calm down soon, I was *really* gonna lose it.

"Okay," I said to myself as calmly as possible, "just relax and pretend that you're at Barneys."

Just the word "Barneys" was enough to get the magic working.

"Now," I murmured to myself, "they're having a big sale and, guess what, there was a glitch on your tax return and you just got a ten-thousand-dollar refund check in the mail."

My breathing eased as I imagined myself trolling the aisles

at Barneys, my ten-thousand-dollar check burning a hole in my *real* Hermès Birkin bag—just like the one I'd seen Liv Tyler carrying in the photo splash pages of *In Style* magazine.

"And now, for the pièce de résistance: the sunglass counter," I crooned to myself.

Some women get their kicks from shoes, others go googly-eyed at the mere mention of Pashmina, but for me the conspicuous consumption item I love above all others is sunglasses. Chanel, Dolce & Gabbana, Chloe, Prada . . . You name the designer and I *already* love the sunglasses they make.

In my imagination, I stood at the sunglasses counter, my mouth watering at all the loveliness surrounding me. I smiled at the girl behind the counter and—unlike every other time I've been to Barneys—the girl smiled back.

"I want to try them all," I said matter-of-factly and the girl nodded.

"As you wish."

And then she began to pull out tray after tray of the most delicious-looking delicacies of the sunglasses variety. As I reached for a huge pair of Fendi shades, I felt a tap on my shoulder—

"Are you okay, Calliope Reaper-Jones?"

I blinked, the sunglasses counter at Barneys faded away, and reality settled itself back on my shoulders.

Senenmut squatted beside me on the floor, concern washing over his features.

"Yeah," I said . . . and then I started to cry.

I don't know why I turned into a big old crybaby like that. It wasn't like I even knew I *wanted* to cry. It just happened. Senenmut wrapped his arms around me and pulled me into his lap.

"Hush, now," he whispered in my ear as he stroked my hair. I buried my face in his chest, then pulled away when I remembered how bloody I must be.

"Do not worry about the blood, little one," he said and I rested my face back in the crook of his arm.

It felt so good to be held like that. It was like I was a child again in my father's arms, being gently rocked to sleep. I hadn't realized how much gentleness was contained inside Senenmut until that very minute. As he hushed and held me, my eyes roamed the room, each wall of hieroglyphics bleeding into the next as tears blurred my vision. For some reason my gaze lingered on the statue of the man and the girl. I couldn't tear my eyes away from it—and the more I looked, the more I wondered.

"Is that you?" I asked in a whisper.

"Is what me?"

He followed my gaze to where the statue sat in the corner. He didn't answer me at first, just stared at the stone effigy.

"I was the girl's tutor . . . and her mother's lover," he said softly, his eyes shining.

"You were more than that, weren't you?" I asked, but it wasn't really a question. I felt the truth circling me like a ghost.

"You were her father, too."

Senenmut slowly nodded.

"When Neferura died, it was like a giant hole opened up in my heart that could never be filled," Senenmut said, his eyes locked on the statue. "But I understood then, as I do now, that such is life. We must be thankful for the time we have together and that is all."

It was awful, listening to him talk about the death of his child so bluntly, the grief still raw in his words.

"Hatshepsut did not understand this," he continued, swallowing back his pain. "She was utterly destroyed by Neferura's death. Her mind became filled with rage at the Gods and she swore that she would trick them out of her own death as revenge."

Senenmut's words rang true in my brain and I began to better understand the series of events that had led the two of us to this place and time.

"At first, she hated anything that reminded her of our daughter—and that included me," Senenmut continued sadly. "But in time, she allowed me back into her heart. At least,

I thought she had . . . until the day she condemned me to death."

"She's not well," I said, thinking about the frenzied creature that had nearly beaten my face into a pulp.

"She lost her only child," Senenmut said, as if that was answer enough.

Damn it, he was right, even if I didn't want to admit it. I might not have had any kids myself, but I *could* imagine what losing a child would be like—and the grief could definitely send you into a spiral of insanity if you let it.

"I know why she condemned you to death," I said quietly. "And you're not going to like it."

Senenmut released me and I sat back, my spine against one of the brick walls for support.

"Please tell me," Senenmut said, his pain brimming on the surface of his face for all to see.

I sighed, cleared my throat, swallowed hard . . . I did everything I could think of to forestall the inevitable, and then, when there was nothing left, I spoke:

"It was because of you and me. Her guard, Mustafa, saw us together and I'm pretty sure he was the one who shot the arrow at us."

"That son of a—"

"Wait—there's more you should know," I said, interrupting him. "Mustafa is not a man. He's a Minx; a mischievous, shape-shifting creature with a really bad attitude—"

Senenmut opened his mouth to protest, but I held up my hand for him to let me continue.

"I know all of this because I've *met* Hatshepsut and her Minx before, in *my* time. She goes by the name 'Madame Papillon' now and she's a noted aura specialist in the magical community. She came to my apartment recently, supposedly sent by my mother and father, to help me learn to control my magical abilities. But I think it was all a lie. I think she *actually* came to warn me off finding you."

"How could she even know that you would be looking for me?" Senenmut asked uncertainly.

"That's the part I haven't figured out yet, but when you said that she wanted revenge on the Gods, that she would cheat them out of her own death, something clicked in my head."

Senenmut stared at me. I could tell that he was having a hard time reconciling his version of Hatshepsut with the one I was now painting for him.

"It makes me think that someone's set me up," I said. "That Cerberus was told by someone else to ask me to find you—and for some seriously ulterior motives."

"But why—"

Senenmut's last words were interrupted by the sounds of voices at the entrance to the tomb.

"We have to get out of here," I said, bracing my back against the wall and pushing myself up on to my feet. Senenmut was instantly beside me, his right arm draped around me supportively.

"This way," he said, guiding me toward the statue.

He reached out and pressed something on the top of the statue's head then put his palm against the bricks. A section of the wall slid open and Senenmut carried me inside, the voices cresting just as the wall slid back into place.

I tried to look around me, but the darkness was absolute. I felt Senenmut's hand at my waist, steadying me. But for that slight bit of human contact reminding me of where I was, I could've been in outer space.

"Look," Senenmut said, his voice a hiss in my ear as he pressed my face forward and I found that I could see again.

We were in some kind of secret chamber, spying on the entranceway we'd just left behind us through hidden peepholes in the wall. I remembered that Cerberus had said Senenmut was an architect and part of me wondered if he'd built this tomb for his daughter. It seemed like a pretty likely bet since he knew where all the secret chamber hideaways and stuff were hidden.

"Did you design—" I started to say, but Senenmut shushed me.

I didn't try to ask any more questions. Instead, the two of

us stood silently against the wall and waited for the drama to unfold.

It was funny, but I was really starting to like the guy now that there were no more secrets between us. I was glad that Cerberus had sent me to help him. It was wrong that he had been trapped in the Jackal Brothers' personal torture chamber for all those years, and I was pleased that I had helped to set things right for him again.

The first person to enter the chamber was the past Senenmut, followed by two guards carrying long spears. One of them shoved him hard in the back with the butt end of his spear, causing Senenmut to trip and fall forward onto his knees. He didn't cry out or whimper; he just picked himself back up and stood in the center of the room, defiant.

I compared this version of Senenmut to the one that I knew and found them to be of the exact same character. The only difference between them was that *this* Senenmut looked less hardened by the ravages of suffering. Otherwise, they were practically the same person.

A few moments passed and then Mustafa entered the room. He looked like one of God's avenging angels with his right hand clutching a gleaming scimitar and his slick, midnight-hued body blending in with the shadowy darkness of the tomb.

"Where is the girl?" he asked the other guards, but neither of them had an answer for him. He thought for a moment, then nodded.

"She must have revived and escaped," he said and the other guards agreed enthusiastically. "No matter. We have the man we want."

"The man you want?" the past Senenmut asked, truly perplexed by his predicament. His yellow cat eyes flicked from one guard to the next before finally landing on Mustafa.

"Please tell me why I am here."

Hatshepsut's head guard laughed. It was a horrible, cackling sound that started in his belly and overflowed into his throat and mouth like bile. I wanted to cover my ears, but I was too scared to move.

"Because the Pharaoh Hatshepsut wishes it so," Mustafa said after the laughter had subsided.

I silently gasped, surprised that Senenmut had never mentioned that Hatshepsut was one of the great Pharaohs of Egypt. Now all the cross-dressing stuff made total sense.

It also kind of made me pity her a little bit, too, because I, of all people, knew how hard it was to live a lie. The stress of constantly hiding the truth inside yourself wore away at your nerves, making you a miserable mess and highly susceptible to irrationally blowing up at the most insignificant of causes.

"Please tell me what I have done," Senenmut said defensively, but he was answered only by silence.

"Bring in the priests," Mustafa intoned, and one of his minions disappeared, only to return with two cowering priests dressed in the same white linen sheath that I had on. They were both older men with shaved heads and long faces—and neither of them looked happy about being there.

"I am sorry, Senenmut," one of the priests started to say, but the guard shoved him and he lapsed into silence.

"I beg of you, please let me speak to Hatshepsut," Senenmut said, and now I could see fear beginning to overtake him. I don't think the poor guy had believed any of this was really happening until they'd brought in the priests.

"Silence!" Mustafa said, raising his scimitar.

I could feel Senenmut tense beside me. He knew exactly what was going to happen next. The flat of the blade struck Senenmut across the side of the head and he fell to his knees.

"No," my Senenmut cried, pushing forward with his hands, trying to open the secret door and save his past self.

I reached out and grasped his wrist, then slipped my hand into his larger one.

"You can't stop it," I whispered, my voice soft against his cheek. "Fate is fate and you can't change it. No matter how much you want to. You'll only make it worse."

Suddenly, the tension eased out of Senenmut's body and he slumped against me, defeated.

"Please," the other Senenmut was saying, his eyes large and round as he begged for his life, but the guard only laughed.

"So has the Pharaoh willed it, so it shall be."

He struck Senenmut once more across the side of the head and the past Senenmut fell forward, unconscious. Suddenly, one of the priests rushed up to Senenmut's prone body, cradling it in his arms.

"I know what you are!" he screamed at Mustafa. "And for this wickedness that you would perpetrate, I curse you *and* your Pharaoh. May Bast punish your wickedness and send you screaming into the mouth of Ammut, Eater of Souls, at your judgment day!"

"You know nothing, stupid priest," Mustafa said and sliced the priest's throat wide open with his scimitar. There was a loud *hissing* sound, and then the ground began to rumble. The shadow of a large cat shot across the far wall of the tomb, causing Mustafa's minions to shrink in fear.

A low, melodious voice filled the chamber, and I squeezed Senenmut's hand, my gut rumbling with nausea at the sight of the priest's blood soaking into the carefully bricked floor.

"You have been cursed in my name," the voice—Bast's voice—intoned, "and I will be your shadow until the day you meet Death, and then I will be your demise!"

This sent the minions running in terror from the chamber, leaving only a defiant Mustafa to hold his ground.

"So be it!" Mustafa screamed at the cat's shadow, continuing the bloodbath by raising his scimitar high in the air and then slicing it down through the skull of the remaining priest.

"We need to leave," I whispered to Senenmut, fear etched in my voice. "Like, now."

I slipped my hand into my pocket and pulled out the rubidium clock. I held the cold metal object up to my lips and spoke these words:

"Take me to Hell."

This wasn't like taking a wormhole or getting an Egyptian

God to transport you back in time. This was a totally different experience. It was like one minute we were in a secret chamber in Neferura's tomb and the next we were standing in front of the North Gate of Hell.

"Where are we?" Senenmut asked, clutching my hand even harder than before.

"Uhm, well, we're standing in front of the North Gate that leads into Hell proper," I replied.

"And what's *that*?" Senenmut continued, pointing straight ahead of us.

"*That*," I said nonchalantly, "is Cerberus, the three-headed Guardian of the North Gate of Hell."

At the sound of his name, the giant three-headed dog turned to look at us. The two dumb heads began to bay happily at my return, but Snarly head only watched us intently with his one large eye.

"Hey, I'm back," I said. "And I brought a *friend* with me."

Snarly head only stared.

"This is Senenmut. Senenmut, this is Snarly—I mean, Cerberus."

Still nothing from Snarly head.

"Well, I guess I'd better be going now that the introductions are over," I said, smiling nervously at the huge, three-headed beast.

"Where do you think you're going, Calliope Reaper-Jones?" Snarly head said quietly.

"Well," I said, thinking, "it's been a rough twenty-four hours, so I'll probably just go back to my apartment and take a shower. Relax a little."

"You will do no such thing!" Snarly head bellowed.

"What are you talking about?" I said, confused. "I brought you Senenmut. We're even-steven."

"Check the clock," Snarly head said.

I froze, my mind slowly coming to the realization that something was dreadfully wrong here—and it had something to do with time. Slowly, I held up the clock so that I could read its face.

"How much time is left?" Senenmut asked me.

The ticker tape of numbers flashed once, twice, then came to a stop. There was only one number left on the face of the clock—and it was not a nice one.

"Zero? How can there be zero hours left? We had plenty of time the last time I checked," I said, the hand holding the clock beginning to shake. "It's not possible!"

Then it hit me.

"Oh my God . . . *how long was I unconscious on the floor of Neferura's burial chamber?!*" I screamed at Senenmut.

He looked bewilderedly back at me.

"I do not know. Four or five hours? Maybe more. I was being chased by Hatshepsut's guards, so it took me much longer to get back to you than I intended," he said.

"Oh Jesus," I moaned, covering my face with my hands. What the hell had I *done*?

"Calliope Reaper-Jones," Snarly head said, a sad smile curving the edge of his gnarly-looking dog face. "You are now the Guardian of the North Gate of Hell."

I tried to not to cry as I watched understanding flood Senenmut's handsome face.

"I am so sorry, Calliope," he said, touching my arm tenderly. "I did not know."

I shook my head.

"It's not your fault," I said. "Believe me, if anyone did this to me—well, it was me."

At my words, the two normal heads began to bay, their somber howls faintly resembling a funeral dirge. I felt my hackles rise as their mournful wails froze the marrow right down in my bones. I closed my eyes, trying to squeeze back the burning hot tears that I knew were coming.

Welcome to Hell, Callie.

twenty-four

"This *better* not be happening on my watch!"

I opened my eyes and my heart leapt, sending the tears that were threatening to overflow only seconds before back into my sinuses.

"Kali, what're you doing here—" I said, but she turned and glared at me, her dark eyes belying her annoyance at having to be here at all.

My friend—and Hindu Goddess of Death *and* a member of the Board of Death—stood at Cerberus's flank, her normally placid face contorted into an angry grimace. She was wearing one of her trademark rhinestone-encrusted saris—this one in bloodred—and her long dark hair was pulled into a precise chignon at the nape of her neck. Golden, lotus-shaped earrings fell like elegant dewdrops from her ears, and when she lifted her hand to set it aggressively on her hip, I noticed that she'd glued matching lotus-shaped jewels onto the tips of her French manicure for a little extra bling action.

"Let me take care of this, white girl," she said, her voice low and controlled, like the hiss of a king cobra snake.

I wasn't sure if the pissed-off vibe I felt emanating off her was directed at me, or just caused by the situation—but *boy,* did I hope it was the latter. Kali could be a *particularly* vindictive character when something pissed her off, and I had absolutely *no* interest in finding myself on her bad side.

"Cerberus, I'm here on behalf of the Board, so you better listen to what I'm telling you," Kali said, her right hand forming a fist as she raised it contentiously in Snarly head's face.

With her honeyed skin, amazing bone structure, and haughty demeanor, Kali pretty much intimidated everyone she came in contact with. Bizarrely, because of our first meeting (I threw a *Vogue* magazine at her head) and the fact that I couldn't *help* calling her on her shit, she and I had developed a rather contentious, but respectful, friendship: She liked to call me "white girl," and I liked to treat her with a healthy dose of sarcasm, bordering almost on disdain. Seriously, arguing with a hotheaded Indian Goddess just to see her get her panties all in a bunch was almost as much fun as going to a trunk sale at Saks.

"I won our wager fair and square," Snarly head said, his one yellow eye fixed steadily on Kali.

The other two "cuter" heads weren't as calm; they both immediately started in with this really irritating high-pitched keening noise, their tongues lolling unhappily out of their mouths.

"I am *not* here to argue who won what," Kali said, hand on hip. "So you just calm your big-ass dog-self down."

Snarly head growled, the sound issuing from low in his throat. Kali reached out her right hand and I watched, enraptured, as the jewels on her fingernails caught the light, reflecting splotches of gold sparkle all around her.

"You just watch who you growl at, stank breath," Kali said and she smacked Snarly head hard on the top of his nose.

Snarly head reared back in shock—I don't think anyone had ever *dared* to reprimand him before—and then like a tiny little puppy, he dropped his head and joined his brethren in their high-pitched, whining serenade.

"Don't you start whining at me, dog," Kali continued, incensed by Snarly head's bad attitude. "You had better listen and quit that bad attitude crap before you really piss me off."

I had spent enough time with the gorgeous—and pigheaded—Goddess to know that when Kali wanted you to do something, you'd better damn well do it—or else there'd be Hell and a half to pay.

"You've been the Guardian of the North Gate of Hell for over, like, three millennia and no one's ever been displeased with your work," Kali said, breaking into Board of Death–ese. "Because of your near-perfect record, we *are* willing to have your position conferred onto another being . . . *if* that is truly your wish."

Oh, crap, I thought as I felt the nails of my Afterlife coffin being hammered in place with Kali's every word. She hadn't come to rescue me; she'd come to put the official Board of Death seal of approval on the transfer!

I opened my mouth to protest, but Senenmut—whom I had forgotten was even there—stayed my mouth by putting a warning hand on my shoulder.

"Just wait," he whispered in my ear. *"Let it play out."*

I tensed, wanting to do what *I* wanted and ignore his probably good advice. Instead, I took a deep, calming breath and tried to relax.

"Okay," I said finally, and Senenmut squeezed my shoulder.

I would do what my Egyptian friend said: *I would wait*—even if it went against everything I stood for. I was definitely of the act-before-you-think school of getting yourself in trouble, but I did what he said and kept my mouth shut.

In the end, it wasn't like there was anything I could *do* about it if Kali decided to sell me out to Cerberus. I had made my own bed and now I was gonna have to lie in it—even if it did smell like wet dog.

"We, of the Board of Death," Kali continued, looking in my direction now, "will allow you out of your contract, but we will *not* allow you to forfeit your position to a half-human being."

Yes! I shrieked inside my brain. *Yes, yes, yes! I was saved! Thank you, half-human blood running in my veins!*

Never in my life had I been prouder of my half humanness than I was at that moment. I had always valued the human part of myself above all else, and now I was being rewarded for it—yay, me! Then, suddenly, it dawned on me that *maybe* this half-human thing might've saved me from a fate worse than Death, but it wasn't *really* a compliment. Maybe because I was half-human, the Board of Death didn't think I was *worthy* of being the Guardian of the North Gate of Hell. Maybe I was some kind of maligned half-breed that no one wanted to trust with any of the important stuff.

With that thought now firmly entrenched in my craw, I didn't know if I was supposed to be celebrating . . . or slicing my wrists—although I meant it only in a figurative way.

"What I'm saying, stank breath," Kali said, returning to her normal mode of speech, "is that if you want out, *we* will find someone to replace you. No wager involved."

The three heads instantly stopped whining as Snarly head rested his monocular gaze back on the Hindu Goddess.

"All you gotta do is say the word, stank breath."

Snarly head considered his answer for a moment, his fierce, yellow eye never leaving Kali's face. It was like he expected to find some kind of "catch" in her offer and was quickly trying to weigh every possible outcome to see wherein the deception might lie before he made his decision. The other two heads, more relaxed now that they'd found their escape from eternal toil was still on the table, began to take turns licking their balls.

It was such an incongruous image: Snarly head locked in an intense mental struggle over whether or not to accept Kali's offer, while his two brother heads blithely took care of their body's baser needs. Watching the giant, three-headed dog, I was glad that there was only *one* of me to worry about—*and* that I didn't have any balls to lick.

After what seemed like an eternity, Snarly head blinked, signaling that he had made up his mind.

"We accept the offer."

Kali nodded.

"Then you're free to get outta here."

But the huge, three-headed dog didn't move a muscle.

"We would like to know who, if not Death's Daughter, will take over our position?"

"What's it matter to you?" Kali said, her bitchy side coming out in spades. "You don't give a damn about the job, stank breath."

Snarly head sighed.

"It matters to us."

Kali shrugged her shoulders.

"I guess if you *really* wanna know, stank breath—"

She snapped her fingers.

"Show yourself!"

There was a ripple in the ether around us and suddenly Runt was sitting beside Kali.

"Hi, Dad," Runt said, her newly born voice as absolutely adorable as the rest of her. She might have only recently learned to talk, but there wasn't an ounce of insecurity in her words.

"You can talk?" I whispered, feeling like a particularly bad parent because while I'd been traipsing around Las Vegas, Ancient Egypt, and the Afterlife like an itinerant mom, I had neglected to be there to witness her first words.

Argh, it made me want to kick myself!

Runt nodded her head and wagged her tail, proud of her new ability. With her pink halter (the one I had magicked into being for her when we first met) and her dark coat all shiny and soft in the afternoon light, I thought the little hellhound looked so much more like a full-grown dog than a puppy that it made me wanna cry.

"I got my voice early," Runt said happily. "I think it was from watching the History Channel with Clio."

I nodded, but once again I felt like a heel for letting Clio be the one who did all the raising of our shared hellhound pup. It was one of the only times in recent memory where I actually found myself wishing that I didn't live in my Battery Park City apartment. If I lived somewhere less selfish—like Sea Verge, maybe—then *I* could've been the one watching the History Channel with Runt.

"Giselda?" Snarly head said, his one yellow eye popping wide open. "Your voice is beautiful."

Snarly head was right. Though she was teeny tiny in comparison to her father, there was just something regal and beautiful about the puppy's voice. In fact, if I had just closed my eyes and listened, I would've realized that Runt sounded *exactly* like Cate Blanchett in that movie where she played Elizabeth, the Queen of England.

So much for the History Channel, I thought. *More like the Movie Channel, if you ask me.*

My cute little puppy nodded and Snarly head bent down and licked her on the cheek.

"My precious little girl is all grown-up," Snarly head said jubilantly. The two other heads seemed equally excited by Runt's vocal maturation, each taking a turn licking Runt's face and making her giggle.

"Uck, family reunions make me sick," Kali said, rolling her eyes.

"But why are you here, daughter?" Snarly head said as his gaze passed from Runt to me and then, finally, to Kali. I could tell by the fiendish look in her eye that Kali was enjoying this—increasingly—awkward situation immensely.

"Allow me to introduce you to your new replacement," my honey-skinned friend said, her dark eyes brimming with black humor.

"Your daughter."

Snarly head's one eye flared in barely concealed rage.

"How dare you—"

"How dare I *what*?" Kali said belligerently, cutting Snarly head off with her quick, offensive retort. "You're the stank breath who wants out of his contract, so bite me. I get to do whatever I please because your sorry ass made an illegal wager, butt wipe."

"But I only—" Snarly head started to say, but Kali wouldn't let him get a word in edgewise.

"I let you out of your contract. I did *not* have you sent to

Purgatory, so you better be thanking me instead of arguing with me."

Snarly head saw the writing on the wall. He knew that no matter what argument he put up, Kali had the upper hand and she was *not* gonna let him off the hook so easily.

"Daughter, don't you see what they are doing to us?" Snarly head said, changing direction to try to persuade Runt to join his side. "They have subjugated our kind to subservience since the dawn of time. Finally, I am free and can rally our tribe to forsake their chains of bondage. Don't sell yourself to these people. No matter what they say, they will abjure from what they have promised you. On that, you can count."

I was surprised by Snarly head's words. I suppose I had just always *assumed* that Cerberus was the Guardian of the North Gate of Hell because he wanted to be, not because he was under contract to my father or something. Even worse, it sounded like whatever this contract was, it wasn't even being honored properly. Snarly head and his two brother heads were being forced to do a job that they hated and weren't being correctly compensated for.

"But Dad, they haven't promised me anything," Runt said, cocking her head adorably. "I just want to help Callie."

Well, that one brought the tears back on.

"I could talk to my dad," I said, swallowing hard to hold back the emotions that were threatening to overwhelm me.

Snarly head only glowered.

"You think your father has any say over what happens to the minions of Hell?"

"Honestly, I don't know *what* the dealio with you and my dad is," I said hastily. "I guess I just thought because my dad was Death and Kali and the Board were involved—"

"You thought incorrectly," Snarly head interrupted me, his great yellow eye unblinking. "If *only* our lives were in the hands of your father, a leader known for his compassion and respect for the creatures under his dominion."

"Well, if my dad can't help you," I said, not really sure

where I was going with all this, "maybe I could talk to someone else who *could* help you."

Snarly head chuckled, but it wasn't the kind of Santa "ho-
ho-ho" sound one imagined when one thought of the word
"chuckle." This chuckle was bitter, full of longing and pain—
and terribly, terribly sad.

"And who might that be?" Snarly head asked disdainfully.

"Well, uhm, I might know someone who could help you,
maybe," I fumbled. "It's a long shot, but, you know, sometimes
the long shot pays off."

Kali and Senenmut looked at me like I was crazy, but I tried
not to let their lack of confidence make me feel bad. I had never
really done anything to make either of them think I was more
than a whiny little brat. I was pretty sure they were wondering
what kind of connections I could possibly be referring to when
I said I knew someone who might be able to help.

Well, I knew one being who could help Cerberus, and even
if I wasn't totally sure how to get in touch with him/her, I figured it was worth a shot if it meant that neither Runt nor I
would have to take over Cerberus's boring job.

"I have a friend upstairs," I said quietly. "A *special* friend."

Now everyone was staring at me.

"Not *that* kind of friend," I said quickly—not wanting
them to think I was getting it on with this "special" friend or
anything.

I hesitated now, feeling like an utter fool. I mean, what if I
tried to contact my friend and he/she didn't answer me—or
even worse, blew me off or something? Just the thought made
me cringe inside.

I took a deep breath and gave Runt a quick smile.

"It's God," I said finally. "You know, the guy/gal upstairs
with the RuPaul voice?"

Snarly head did that horrible chuckling thing again and I
gritted my teeth at the sound.

"You think the Creator would listen to you, a mere half
mortal with middling magical ability at best?" Snarly head
said.

I looked down at my feet, embarrassed. Cerberus was right. I was about as magically adept as a peach pit.

Then I felt Senenmut's hand on my shoulder.

"Calliope has more magic inside her than all of us here combined," he said.

I turned to look at my new friend and something inside me—I was pretty certain that it was just plain old gratitude—made me want to cry. I didn't understand how someone I barely knew could actually have faith in me when everyone else just considered me a screwup.

"He's right," Runt chimed in—and my heart soared at the hellhound pup's words. "There's something special about Callie, whether she knows it or not."

I looked over at her, my eyes brimming.

"White girl is a pain in my ass, but she does *not* back down from a fight," Kali said. "Believe me, I know from experience."

I giggled at Kali's words, trying not to cry even though I could feel the tears prickling the backs of my eyes and trying to run out my nose.

"You guys," I said, wiping my eyes with my hands, as I'd lost my purse on the trip to Ancient Egypt—and the wad of Kleenex that I always kept inside it.

Snarly head watched me curiously.

"You would go and talk to God on our behalf?" he said, the words slipping out of his mouth unbidden.

I nodded, reaching out and patting Runt's head.

"You and Runt are my friends," I said. "Of course I'll help you."

Snarly head sighed and lowered his head. I stood there, not sure what he meant by the gesture. It was Runt who nudged me forward with her nose.

"He wants you to stroke his head," she said quietly.

I swallowed hard, remembering my first encounter with Cerberus, the three-headed Guardian of the North Gate of Hell. I had been terrified of the giant hellhound, afraid that he would eat me whole the first chance he got. Now here I was, petting the damn guy's head.

You just never know where life is gonna take you, I mused as I held out my hand and tentatively petted the giant dog head. After a few moments of patting, I started to get comfortable, even scratching behind his gnarly-looking ears a little bit.

"Thank you . . . friend," Snarly head said finally as he lifted his face so that his one eye was directly in line with my own two eyes.

"Anytime," I replied, liking immensely the new direction our relationship was taking.

"So, you wanna stay now, do you," Kali said, hands on sari-clad hips.

It wasn't really a question.

Snarly head turned to his other two heads—who only panted, pink tongues lolling out of their mouths.

"Yes. We will stay," he said, looking at me, then Runt. "For now."

"So be it," Kali said before turning to me. "Okay, I'm outta here, white girl."

"Wait," I said as I walked over and slipped my arms around the imposing Goddess. She stiffened for a moment, then slowly relaxed into the hug.

"Thank you," I whispered in her ear. "I know you didn't have to do this."

She nodded, but when we pulled apart, she had a funny little smile on her face.

"Later, white girl."

And with those three little words, she disappeared into nothingness.

"You have to go home, Callie," Runt said in the wake of Kali's departure. "Jarvis and Clio need you."

"Is something wrong?" I asked nervously.

"That cat," Runt said, shaking her cute little puppy dog head. "I don't like how she's insinuated herself in with Clio. Jarvis seems to understand that she's bad news, but . . ."

She trailed off.

"I got it. You don't need to say another word."

I turned to Snarly head.

"May I keep Senenmut for a couple more hours? I wouldn't ask, but it's really, really important."

Snarly head considered my request for a few moments, then nodded.

"Giselda may stay with me until he returns?" Snarly said. "Not as insurance that you *will* return, but because I have missed my little girl."

I gave him a crooked smile. It made me happy that he'd missed his kid and wanted to get to know her again.

"Uhm, well," I said, "it's really not my call. I think you're gonna have to ask your daughter what *she* wants."

"You don't mind?" Runt said, surprised.

I shook my head.

"You're your own person, Runt," I said. "You don't need me to make your decisions for you."

It was true—and doubtless the wisest thing I had ever said. I didn't *need* to feel like a jerk for missing Runt's first words. I was her friend, not her parent. She didn't need me to boss her around or act like I owned her. She was a sentient being in her own right, and her decision-making process was probably way more mature than mine anyway.

I squatted down beside her and rubbed her ears, glad that we belonged *with* each other, but not necessarily *to* each other. I knew we had a very special bond, one that would not be easily broken, no matter *what* happened to us in the future.

"I want to stay," Runt said tentatively as she looked from me over to her dad.

"Then be a good girl for your dad," I whispered as I pulled the soft, black-furred puppy into my arms and pressed my cheek against her soft muzzle.

"Just don't forget me," Runt said softly. "I wanna come back soon."

"Of course," I said, scratching her ears. "You're an honorary Reaper-Jones now—whether you like it or not."

Giving the hellhound pup one more kiss on the top of her

head, I stood up and watched as she trotted over to her father and sat back on her haunches beside him.

"See you later, then, alligator," I said as Snarly head licked Runt sloppily across the side of the face.

I truly didn't think I had ever seen anything cuter.

twenty-five

"Hey, Mr. Mom, how about a wormhole outta here?" I asked, very glad to be getting out of Hell in one piece and without a new job looming on the horizon. I shuddered, not wanting to think about how close I had come to losing everything that was important to me in one fell swoop.

"It would be our pleasure to send you home," Snarly head said, giving Runt a knowing look. "Giselda?"

Runt issued a short bark, then gave her tail a furious wag. Suddenly, I heard a tinkling sound—like a thousand tiny fairy bells ringing in concert—followed by a dry breeze that counteracted the saturating sweatiness that I disliked so much about Hell. The dryness enveloped me, sending pleasant shivers up and down my spine, and I smiled, a sense of well-being permeating my entire body. A shimmering doorway magically appeared before us, splitting apart the air and radiating so much love and happiness that I wanted to sing with joy. My mind was filled with images of butterflies and unicorns and ice cream cones that dripped their sticky sweetness all over your hands when you tried to eat them.

It was like being shoved bodily into the overecstatic mind of a seven-year-old girl (which was *kind* of what Runt was), which was both fascinating and kind of frightening at the same time.

I had come across this kind of doorway before—both times at Runt's behest. She was the only being I had ever met who could make traveling through time and space a pleasurable and satisfying experience, rather than a gut-churning, mind-ratcheting event. I decided that if I could learn to open a wormhole/doorway the way she did, I wouldn't dread the prospect of time/space travel so much anymore.

"See you on the other side," I said to Runt as I took Senenmut's arm and we walked into the yawning chasm of light.

the only problem with Runt's mode of transport was that after all the happiness and well-being you experienced inside the doorway, it was major emotional-letdown time when you actually reached your destination—which for us happened to be my dad's darkened library. Whether you wanted it or not, you were left with a big, gaping hole in your heart where all the butterflies and unicorns and ice cream cones had, until just recently, resided.

I could see from Senenmut's face that I wasn't the only one who was affected by the loss of all the seven-year-old-girl stuff. I could only imagine that the experience was even harder on Senenmut than me because I had never lost a child before.

Especially a young female child.

Senenmut's usually handsome face was ashen in the evening light, both hands curled into tight fists that he held rigidly at his sides. I couldn't decide if it was anger or grief that consumed him so completely, but whichever emotion it was, I was glad it wasn't directed at me. I knew that sometimes the only way to diffuse such strong emotion is to share it with someone else—even if it is only through the means of touch.

"It's okay now," I said, grasping Senenmut's arm, causing him to instantly relax his hands. He gave me a tight smile and nodded, all the sadness pooling in the depths of his yellow eyes.

"Thank you."

I smiled and squeezed his arm once more, then turned on the bronze standing lamp that stood beside the grandfather clock. It barely emitted enough light to half illuminate the room.

"Where are we?" Senenmut asked curiously.

"My dad's library," I said.

"You're back, thank goodness—"

I turned to find Jarvis in the doorway, his face strangely passive. He had changed clothes since the last time I'd seen him, so that now he was wearing a thick brown Windbreaker, a white thermal shirt, and a pair of boy-sized corduroy pants. This gave me pause, as I had never seen Jarvis wearing anything less than Armani.

"Yep, home again, Jarvi—and what the hell are you wearing?" I said, my face twisting into an incredulous smirk.

I found myself wishing once again that I hadn't lost my purse, so I could've pulled out my phone and taken a few blackmail-worthy pics of Jarvis's wardrobe—for posterity, of course—even though I knew he would've gutted me if I'd even *tried* to go all paparazzi on his ass. Still, there was something really bizarre about seeing Jarvis dressed in Salvation Army castoffs, and the whole thing just begged to be documented.

Jarvis turned red as he caught me staring at his clothing choice.

"I'm in *disguise*," he spat back at me defensively, pulling on the zipper of his light jacket.

"In disguise for *what*?" I said, snickering. "You look like an American Apparel ad gone bad."

Jarvis pulled out his pince-nez—trying to regain his dignity, I supposed—and glared at me through the glass, which served only to make me snicker louder because he looked so absurd.

"Oh my God, I wish I had a camera," I moaned as the snickering became full-fledged laughter.

"Just shut up," Jarvis said as he prissily slipped the pince-nez from his face and put it back in his pocket.

I guess he'd realized how silly he looked trying to mix hip-hop hobo with dandy chic.

"Why are you in disguise anyway?" I asked.

Jarvis sighed, flipping on a few lamps before sitting down in one of my father's leather wingback chairs and patting its arm. It took my eyes a moment to adjust to the extra light flooding the room, but out of the corner of my eye I caught a flash of fawn-colored fur streak across the Oriental carpet, pass the carved mahogany fireplace—which instantly burst into flame—and land gently upon the proffered arm of the chair.

A moment later, Clio followed the cat into the room—and I almost choked.

She had on a low-cut red halter top and a pair of supershort daisy dukes that made her look like a white-trash trailer-park princess. I had *never* in my life seen my younger sister dress this way, and frankly I was shocked at her choice of attire.

"Oh, you're back," Clio said absently as she came to stand behind Jarvis's chair.

I didn't know what to say. The Clio I knew and loved would never behave (or dress) like this. I was beyond certain that Bast was responsible for this new change in my sister's personality.

"Uhm, yeah, we're back."

Clio's eyes bounced away from me and flicked over Senenmut in a way that almost made me blush.

"Don't you have a boyfriend?" I blurted out, but Clio merely shrugged.

"Oh, do I?"

Jarvis spoke up, his words *sort of* diffusing the tension.

"I suppose that we must let Bast fill you in on our wanderings," Jarvis said softly as he reached out to stroke the back of the Abyssinian's neck.

It kind of creeped me out the way Jarvis was petting the cat. I mean, he wasn't usually this demonstrative, and when we'd last talked, we'd both pretty much agreed that we didn't care for the Queen of the Cats . . . and now this?

Weird.

"I don't think I want to hear what *Bast* has to say," I murmured, my jawline rigid as I tried to contain my annoyance.

It seemed that while I was gone, trying to save Runt from what I thought was a permanent return to Hell, Bast was busy ingratiating herself with all my friends and family.

And trying to control their minds at the same time, I thought angrily.

Clio left the safety of the wingback chair and moved toward me, her eyes catching mine as she stepped closer.

"Callie, you have to listen to Bast," Clio said, putting her arms around me and squeezing. "She didn't know we were her allies before."

"Allies in what?" I asked testily, shaking away Clio's comforting embrace. "I don't understand what you're talking about."

Clio shrugged at my unwillingness to be reasonable and sat down on the leather couch in front of the fireplace. She gave Jarvis a meaningful glance, but he only shrugged.

"Calliope," Jarvis said, continuing to stroke Bast, "I think you would do well to listen to what Bast has to say."

I opened my mouth to answer him, but something stopped me—Jarvis *never* called me by my first name without trying to add a Mistress or Miss in there somewhere.

"My dear, I think by now you know the reason that I am here," Bast said abruptly from her perch on the delicate arm of Jarvis's wingback chair, her amber eyes like liquid gold in the firelight.

"It's the curse. You wanted me to find Senenmut so that the curse the dying priest spoke would be set into motion," I said gamely. It was only a guess, but I was pretty sure I had just hit the bull's-eye.

Bast blinked, then sat back on her haunches to get a better look at me. I found myself entranced by the cat's luminous eyes, so much so that I almost walked over to Jarvis's chair and petted her. Only the knowledge of how much sneezing would be involved with the gesture kept me hanging back at a safe distance.

"Yes," she said, her voice like crème caramel to my ears as she began to purr. "Hatshepsut and her Minx must be destroyed."

"And that is precisely why I am wearing this disguise," Jarvis added tersely.

"What are you talking about?" I said.

"When I told Bast that you had been paid a visit by Madame Papillon, the noted aura specialist," Jarvis said, "she was convinced that this could not be the case."

"The real Madame Papillon hasn't practiced in years," Clio said. "She was ninety-four and not immortal. Bast and Jarvis just returned from her home in Wellington, New Zealand, where sadly they were informed that the old woman had recently *died*."

I turned back to Senenmut to see what he thought about this new piece of information, but he was intently staring at Clio, his eyes narrowed.

"Yeah, well, you're already preaching to the choir," I said. "I figured all that out when Senenmut and I were back in Egypt. Besides, I know why Hatshepsut pretended to be Madame Papillon anyway: to warn me off you."

I pointed to Bast.

"If I thought cats were my weakness, then I would steer clear of you and the curse might never be enacted," I continued.

"Or at least that was Hatshepsut and her Minx's hope."

Jarvis and Clio exchanged another look.

"Yes, I believe you are correct," Bast said, purring quietly. "But sadly, that hope was not correct. By the very *action* of trying to deceive you, they have now brought forth their own demise."

"None of it really surprises me," I said. "We already know that the Minx lied to Hatshepsut in order to get rid of Senenmut, so it only makes sense that it would try and trick me, too."

Both Clio and Jarvis were staring at me and I couldn't help wondering what the two of them were thinking.

"Minx are succubi," Bast said suddenly, her voice low and harsh. "Their very survival depends on the continued existence of their host."

"Wait—so as long as Hatshepsut remained alive . . ." I said but stopped, thinking—there was one important piece missing here.

"Why was Senenmut stuck with the Jackal Brothers?" I said abruptly. "He *should've* been judged and sent into the Afterlife."

Bast nodded, pleased at my progress.

"Oh my God," I said as the final piece snapped into place. "Senenmut was a sacrifice! So that Hatshepsut—and through her, the Minx—could gain some kind of immortality."

"Yes!" Bast purred.

"You said that she had sworn to outwit the Gods." I turned to Senenmut for confirmation. "That she would keep Death at bay as revenge for the Gods taking her daughter—"

"That cannot be," Senenmut said, his voice tremulous. "Hatshepsut could not do something so terrible to me."

I felt awful for the guy, but I couldn't do it. I couldn't lie to him and tell him that the woman he loved *hadn't* destroyed him for her own gain.

"I think part of her hated you because you were her link to everything she had lost," I said softly.

Senenmut shook his head.

"No."

But there was no weight to the word. He looked drawn and defeated as he sank down in the other wingback chair and pushed his face roughly into his hands, sobs racking his strong, able body.

I wanted to go to him, but Bast caught my eye and shook her head.

"Leave him be. He has much to process."

"So, now what do we do?" I asked Bast.

"It seems only natural that you would invite the false Madame Papillon here so that you could set a trap for her and her

Minx," Bast said, her voice as smooth and sexy as silk. "Does it not?"

"Okay, *say* I invite them here," I said, trying not to look at Senenmut's hunched form. "What do I give as my reason for wanting to get in touch with her? I mean, it's not like I can just call them up and say: I miss you. Let's hang out."

Bast, still purring, sat back on her haunches, away from Jarvis's touch.

"Summon Hatshepsut under Madame Papillon's name. Tell her that you would like to have the magic lesson she promised you. I believe *that* will be an offer that she and her Minx cannot afford to pass up."

"Fine," I said, "but only on one condition."

"And what is that?" Bast purred as she hopped off the arm of the chair and skulked dangerously close to where I was standing.

Immediately, my nose started to itch.

"I want Daniel's Shade back."

Bast paused, her tail flicking arrogantly behind her.

"Oh, is that all," she purred. "Of course you may have him back, my dear . . . *of course.*"

jarvis had insisted that the best way to summon Madame Papillon was to invoke a calling spell. Now, I had never in my life done a calling spell before, so I left the logistics of the thing up to Jarvis and Clio—who were *much* better at the magic stuff than I was. Together, they decided that the best place to invoke the spell was outside by the cliff's edge—you know, the really creepy place where the three benches overlooked the water? I thought this was an odd place to do an invocation, but since Senenmut had chosen the same place to call up Nephthys, I just assumed that the benches had some kind of magical vibe surrounding them.

So, as the two of them—plus Bast—went outside to prep the spell, I waited in the kitchen with Senenmut.

* * *

in the overwhelming brightness of the kitchen's recessed lighting, the poor guy looked like he'd just gotten hit by a Mack truck. His eyes were lusterless in his ashen face, and dark smudges circled them like desiccated leeches. The defeated slope of his shoulders belied the misery that was eating him from the inside out.

"Want some hot chocolate?" I asked. Senenmut only glanced at me blankly. It occurred to me after the fact that the guy had probably never even heard of hot chocolate before.

"It's really good. I'm gonna make some anyway, so you can try mine, and if you like, I can make you some, too." I said, my maternal instincts kicking in.

Senenmut nodded but didn't look very excited at the prospect of this "hot chocolate" I was offering him. As I bustled around the kitchen, pulling milk from the refrigerator and cocoa powder from the ridiculously overstuffed pantry—I guess one never knew when one was gonna have to feed an invading army—I tried to keep an eye on the morose Egyptian. He sat hunched over a faded white wooden stool that was pushed up against the center island, his face in his hands. He didn't move as I poured the milk into a pan and set it to heat on the stainless steel Viking range that was the jewel of my mother's kitchen.

"I cannot believe that Hatshepsut was aware of Mustafa's treachery," Senenmut said, his voice so low that I wasn't sure if he was talking to me or to himself.

I waited, stirring the pan as the milk began to simmer, and figured that if it *were* me he was talking to, he'd let me know when he wanted an answer.

"I thought that I knew her . . . and the woman that I loved would not have betrayed me so willingly."

I took two white china cups and saucers from the cabinet and poured some milk into each one.

"Maybe her need for revenge was greater than her need for human love," I said softly.

"I do not think so," Senenmut said gravely, looking up at me for the first time.

I didn't answer as I stirred a couple of spoonfuls of cocoa powder into one of the cups of milk and set it in front of him. I did the same for myself, then took the stool beside him.

"Maybe you just didn't know her as well as you thought you did," I said, taking an exploratory sip of my drink—which was delicious—and trying not to burn the roof of my mouth at the same time.

Senenmut watched me sip my drink, then looked down at his own cup of hot chocolate.

"You said I could try yours first."

I shrugged.

"I lied. It's cocoa. I promise you you're not gonna want to share it, either."

This made Senenmut smile, but only for a moment, then the smile disappeared as quickly as it had come.

"Do you really believe that it is a good idea to bring Hatshepsut and her Minx to your home?" Senenmut asked, sniffing the cup of cocoa curiously before sipping it.

"I don't think I have any choice," I said. "I either confront them here, where I have a little support, or at my tiny apartment, where I don't."

Senenmut nodded and took another sip of cocoa.

"This is very good."

"Cocoa's the one thing I'm pretty good at not screwing up," I replied, pleased that Senenmut liked my little hot chocolate pick-me-up.

We sipped our drinks in silence, each lost in our own thoughts. It was really nice not to be alone as I waited for Clio and Jarvis to summon Hatshepsut and her Minx.

Out of nowhere, Senenmut said, "Do you trust Bast?"

I picked up my cup and drank what was left of my hot chocolate then I stood up to put my cup and saucer into the sink.

"No, I think she's up to something—and I also think she's got some kind of weird hold over Jarvis and my sister."

Senenmut nodded.

"Yes, I think that you are right, only—"

He paused, thinking.

"What? Go on," I said.

Senenmut shook his head.

"It may be nothing—" he started to say, but was interrupted by a faint knocking sound. Startled, I turned around to find Clio standing at the window in front of the kitchen sink, gesturing for us to come outside.

"I think it's time," Senenmut finished instead, leaving me to wonder exactly what it was he was going to say before Clio interrupted him.

As we left the safety of the kitchen—and the comfort of our hot chocolate—my Egyptian friend's comment about Bast stayed with me, scratching at my brain like an itch that wouldn't go away.

twenty-six

Clio was unusually quiet as Senenmut and I followed her across the grounds toward the cliff's edge, the roaring of the waves below us like white noise in my head. I guessed everyone was feeling kind of tense, because the usual joking banter Clio and I would've fallen into was replaced by silence as we moved toward the benches. I wrapped my arms around myself, my mohair sweater not even pretending to keep me warm. I realized I should've grabbed a jacket before we went outside, but I didn't think anyone would take too kindly to me running back to get one.

It was already cold out—and the buffeting winds only made it worse, whipping the longer strands of my hair into my face, stuffing my mouth with the foul taste of dog drool and sweat. *Yuck!*

The only light came from the fullness of the moon, which hung round and distended above us, making me wonder what exactly it was we were about to give birth to by inviting Hatshepsut and her Minx to Sea Verge.

Even though he *was* acting kind of weird, I trusted Jarvis implicitly, and since he had signed off on the experiment, I wasn't worried about biting off more than we could chew. Still,

once they *did* arrive—and under false pretences, mind you—
how they heck were we gonna contain them? The Minx in its
Mustafa form had already proven to be a wily adversary—and
I didn't know *what* Hatshepsut would do once she laid eyes on
her long-lost lover, Senenmut.

Things could go to Hell in a handbasket pretty damn
quickly if we weren't careful.

Senenmut took my hand as we got closer to the cliff's edge—
and my first thought was that he was just being friendly—but
when he gave my fingers a metacarpal-crushing squeeze, I
had to stifle a yelp. I looked over at him angrily, not sure what
game he was playing at, but he merely shook his head, his eyes
wide with fear. He indicated with his head, and I followed his
gaze. Jarvis and Clio had encircled the benches with a fine white
powder that I couldn't place but guessed was crushed bone.

"What is it?" I hissed at Senenmut, but he only squeezed
my fingers harder to shut me up as Clio turned to see what the
trouble was. I flashed her a wide smile, which she seemed to
accept.

"All good," I said. "Just tripped over myself for a minute
there."

This got another harsh squeeze from Senenmut, who had
slowed his pace down to half speed, pulling me with him as he
decelerated.

"Fine," I mumbled under my breath. "Don't tell me what's
going on."

But by then, I was starting to feel kind of nervous about the
scene that lay ahead of us, too.

I spied Jarvis standing just within the circle of bone powder
over by the cliff's edge, Bast sitting primly on his shoulder.
That was so *not* a Jarvis move. Still, even with my growing
misgivings, I forged ahead, glad that I at least had Senenmut
in my corner.

"What's with the circle?" I asked Clio as we neared our
destination.

"It's for the spell, silly girl," Clio replied.

Her voice was light, but it worried me that she chose not to turn around and look at me when she spoke. Besides which, what seventeen-year-old girl living in the twenty-first century *ever* used the term "silly girl" in reference to an older sibling? I would've expected that kind of terminology from Jarvis, but Clio? *Never*—no matter *how* many Paris Hilton reality shows she decided to watch.

"I've never done a summoning spell before," I said, "but it seems kind of weird to have to use ground-up bones just to make what amounts to a toll-free long-distance call."

Senenmut and I had reached the edge of the circle, but instead of following Clio inside it, we had each made an unconscious decision to stay as far away from the bone meal–covered part of the ground as possible.

"You have to step inside the circle for the spell to work, Callie," Clio said, beckoning me forward.

"I don't think so," I replied, my feet staying firmly where they were.

"Why not, Calliope?" Jarvis said—using my given name again—as he reached up to stroke Bast's neck. "The spell won't work if you don't step into the circle."

"Step into the circle," Clio said, more resolutely.

"Yes, step into the circle," Jarvis chimed in.

"Would you guys *please* stop with all the repeating," I groaned. "You're giving me a headache."

Senenmut squeezed my hand again, forcing me to look away from Clio and Jarvis.

"What?" I hissed, annoyed.

"Don't look them in the eye," he whispered.

"Why?"

He sighed.

"You ask too many questions, Calliope Reaper-Jones. Just . . . don't do it."

"Fine," I said, exasperated.

Out of the corner of my eye, I saw Clio lean forward to whisper into Jarvis's ear.

"Whatcha talking about?" I asked innocently, and they both

quieted down instantly. I waited for one of them to answer me, but neither of them seemed inclined to speak.

In the end, it was Bast who replied for them.

"What they say about you is true, Calliope Reaper-Jones," she purred, her tail swishing wildly against Jarvis's shoulder.

"Thanks, I guess," I said, not sure if that was a compliment but deciding to take it as one anyway.

"It is not a compliment," Bast hissed at me, jumping off Jarvis's shoulder and landing gracefully on the grass, her long, dark tail twitching as she slunk toward me.

I so do not like that cat, I decided for, like, the millionth time.

"You are impetuous and impertinent," Bast continued as she crossed the circle and jumped up onto one of the benches, her brown coat a dusty charcoal in the shadowy moonlight. "And you have no respect for those who are vastly superior to you."

"What? Like you?" I snorted. "You're a cat, lady. You walk on four legs. So go suck on an egg because you're no more *superior* to me than you are to anyone else around here."

She hissed at me, flashing a set of razor-sharp incisors that glinted pale white in the moonlight.

"No matter," Bast said, calm again. "You've done exactly what I wanted you to do. And you've made the whole thing so much easier than I even expected."

"To ashes with you!" Bast suddenly hissed at Clio and Jarvis. They both turned to look at me, terrified.

"What the hell—" I started to say, but my words were cut off by a flash of green light so bright that I had to close my eyes to keep my retinas from being scorched. Even with my eyes closed, I couldn't escape the terrible *roar* that filled the night, nor could I drown out the cacophony of agonized screaming that followed.

When I found myself able to see again, I discovered that the whole area within the circle was glowing in shades of electric lime. I watched, horrified, as the lime green light enveloped Jarvis

and Clio, their bodies flaming a bright shade of purple as the spell
Bast had cast began to melt the skin right off their bones.

I couldn't believe what I was seeing. It was like being
trapped in a bad dream or watching a horror movie in slow
motion. You know what's happening, but you're utterly helpless to do anything about it. I tried to make my feet move, to
run forward and save my sister and my friend, but I was rooted
in place, unable to make my body do anything I told it to. It
was like the weight of the whole world was pressing down on
me, holding me rigidly in place.

Then, without warning, time suddenly snapped back into
normal speed and I was in control of my body again.

"Clio!" I screamed, my heart thrumming inside my chest as
I watched my baby sister being burned alive like a witch.

I started to run into the circle, thinking that maybe I could
save them if I could only reverse the spell or pull them out of
the light before it consumed them entirely, but Senenmut
caught my arm and pulled me back. I struggled against him,
hot tears splashing down my face.

"Let me go!" I screamed, pushing and kicking at him, trying to force him to let me go.

But he held me tight, letting me rip at his skin with my
nails. Not flinching as I strained against him.

"No! Please, God, no!" I wailed, covering my face with my
hands as I tried to hide from the horrible image of my sister's
face melting like candle wax.

"Clio . . . !"

Her name was a whisper on my lips as I slumped against
Senenmut, my head throbbing in time with my pulse.

They were gone—reduced now to nothing more than a pile
of ashes for the wind to steal.

I could feel unconsciousness looming over me, my brain
wanting to blot out the horror of what I had just seen, but I
fought it.

"Calliope," Senenmut said, whispering into my ear and
dragging me away from the brink of the blackness that threatened to consume me.

I shook my head, my brain on fire with what I had just witnessed, the death and destruction that could never be undone.

I heard someone crying—not realizing that that someone was me. My stomach was in my throat, a sense of unreality overwhelming me. Senenmut held me as the sobs stole over my body and white-hot grief seared my brain. All I could think about was my little sister, her face, her smile—

Then a thought came unbidden into my mind, one so true and cutting that it made me catch my breath. I shuddered as it sliced me apart from the inside out.

It should've been me.

It should've been me.

The sobs consumed me and I shivered in my grief. I had never experienced anything like this before. It was the most horrible feeling in the whole world and it was mine to deal with for the rest of my life.

The fight left me then. It was all I could do just to keep myself from coming unhinged. If Senenmut hadn't been holding me, I would've crumpled to the ground at that moment and never gotten up again.

I was truly defeated.

"Calliope Reaper-Jones, look at me," Bast called, and there was nothing I could do but comply.

Clio and Jarvis were gone. Not even a trace of their bodies remained within the circle—the wind had seen to that. Grief and resignation squeezed my heart.

But then another thought filled me—this one not so self-destructive—and it was like a match igniting an uncontrollable fire.

Revenge.

My whole brain smoldered with the word. It overtook me, filling my soul with its song until it was all I could do to keep myself from racing into the circle and strangling the Queen of the Cats with my bare hands. I had never wished for the power of Death before—the opposite, even—but now my body crackled with the need to murder the creature that had destroyed the best part of me.

"You fucking bitch," I screamed, the words leaping from my mouth, drenched in spittle. I tried to break free from Senenmut's grasp, but still he held on to me, restricting my need to destroy.

Bast purred as she skulked across the bench, her tail swishing like a scythe behind her. Suddenly, she jumped onto the middle bench—the one with the inscription under the bottom that had creeped the bejesus out of Clio and me when we were little—and sat back on her haunches.

"You have lost, Death's Daughter," she purred. "And now you will do what I tell you to or I will rain down more death and destruction on your family."

At those words, I felt Senenmut's body tense and—without warning—he let me go. I was so surprised that I just stood there, immobile. Before I could pull myself together, Senenmut had moved beyond me, his body a dark streak as he propelled himself toward the cat.

Bast hissed, raising one of her paws up so I could see the glint of exposed claw. There was another flash of green light, this one directed outside the circle, and before Senenmut could reach her, he was suddenly thrust backward into the air, his body hitting the ground with a sickening *crunch* that would've signaled the endgame for any living man.

I raced over to where he lay in the grass, but there was nothing I could do for him. His eyelashes fluttered for a moment, then stopped as a trickle of blood slid down the side of his face. I stood up, livid now, and marched back over to where Bast was sitting, casually licking her paw.

"You can't do this!" I cried, rage and frustration filling my body with adrenaline.

"What do you mean I *can't*? I already have," Bast purred, pleased with her nasty cat self.

Of course, she was right—but that didn't mean I wasn't going to pay her back heartily for her trouble.

"What do you want from me?" I said, my voice emotionless.

Bast lifted one of her back legs and began to smooth the fur on it thoughtfully with her tongue. Her casualness in the face of so much slaughter enraged me.

"Hmmm, what do I want?" she mused as she cleaned herself. "I suppose that what I really want, Calliope Reaper-Jones, is you."

"Never," I hissed at her, but she seemed unmoved by my anger.

"I want to be human, and your body is the perfect vehicle for my needs," she continued quietly.

"Why me? You could have any body you wanted," I said tersely.

Bast purred even louder.

"I wanted an immortal body, and there are fewer of those lying around than one would think."

"I won't give it to you," I said evenly. "Not ever."

"Oh, but I think you will," Bast said, and suddenly I felt two sets of strong arms slipping around me and lifting me off my feet.

I tried to struggle, but it was no use. Whoever had me was much stronger than I was. I threw my head back to see who my captors were and my heart lurched.

I was being held by the last two creatures in the world that I wanted to see right then.

"Fancy meeting you boys here," I growled through clenched teeth as I stared at the Jackal Brothers in all their loincloth glory.

Neither of them replied to my more-than-hospitable greeting.

"Thank you," Bast said to the two Egyptian Gods as they walked me across the line demarcating the circle and the real world, unceremoniously dumping me on the bench beside the Queen of the Cats.

"Okay, you win," I said, stalling for time. "I'll do what you want, but you have to tell me *why*."

Bast jumped into my lap, her weight pressing into me as she curled against my thighs, her bright, gold-flecked eyes drilling holes into my brain as she kneaded my pant leg with her paws. My nose began to itch and I sneezed so loudly it almost drowned out the crashing of the waves below us.

"No sneezing," Bast said, flicking her tail right up under my nose.

Instantly, the urge to blow my brain out my nose was gone. I almost said thank you out of ingrained politeness, but I bit my tongue. I wouldn't give that bitch a thank-you until Hell froze over.

"You have become quite famous within the supernatural community, Callie—may I call you Callie?" Bast asked sweetly.

I nodded, not trusting my mouth. I was liable to spit at the cat rather than be civil.

"After all the publicity you received when you saved your father's life, the Minx saw your picture and recognized you as the girl it had seen with Senenmut in Egypt those many centuries ago," Bast said. "It had been waiting so long to meet Death—and then to discover the girl from Neferura's tomb was actually Death's Daughter . . . Well, with your arrival, it knew that the curse against it and its host, Hatshepsut, would soon be invoked and they would be damned forever by my wrath. Its only hope to subvert the curse was to convince you that cats were your mortal enemy—and that you must stay far, far away from me."

She paused for effect, and it was all I could do not to throttle her right there. I looked over at the Jackal Brothers, who stood just outside the bone powder circle (smart guys), watching us. I knew if I even lifted a *finger* against the cat, they would attack: another reason to remain calm in the face of rage.

"It was only after the Minx had met you that it realized exactly how much power you really possessed. It decided, unbeknownst to Hatshepsut, that you would make an even better host than she had. You were a true immortal, after all, and Hatshepsut was not."

"But she's lived all these years—" I said.

"At the behest of Anubis and Bata. In exchange for Senen-mut's eternal soul, she was given the gift of long life—but *never* immortal life."

"The Minx told you all this?" I asked, surprised.

Bast rubbed her cheek against my leg, marking me with her scent.

"Not in so many words, but it was only inevitable that I would find out its plan, that it would come to me, asking for mercy, and I would pretend to offer it help in its quest. After all, it was my own curse that meant the Minx's undoing . . . and it was to my brothers that it was beholden."

Oh, shit.

twenty-seven

"Anubis and Bata are your brothers?"

"Half brothers. Does that surprise you?" Bast purred.

I shook my head. At that point, nothing would've surprised me anymore.

"So, that's why we were sent on that wild-goose chase to Las Vegas," I said. "That woman in Target was never Hatshepsut."

"Of course, my stepmother, Nephthys, wouldn't send you to the *true* Hatshepsut, though she did guide you to the next best thing—"

"Hatshepsut's *daughter*," I said, understanding now why Senenmut had felt such a strong pull toward the young woman at the Target.

She was the reincarnation of his daughter.

I wanted to cry all over again. To be so close to someone you once loved and not to be able to connect with her was the worst kind of torture. For the first time, I understood why humanity feared Death so much. It wasn't the pain or the fear of the unknown that was so terrible. No, it was the eternal loss of those you held dear to your heart that made it unbearable.

Clio filled my thoughts again, tears prickling at my eyes,

but I ignored them, focusing my attention back on the creator of all my suffering, silently stoking my rage.

"I told Senenmut his Gods wouldn't help him," I said under my breath—and I had been right.

The Gods may have worked in mysterious ways, but they would always do what was best for themselves in the end.

There was one question I needed to ask before we went on, and it concerned someone I loved. I had to know how Daniel fit into the whole scenario.

"So, tell me why you were at the Hall of Death."

I guess it was more of a command than a question, but Bast didn't appear offended. Whiskers trembling, she nodded her head, seemingly pleased by my words.

"Your friend Daniel asked me to help him steal his Death Record. Since I was *your* father's spirit guide, he assumed that he could trust me, that my dislike of the Devil matched his own, and that I would help him in his quest to stage a coup against Hell."

What?!

"Of course, he made a terrible error in judgment," Bast continued. "He didn't know that I had already made a deal with the Devil eons ago. Believe me when I say I will not be some human's lackey any longer than I can help it."

It was dizzying how much information was being thrown at me at once.

"Wait a minute. You were the one who had Cerberus sic me on Senenmut, weren't you?" I asked, the whole plot starting to reveal itself to me as I spoke.

"Yes, when the Minx recognized you for what you are, it saw its opportunity to ditch Hatshepsut and, with her, its tie to my brothers. When Anubis and Bata discovered the Minx's plan, they came to me, their all-powerful sister, for help."

"And then *you* saw *your* chance and grabbed it," I finished for her.

"More like clawed it, my dear," Bast purred.

Yuck, evil cat witticisms make me want to barf.

"You set Hatshepsut and the Minx up," I continued. "You

figured if I thought they were the bad guys, then of course that would *only* make me trust you more."

Bast purred.

"Well-done, Callie. You have proved to be a fantastic little detective. But now, can you deduce what will happen next?"

The only thing I could see happening next was that Bast would do some weirdo spell and steal my body. God, I had been a patsy from the very beginning, played like the kind of cheap toy accordion you just throw away when it finally goes out of tune.

"Where's Daniel?" I asked abruptly. "I want to see him before you steal my body."

"I suppose I can humor you," Bast purred. "After all, he's right here."

She jumped off my lap and onto the ground. She began to cough, her whole body rippling back and forth as she hacked up what appeared to be a hairball, but upon closer inspection proved to be nothing of the kind. It was Daniel's Shade, all crumpled and pretty gross-looking after hours inside Bast's stomach.

"Body and soul are one again!" Bast hissed and a ball of bright purple light enveloped the gross, mottled thing that was Daniel's Shade. There was a flash of lightning and I screamed.

"Daniel!"

His body lay in the grass, naked and wet. I crawled off the bench and kneeled down beside him, cradling his head in my lap.

"Daniel, wake up," I said, kissing his eyes and his lips, overjoyed that he was in my arms, whole and unharmed.

"Callie," he moaned softly as he opened his eyes.

I bent down and kissed him again—and this time he responded, albeit weakly, in kind.

"Enough," Bast said as she prowled in front of us. "Seize them!"

I was ripped away from Daniel by Anubis's strong arms, while his brother grabbed Daniel, hoisting him onto his feet and throwing a light linen robe over his head to hide his nakedness.

"We will begin the transformation now," Bast said. "Bring forth the other bodies."

Anubis's brother, Bata, sat Daniel down on the farthest bench and walked out of the circle. Daniel was still so haggard that he could barely sit up, so I struggled out of Anubis's grasp and ran to him.

"He's too weak," I cried. "Let me help him."

Bast swished her tail and Anubis stepped away, letting me take the seat on the bench beside Daniel. I pulled his frail body forward, letting him settle his full weight against me.

"Thank you," he whispered, closing his eyes wearily as he leaned against my shoulder.

Just as his breathing started to quiet, I heard crashing on the pathway leading from the house. I looked up, wondering what had caused the noise, and then my eyes caught sight of something unimaginable.

Coming toward me—somehow still alive—*were Clio and Jarvis.*

I didn't know if I was imagining things or if I had just completely gone crazy, but if what I was seeing was real, then you could put me in a straitjacket and lock me away forever and I'd be fine with it.

"Get your damn hands off me!" Clio said, her voice sharp with anger as Bata pushed her down the path.

She and Jarvis both looked worse for wear. They were each clothed in the same kind of robe as Daniel—and neither of them seemed very pleased about it.

"Do what the girl says and unhand us," Jarvis added as he tried to keep pace with Bata's long strides.

Just hearing their voices was a revelation. I couldn't believe that I had been given such an amazing second chance. I vowed right then and there to be nicer to both of them for as long as I lived.

"Who was in the circle?" I asked, turning to Bast—although I was pretty sure I already knew the answer to my own question.

"I promised Hatshepsut and the Minx that if they helped me steal your body, I would then bestow them bodies in return," Bast said, her eyelids half-closed as she watched me. "But I tricked them. Instead of spelling them into real bodies, I created *the illusion* that they had been placed into your friends' bodies."

"And then you destroyed them the first chance you got," I said.

If I hadn't been so upset, I would've realized much sooner that Bast *couldn't* destroy the real Clio or Jarvis without knowing what their weaknesses were first, since they were both immortal.

Damn, I could be dense sometimes.

"They had to be dealt with. Besides, I had other plans for the bodies," she purred. "My family has been stripped of its real power for centuries. I think it is high time that we made our return—and Death's Daughters will be the vessels of that triumph!"

"Callie!" my sister cried as she and Jarvis were thrust unceremoniously into the circle with me.

Clio immediately ran over, grabbing me around the neck and nearly choking the life out of me, and then I felt Jarvis's arms join Clio's, so that we were in some kind of weird, three-way "I really missed the crap out of you" hug. I felt the tears pooling behind my eyes and this time I just let them flow.

"I thought you guys were dead," I whispered, my throat constricted by emotion.

"We thought you were, too," Clio said as she released me. "Bast got me before you even left, and then once Kali came to get Runt, she went after Jarvis, too. She's had us down in the cellar with Anubis and Bata ever since."

Well, at least now I knew that the *real* Clio wasn't a sucker for Paris Hilton, after all. *Whew!*

"They plan on stealing our bodies," Jarvis said, sitting down on the other side of Daniel and relieving me of some of his deadweight. "Because we're immortal—and because they think one day you will ascend to the Presidency of Death, Inc."

"I know," I said. "I was so stupid not to see it sooner."

"It's not your fault, Cal," Clio said. "Bast fooled all of us—"

Suddenly, we were interrupted by a thunderclap that ricocheted in the air above our heads. We all looked up—except for the comatose Daniel—to see the night sky filled with shooting green waves of power that kind of resembled the aurora borealis on a clear night.

"What in the world—" Jarvis started to say, but another thunderclap drowned out the rest of his words.

I watched as Bast and the Jackal Brothers prostrated themselves on the ground, their faces pressed into the dirt. Another thunderclap rent the air—sending a sizzling buzz into the ether that made my hair stand on end with static electricity—and I saw the large red bird with the midnight-colored beak circling in the air above us.

"Look!" Clio said, pointing at the bird as it made a couple of loops in the air before swooping earthward. Clio and I ducked as the bird shot over our heads and landed on the ground in front of the bone powder circle.

The bird screamed, then thrust itself forward, its feet touching the earth only for a second before it began to transform, its body elongating like Silly Putty into the red-robed form of a statuesque woman, her long black hair cascading down her back.

"*Nephthys,*" Jarvis breathed, staring at the beautiful woman that stood erect before us.

Her face was as pale as alabaster, high-arched eyebrows giving her face an almost *surprised* look. She had high cheekbones that looked as sharp as razor blades and pouting, pale pink lips the color of Japanese cherry blossoms. She held a long black staff in her hand that was more armament than walking stick. It was carved out of pure ebony, its asp head so lifelike it might have been a living snake dipped in black paint.

Bast and her brothers were instantly on their feet, approaching the powerful Goddess with what appeared to be tentative caution.

"O great Mother, we did not expect you here or we would have prepared—" Bast purred, but Nephthys only glared at the cat.

"SILENCE!"

Once more I watched as the three siblings prostrated themselves on the ground with reverence and—if I wasn't completely crazy—with some fear, too.

"We did not mean to offend you, Mother," Bast said, her cat's face pressed into the dirt.

Nephthys didn't reply, only paced vengefully back and forth in front of her three errant children.

"Mother . . . ?" Anubis squeaked, and I almost giggled as I remembered the strong, terrifying voice I was used to hearing issue from his mouth.

Nephthys stopped in front of Bast and the cat cowered before her. She raised her ebony staff, resting it against the back of Bast's head. I wanted to cheer. Finally, someone was gonna show the goddamned Queen of the Cats who was boss.

"That one will be mine."

I gawked as Nephthys lifted the staff away from Bast's head and pointed it at me.

Now Bast's stepmommy wants to be me? Jeez, what the hell made me such a hot tamale these days?

"Look," I said, "you guys don't want to be me. I have a crappy job that I only kind of like, a teeny-tiny apartment, and a wardrobe that could use a lot of bulking up—"

"Silence!" Nephthys said, lifting the staff so that it pointed directly at my heart—not a great sign. I closed my mouth, opting for silence as the wiser choice in the situation.

"I will take that body," Nephthys said again, lowering her staff and walking toward me.

She reached out a long, bony hand and lifted my chin up with her fingers so that she could look into my eyes. Then, before I knew what was happening, I was being lifted into the air via my face. I struggled against Nephthys, but she was much stronger than me and it was no contest.

"Callie!" Clio screamed, grabbing for my arm, but Anubis

and Bata were upon her in an instant, pulling her off the bench and away from me. Jarvis had his hands full keeping Daniel upright and there was nothing he could do to help me anyway.

Nephthys stared deeply into my eyes, her intense black irises like two glowing pools of nothingness. I can't say that the feeling she engendered inside of me was *terror*, per se, but it was pretty close. Actually, it was more like my whole soul shriveled up at the stark desolation emitting from her fathomless eyes.

I think that describes the experience pretty well.

Now I knew why her children were so frightened of her. She was hands down the scariest Goddess I'd ever come across—and I'd met quite a few of the ladies over the past few months.

"εἴστε ορυχείο."

She spat these words in my face. I had no idea what they meant, but I deduced from context that they probably weren't friendly words of encouragement.

Suddenly, I felt something like fire pierce my sternum and I screamed as searing hot pain shot through my body. Nephthys's eyes sparkled with excitement as she rammed her staff deeper into my chest, penetrating my heart. I looked down, feeling sick to my stomach at the sight of the great ebony staff protruding from my rib cage.

"Please," I groaned as blood began to pour from my mouth, trickling down my chin and onto the ground beneath my swinging feet.

"εἴστε ορυχείο!" Nephthys screamed, her head thrown back so that her voice shot up to the heavens.

I felt drowsy as my heart stopped pumping and my feet stilled. All I could do was stare at Nephthys as my body slowly began to shut down.

"Exhale!" Nephthys commanded me, but with my last few ounces of strength, I shook my head.

"Exhale!" she screamed, thrusting the staff farther into my body.

I couldn't help myself. I opened my mouth as an unbidden scream of pain escaped my throat. Nephthys smiled, revealing sharp yellow teeth all in a fixed row. Suddenly, her tongue spilled out of her pink mouth, snaking toward me with a barely contained ferocity.

I knew *exactly* where that tongue intended to go, so I tried to shut my lips to fend it off, but she was too quick. I gagged as I felt her tongue, wet and warm, probing inside my mouth with erratic dexterity before slipping slowly down into the inner reaches of my gullet.

I felt something snap inside me, and I was filled with the bizarre sensation of my body being ratcheted into two. Then, as abruptly as it had begun, her tongue receded, pulling itself out of me and sliding back into her mouth.

Nephthys leaned forward, her hot breath sour in my face.

"You are mine."

She opened her mouth again, and this time I smelled the foul stench of her decaying soul as it burst from her mouth in a wisp of stinking vapor and slid stealthily toward my own lips.

"No!"

Nephthys's eyes flicked to her right, but she was too late. Senenmut was almost upon her. She tried to pull her staff out of me and use it to defend herself, but Senenmut slammed into her, pinning her to the ground.

I fell backward, her staff still inside me, and as I lay on my back on the ground, my senses became heightened. The stars hanging in the midnight sky above me were brighter than I had ever seen them. I heard the cool hiss of the water below me, only now it seemed to be whispering my name quietly to itself.

"Calliope! The staff!" Senenmut screamed as he thrashed on the ground with Nephthys.

I reached up with both hands, grasping the coolness of the ebony staff. Part of me wanted to just close my eyes and give in to the encroaching oblivion, but I couldn't do it.

I yanked the staff out of my sternum.

The pain was blinding and I screamed again as I heard a

sucking sound, and then a great rush of air from my lungs let me know the staff was finally free from my body.

I rolled onto my stomach, clutching the staff, only to find myself face-to-face with my archenemy, Bast. The cat's teeth were bared, her eyes intent on the staff in my hand.

"Bugger off," I said as I raised myself to my knees and thrust the staff out in front of me just as she made a leap for my face.

I struck her head with the ebony stick the same way a major leaguer snaps a fastball out of the park. I could feel the bones in her skull crack and her body dropped onto the ground, motionless.

Since she was immortal, I knew that it would be only a matter of time before her body mended itself and she was back on her feet again, so I nailed her with the staff a few more times for good measure.

"Calliope!" Clio screamed and I turned to see Nephthys sitting astride Senenmut, throttling him with both hands.

I sucked in a deep breath and pushed myself to a standing position, using the staff for support.

"Hey, *bitch*!" I screamed. "Look what I got!"

Nephthys, her hands still clutching Senenmut's throat, turned to look at me. I used the opportunity to plunge the end of her staff deep into the socket of her left eye, a nice, crisp crunching sound filling my ears as I slammed the staff into her brain.

She screamed, swinging her head back and forth, the staff moving with her like a price tag. Anubis and Bata released Clio and ran to their ailing mother, but she pushed them away angrily.

"My eye!!" she screamed as she pitched forward onto the bench, her body spasming wildly.

Luckily, Jarvis had been able to pull Daniel away from the bench and out of the circle, so we all watched, safe but fascinated, as the bench cracked in half and the earth below it gave way, sending the horrid Goddess plummeting down to the waiting sea.

"What the hell is going on around here, white girl?"

We all turned around to see Kali and Indra standing by the path that led up to the house. Kali had a dagger in each hand and Indra was carrying a short bone scepter with sickly sharp diamond blades on each end of it.

"I think we got it under control," I breathed, my chest making a sucking sound as I spoke. I looked down at the gaping, bloody hole in my chest and blanched. Suddenly, Senenmut was beside me, holding me up by my waist as a complete and utter blackness threatened to consume me.

"Totally under control," I rasped, pushing Senenmut away as I gave Kali a rakish grin. Then my eyes rolled backward inside their sockets and I pitched forward.

It was Senenmut who caught me, holding me tight so that I wouldn't smash into the ground. But by then, I was nearly unconscious, so it didn't really register when he whispered these final words of farewell into my ear as he held me close:

"Thank you, my friend."

epilogue

I stood in the middle of my living room, trying to decide what to do with the nearly naked men coasters. They were strong reminders of the visit that Hatshepsut (pretending to be Madame Papillon) and her Minx had paid me, and frankly I kind of wanted them out of my apartment.

It was hard to believe that Hatshepsut and her Minx were no more. Even now, it was hard for me to think about their deaths because it reminded me of how incredibly close I had come to losing Clio and Jarvis—and that was something that I never wanted to experience ever again.

The one nice thing about your sister dying—and then not dying—is that you get the chance to do things a little differently than you did before. So, when Clio finally confessed to me that she had been seeing Indra, I didn't freak out or get all big-sister bossy on her; I just told her that I was happy for her—and that if he hurt her, I'd cut his balls off.

Actually, I had kind of gotten over my bad first impression of Indra. In the end, he had been the one to alert Kali that something was fishy over at Sea Verge. Apparently, he'd been trying to get ahold of Clio all day, and when he finally *did* get her on the phone, she acted like she had no idea who he was. Needless to say, Indra had not liked that one little bit.

All I can say is that I was glad that he and Kali had gotten there when they did because it took their combined forces to finally subdue Nephthys and her brood. Once they had gotten them all corralled—and dredged out of the water—Kali had called in a team from the Psychical Bureau of Investigations to transport them over to the Purgatorial Court for arraignment.

I was out cold at the time, but I had heard about the aftermath from both Clio and Jarvis, so I also knew that Kali had taken custody of Daniel and Senenmut, intending to take them before the Board of Death for evaluation.

The one thing I felt really bad about was that I didn't get to say good-bye to Senenmut. After careful consideration, the Board of Death had sent him directly to Heaven, where he would then be expeditiously returned to the recycling pool of souls.

I had wanted to tell him thank you for all that he'd done for me; that without his influence, Bast and her cohorts might well have gotten the upper hand and I would have ended up with no body and no Clio and no Jarvis. I also wanted to tell him how sorry I was for how Hatshepsut had treated him; that I didn't think *anyone* deserved to suffer the way he had—especially someone as kind and caring as he was.

But after all the crap he'd been through, I guess that maybe the best thing for him *wasn't* to linger around waiting for me to say good-bye. Maybe the kindest cut had been to give his soul a rest from all the terrible things that it had endured.

I was suddenly pulled out of my maudlin thoughts by a loud knock at the front door.

Forced into action by unexpected company, I grabbed my trash can out of the kitchen and dumped all the naked man coasters into it. I was just replacing the can under the kitchen sink when I heard another knock. I raced over to the door and put my eyeball up to the peephole.

Nervousness flooded my body as I recognized my visitor.

"What're you doing here?" I asked, opening the door wide so that Daniel could come inside.

He looked a lot better than the last time I had seen him—well, at least he was conscious this time.

"I was just in the neighborhood," Daniel said, following me back into the living room and plopping down on my couch as I stared at him, surprised to realize that this was the first time he had ever been in my apartment before.

Even though it was nearly one o'clock in the afternoon, I was still in my floral print pajamas, my hair a rat's nest of tangles. Luckily, I *had* brushed my teeth, but that was as far as my good hygiene went. I was *supposed* to be spending the day cleaning, but it had been a superbusy week at work and my whole body, especially the spot where the staff had pierced my rib cage, still felt kind of funny, so I had mostly been lying on the couch reading back issues of *Marie Claire* and *Elle*—hence the PJs.

"Actually, that's not really true," he said as I sat down on the couch beside him, my hands in my lap. "I wanted to see you . . . to tell you thanks."

I shrugged, embarrassed.

"No one seemed to know what happened to you," I said finally, changing the subject. "I asked Kali, but she said that your fate was top secret and to mind my own business."

"I didn't just come here to say thanks. There was some other stuff that I wanted to explain to you," Daniel said, looking sheepish.

"Oh?" I said.

He nodded.

"Nice PJs, by the way,"

I rolled my eyes, embarrassed again.

"I didn't know I was gonna have company, so you're lucky that I even brushed my teeth."

Suddenly, Daniel reached out and took my hand. I stared at our intertwined fingers and my heart started to beat faster.

"Callie, I want to apologize—" he began.

"For what?" I said, interrupting him. I was starting to feel pretty nervous being in such close proximity to the guy I was kind of in love with.

"For not being straight with you from the beginning."

His ice blue eyes found mine and I struggled to catch my breath.

I shrugged.

"Don't shrug like that," Daniel said. "What I did to you wasn't cool. It's just that I didn't want to burden you with all my troubles because . . . well, I really liked you."

I couldn't breathe. Seriously, my lungs stopped working.

"I didn't know what you thought of me. I was the Devil's protégé, and a few of the times that you thought you were spending time with me, it wasn't, well, actually me."

I squeezed his hand.

"I know. The Devil told me."

Now it was Daniel's turn to blush.

"It was really hard for me," he said, "being stuck in my body, watching everything the Devil did, but unable to have any control over it."

I had experienced the body-swapping stuff a few times, so I knew *exactly* what he was talking about.

"And then you came along and I knew the Devil was going to try and seduce you, use you to destroy your father—"

"Really?" I said. That was new information to me.

"That's why I ran away and came after you. You see," he said, looking down at our intertwined hands, "I liked you from the very beginning. You didn't just crumble into a pile of mush when the Devil turned on the charm—"

Little did Daniel now how incredibly close I had actually come to succumbing to the Devil's dubious charms.

"And you were really funny, too," he finished. "I don't know. I just thought you were cool, so I did everything I could to try and help you."

I squeezed his hand.

"You don't have to apologize for that stuff, Daniel. If anyone understands how incredibly insane the Afterlife is . . . well, it's yours truly."

Daniel smiled.

"Now," I continued, "there's one part that I don't understand about the whole Bast thing. Why did you need her help to get your Death Record?"

Daniel sighed, letting go of my hand, so he could run his fingers through his hair in frustration.

"I needed someone to help me split my body and soul apart. It was the only way to get in and out of the Hall of Death undetected," he said. "The funny thing was that I didn't know how I was gonna do it and then one day Bast just appeared and said she would help me. I would become a Shade and she would use my body to steal my Death Record."

"I don't understand. Why didn't Bast just *get* it for you?" I said, confused. "Why did she have to use your body?"

"Unless you know the right spells, the only Death Record that you can call out is your own."

Well, that made sense—and that was why I had seen Daniel's body searching through the Death Records, but he hadn't noticed me.

"You sent me up there to watch over things, didn't you?" I said, finally getting it. "You saw me in the waiting room and you didn't trust Bast—"

"And you and I were still connected because of the coalescing," he finished for me. "Sorry about that, by the way—and yes, I used you to keep tabs on the cat."

"But *you* didn't know about the curse," I added. "You had no idea that it was really Bast using *you* as bait to get *me*."

Daniel gave me a weak smile.

"She engineered the whole thing because she knew you had to come to the Hall of Death to find Senenmut."

It was amazing to think about all the subterfuge and manipulation that had gone into Bast's plans. It kind of made my head hurt just thinking about it.

"So, are you still worried about burdening me with all that trouble you were talking about?" I said, teasing him.

He sighed.

"Yes and no. I see that you're pretty good at handling the tough stuff, but what I plan on doing is serious business and I don't want to get you mixed up in it."

"Why don't you let me be the judge of what's good for me," I said. "Please, Daniel, trust me . . ."

I could see that it was hard for him to let his guard down, to trust that another person (or God) wasn't just using him to further their own nefarious plans.

"I'm going to Heaven, Callie, and I'm asking God to grant me the Protectorship of Hell until I can figure out away to make the Devil resign his position," Daniel said. "He's a bastard. I'm sure between Cerberus and some of the other denizens of Hell that you've met, you know what I'm talking about."

I did.

When Runt had returned from spending time with her dad, she'd filled Clio and me in on how bad it really was down there. Needless to say, it only made me recognize that I needed to get on the stick and figure out how I was gonna stage this whole meeting thing with God that I'd promised Cerberus.

But maybe, just *maybe*, I had found a way to get the ball rolling on that one. It only took me a minute to make up my mind before I asked for my favor.

"Uhm, I know this is a weird request, but can I go with you?"

"You want to come to Heaven with me?" he asked, confused.

I nodded.

"Why?" he said, staring at me.

"Because I promised a friend that I would try and intervene on his behalf with God," I said. "And I think it kind of goes hand in hand with what you're going to see God about because . . . the friend in question is Cerberus."

Daniel laughed.

"Really? You're kidding?"

I shook my head.

"So, can I come?"

"It would be my pleasure to escort you to Heaven," Daniel said, a huge grin on his face, "but first I wanna ask you . . ."

He paused, looking down nervously at his hands.

"What?" I said, touching his arm.

He looked up at me then, his eyes dark and hungry. They locked onto mine—possessing them, even—and I shivered.

"Calliope Reaper-Jones, may I kiss you?"

All I could do was nod. He leaned forward, his lips barely inches from mine and whispered:

"You're even lovelier than I remembered."

And then he took my mouth with his—and it was the sweetest, most intense kiss I had ever experienced.

"Again," I moaned, my body racing with need as he pulled away to take in my bruised lips and wanton eyes. *"Please don't stop . . ."*

He grinned and pulled me closer, his hands snaking underneath my PJs to touch my bare skin.

"Just kiss me," I begged as his body pressed against mine, like we were made to fit together.

And so he did.

Again.

And again.

And again.